Between the Monk and the Dragon

Between the Monk and the Dragon

A Parable

JERRY CAMERY-HOGGATT

RESOURCE *Publications* • Eugene, Oregon

Resource Publications
An Imprint of Wipf and Stock Publishers
199 W. 8th Ave., Suite 3
Eugene, OR 97401
www.wipfandstock.com

ISBN 13: 978-1-62032-410-3
Manufactured in the U.S.A.

For
Kelly

and for
Josephine

Sometimes one wonders
whether the dragons of primeval ages
really are extinct.

—Sigmund Freud

It does not do to leave a live dragon
out of your calculations,
if you live near him.

—JRR Tolkien

The Medieval Horarium

6:00—Vigils First communical prayer

6:35—Lauds Morning prayer

9:00—Terce Midmorning prayer

12:00—Sext Midday prayer

3:00—None Mid-afternoon prayer

6:00—Vespers Evening prayer

8:00—Compline Night prayer

The seven daily prayers are called the *divine offices*.
The regular meeting of the members of a monastery is called *Chapter*.
The Benedictine Grand Silence is observed between Compline and Vigils.

Caput Primum

BOOK ONE

I

FLETCHER DUG THE WOLF pup out of the burrow, withdrew his hunting knife from its sheath, and then paused, aware of the pup's tiny head and its soft fur against the rough calluses of his palms and fingers. He thought for a moment of his own child, equally as helpless, but his own child had taken his wife from him, and this pup had done nothing except to be born. He braced himself to do what his sense of duty told him had to be done, then took the pup's head firmly in one hand and slit its throat in a single firm stroke.

It was something he had done many times with larger animals, but this was somehow different. The knife entered the throat too easily. Fletcher felt something horrifying within himself, felt the gorge rise within his throat, had all he could do to keep his stomach down. A wave of anger surged over him. He dropped the knife, and grasping the pup's head in his right hand and the body in his left, he wrenched its neck like a chicken. There was blood on his tunic, blood on his hands. Fletcher counted six or seven droplets of blood in the air, and beyond them a spattering of others too tiny to add to the count. A strange silence fell over the glen like snow falling on the marshes. He saw his own hands, covered now with blood, he saw the carcass of the mother wolf tied to the rump of his saddle, he saw the arrow, his arrow, that had killed her, he saw Alysse, her hair shimmering in the morning breeze, her smile an eternal beacon that called to him from somewhere deep in his dreams or maybe from the other side, he saw her dressed as the Virgin Mary, with lighted candles flickering at her feet, he saw her giving birth and then dying, her last breath the sigh of life fading from her body, he saw the girl an infant covered in mucus mixed with the blood of the wolf pup, he saw the girl older, maybe ten, poring over a book by the light of a candle in a corner of the hut, he saw the candles of the church where Alysse's body lay waiting a funeral and a simple Christian burial within the monastery walls.

Just the day prior, Fletcher had tracked the pup's mother deep into the king's forest, where he had caught sight of it silhouetted against the grey English sky, sniffing the wind as though it somehow sensed that there was danger nearby. It was odd for a wolf to do that. Usually wolves kept a low profile, preferring to blend into the grasses and heather of the forest. Fletcher had stopped his horse and dismounted a hundred paces off, down-wind.

It was unusual that there should be a hunter in an English forest on the day before the Feast of the Annunciation in this year of the Lord 1253, and it was unusual that in this forest the hunter should be a commoner, but John the Fletcher had been sent on precisely this errand by the sheriff of Warwickshire, within whose jurisdiction the forest lay. The wolf had been wreaking havoc on farms in nearly a ten mile radius. There was concern for the farm fowl but even greater concern for the smaller children, and the farmers had appealed to the sheriff and then beyond the sheriff, but it was only after Prior Robert, titular head of the Monastery of St Cuthbert and St Chad, had added the voice of Christendom to the voices of reason and pleading that the sheriff had obtained rights of warren to engage in the hunt. His reluctance had been understandable—the shire bordered royal lands, the forest in which the wolf had found refuge was the king's own demesne, and it was forbidden to hunt there except at the king's pleasure. The sheriff had been granted the warren only on the condition that he send his own sergeant, and that any other found hunting there should be brought bound to the stockade and made an example.

"And keep an eye out for hunters in the forest, John," the sheriff had grunted, reinforcing this secondary responsibility. "Somebody's poaching the king's game. The forester says there's a hunter's bivouac in that mound near the north fork of the river."

Fletcher had acknowledged this instruction with a grunt of his own. Poaching in the king's demesne was serious business. A nobleman or knight caught hunting without permission might be released with a heavy fine or the loss of his title or liberty, but a peasant or villein—who had neither gold nor freedom to lose—might rightly and justly expect punishment by maiming, the lopping of a hand or the blinding of an eye.

The wolf had raised its head for a better sense of the breeze, but in doing so had exposed its position.

Without taking his eye off his quarry, Fletcher withdrew his bow and an arrow from the quiver he wore diagonally across his back. Had it not been for an intervening stone outcropping the wolf would have been easily within range, and as he seated the arrow in its place Fletcher thought that even a clumsy archer might bring down such a target. He steadied his left foot against a fallen log, but with his eye on the wolf he failed to note that the underside of the log was rotted out. When the log collapsed beneath his weight, the wolf caught the sound and was gone. It was gone, but not before Fletcher discharged his weapon. The arrow caught the wolf in the flank. Fletcher heard a yelp of pain, and then scrambling in the brush.

When he reached the brow of the hill, all he could find was a thin trail of blood and the oddly mixed and dragging paw prints made by three good legs and the one crippled by the arrow.

He went back for the horse, but did not mount. Instead he walked the horse along the ridge, picking up the trail where he had left off, then following the prints and blood down into the glen until the trail disappeared completely in the swift water near the north fork of the river. The wolf was wounded, but how badly he could not tell, and it had enough of its wits about it that it managed to lose both the hunter and the horse by taking to water.

Fletcher worked both sides of the river for a mile or more in either direction, looking for the wolf's prints in the mud of the riverbank and then just beyond the heavy boulders that lined the water's edge. The fork in the river only complicated things because it added two additional banks where the wolf might have left the water, and the spring snow melt had swollen the river and increased the chances that the animal had drowned and been carried down one of the two rivers. Fletcher moved methodically down one bank, then up another, and only when the light began to fade did he decide to withdraw. He would return in the morning with one of the sheriff's hounds that might pick up the trail by scent.

The return to the village was slowed by only one distraction. Just off the path Fletcher spotted a hunter's bivouac. As instructed, he stopped to investigate, though he did not spend more than a moment;

he paused only long enough to note its location and check briefly inside. It was low-slung, hunkered down into a little mound of earth like an animal's lair, large enough for two or three good sized men to spread out protected from the weather, with its back directed toward the road and its opening masked by a stand of tall trees.

What he did not see was that high in one of the trees there was a small wooden perch, placed there as a lookout for game or authorities by the hunter who had built this secret shelter within the king's demesne.

What he did see chilled him to the bone. Within the bivouac, on a short peg driven into the wall, there was a girl's coat, no doubt left there because the spring day had turned warm. This bit of evidence he read as easily as a monk reads Latin. The coat belonged to his sixteen-year-old-daughter, Elspeth.

Elspeth swung down from the crab-apple tree and gathered up a half-dozen small apples she had picked and dropped into the grass. Then she sat on a rock beside the river that ran through middle of the forest. She drew her head back and tried to roll the apples one at a time down the bridge of her nose. *The trick*, she thought, *is to hold perfectly still. Easier said than done, though, but worth the effort*—why, she did not know. As she finished with each apple she threw the core hard across the river, trying to reach the other side.

This did not last long. There was a moan or a yelp coming from the underbrush on the other side, beneath the low canopy of branches. Something was hurt. She touched the hunting knife at her waist, then moved down the river to a little bridge of rocks, then threaded her way carefully across to the other side.

It was a wolf, badly hurt with the broken shaft of an arrow in its flank. It did not take a hunter like her father to know that the wolf was dying.

Elspeth wondered what any person of compassion should do in such a case. There was little danger of being bitten; the wolf was too far-gone for that. It was obviously in great agony. She sat on the edge of the river and chewed a long blade of grass and thought, but her thoughts were troubled by the agonizing whimpers from the animal on the bank.

"Poor thing," she said. Then she rose and withdrew her knife from its sheath.

"There," she said. "Not long now. Hold on." She wiped her forehead with her sleeve, held her breath, and then with a single hard stroke she had the throat cut, and the beautiful animal closed its eyes and was gone.

A breeze came up and ruffled its fur, and Elspeth drew her hand back quickly. Only moments before, the animal had been warm, quivering, probably as much in agony as in fear, if it felt fear. It had throbbed with a beating heart. She had killed chickens, and had even helped her father slaughter a hog once, but never before had she killed anything so wild or so beautiful. The animal was magnificent. She turned to go, but something caught her eye. A row of heavy teats on the animal's underbelly told her there were pups somewhere. The teats were full and round, and obviously in need of suckling. She whistled then, and muttered, "You're a mama."

She climbed a boulder that lay hard on that side of the river, taking care to keep her profile low in case the hunter might still be near. Deepening shadows covered her movements, but they imposed an urgency of their own.

She started up the bank of the river, stooping low as she walked, looking out for the animal's tracks but moving quickly because of the encroaching darkness.

"What kind of man shoots an animal and then leaves it to die like that?" she said to herself, spitting disgustedly into the dirt because she already knew the answer. From the markings on the shaft of the arrow she knew what kind of man had done this. The hunter had been her father.

It was not difficult to find the lair. Elspeth tracked back along the river until she found where the wolf had entered the water, then along the trail of prints and blood to the place on the bluff where the wolf had taken the arrow. Somewhere along the way she found part of the shaft wedged in among some branches where apparently the wolf had rubbed its shank until the arrow had broken off. She continued this line of movement, reasoning that a wounded female would lead its attacker away from its pups. She found the lair just a little way from the bluff, nestled in beneath the ruins of an old Roman wall.

She crouched, not wanting to attract the attention of the wolf's mate. The lair was concealed behind some low-lying branches of an elderberry, barely a stone's throw away, and she moved in cautiously. There was only a single pup, barely visible in the darkening light. The pup was the size of a small cat, and when she drew it out it was unable to open its eyes.

"There," Elspeth said softly. "You've got no mother." She stroked the pup's fur cautiously, keeping her hand well back of its head in case it might lunge and bite her. "Don't worry, baby, I won't abandon you, not when you've got no mother." She knew enough about the forest to know that without a mother the pup would starve, but she also knew enough about the village to know that it had no future there either. There were dangers either way, and not just for the wolf. From the dogs in the village. From her father. From Sheriff Ranulf, who would want to know what she was doing with a wolf pup—if she were caught. Of these, she feared her father the most. There was no telling what he would do if he discovered she had been in the king's forest.

"You're hungry," she said, though she did not really know that. Perhaps the pup had stirred this first inkling of maternal instinct in her. "I'll feed you," she added, then said reassuringly, "gruel—goat's milk and boiled oats. Bet you never had goat's milk and boiled outs."

The journey back to the village went quickly enough. On the way she stopped at the bivouac for her coat. She wrapped the pup in the coat as long as she was on the road that led into the town of Warwick, but at a certain place the road forked off to a footpath to Wharram, the village where she lived with her father. In Wharram she held the coat before her like a sack of potatoes. Surprisingly the pup remained still, so no other of the villagers suspected anything that might run afoul of the law or normal custom.

At the hut she tried to feed the pup gruel, but when she met with little success she wrapped it in a cloak and placed it in a box beneath the lean-to that had been built on the back wall nearest the fenced enclosure where she and her father maintained their meager collection of livestock. She placed a rough plank over the top of the box to serve as a lid, fed the other animals, then went inside to fix supper.

John the Fletcher was a large man, angular and strong, barrel-chested, with arms as long and as thick as an ox-yoke. He had a hawk-like face, with sharp features—a hooked nose that had been broken in a fight, and a strong chin with a heavy black beard. He had his Welsh mother's unruly black hair and thick eyebrows. None of this you noticed when you saw him. It was as though these traits, each of which might have been prominent in another man, God had added in as an afterthought, something that would have dawned on you after he had left: "Oh, yes. He was like that, too." What you noticed were his eyes. Fletcher's eyes were black, sharp, piercing. They were deep set like onyx into that rugged Welsh face. They were as bright as they were dark, and they stood in such striking contrast to his other features that they held you captive for a moment. They seemed to miss nothing. He could spot an egret or a crane a mile off. The villagers sometimes said that he had eagle eyes, a reputation he had nurtured. The sheriff had been impressed enough to call upon his uncanny ability to spot even the slightest movement on the horizon.

Fletcher had been sent to the shire by his parents when he was quite young, and he had brought nothing with him when he'd come. No tools, no skills, fewer words. An apprenticeship to a bookbinder had ended in disaster—he was no good with books—but he could work miracles with a bow and arrow, like what he remembered of his father before he had been sent away. Fletching arrows and archery were in his blood and fingers. For a time, his grandfather had been the Welsh king's personal archer and a skilled huntsman before he lost three of the fingers on his left hand when the cranking mechanism of his cross-bow had broken during a border skirmish with a band of marauding Danes.

He believed it was his mother who had arranged the apprenticeship with the bookbinder, though he did not know how she had accomplished this. She was unlettered, and the English village of Wharram near Warwick was a good distance from the Welsh border. He could not name the village where he had been born, and had only the dimmest memories of his parents. The bookbinder had done the finish work for the scriptorium of the Monastery of St Cuthbert and St Chad. It was a slow, demanding craft and John's thick fingers had found no friend among the quires and glue and thread that marked the bookbinder's trade. To make matters worse, he saw no use for books, and had stoutly refused to learn to read. Books were nothing more than dead markings on a page that confused a man's spirit and made him discontent with the lot to which he had been assigned by Almighty God.

When the weather was fine he had played truant, which had displeased his master and brought beatings down upon him. When he had grown large enough to strike back he had been ejected from the bookbindery in disgust. Well and good. He hated the man. Instead, he returned to fletching arrows and archery the way his father had taught him in his early youth, before he had come to the shire.

It was from his father and grandfather that John the Fletcher had inherited his skill with the bow, not to mention his eagle eyes. Like them, he was master of both longbow and crossbow, this latter weapon introduced from Italy—lately made wicked by the addition of a steel bow, which added power and range, and by steel bolts with chiseled points for maximum penetration. Unlike its cousin the longbow, the crossbow could be carried loaded, it could be drawn and aimed with the archer lying prone, and it delivered its bolt silently, all of which made it an ideal weapon for hunters and assassins. A skilled marksman with a good eye and a steady hand could place a bolt through solid armor at three hundred and fifty paces. But the crossbow was slow. It had to be cranked back, rather than drawn back, and when speed was necessary an archer always preferred a longbow. British archers were unmatched in the whole of Europe; any one of them could fill the air with a steady river of arrows, the second arrow following so closely on the first that it was aimed and in the air before the former had struck its target. It was among such men that John the Fletcher was considered a master bowman. Once, with a longbow he had brought down a wild boar that had charged his party at full run twenty paces to his left.

So skilled was John Fletcher with either weapon that he had eventually been promoted to the rank of sergeant in the service of Ranulf, Sheriff of Warwickshire, perhaps the highest rank afforded a man who could not read. He had been an energetic man, had worked hard, had had hopes of living as well as any man born to a peasant's modest station. That was before Alysse died in childbirth, leaving him with a broken heart and a pitiful, squalling baby girl whom he had kept alive with rough lullabies and a thin gruel of goat's milk and boiled oats. (Thank God for the women of Wharram—especially Sarabeth—who had watched the baby when he had had to work.) After Alysse's death he made no further attempt at progress, but simply accepted his station as the will of God.

Alysse had been dark and spirited and comely, the love of his life and now the angelic figure who haunted his dreams both waking and sleeping. Her high cheekbones and broad forehead had framed eyes that could have lighted the way home for mariners lost in the great sea.

Fletcher tried to think of the child as Alysse's gift to him, someone for whom she had given her very life, but when he was tired or discouraged his perspective shifted and he saw the child as an intruder, a thief, who had taken its mother's life in the very act of being born. Its first lusty squall had drowned out its mother's dying sigh, so that when Sister Bertrice the midwife turned from the child to its mother she discovered that Alysse had quietly slipped away, like a messenger who leaves a package on the doorstep and moves along to another errand in a different place. To John it seemed as if the child had stolen its mother's breath from her.

Sister Bertrice had handed him the squalling baby while it was still covered in its mother's blood and what John thought was mucus from the birth canal. There was an urgency to her movements that made him panic. Why had she done this? The blood on his hands shocked and horrified him.

The panic was over in a moment. When Sister turned back, the look in her eye and the change in her manner told him that Alysse was gone.

His life itself was gone.

"I'm sorry," Sister had said then. "God took her. I did all I could. It seems you can't have both, John, but she got you a fine, strong child."

"Boy," he had said, not really asking. He had not looked, had been afraid to look, and had been distracted by the urgency of Sister's movements.

"A girl," Sister said. She cleaned her hands on a towel. "I'm sorry, John."

Fletcher stood there numbly. *Why would God take Alysse, and not me instead? Or the baby? What am I going to do with a baby? I don't need a baby. Especially not a girl. Not without Alysse. Why take Alysse, and not the baby instead? With Alysse alive they could have tried again for another child, at another time.*

Sister took the child gently, washed it and wrapped it in the blanket Alysse had folded and left ready on a chair near the bed. "Now take the child outside. Send for Sarabeth; she'll know what to do. I got work to do here." There was a pause in her talk as she handed the baby to Fletcher. "Hold its head like this," she said.

John had tried to hold the baby's tiny head, but it was awkward. The baby's muscles did not work, and it was so small it seemed to get lost in his large hands, and then he was aware that it looked so fragile and its skin was wrinkled but so soft there against the rough calluses of his palms and fingers that he thought for a moment that it had none of him in it and all of Alysse, and he was overcome by the helplessness of it and he had felt helpless to care for it too and he wanted it gone. But then again, as fragile as it was, it had been strong enough to steal its mother's breath from her. It had taken her life and his too. He held his breath for a moment, thinking of Alysse's breath, now forever drowned out by the breathing of the baby. He felt the gorge rise in his throat. It would be so easy to drop the child. Or wrench its neck. Who would know? He could call it an accident.

As deep as it was, this reaction was also fleeting, a momentary pause in the normalcy, and it raised an equally fleeting revulsion within him. How could he have thought such? But the death of Alysse had not been normal; nothing would ever be normal. Not now. How was he to raise a child without Alysse?

". . . Father Athanasius." Sister was saying something.

"What? What was that you were saying?"

"I said to have one of the children bring Athanasius." As she said this she bent over Alysse's body and quietly closed the eyelids. She crossed the girl's hands above her heart.

"Yes. Father Athanasius . . ." Fletcher said, and left the midwife to the sorry holy work of cleaning up after the birth and the death, preparing Alysse's body to be moved to the monastery church to await the funeral mass and after that the spring thaw when the ground would open up to receive all that remained of his dreams and hopes and happiness.

Thus had begun a long nightmare of grief. Was this what the priest had called The Dark Night of the Soul, this asking questions for which there are no answers, this waiting to forget but never forgetting, this wound that would never heal, just as Alysse herself would never return to him no matter how—or how long—he waited; this loving the child because it was Alysse's dying gift to him yet hating it too because of the terrible price it had exacted by its birth?

Already by nature a private man, Fletcher withdrew more deeply into himself, closing off the wound from light and air and healing. Is it right even to want to be healed from such a wound? The loss had changed him, and that had been the infant's doing too. To be healed of such a wound was to release his wife to the past, and he could not bring himself to do that. Worse, it was to forgive God, and he did not want to do that either. But then, who was he to think such thoughts? The wound did not fester, did not torment him, did not leave him crippled or ashamed, not like that bookbinder had left him ashamed, but it did not heal, either. It was a sweet dark place within him, a cave for the soul, a kind of hermitage where he could escape alone into the quiet comfort of his grief.

Even now, sixteen years later, Fletcher still slept on his own side of the canopy bed he had made as a marriage gift for Alysse, the bed in which she had come to him as a bride and then had left him as a mother—victim of her own infant. He still woke up at night listening for her gentle breathing or the soft crackling of the straw in the ticking as she shifted her body in her sleep. What he had instead was the girl, sleeping in her own bed, filling the air with the ebbing breath of early womanhood.

Sometimes the girl awakened him with night terrors. Once when she was maybe six she had cried out, "Mama!" in her sleep. That was an odd thing. How could the girl miss a mother she had never known? Elspeth had never smelled her mother's hair, or tasted her sweet kisses, or dreamed with her of growing old together. For that matter the girl had never known her father the way he was before he had been forever changed by her mother's death. How could she understand what she had taken from him? The cry had left Fletcher hollow inside, aware more than ever that what he had to give was not what the girl had needed.

So now, sixteen years after Alysse had been taken from him, when the girl was nearly a woman and was apprenticed to that bookbinder's son and his seamstress wife, still she filled a void inside him. How old would Alysse be now? He had kept track—count nineteen years from the age of the child. The girl, three; Alysse, twenty-two. The girl, seven, Alysse, twenty-six. When the girl turned sixteen, Fletcher thought of Alysse: thirty-five. What would Alysse have been like at thirty-five? Would her body have rounded and softened with age as had the bodies of the other wives in the village, many of them her childhood playmates, whose children played with her daughter? Would her eyes have crow's feet, as theirs had crow's feet? Would her voice have deepened in tone? What of her laugh? The dying of her laughter had taken the summer breeze from his heart. As a child the girl had laughed like her mother and had never been able to understand why such laughter should move her father to tears.

Sometimes when he thought the girl was not looking, Fletcher found himself gazing at her. She had Alysse's same dark Welsh hair, worn long and braided down her back like her mother, but at night cascading loose in a way that framed her mother's dark eyes; she had her mother's tight build, with wiry arms and the long, slender fingers that had so easily mastered the seamstress' craft. In her apprenticeship she was learning two trades—with equal facility she was learning to stitch dresses for ladies or quires for books, however the need arose. Alcera, the seamstress who was teaching her to sew, had also taught her to read—Alysse had been able to read, and had dreamed as much for her child and how could he deny his dead wife her single strongest wish? But that had been a disaster because it had quickly filled the girl with ideas about moving beyond her station, ideas that Fletcher knew were stupid and dangerous, especially for a woman born and raised a peasant.

He had tried to do right by Alysse, and hoped that he had raised a daughter Alysse would have been proud to own. Recently he had managed to arrange a marriage for the girl with a good Welsh boy named Meurig something from Aberystwyth, a tradesman with a good skill, the son of a silversmith, but Elspeth had said something about his having no more authority over her than what she might give him of her own free will, and that she counted the betrothal a mistake. Fletcher blamed the books for that. Such things make a woman proud and give her ideas about being better than her man, and more than once he had threatened the seamstress with physical harm if she did not desist.

Alcera had proven difficult on this question of teaching the girl to read, insisting that she had every right to train the girl's skills as she pleased, and that she, Alcera, had given Alysse her solemn promise while the baby was still in the womb. An obstinate woman, Alcera, and no model for his daughter to copy, but in the end it had been Fletcher himself who had finally relented out of respect for the wishes of his wife, and the semblance of friendship with Alcera's husband Levente. He and Levente had grown up in the same household, if not as brothers or even as friends, at least as two boys who had both been shaped by the same man—Levente's father had been Fletcher's master, and a hard taskmaster to them both.

But there had been compensations, too. Levente and Alcera also allowed the girl to return home each night to the hut in Wharram since there was no grown woman in the house to tend to the needs of her father. Fletcher believed that this apparently generous arrangement on Levente's part benefited the giver more than the recipient because it allowed him the benefit of the girl's service without the expense and trouble of maintaining her board.

Fletcher paused long enough at the gatehouse to file a verbal report that he had spotted the wolf in the forest, but had lost the trail in the thinning light. He arranged for a hound and its handler to be ready at first light, then headed to the hut that he shared with his daughter in the village of Wharram, nestled in a hamlet a mile beyond the foregate.

It was quite dark by this time, and he made his way home by the light of a torch he had taken from the sheriff's storehouse of weapons and equipment. In his left hand he carried a loaded crossbow. He threaded his way among the rows of half-timbered houses owned by the merchants, out along the lane past the cottages, and then the huts that ringed the outskirts of the town.

Just before he turned down the path to Wharram, he stopped for a flagon of ale at a dimly lighted storefront at the edge of the town. It could hardly be called a tavern, more a small thatched hut where one could buy ale. A crudely lettered sign above the door gave name, though neither Fletcher nor any of the other patrons could have read the words: *The Pint and Ploughman*. The windows were shuttered to ward off the evening chill. A bit of light came from several candles set out in a row along the center of an ancient wooden table, and there was a small fire in a fireplace set well back beyond an interior wall. The proprietor's name was Willem—an old friend.

Most of Willem's regular patrons had snuffed their torches and left them outside the door. Fletcher added his to the others and stepped inside for a drink. He had known most of these men since childhood; they were lifetime neighbors and frequent comrades in arms. Willem's sister Sarabeth the serving woman had tended to his child when she was born, and sometimes when she was sick with fever. She brought his ale before he asked, and he tossed the proper coins across the table without a word. The ale was thick and bitter, but it eased the pain he felt as he thought of Alysse, and it always stiffened his resolve to do right by her daughter despite what she had done to her mother. Ale—a good thing given to men, a gift of God and the barley fields. Calmed his nerves to do right by the girl.

But she has a stubborn streak in her, thought Fletcher, and the streak was made worse since Alcera had taught her to read. The girl went into the king's forest, she talked back to him, she came and went as she pleased, she refused to do her duty with that Welsh boy Meurig, with whom he had made what any sane person would agree was a good match. She walked about the village like she was somebody, better than their neighbors, better than him. Once she had even looked Sheriff Ranulf in the eye and told him to take his hand off her arm. It was an arrogance unbecoming a girl of her station, and it left Fletcher speechless and ashamed in the presence of his friends.

"Another flagon, Sarabeth," he said as he placed a stack of coins on the table.

Fletcher tossed it back in a single swallow, rose, lit his torch at Willem's fire, retrieved the crossbow, and made his way down the path that led to the village where he and his daughter shared a hut and a lean-to shed, but little else beyond the common bond they both had with Alysse.

The hut was a typical peasant's affair—a single room under a thatched roof, built on a slightly excavated pit about four feet in depth. No castle, but good enough for a working man and a girl. It got them through the cold Warwickshire winters. There was a small lean-to attached at the side, and then behind that an enclosed pen for what few animals they possessed. A chicken coop and a privy marked the far corners of the property. Like many of the huts in the village, this one had a grape arbor on the south side; he had planted it there to provide a gentle shade of the mixed and brilliant layers of green that cut the summer sun.

Everything seemed to be in order. Tools and farm implements were stacked against one wall. A bag of un-ground wheat rested against another. Candles were already lit. The girl had made a small fire against the evening chill. On the wall near the door was a series of small pegs, on one of which hung the girl's coat, retrieved from the bivouac, just where it had hung that morning.

Fletcher said nothing as he sat down to the supper of grouse and some gruel the girl had prepared. Finally, his belly full of food and ale, and his limbs tired and aching from the hunt, he readied himself for bed.

Elspeth sat at a rough bench he had made for her mother, brushing her long hair with her mother's combs. Lately, she had taken to wearing her mother's dresses, too, and tonight she wore her mother's nightclothes. He had saved these in a trunk beneath the bed because parting with Alysse's clothing was more than he could bear, but the girl had found them and had asked permission, but even so when she wore them he found it disturbing. Who did she think she was?

But he said nothing about that. He was no good with words, and there was little place in his house for talk. Women talked. Men said what needed to be said with their tools and weapons. Hunters bided their time and waited. Farmers plowed and planted, and then bided their time and waited. It was the women who filled the air with talk. But there were serious matters to discuss and so at last he broke the silence: "The sheriff says there's a poacher in the king's forest. Told me to keep a lookout." His voice was gruff, and still laced with traces of the Wales he had left behind when he was a boy. He unbuttoned the top button of his shirt and pulled it off over his head, replacing it with a woolen nightshirt.

Elspeth set down the brush and turned to him. "You were in the forest today?" she asked, but she turned her eyes aside and Fletcher thought she probably knew the answer already. She stood and came to him, placing her hand on his shoulder.

"There was a poacher in there. Maybe more."

"Any idea who that might be?" said the girl, quietly evading the potential accusation. She picked up the brush again, ran it casually through her hair.

"Certain of one of them." He looked at her hard. "The sheriff catches a commoner in the king's forest, and he's got to make an example of him. Won't have a choice."

"What kind of example?"

"An eye or a hand is hard to replace."

"So you think there may be more than one?"

"At least one." He looked at her coat hanging on its peg.

"What kind of fool poaches the king's game?"

"I'm going to try to warn him off first. He's got too much to lose; a warning'll give him time to reform before it's too late."

"And if he doesn't?"

"Then I'll do my duty." Fletcher felt his forehead cloud over, and the look he gave was intended to send a shudder down the girl's back. If his eyes had been crossbows, they would have dropped her in her tracks. He jutted out his chin and nearly growled out his final remark: "Remember, girl. You don't want to challenge me, understand? You'll learn the hard way, you will."

Elspeth stepped back and curtsied to her father. "It doesn't do to threaten me, sir," she said, smiling. She ran the brush through her loose hair again and smiled at him, her teeth an even white row of gems, like the string of pearls the sheriff's wife sometimes wore. "My father works for the sheriff, sir."

"Not for long if you're caught in the king's forest."

She bent down and kissed him on the forehead. "If I hear about anybody poaching in the forest, I'll bring you word. I promise."

I promise, she says! I'll bring you word, she says. Answers like that infuriated Fletcher because they were so patently dishonest. "And keep clear of the forest yourself," he had said to her to reinforce the warning. "Understand me?" Even as he said it, he thought the girl was developing the same hard, distant look he had seen in her mother, but he did not ask what was troubling her. Was it dissatisfaction? Was it fear? *Let her be afraid*, he thought, *if fear keeps her out of the forest.* But he knew it wasn't fear he had seen. That was what he thought about as he pounded his straw pillow into a tight ball, pulled the rough cover up around his chin and snuffed the candle. There was something brewing in the girl, something unrelated to the bivouac and the girl's presence in the forest that day, something perhaps only Alysse could have understood.

Ah! Alysse. The very thought of her name flooded his mind, drowning out his worries about the girl. As Fletcher drifted off to sleep he thought only of Alysse.

THERE WAS A PRESENCE in the hut, but Elspeth could not quite make out what it was. The air had grown stale and heavy, and dim with sleep her memory was more of an obstacle than a help as she tried to locate the presence and figure out what it was. She smelled something hard. Tar maybe. But it was somehow *exhaled*, the breathing discernable as a faint rhythm in the air. The feeling of alarm grew within her until she slowly began to feel trapped, enclosed, smothered. After a time she realized that her heart was beating hard and erratic, then almost wildly. Whatever it was, it *breathed*, and she had taken in the smell of it in her sleep, had taken part of it into herself, and for a moment she thought she would be sick. She swallowed hard against that. She felt flushed and sweaty in her bedclothes.

Then there was a movement in the corner of her eye—a subtle, undulating movement in the thin sliver of moonlight that leaked in through a crack in the window. What was that? A tail? Did she see a tail? Or the outline of a tail? It was too large for a lizard. It slipped silently out of sight around the corner of her father's canopy bed. There was an animal in the hut, and she knew instinctively that it was dangerous. She pulled the covers closer around her, and groped in the dark for a knife or something she might use as a club, but there was nothing at hand. She squinted into the dark corners of the hut to see if she could gain some sort of clue about what it was.

It had been the hard smell of tar that had awakened her; she now knew it for certain. What was it? How did it get in? Where was her father?

What she said next she said very quietly. "Father." That was all, just the one word. *Father.*

He emerged from behind the canopy.

She said—again, very quietly—"There's something in the hut." If she closed her eyes she could see it again. She described it to her father—the smell of tar, the shimmering, the tail slipping around behind the bed. "It's some kind of animal. It's got a lizard's tail, I think. No, it's too big for that. Too big to be a lizard. I think it's in the corner. On the other side of your bed."

Her father stood up in the dark, moved quietly to the doorway to retrieve his crossbow. He could not load it there in the dark and instead hefted it above his head like a club. Then he moved to the bed, calmly pulling it around to expose the space between the bed and the wall.

Nothing.

The space was empty.

He opened the door to gather a little more moonlight, and then used his flint kit to light a small lamp. When he left the door open, she thought perhaps it was because a trapped animal is more dangerous than a free one. She thought about the pup in the box outside.

"Nothing, Els. There's nothing there." He held the lamp low and looked under the bed, waving his arm in the small space to show her there was nothing there. "Look for yourself. Nothing. No lizard, no creature. You've had a bad dream."

A small breeze came in through the open door, chilling the sweat against her skin. "It was here. I know it was here. Right there, behind your bed." She went, knelt, looked hard beneath the bed. Nothing. She took the lamp and made a careful inspection of the hut. Nothing. Beneath the two beds. Behind the table. Nothing.

"Go back to sleep, Els," her father insisted. "There's nothing here. You're safe. You've just had a bad dream. Go back to sleep."

It was a long time before she drifted back to sleep, and even wide awake she relived the dream. It had all seemed so very real, so vivid, as though she could reach out even then and touch the creature, but it was gone as quickly as it had come. She sat on her bed with her back to the wall and stared out the open window at the corner tower of the town, and wall of the monastery and the convent, all of it outlined against the sky by the glow of the moon. Even the fresh breeze that came in through the window could not clear from her memory the smell of tar that seemed to linger in the air like a stain.

WHEN FLETCHER WOKE, HIS tongue tasted sour and dry and he thought for a moment that he had been chewing on lemon rind. His head throbbed in a kind of incessant marching beat. His woolen nightshirt clung to his body from the night sweats, and the sticky throbbing heat nagged at him, forcing its way past that fragile barrier between things remembered and things dreamt.

He had told the girl she had had a bad dream, something about a creature in the hut, but there was more to it than that. He should have known this moment would come. He had sensed something was disturbing in the girl. There was that defiance, that flash in the eye, that granite set of the girl's jaw.

Fletcher knew more than he had told the girl. That was no dream. What she had described was a dragon. It might still be there; dragons could almost disappear at will. The defiance in the girl had drawn a dragon into the hut.

He wasn't sure he wanted it gone. Not yet. He wanted to see it for himself first.

But the light had grown strong, and Fletcher forced himself to clear his head to get up. The wolf was waiting in the forest. He dressed and headed for the stockade, taking with him a hunk of the long-bread the girl had set out for his breakfast.

No sooner had Fletcher gone than Elspeth was on her feet. She dressed quickly, her fingers trembling in the morning cool. Before the sun was fully up she had quietly gathered the wolf pup from its box in the shed and returned it to the forest.

AT THE FOREGATE, THE stable boy had already saddled his horse. Fletcher slipped the crossbow and a quarrel of bolts into one of the saddlebags, and in the other he put provisions for himself and Aelric, the handler for the dog. As he mounted, he took up a longbow in one hand and a quiver of arrows for his back.

Aelric rode a second horse. There would be time for walking when the hound had picked up the wolf's scent.

"So John, what's our quarry today? Two legs or four?"

"I put an arrow in a wolf last night near the north fork of the river."

Aelric laughed, an insidious little laugh that made John want to spit. "The great John Fletcher didn't take him out with his first shot?"

"Shut up, Aelric," Fletcher said without looking at the man. He finished tying off his saddlebag, then mounted. "I put too much weight on a rotted log. The log broke just as I released the bowstring. I lost his trail when he took to the water. He can't have gotten far. We'll start where he went in. The hound can pick up his scent there."

They rode in silence until they were beyond the foregate. Fletcher thought about the girl. He knew all too well what kind of creature the girl had seen. Fletcher himself had been burned by such a creature when he was a boy. The bookbinder had kept a small dragon the way some people keep snakes as pets because they are fascinated by the beauty of their scales or the sinuous way they moved.

The bookbinder's dragon had held a similar fascination for Fletcher. Dragons are intelligent creatures; part of their nature is their ability to mimic other natural phenomena—a rock formation, a stand of trees, another animal. It was a state the bookbinder had called the "mime." Or they shift colors to match their surroundings the way a chameleon changes colors, only dragons do so exquisitely, and by holding themselves stock still they can perfectly disappear. As he rode beside Aelric, Fletcher was fully aware that this outcropping of rock or that stand of short trees might well be a dragon, or even a roil of dragons, in a state of mime. When it was still a kit the bookbinder's dragon had been known to mime cats and then dogs, and once when it was larger it mimed a small shed, so that few if any of the villagers had even known that it was there. In fact, few of the villagers had ever seen a dragon—more correctly, few were aware of having seen a dragon—and fewer still were courageous enough to believe they existed. To see one, you have to be looking for it, and you have to be willing to face the reality that something beautiful can also be terrible. People seldom look for creatures they're afraid to believe exist.

But there was evidence of dragons even so—the mime had its limits. No living thing stays stock-still forever, and sooner or later even dragons have to breathe. When dragons flew overhead on a starry night their shapes could sometimes be discerned as a darkening of the stars, but it was a darkening that said *dragon* only to those who looked very intently and patiently. What's more, a dragon's mime might trick the eyes, but not the nose or the ears. They give off a distinctive odor—hard like tar. They leave footprints. And then there is the bellowing, but even that was a kind of camouflage. The bellowing of dragons is often taken for thunder.

Sometimes when the wind shifted Fletcher smelled the hard, acrid smell of tar and knew that somewhere nearby there was a dragon, no-doubt standing stock still but tracking their movements with its eyes. In the old days while he had still been indentured to the bookbinder, Fletcher had known of a small roil of dragons that nested in a cave near the village, but he had said nothing to the authorities because the creatures held a peculiar fascination for him. Something terrible can also be beautiful.

The bookbinder's dragon had grown larger as Fletcher and Levente had grown larger, all of them kept in the same house, all kept against their wills by a demanding and angry taskmaster.

"Know anything about dragons, Aelric?" asked Fletcher, breaking the silence only when they were well away from the town.

Aelric laughed again, that same high-pitched nervous way John found annoying and revealing at the same time. "Dragons, John?" he said. His eyes shifted quickly from side to side and his body dropped a little closer to the saddle and the protecting bulk of the horse. "There ain't no dragons. Not now, if there ever was any." He glanced behind himself and then stared at the dog, which had frozen in position, point-ing at a small outcropping of rock that loomed from a bluff that had ap-peared on the left, casting a long morning shadow onto the trail ahead of them. "Back," he said to the dog. The animal let out a low rumble, then returned to its place on the trail. The hair remained raised on its back.

"Don't believe in them then?" said Fletcher. Aelric had stopped to let his horse piss, and Fletcher had to twist around in the saddle to be heard.

"Never seen one, that's all," said Aelric, catching up. "Got no time for some creature I never seen. Don't want to see one, not in my lifetime."

They rode more deeply into the shadow of the bluff. Aelric looked back in the direction of the outcropping, but with the change of per-spective it had disappeared from view.

"Maybe you're not looking in the right places," said Fletcher.

"No such thing as a right place. Why would I look for a dragon? They're dangerous." Then, as an afterthought, he added, "I'm not saying I believe in them though."

"Dangerous, but oh so beautiful," said Fletcher. The bookbinder's dragon had been a marvel. "Dragons are weird beautiful, like something you'd see in a dream. Nothing else like them. Nowhere."

"Beautiful and dangerous then, but neither if they're made up out of some storyteller's head." Fletcher noticed that Aelric drew his mount a little closer to his own, and kept darting his eyes across the countryside.

Fletcher thought about the time he had been burned. He might have been ten. Maybe eleven. At the time, the dragon was the size of a small cat, but it was more lizard-like, with layers of fine scales that reminded him of the trout he sometimes caught in the river. The scales were iridescent silver, and so fine he imagined the animal's hide might feel smooth to the touch. It could have been a lizard, except for the talons and the wings—and the fact that it could disappear. The wings were disproportionately large, so that they almost looked comical. They were locked into the pronounced and protruding bones of its shoulder blades. The bookbinder kept the dragon in a cage, but when he let it out for exercise, it had to struggle to maintain its balance against the weight and distended length of the wings. Its belly was low to the ground, so that as it made its way across the floor of the bindery, it swayed from side to side, and sometimes even fell over, and as a young boy Fletcher had felt a kind of sympathy for it, and after a while even something like affection.

When he brought it morsels of bread from his dinner-plate, the dragon had made a cooing, clucking sound like a hen might make, or it would purr like a cat, the rumble coming up from deep within its belly.

But once, as he fed it, the dragon had responded to his outstretched hand with a blast from its nostril-flame, which was how Fletcher discovered that an animal can be both dangerous and beautiful at the same time, that something beautiful isn't automatically safe or good. When he had reported this event to the bookbinder, the man had blamed him rather than the animal. "That can happen," he had said. "Watch yourself around my dragon."

"I got burned by a dragon once. When I was a boy," said Fletcher simply.

Aelric turned in his saddle and looked at him, hard, then snorted: "You seen dragons, have you!" As he said this he rested his hand on the butt of the crossbow he had brought in his saddlebag. The trail led closer to the bluff.

"They've got this weird way of disappearing," Fletcher insisted. "Like lizards and horny-toads. And snakes. A snake holds perfectly still against a flat rock, it disappears. Dragons do that, too."

Just then a flock of grouse shot up from the brush beside the path in front of them. They had held so still and the coloring of their feathers had blended so perfectly with the bushes that the hunting party might have passed them by completely if the hound had not caught their scent and run out to rout them from their nest. Fletcher said nothing. What more needed to be said?

Levente, who was older, had challenged the bookbinder about the danger. "It burned John," he said. "It could burn one of the farm animals, or even a child. What if it burned somebody else, maybe worse than it burned John?"

The man had been unmoved. "A dragon's no more to blame for that than a wolf is to blame for eating sheep. It's their nature."

"We don't keep wolves as pets," Levente said. "And we don't let wolves run freely through the countryside, eating people's farm animals. We hunt them down and kill them."

"That we do," the bookbinder had said to him, "but if we kill them all, the farms get overrun with rodents. Even wolves have their place in God's creation. But I haven't let my dragon run free now, have I?"

"But somebody could get hurt," Levente protested, but Fletcher knew the protestations would have no effect on his father.

"Would you give up the fire crackling in your hearth on a cold winter's night just because somewhere, sometime, somebody else's fire got out of hand and burned his house down?"

"But a person takes precautions."

"Right," said the bookbinder. He shook a sharp-pointed awl at Fletcher. "My point exactly. Mind yourself around my dragon."

That he had done. Once, the dragon had broken its holding chain and escaped, only to be recaptured and returned by the bookbinder.

Fletcher had felt sympathy for the animal then, and brought it food. It was too large to be confined in such a place as the bookbindery. It was a living thing, a marvel, as near to perfect as any creature Fletcher had ever seen, before or after, but terrifying and mysterious nonetheless. By then he had realized that he was held captive in the same way as the dragon—the bookbinder was a hard man—and he wanted freedom for himself and the dragon both. In an odd way, he identified with it.

Fletcher and Aelric rode in silence after that. Fletcher was not afraid of dragons, not for himself, but he did worry about the girl.

With the hound it took no time at all to locate the carcass of the wolf. It had made its way farther downriver than he had expected, had proven extraordinarily strong. It was a large animal, and would have been beautiful were it not that its pelt was matted with blood and mud and dirt. Perhaps the arrow had opened an artery. Fletcher raised the carcass slowly and turned it over to inspect the damage the arrow had made in the pelt. The shaft of the arrow was broken, but he would re-cover the tip later when he skinned it. The pelt would go to the sheriff. He would give the rest of the carcass to Aelric for the hound.

"John, look here," said Aelric. He pointed to the wolf's throat, which had been cleanly sliced through with a knife. "I thought you said you put an arrow in it."

Fletcher indicated the broken shaft in the animal's shank. "Some-body else did that."

"A poacher in the king's forest!" Aelric gave a low whistle.

"A poacher would've taken the carcass," said Fletcher flatly. He ran his hand along the animal's back, stiff now in death.

"Why cut its throat but leave the pelt behind?"

"He didn't come to take the wolf, only to kill it. Probably a farmer who'd lost too many chickens." But maybe Elspeth had done this, which was more disturbing.

"Why not skin it anyway?" asked Aelric. "It's a pretty thing." He glanced at the hound, then ran his fingers through the wolf's thick fur.

"And be caught in the act or later with the evidence in his hands?" Fletcher said. "Maybe he heard someone coming." He let out a low whistle. "Look here at its belly. This wolf had pups." As he talked he cleaned off the carcass as best he could and slung it up on the horse behind the saddle. With a rope he tied it to a pair of iron rings that hung behind the saddlebags.

"Home now?" asked Aelric.

"Not yet. While we got the hound we've got to find the lair and kill the pups. And a mother wolf means a father wolf. Let's hope we find him, or else we'll be hunting again tomorrow."

They found the wolf's lair on the edge of a small glen, near the ruins of a Roman wall, not far from the rise where she had taken the arrow. When the wolf had led him down river she had taken them away from her lair, a mother's instinctive movement even in dying to protect her young. It was a beautiful and sacrificial thing, something he admired in the animal even as he realized that its blood was on his own hands. He caught an image of a squalling, bloody baby Alysse had left him.

Footprints leading up to the lair told him someone had been here, too. The opening had been widened by a solid, stomping kick. Had Elspeth done that? She did not seem heavy enough, but then again, she was a tough girl who often did things that surprised him.

Within the lair, deep back, he found a single pup. What that meant was hard to tell. Had there been other pups? Had Elspeth taken them? Why? What had she done with them? And why leave this one? Perhaps she had decided to scatter the litter, hoping to give them a better chance of survival, and had simply missed this one. Either way, without a mother it was likely to starve. That was the way of the forest. Some creatures live, some die.

Despite himself Fletcher rankled at that. A pup without a mother was evidence enough that there was something wrong with the world. Should he leave this tiny creature at the mercy of the elements? It would soon enough be a meal for some forest creature, and if not that, then it would starve. And if it survived somehow, he and Aelric would be back hunting it as a mature animal, only later in the year, maybe in winter when the natural game in the forest would grow scarce and like its mother it would make its way out of the forest to fill its belly with chickens and farm animals.

He withdrew his hunting knife from its sheath, and then paused for a moment, aware of the pup's tiny head and its soft fur against the rough calluses of his palms and fingers, and in his mind's eye he pictured Elspeth as a baby, equally as helpless, but Elspeth had taken Alysse from him, and this pup had done nothing except to be born. Elspeth had grown defiant, and he could lose his job if the forester caught her in the forest. She was risking everything—she was nothing but trouble, right from the start—she had taken Alysse from him—he could wring the girl's neck. He braced himself to do what his sense of duty told him had to be done, and then took the pup's head firmly in one hand, and prepared to slit its throat in a single firm stroke.

What happened next you have already heard. The knife went in too easily, and Fletcher was overcome by a mass of crowding images of tragedy. His arrow that had killed the pup's mother. Images of Alysse in childbirth, the infant, the girl, the Blessed Virgin, Alysse calling out to him from the other side, her body in its coffin awaiting burial.

From somewhere far off Aelric was saying something. "John, are you alright?" Aelric was shouting now. "Fletcher!"

When he came to his senses he was holding the pup in his hands, alive—tiny, helpless, but alive. The knife was lying in the dirt near the mouth of the lair.

II

FLETCHER SET THE PUP down, then went to the edge of the glen and emptied the contents of his stomach. He rinsed his mouth from the water bag on his saddle, spitting over and over again, trying to wash the terrible taste of tar from his tongue. "I can't kill it, Aelric," he said, coming back. "It's got no mother and it'll probably starve to death, or even end up supper to some larger animal, but I can't kill it." He waited for his breathing to slow and his heart to stop its wild terrified beating. What was that? Why would a pup affect him like that? He'd killed a hundred wolves, for Christ's sake. Including pups—when he'd had to. What was this about?

"You're in charge John," said Aelric, shaking his head. "What's next?"

Fletcher rinsed his hands with water from the water bag, and splashed water up on his face. Then he mounted his horse and led off in the direction of Warwick

"Not a word, Aelric," he said.

"You're in charge," Aelric said again.

Returning from the forest, Elspeth came upon three of the village boys, the one in the middle a strapping youth named Jason, who snatched her up by the waist and held her aloft for a moment.

"Put me down, Jason, you ruffian," said Elspeth, laughing. She pounded his chest.

"Sit with me in church, Els," Jason pleaded. He continued to hold her aloft, and she realized he must be incredibly strong. "I'll put you down if you'll promise to sit with me in church."

"It would be improper. I'm betrothed, remember, and my father would not allow it."

"You let me deal with your father, Elspeth." He set her down on the road, and he and the other boys stepped into pace beside her.

"Nobody deals with her father," one of the other boys said. He held his arms up in a mock stance of a man aiming a crossbow. Then he pulled the imaginary trigger.

Jason jumped him over the top and knuckled him under the ribs. "He shoots me dead, I'll come back and drive him mad by knuckling him in his dreams."

"Alin's right," said the other boy soberly. "He's already a madman."

"He's not," insisted Elspeth. "He's a man of his word. And a gentleman."

"A gentleman who'll break every bone in Jason's body if he sits beside you in church," Alin said. He picked up a pebble and threw it hard into the brush, startling a small grouse out of hiding.

"He's made commitments," said Elspeth. "He's a man of his word. And he's given me over to a Welshman, and would not think kindly of a village whelp who would try to intervene." Even as she said this, she knew that the marriage would not take place. It was an imposition, something she would prevent, but Jason did not know that, and she sometimes used the betrothal to her own advantage in conversations like this one.

"I'm seventeen," said Jason defensively. "I've got my own flock already. I'm full-grown by any standard."

Elspeth was unimpressed by this claim. "Are you man enough to deal with Meurig ap Gwynedd?" she asked.

"Bring him on," Jason replied, but just then they came in sight of Elspeth's hut, and he stopped before he could be seen by her father. Just before he left, he reached out and grabbed Elspeth by her braided hair, forcing a kiss. "You're mine," he said. Then he turned with the other boys and ran for the village.

Elspeth aimed an imaginary crossbow of her own and pulled an imaginary trigger. "So much for manhood," she muttered as she continued along the path.

As he thought about it, Fletcher realized he didn't have it in him to confront the girl about the pups. At least not directly. He had had his say last night at supper. Today he was too tired from the hunt to bring it up again. It was none of her affair. A man's work, that's all. He skinned the wolf, gave the meat to Aelric for the dog, set the pelt aside for the sheriff, and made his way back up the path to Willem's pub for ale. One flagon. Two. Maybe more. He couldn't remember and he didn't care. He hardly saw the flagons, said hardly a word to Sarabeth, but he was in a bad way as he stumbled back to his hut in the dark.

Elspeth had a small fire going, and a stew. "I was worried about you," she said.

He pulled out a chair and dropped heavily into the seat, spreading his legs to steady himself.

"Eat some stew," she said. "You'll feel better."

Fletcher said nothing. Who was she to tell him what to do, or how to feel better? "Don't want stew," he said heavily. He was having trouble forming up the words. "Bring some of that beer. We've got beer, don't we?" His speech was slow and slurred like the mud in the river after a storm.

"You've had enough," she said quietly.

"Who are you to tell me anything?" he demanded. "What do you know? About life? About anything? You think you're so smart. What? Because of that bookbinder and his wife? You're a girl, not even a woman. You're like your mother."

"Father, don't . . ." she said.

"I thought you wanted to know about your mother."

"I thought you loved her."

"She was too good for us little people. Sat around reading while the other women worked. Puts ideas into her head. She starts imagining things, having dreams, thinks they're real, that's what she does."

This tirade lasted until the light in the hut had faded so badly he had to grope to find his bed, stumbling in fully dressed.

Elspeth removed her father's shoes and set them by the door, then went to her own bed. Before he had finished, her father said something that troubled her even more deeply than his drinking or his going on and on about her mother: The creature in the dream had been a dragon. And then her father had added angrily that she could not—must not— tell anybody about the dragon in the dream. The sheriff would catch wind of it and think she had gone mad. "Not a word," he had said. "Not to Alcera, not to Levente, not to anybody." She would be taken away from her father. Does having dreams about a dragon make one crazy? Had she gone mad? Would they take her away?

She sat up in bed and leaned her back against the bedstead of her small cot, arms wrapped around her knees, trying to tease out memories of what had happened in the dream about the dragon, but the dream was too far gone and she could not recall the details. Even so, thinking about it she had trouble going to sleep. What if the dream returned? She threw back the covers to cool her sweating ankles. She rose and went to the window to open the shutters and draw some air into the room. It wasn't far—three or four steps—though it seemed to take forever. She felt as though she was walking in slow motion, the way a jester might walk in one of the festivals at the castle. It was a struggle to get to the window.

Even so, she was careful not to wake her father. She remembered pausing to catch her breath, then opening the shutters slowly, stopping just short of the spot where she knew they would creak.

Through the open window, moon-beams had cast a soft glow around the hut. She paused a moment to breathe in the air and let her heart stop pounding. In the distance, outlined against the sky above her she could see the towers of the Monastery of St Cuthbert and St Chad, the high belfry a finger pointing toward the heavens, and beside the monastery the lower walls of the Convent of St Elizabeth, then the town, and nearer, to the left, the foregate where the sheriff's armory was kept. Beyond the wall of the convent, the river made a ribbon in the moonlight, a silvery snake that bellied up to the bluff on one side, then stretched lazily across a woven tapestry of fields and farm houses, curled down beside another sleepy village, dropped rapidly into a steep ravine and finally in the far distance laid the tip of its tail in a lake that glistened silver in the bright moonlight.

Elspeth turned to go back to bed. The hut was still lighted by the dying embers of the fire in the fireplace where she had cooked the evening meal for herself and her father. On the table was the long-bread she had set out for their breakfast. She could hear her father's breathing behind the curtain of the canopy bed, heavier than usual, but regular and deep. Elspeth had always taken comfort in her father's night breathing. Its regularity had the effect of a clock—like the tower clock at the church. Her father's night breathing measured off the night almost without variation. Everything was as it should be. She thought about the creature, the dragon. Would it come back?

A breeze came in through the window, ruffling her hair, then her bedclothes, then the curtain on her father's canopy bed. Within the bed behind the canopy there was a soft glow, like the embers of the dying fire in the fireplace, but it ebbed and flowed in a rhythmic pattern, regular and deep like her father's breathing. The only thing like it she had ever seen was the pile of coals in the forge at the blacksmith shop, flowing and ebbing with the movement of the bellows. She held her breath and slipped quietly in for a closer look. With one hand she steadied herself against the bedpost, and with the other she drew back the canopy—ever so gently—to see what made the glow in her father's bed.

What she had seen was not her father at all, but a large animal, sleeping. She had watched in silence as the animal rolled over. It looked like a huge lizard, but larger than any lizard she had ever seen. Its upper back was covered with scales, like a trout maybe, which gave way to plates beneath on the creature's underbelly. Its back was dark green, with an iridescent shimmer of yellow, but beneath, in the underbelly, the green lightened until it was almost white. The creature had four legs, the hind legs large and strong, the forelegs very small, with claws instead of feet. Each of the claws had three large talons, each talon the size of a man's finger.

On its back were disproportionately large wings, too large for the body. From the size of the wings, Elspeth guessed that the dragon was still young, a pup or a kit, she did not know what to call it. A creature with wings of that size would need to be much larger in the body or the wings would be unworkable. Even so, the dragon was not small. She had the impression that if it were stretched out to its full length it might be larger than she was. On its head were two pointed, scaly ears, and large bulges where its eyes protruded slightly. The eyes were glazed over now in sleep, but were still fully visible behind thick, clear membranes. There was something familiar about the eyes, and Elspeth later remembered thinking that it might be the way they reminded her of a lizard she had once brought home from Alcera's garden.

The glow came from the dragon's nostrils. It was very calm, very steady, flaring and ebbing rhythmically as the creature slept. In some ways the consistency of it was even reassuring, like her father's night breathing, but had that hard smell about it, like tar. Elspeth backed up slowly, not taking her eyes off the sleeping creature. "Father," she said once again, calling out quietly as she had done before.

Fletcher lay in his bed and tried to picture Alysse in his mind's eye, but all he saw was what he could remember of the girl she had been when she died—forever nineteen years old, forever gone. He fingered his bedclothes, imagining they were the cloth of her skirt. He searched his memory for the smell of her hair and the look of joy he had seen in her eyes on their wedding day. He laid his head back on the hard pillow, imagining so vividly Alysse's lap. He listened for her breathing and the soft rustling movement of the straw in the ticking of the mattress.

Such imaginings were more difficult now. So many years had passed, and with each year it became harder and harder to remember. He had heard that there were artists who could draw or paint an image of a person that preserved the memory perfectly, but he had never seen such an image. Such extravagances were only for the royals and the landed gentry, or those among the merchants who had money and had traveled outside the shire, but they were not for poor men like archers.

The only things even remotely like such images he had ever seen were the stained windows and paintings and statues of the Blessed Virgin in the monastery church where the villagers gathered for mass, and he sometimes stood transfixed before the statue of the Virgin, imposing what details he could remember of Alysse's face and shape upon the holy artifact until the mother of God and the mother of his child would blend together into a single image in his mind. He sensed that somehow this was a sacrilege, but both women were holy to him and he had continued the practice nonetheless, telling no one. Sometimes he wondered how the one woman could have given birth to so blessed a child while the other had birthed only this agony of a daughter for whom he could find no place in his broken heart.

When he could bring himself to pray he asked that the Virgin would carry word of his grief to his wife, but those were rare times. He seldom found the words for prayer.

In recent years there had been another source of agony. As the girl grew she had taken on her mother's features—the line of her jaw when seen from behind, the way she held her head as she looked at the sunset, the sound of the mother's laughter a distant echo in the laughter of her child. At night it was the same. Sometimes Fletcher gazed at the girl's form, sleeping in the other bed, but he saw the form of Alysse there, too, and he wished she were sleeping beside him in his own bed, so that each night before he fell asleep he had to force himself to remember that it was only Elspeth's face he saw, this imperfect imprint of her mother, this face of the girl who had forever taken his Alysse from him. She owed him something for that.

The following day, returning home from his rounds, Fletcher entered the town through the north gate, dismounted, then led his horse past the town-side gate of the monastery and the south transept of St Cuthbert's Church. If he were not distracted by his concern for Elspeth, he might have entered for a moment's reflection and prayer, or at least to pause before the church, if only to draw comfort or guidance from the nobility of its architecture and the sacred art with which it was adorned. He wondered how many of the villagers had noticed that he often paused to mutter prayers before the statue of the Blessed Virgin. Tonight he passed in silence.

St Cuthbert's Church was the jewel of the monastery grounds, a soaring structure of solid granite, with a wonderful red and white rose window overlooking the high altar in the chancel, scenes from the lives of Jesus and the Holy Apostle Paul displayed in six pairs of stained glass windows with pointed arches running down the ambulatories on either side of the nave, and a fine set of Old Testament scenes set into the north clerestory windows high above, so that even in the dimmed and slanting evening sun the stone walls often seemed pierced with colored light. Outside on the spires were finely carved grotesques and gargoyles, intended, the priest said, to ward off demons and dragons should they appear.

If the church was the jewel of the monastery, the altar was the jewel of the church. It was high, gleaming, its paneled triptych gilt in gold. Set into the panels were shallow carvings of biblical scenes, the crowns sometimes set with jewels. The altar was the pride of both the monastery and the congregation of townspeople and villagers. Whether it was due to the general superstition of the peasants, or the fact that Warwick was far enough from the beaten path that the bolder sort of bandits picked more accessible targets, or were simply afraid of getting caught, it had been a wonder to him and a tribute to Sheriff Ranulf that the sanctuary was unlocked day and night, quite open and unguarded, and yet the jewels of the high altar of St Cuthbert's Church remained untouched. Perhaps they were protected by the unseen hand of God.

Through an open doorway in the transept Fletcher caught a fleeting glimpse of an old monk, silently lighting candles in preparation for Vespers, and then, deeper within the chancel, the niche that held the statue of the Blessed Virgin. In the moment it took to take in this scene his mind flashed back with its usual dogged persistence to the single most momentous occasion of his religious experience—the funeral of his beloved Alysse. The flickering candles brought it all back. The coffin, the funeral march, the monks in the choir, Father Athanasius' funeral homily preached all in Latin but translated for him by one of the brothers, the deep and unsatisfying sense of hollowness within him when it was over.

All of this transpired in only that moment it took to walk past the open doorway of the church. He continued through the foregate, released the horse to one of the sheriff's grooms, and headed home. The path took him past *The Pint and Ploughman*, where he stopped for a drink to clear his head.

"Ale." That was all he said to Sarabeth. She brought a flagon in silence. He failed to notice the way she fussed with a stray lock of her hair in the thin light of the doorway, or the bustling physicality of her body as she reached across his right shoulder to set the flagon before him on the table. There were so many troubles that required his attention, not least among them the emerging difficulty with his daughter, who was approaching womanhood with a petulance unbecoming a peasant girl in the year of the Lord 1253.

If nothing else, the goings on in the king's forest told him the girl was hiding something from him. He could abide a strong-willed child, but not a liar. Then there was her obstinate refusal even to talk about the marriage he had arranged for her with that boy in Aberystwyth. There was the dragon the had appeared in the hut. Beneath it all, tugging strongly at the corners of his mind, was that troubling business with the wolf pup, with its flickering rapid-fire images revealing a deeply disturbing connection with Alysse, just as everything he did or said was connected in one way or another with Alysse.

When he looked up finally from the flagon of ale, Sarabeth was seated opposite him at the table, watching him intently. She was a large, rawboned woman whose ruddy complexion and long braid of thick red-gold hair reflected her Scottish ancestry. For all the energy she usually exuded, Sarabeth was also capable of that deep inner quiet of a woman accustomed to waiting. The world had not rewarded her wait, so that even though she was now past her prime, Sarabeth had known neither the pleasures of marriage nor the joys of motherhood. What maternal instincts she possessed she lavished on the patrons who frequented her brother Willem's pub for ale, man and woman alike, but among these she paid special attention to those who were without the care of a wife at home, such as John the Fletcher who in his loneliness had occasionally sought out her help or advice about what to do with his daughter, Elspeth.

"So, John," she said, eyeing him with more than her usual circumspection. "What's troubling you tonight? You've got that look on your face again."

He did not move, but simply looked at her. She always made such a fuss when he was there.

"Don't you know I worry about you so?" Sarabeth was saying. Her voice rippled from her, deep throated and smooth like aged brandy, set off against the hubbub and clatter of the pub by the rolling lilt of her native Scotland.

"I was thinking about a funeral mass a lot of years ago," he said.

"Alysse," she clucked. "You'll not move along from that now will you?"

He sat silent as she talked.

"Aye," she said. "I remember it well enough myself. Quite vividly as it happens. You alone on the mourners' bench. Willem and I sat in the transept. I held the baby, remember? I remember pulling my blanket up around her against the winter chill. Sister Bertrice sat there beside us, remember?"

Fletcher drained the flagon. Sarabeth was back in a moment with a pitcher.

"Could I tell you something, Sarabeth, just between the two of us?" he said. "I remember watching you there. I even thought at the time that except for your face, it could have been Alysse sitting there, holding the child before its baptism." For a moment the scene flashed across Fletcher's troubled imagination. The baby dressed in a white baptismal robe. The candles gone, the church festooned with banners. The chant, while serious, would have been full of hope.

Somebody at the back of the pub called for Sarabeth's attention. When she returned, she sat down beside him. "The funeral. What time did it begin?"

"I remember the bells tolling Sext." Sarabeth's question thrust him headlong and heart-long back into the nightmare. In his mind's eye he saw a faceless acolyte whose solemn ministrations with the incense brazier had filled the air with the thick sweet smell of a church in mourning. Then came the coffin, a simple lead-lined wooden box that had been made by one of the monks in the monastery woodshop. He remembered wanting to crawl inside it, to join Alysse in the sweet oblivion of the box, but could not because he had to care for her baby. Behind the pallbearers filed the monks of the Monastery of St Cuthbert and St Chad. Then the other acolytes, the sacred scriptures, and last of all Father Athanasius. Athanasius carried an incense brazier on a silver chain, singing the words of the liturgy in high-pitched Latin, swinging the brazier systematically in the direction of the various sectors and rows of the worshippers, blessing them with the heavy smells and sounds of the Christian burial rite.

"Father Athanasius officiated, remember?" he went on.

"Who can forget Athanasius, God rest him?" said Sarabeth. Athanasius had been the priest at St Cuthbert's for as long as anyone could remember, since the turn of the century even, until the inevitable infirmities of old age had forced him from his pulpit. Fletcher looked around the hut at Willem's patrons. There was hardly a man or woman there whom Athanasius had not baptized. He had buried most of their parents, and some of their husbands and wives, and sadly one or two of their children. It had been Athanasius who had officiated at his marriage to Alysse, and Athanasius who had baptized their child.

But on the day of Alysse's funeral, Fletcher thought, it had also been Athanasius, acting the role of pallbearer to his hopes and dreams, who had announced Alysse's death and in this sacrament prepared her soul for paradise, even as later on in the spring it had been Athanasius who had consigned her body to the earth.

"Yes," said Fletcher. "Who can forget Athanasius?"

"Don't remember his sermon, though" said Sarabeth. "That much was forgettable." She laughed a little, awkwardly.

"They were all forgettable," John replied. "He preached in Latin. Remember?"

"Aye. Not like Father Thomas." The new priest occasionally lapsed into English.

"Want to know what he said?" asked Fletcher, suddenly needing not to be alone.

"Don't tell me your talents extend to Latin, now."

"I'll tell you if you'll fetch another phitcher of ale." He was unaware that he had slurred the word "pitcher," but was alert to the blurring of the images in his mind's eye. The flames of Willem's candles, only moments before bright and crackling in the evening light, were now softening into an unreliable glow. In Fletcher's mind's eye, Willem's candles illuminated the movements of the monks in the church, and in their unsteady flickering light the shapes of their habits blended into huge ghostly shadows cast up against the walls of the chancel.

Sarabeth poured another drink. "Now," she said. "Tell me how you know Latin."

"Never said I knew Ladin," said Fletcher. "Said I knew what Fatherr said in his sermon."

"Alright, then, John," said Sarabeth. "Tell me that, then. But first tell me how you know."

He drank from the flagon, setting it down hard on the table. "One the monks transslted, doan remember which one."

"Brother Constantine?" she said. "He sat next to you."

"Righ, Constantine. It was Constantine translated Athnasius' serm'n for me. When th' other monks filed into the chancel, Constantine slipped in beside me on my pew. Whispeered everything right in my ear."

Fletcher was recalling the way the funeral entourage had processed down the north ambulatory, behind the final pew, and then up the center aisle. The pallbearers had set the coffin on a bier that had been placed at the point where the transept intercepted the nave. They then continued on to seats in the chancel, each one in turn bowing to the crucifix that hung above the high altar. As they mounted the short stairs to the chancel, unexpectedly Brother Constantine had broken ranks and had taken a place beside Fletcher on the mourner's bench. He was a small man, and his movements within the church had hardly been noticed by the other mourners.

All of this recollection Fletcher had kept in a tight bundle inside him, as if by clinging to the details he could keep them from fading in his mind. But tonight, what time and an aging memory could not accomplish was quietly being turned into a finished work by the powerful numbing effect of the ale.

"Probly this monk—Constantine—had hell to pay in Shapter."

"Now that you say it I remember the prior's frown!" said Sarabeth. Prior Robert had more than frowned; he had indicated his displeasure with a heroic scowl. He had been a much younger man then, and freshly installed in his office had been distracted from his duty to offer pastoral care by an unusually large preoccupation with his new authority.

"He give a look that wuld'v had the devil doing penance," Fletcher said, "but Constantine only smiled and nodded and settled in quiet."

"Tell me about the sermon," said Sarabeth. She poured him out another flagon of ale.

He concentrated hard on what she had said. "Lemme think a minit," he said. He reviewed the entire stock of his memories, running through them the way he might inventory a shelf of crossbows, but raggedly because of the ale. He remembered being thankful for the presence of another warm body beside his own. On every prior occasion he cared to remember, the space beside him at mass had been filled by Alysse herself, now reduced to a body in a coffin not more than a foot or so before him. He remembered almost reaching out to touch it, but shrinking back when Constantine whispered something in his ear too quietly to make out.

Then he started to cry, unashamedly because this was Sarabeth who would not think ill of him no matter what he did, and because the opinions of the other patrons did not matter to him.

Athanasius' funeral sermon had been reduced to a short homily, no doubt because Alysse, while well known and loved in the village and town, had not been a woman of consequence. A short homily was adequate for the wife of a peasant; the husband would not understand the Latin in any case. Athanasius had not reckoned on Constantine translating, but that little mattered.

"Athanasius said that we ought not to grief as those who got no hope." The tears were coming freely now. Fletcher did not care that Willem and the other patrons were watching him, maybe listening to what he said. "He said that Chrishians who die baptized and shriv'n are raised incorrubtible in the fin'l resurrecshun." Fletcher thought about Alysse's body, encased in its lead-lined coffin, already in that process of decay that is the end of all living things. Surely the hope of a bodily resurrection in paradise did much to allay the grief of those who are left behind. Even as his memory grew fluid and imprecise, still he was clear enough to know that Father Athanasius' words had been intended to ease the old priest's own doubting heart, his boney fingers raised in oratory, his own thick cough reminding the parishioners that the decay of the grave sometimes swallows us even while we live.

Then Sarabeth was saying something to him, but he couldn't make out what it was. He tried to stop the flow of images and confusions and tears to concentrate on what she was saying, but he couldn't do that now either. Sarabeth had slipped around on his side of the table and was cradling his head against her shoulder. "It was wrong, Sarabeth," he said. "Shoulda been me, died."

"But God has his reasons, John," said Sarabeth, stroking his black hair with her hand. He thought that was what she said. Maybe something else. "Shhh, now, God has his reasons."

It wasn't God's faull, he thought. *It was the faull that girl, that child. The girl did this to Alysse.* "Lea me 'lone for a few minutes, will you Sar'beth? I wanna thing thiss through."

Sarabeth disentangled herself from him and gently laid his head down across the table, and there, with the softly swirling sounds and bittersweet smells of *The Pint and Ploughman*, John the Fletcher dreamed the never-ending dream of Alysse.

He dreamed of the old priest stepping down from the high pulpit. He dreamed of Brother Constantine whispering that he would remember John and the baby in his prayers at Vespers, and then of Sarabeth bringing him the child. He dreamed of Alysse's coffin being taken to a crypt in the apse to await interment after the spring thaw. He dreamed of the other deaths that winter, other bodies consigned to temporary crypts in the apse, and of their burial in the sacred monastery grounds after a special funerary mass when the thaw made it possible to open up the ground.

Then he woke up, startled, clear only that he was in little condition to move. Willem and Sarabeth were locking up. He stood and warily made his way across the floor toward the door of Willem's pub.

"Better let us come along," said Willem. "We'll get you home, and in bed too."

Willem slipped Fletcher's right arm over his shoulder and Sarabeth came along the other side. With his free hand, Willem picked up a torch to light the path. It was dark already, and would be darker still when they made the return trip back to their hut.

As they made their way along the path, Fletcher tried to engage them in conversation.

"Iss a sinn?" he asked.

"Is what a sin?" asked Willem.

"What idiot priest said," said Fletcher, taking some clarity from the cool breeze that ruffled his hair and kicked up the branches of the trees. "Iss a sinn to grief?" What Fletcher did not bury, could not bury, was his sense of confusion and loss over this woman whose life had made his own complete. The priest's words, intended in their own way to comfort and encourage, had left him confused about the very grief they were designed to allay. And so he wondered if it was sinful that he still grieved. If it was, then it was a sin of which he would not repent; he had no choice but to live with this guilt.

"If not a sin, then a shame," said Sarabeth, as she shifted her weight to get a better grip. She slipped her arm closer around his waist.

Willem was more philosophical. "If you want an answer to a question like that, you should ask the idiot priest."

But Fletcher knew there were many questions he would not ask the idiot priest. Where was Alysse now? Did she miss their baby? Did she miss him? Where is the justice of a God who would take a mother and leave the child? What was the sense of that?

When Elspeth got home, the hut was empty and in disarray, as though her father had left in a hurry. The gate was unlatched, and the goose was in the lean-to tearing open one of the sacks of grain that had been stored there for grinding into flour. Inside the hut there was a half-eaten loaf of bread on the table, and her father's bed had been slept in but not made. At an earlier time in her life she would have found this worrisome, but lately, as the sheriff had come to rely more heavily on her father's skills as a watcher and hunter, he had been called to service on increasingly short notice, and had had to stay sometimes late into the night. He left word when he could, but that was the exception rather than the rule. He could leave no note because he could neither read nor write.

What Elspeth did at such moments varied with her mood and her level of hunger and whatever she read in the subtle clues her father might have left behind. Usually she simply waited until her father got home to prepare their supper. Sometimes she nibbled on whatever fruits or vegetables were at hand to curb her appetite, but sometimes, when the appetite began to gnaw with a sixteen-year-old's peculiar voraciousness, she simply went ahead and cooked, keeping her father's portion hot on the fire until whatever hour he got home. It was an imperfect system, but in the absence of written communication it kept them both fed.

Elspeth corralled the chickens and then scattered pieces of the bread near the chicken coop. She caught the goose and returned it to its pen. Inside, she made her father's bed, swept the floor, and then started a small fire to warm the hut while she waited for her father. The sun set. The evening breezes turned chilly.

She started supper, chopping the ingredients for a thick gruel and setting them on the pot to boil. Still she waited. Still no sign. From time to time she returned to the pot to stir the gruel so it wouldn't burn on the bottom. She was stirring the pot when she heard the sound of voices on the cart path outside. Willem. Sarabeth. Her father. Willem's voice and Sarabeth's were clear and distinct—she would have recognized them anywhere—but the voice of her father was muted and slurred and it took a moment for her to realize who it was. She thought at first that her father must be sick, and she had the door open before they arrived, and had pulled a chair back from the table and thrown back the covers of the canopy bed in case they needed that instead.

Her father was muttering something about "idiot priest" and "phurgatory" and "'Lysse," all of which told Elspeth nothing at all except that the man was not sick, but drunk. Very drunk.

"I have him now," she said to Sarabeth and Willem. "I'll see his bar bill is paid in the morning."

The three of them moved Fletcher to the bed and Elspeth pulled off his shoes and lifted his legs up onto the bed. Fletcher was sweating heavily now, and Elspeth was aware that he might be sick. She turned to look for a bowl. When she turned back, Willem and Sarabeth were closing the door behind them. She heard something that sounded reassuring—not to worry about the bill, all would be well—but was called back to the bed by the sound of her father retching into the bowl.

Then she heard sputtering at the fire. She turned back quickly to see that the gruel had boiled over and was spilling out in sporadic bursts and pops, threatening to douse the flame. Elspeth grabbed at the pot handle to stop the spilling and more importantly to salvage what she could of the gruel. It was a quick unplanned urgent gesture, and in her hurry she neglected to pad her hand against the heat. The searing pain of the burn was instantaneous; she later discovered that it had left a long red welt across three of her fingers and a part of her palm. She jerked back, upsetting the tripod that held the pot over the fire, falling backward against a chair. The gruel spilled out onto the floor, making a large steaming mass across both the floor and her dress, giving her another shot of pain, this one less intense but distributed over a wide area on her left leg. Worse, she twisted the leg as she fell.

Her father was upon her then, lunging at her, stepping into the steaming gruel, his fists flailing. Elspeth tried to get to her feet, but the twisted leg did not support her weight. Her father brought a chair down hard across her back. The chair splintered into six or seven large pieces, all of them sent flying or sliding across the floor. He slipped and came down hard on his right knee in the steaming mass.

Then it was over. The gruel, thinning as it spread, had cooled very quickly into a terrible but harmless mess. Her father, sick from the pain and the alcohol managed only to raise himself enough to fall backward onto the bed. Elspeth stumbled outside, and for a while sat spread-eagled by the door catching her breath and trying to think through what she should do next. Then, when the searing pain again demanded her attention, she struggled up and stumbled to the well, where with her unburned left hand she drew up a bucket of cool, clear, healing water.

She went and sat down in the lean-to, pulled wheat sacks around herself for warmth, and waited for either sleep or morning, whichever might come first, to provide relief from her confusion and fear.

It was in one of those fitful, intermittent periods of sleep that she found herself disturbed by the excited cackling of the hens, themselves disturbed by something on the roof. She was sure she was dreaming, but even in her sleep when she held her breath and listened carefully she caught the barely audible sound of a presence, and then a heavy movement above that started on the roof and ended near the chicken coop. She thought at first that a sudden gust of wind might have rustled the leaves in the trees beyond the fence, but the trees closer to the house were absolutely still, and she could see by the light of the half-moon that the movement in the yard was different than wind—closer to the ground, steadier, more substantial. A low growl anchored her attention around the side corner of the house.

In her dream she pulled in her arms and legs, frantically scrambling to hide herself behind the wheat sacks, and then when she had her head covered too she watched out of the triangular opening of the lean-to.

The creature was in the barnyard this time, moving across the tight space where the pathway came close to the corner of the hut. Its tail was stretched out and its spines raised, the way a porcupine might raise its quills when it felt threatened. It had grown. The wings were a better fit to its body now, and she had the impression that it could probably fly. Its eyes flashed, and another low rumble welled up within its throat. The rumble was short and raspy, the sort of sound that would have developed into a roar had the creature been larger and more mature. To Elspeth the rumble was enough. The fear was the same, and it was there from the moment that the dream began. This time the curiosity was gone, and the fear presented itself as her only emotion, intensified and made concrete by the throbbing welt on her hand and the scalded skin on her leg. The creature was something from a nightmare, and the fear gripped the girl instantly.

She rubbed the ache in her back where the chair had hit. Almost reflexively she reached for a metal rod that was leaning against the corner of the hut, not really knowing if such a weapon would be of any use against a creature like this one, but realizing also that doing something was better than simply waiting for the animal to attack. As she did so, a blast of flame shot from the creature's nostrils. She threw the rod. She had not been burned, but was now terrified. She turned suddenly, and scrambled for the space behind the stacks of supplies that were stored in the lean-to.

She cried out for her father like before, but this time she was aware that her father, drunk and sick in the hut, would not come to her aid. The cry, oddly, seemed to be enough for the moment. The creature retreated. There was a long silence, punctuated in the distance by the barking of a dog.

When she woke up she tried to recall the dream. It had all seemed so real, as real and vivid as the throbbing pain in her hand and leg. If her father had not told her that the creature was the stuff of dreaming, she would have staked her life on the fact that it was real. Whatever she might have thought about the reality of the dragon, she knew that the fear at least was real. She prayed for this nightmare to pass, and then, slowly, in what seemed like an answer to her prayer, she felt her spirit calm and her heart slow. Her mind moved to other things. She thought vaguely of the saying she had once heard at church—weeping endures for the night, but joy comes in the morning.

But the danger had passed and there was nothing more to be done. She nestled down deeper into the grain sacks and went back to sleep.

Fletcher's head felt like it had been filled with cotton soaked in creosote, and then split open with an axe. He tried to spit, but his mouth was dry, and nothing came except for the flat acrid taste of tar. His knee throbbed, and below the knee there were scalded places where the skin had been burned. None of this made any sense to him, and he sat for a long time trying to clear his head.

He tried to reconstruct what had happened during the night. The hut was a shambles. One of the chairs was broken. The fire pit and the tripod had been overturned, and ashes were scattered across the floor. Mixed in with the ashes a mess of cold gruel had spread out on the floor in the shape of Warwickshire. The girl was gone.

Then slowly the story came back to him in broken, fragmented images, shattered images like a stained window he once saw in War-wick that had cracked and then shattered under the strain of a small earthquake. He had come home drunk. Must have stopped at *The Pint and Ploughman*, but there was no memory of coming home. The girl had spilled the gruel, and may have burned her hand. It was impossible to tell what had happened first. He seemed to recall saying something harsh to the girl, something about Alysse.

After that, the memory mired in a fog as thick as the spilled gruel.

When Elspeth woke again she was huddled into the farthest, deep-est corner of the lean-to. She ached from the cold and the cramped position in which she had fallen asleep. She reached back and forced her hand against the small of her back, pushing hard to try and warm the muscles. A spasm ran through her right leg. Through the opening she could hear the chickens, and see the sun, and smell the dew that was heavy on the grass. She pulled herself up and out, working her way over the pile of wheat sacks and supplies.

The leg was a problem, and she found a stick to use as a make-shift crutch. In the middle of the yard she found the metal bar she had thrown at the creature the night before. It was fully fifteen feet from the opening of the lean-to. *I must have thrown it hard,* she thought. She was thankful that she had not hit one of the animals.

She did not go back into the house because she had no idea what she would find there. Her father had been drinking, and there had been an accident with the fire. Clots of gruel had spattered up onto her dress, and there was a mess of it dried on her leg. Her hand was now throbbing with the burn from the handle of the pot. A thick angry red line ran diagonally across three of her fingers and the palm, where the welt was already beginning to blister.

She went to the well and tried to turn the handle with her left hand, hoping to draw some fresh water for the welt, but also to delay going into the hut. She could not go to Levente's shop with the spattered gruel on her clothing. Besides, the welt would make it hard to do her work, and it would raise questions she would not want to answer. This dilemma, while painful, suddenly made one thing very plain: She was in danger, and it had something to do with her father, and with her unbidden dreams of dragons.

She considered her options. If it came to it, she could hide in the bivouac in the king's forest, but that would only serve in an emergency. A better plan would be to stock it as a way-station, a place to launch a run for Coventry, or maybe Wales. If she ran, would she take the horrors of the dreams with her?

"What happened to you?" It was Alcera's voice and it was coming from behind her. Elspeth jumped, startled and for some reason embarrassed, as though she had been caught doing something shameful. She turned to see the master seamstress walking along the path. The older woman turned into the yard, closing the distance between them quickly. "You look like you've been in a fight, Els. What happened?"

"I . . ." Elspeth started, but was interrupted. She was aware of deep blushing, ashamed again. The feeling of having been caught at wrongdoing filled her head. She couldn't think clearly.

"She spilled some gruel last night by accident, Alcera." Her father was speaking from the doorway, answering Alcera's question before she could. "When she went to stand up after supper she tripped and fell. Spilled gruel all over herself. It's not serious," he said. "Isn't that right, girl?" he said, looking for confirmation.

"I'll be alright," Elspeth said. "I slipped and fell. I caught my hand on the tripod and spilled everything. You should see the welts on my fingers." She held out her hand for Alcera to see. "I was just coming out to the well for some more cold water."

"Those welts look angry, Els," said Alcera. She turned the hand over, opening the fingers gently for a better look. "You take the rest of the day to see to them. Be especially careful with the blisters because if they break, the sickness will get worse. We'll look for you tomorrow."

"Thank you, Alcera," said Elspeth. "I'll do that and see you tomorrow."

"And keep off that leg," said Alcera, as she continued her journey.

Elspeth limped inside and helped her father clean up the mess from the night before.

જ

After the death of Father Athanasius, the Church of St Cuthbert had a new priest whose preaching had caught the attention of both civic and diocesan officials because of its emphasis on the importance of duty, always a safe topic now that Thomas Aquinas was baptizing Aristotle's Great Chain of Being and making it the basis for a just and ordered society. Human over animal. Husbands over wives. Parents over children. Civic authorities over private citizens. Church over state. Thus Aquinas asserted a fresh claim for the final authority of Holy Mother Church over all things.

Following the Eucharist, Father Thomas replaced the elements, and turned quietly and mounted the high pulpit to deliver his sermon, the movement of his robes causing a faint crackle as he climbed the steps. He was a tall, thin man with angular features and a nose that might have been broken in a fight. What always struck Constantine was Thomas' fingers—they stuck out of his hands like sticks, with large knots where the joints would have been.

Thomas was both a priest and a brother of the monastery itself, where he had lived in cloistered seclusion since the day he had taken vows fourteen years past. He therefore answered to two ecclesiastical authorities—Prior Robert, who managed the affairs of the Monastery of St Cuthbert and St Chad, and Bishop Stefan, whose See at Coventry oversaw the whole of Warwickshire. While Prior Robert rightly supervised the business of the monastery and acted on its behalf in affairs of the world, there were rumors that Thomas chafed at the limits this imposed upon him, and had even chided Robert in private over any steps he might have taken that Thomas thought unwise or theologically lax. Robert, the rumors said, endured Thomas' remonstrations with patience and good humor, and some of the monks thought privately that by doing so he better prepared his soul for heaven.

A simple man himself, Father Thomas was thoroughly imbued with the spirit of the Church, and Christendom was for him the encompassing principle upon which the whole of life turned, ecclesial and secular and familial, so that the very concept of authority outside the life of faith was quite impossible for him to conceive.

Whatever his theological reasoning, and however troublesome for his fellow monks, Thomas assumed full autonomy within the monastery church, and therefore also over the spiritual life of its congregation. He wore his ecclesiastical authority like an oversized habit—he smothered himself in it. It was his brother monks who chaffed beneath it like a hair-shirt.

It was the final Sunday of June, and within the congregation— hosted by the monastery—there was a contingent of military men lately returned from the Holy Land. Father Thomas had chosen for his text St Paul's wonderful admonition to the Romans to obey the civic authorities, thinking that in this one text he could elaborate a whole complex of ideas showing that obedience to authority was God's right and only way.

As always, Father read out the text of scripture in Latin, Jerome's Vulgate having served the needs of the devout for nearly a thousand years. Most of his sermon was in Latin, too, which left it unintelligible to the villagers and townspeople, but the old priest's Latin was not fluent and in his great fervor for the gospel he occasionally lapsed into English. Thus the villagers heard the Word of God. The prayers, the hymnody, and the scriptures, all were sung or spoken in Latin, but then entangled within them were threads of exposition in English. Invariably these moments of enlightenment came when Father was in high fervor, so that they tended to be shouted rather than spoken, driven forward and made compelling, not by any inherent logic, but merely by ferocity and passion. As confused as this style of preaching could be, when the villagers listened intently they could sometimes make out the lines of the old priest's thinking. Between these moments, when the priest returned to his Latin drone, they had ample time to ponder the ways of God and man. For those among them who were unlettered this was the closest they might come to hearing the very Word of God.

"*Omnis anima potestatebus sublimioribus subdita sit non est enim botestas nisi a deo. . .* Let every person be subject to the governing authorities, for there is no authority except from God,'" Father said abruptly, "so it says in our text. But why is this so?" He raised a crooked stick finger and directed it out generally at the entire assemblage of villagers and townspeople and monks who sat before him. "It is because the heart of man is desperately wicked, an unreliable guide in matters spiritual and temporal. It is this wickedness, this terrible fallenness, that tears apart all that is sacred and holy. Because of this wickedness, God has ordained authorities among men—to control the appetites and discipline the passions . . . ." Then he lapsed again into Latin.

As Thomas droned on, Fletcher's thoughts drifted to the sheriff and the order of the shire, and the battle with the Danes that had cost his father his fingers and thus also his trade as a huntsman. Surely his father had not paid this price in vain, but had paid it in the name of order. If the order of society was God's great plan for Christendom, obedience was good and right, but not only, as the priest had said, because it controlled the human appetites, but more importantly because God was a God of order and because God had made society itself, with its inherent structure of king and nobleman, villein and servant and slave, each in his place.

Fletcher quietly patted Elspeth's shoulder, indicating in that non-verbal language fathers share with daughters that the priest had made a good and important point. He whispered the name, "Meurig ap Gwynedd," but Elspeth shrank back slightly, allowing his hand to slip unheeded to her back.

To Fletcher this line of reasoning made sense, not because as a father he wished to be obeyed, but because as a sergeant in the service of the sheriff he had seen first hand the misery caused by masterless men who did not wish to be accountable for their actions. It was not a matter of who was right, but of who held the properly constituted authority—parents over children, baron over villein, king over baron, and Holy Mother Church over all.

". . . Holy Mother Church over all," Father continued, not knowing that his language had been anticipated by this quiet man in the back of his congregation. "It was disobedience that had caused the fall of Adam, and even now brings wars and famines, pestilence and plague, all visible signs of the evil and fallen state of man! Disobedience was the original and primal sin, the very thing for which God drove Adam from the garden!" By this time the priest was red-faced, nearly shouting out his sermon. What was the word he had heard? *Diatribe.* That was it. *Diatribe.*

Fletcher listened and thought about Elspeth and grew as red-faced as the priest, shamefully aware that he was the father of a disobedient daughter. Surely God would punish them both, the girl for her open rebellion against the law of God, and the father for his failure to teach his daughter this primary lesson of the Christian faith!

"Even this is indicated in the natural order, in the relation between animals and men," the priest continued. "For the higher animals are those that can be trained in the service of king and country, while those animals that cannot take training are the very ones that prey upon man, that destroy our crops and eat our farm fowl."

Fletcher thought about the wolves he had hunted and the damage they had done to the villagers' livestock. He thought about the moles and rabbits and rodents that burrowed their ways into the villagers' vegetable patches. He thought about the dragon. Surely the priest was right!

Elspeth usually listened to Thomas only sporadically, if at all. Thomas was a man of God, but he was hard to hear, just as the scriptures were hard to understand, and she wanted and believed she deserved clearer evidence from the maker of heaven and earth. A bird outside flew against the rose window with a nearly silent thud, and clouds now cast varied patterns of light and dark against the clerestory windows above her. The rivering light through the stained glass brought the biblical images to life; they captured her imagination and carried her away to the Holy Land. A willing conscript, she was. Perhaps she might even take the Cross and join the crusades if she could convince her father to teach her the skill of archery. She could dress as a boy! Maybe some nobleman on crusade would be willing to take along a high spirited lad with skill in archery and the ability to read.

"And so also," the priest continued, "when the Holy Apostle Paul instructs wives to obey their husbands, and children to obey their parents, and slaves their masters, he bases that admonition on the primary structure of the created order itself. For to rebel against parents or masters is to sin not only against God, but also against nature. In the same way, he means for those same husbands and parents and masters to train up their wives and children and servants to the holy estate of obedience, and in doing so to raise them from the lower form to the higher, and thus to save their souls!"

Elspeth gazed at the ceiling, hoping for a breath of air, but the church was fully enclosed so that not even the movement of the ushers along the ambulatories provided relief. The women fanned themselves. A not-so-subtle change of pitch in Father's voice caught her attention, and she suddenly sat up and tried to focus.

"*Filii oboedite parentiyus vestrin in domino* . . . Children obey your parents," Father said, "for in obeying your parents you learn the important lessons about obeying the civil authorities whom God has placed over you." Then came more Latin.

Like a ship dragging anchor, this final crescendo of the sermon caught her attention and held fast. So far as she was concerned, it might as well have been the whole of the sermon, and despite her growing sense of independence she found herself filled with consternation and shame because she knew, as her father knew, that she had within her an unrepentant heart and an unbroken spirit. For days now she had thought about running, about leaving him alone in the world, and then she had thought about killing him. It was a tearing of whole cloth, to think like that. He had been sent away from his home as a boy; he had been bereft of his wife as a man. Could she be the one who took his final human contact from him?

But in the last months, since she had stolen the wolf pup, he had grown angrier, more preoccupied, and more unpredictable. Something within him had soured like milk, and she could hardly avoid thinking that in some way it was her fault.

"He who spares the rod . . . . Chastise and discipline the soul . . . . Thus he draws us to Himself . . . ." The words echoed in Fletcher's head as the mass concluded. Such words were all the more painful because he had tried to train Elspeth into a life of obedience, but the girl had been headstrong, like a wild animal, following her baser nature. Now he had that idiot Levente and his wife to reinforce every bad trait in the girl. The harder he tried, the worse she got. Fletcher knew that despite his most serious efforts he had failed miserably in this foremost of a parent's duties—failed the girl, failed God, failed Alysse.

The mass ended. He rose and brushed past the girl in a hurry to get out of the church. Elspeth, limping, had to struggle to keep up. She caught up with him outside in the narthex. They walked home slowly then, impeded by her limp.

Fletcher did not say anything to the girl, and instead tried to piece together the key points of Father Thomas' rambling sermon. From this sermon, or more precisely, from what he understood of it, John Fletcher had in his own way resolved to do better by his daughter. He who spares the rod . . . . Chastise and discipline the soul. . . Thus he draws us to Himself . . . . Chastise and discipline the soul . . . . Thus he draws us to Himself . . . . He who spares the rod . . . .

Several weeks passed. There were fewer problems with wolves in the shire and the talk in the village turned to other things. Fletcher found himself reluctantly thinking about the wolf pup, but not understanding what had happened, or why it had happened, and that had led to a period of deep brooding. The episode with the wolf pup had unnerved him. He had seen something within himself he did not know was there, as real as if he had lived through a waking nightmare. In his darkest moments it all came back. The images, the blood, the wrenching of the pup's neck. All of this had happened only in his mind, but still it horrified him. In reliving the nightmare, he saw himself, too, clearly for once—angry and enraged and as wild as this animal he had almost killed with his bare hands. He did not like it that he had had to beat the girl, but he did not know what else to do to curb her rebellious, headstrong spirit. His treatment of his daughter—but how else could he treat her?—spoke to that same something within him he had not known was there, and he felt dirty and disgusted with himself, like the floor of the sheriff's stable.

These things he kept within his heart, torn apart as it was. One entire afternoon he spent walking alone along the back roads and forest paths of the shire. As he walked he pondered who he could share this struggle with. The priest? He had committed no sin. Elspeth? It would not do to let her see him question himself. The sheriff? It would not do to let such a man think less of him. Aelric was excluded, too, because he did not trust the man's discretion. He thought about the disturbances in his daughter's spirit, which also seemed to be growing, and these disquieted him even more.

When the sheriff's man Caedmon asked him to account for his time, he said merely that he had been keeping an eye on the king's forest.

At first he could not say whether he was troubled more deeply by the images that surrounded the incident with the pup or the appearance of the dragon, or by the growing disturbances in the girl herself, but in time this difficulty resolved itself as concern for his daughter. The girl was the one who had drawn the dragon into the shire. More than anything else this is what filled his thoughts as he trudged home to Wharram late that afternoon.

III

THE SUMMER HEAT WAS on them completely before Elspeth saw the dragon again, bigger and more threatening—fully grown. It was as though the dream were somehow becoming a reality to her, as though something within her was struggling to break free of her imagination and confront her face to face, in real life. From time to time she thought she smelled the stench of tar in the hut, hard and offensive, but always it drifted away, the way a dream disappears when one wakes up. The smell of tar always brought the dream back. She did not sleep well. She drew pictures of the creature on the scraps of paper Alcera's husband Levente had thrown away in the bookbindery.

More than once, while she was in Levente's shop the older woman had asked her what was troubling her. "Something's wrong, girl. Something's troubling you. What is it? You can tell me."

Usually Elspeth shrugged off Alcera's questions, or mumbled something about having had a bad dream, and Alcera was a tough, practical woman who did not like to pry into other people's affairs.

In midsummer the creature was back, emerging from the canopy bed and prowling the hut the way a cat might prowl a room, looking for a place to sleep. Elspeth lay perfectly still in her bed, but with her eyes wide open and her covers pulled up tightly around her chin.

The creature began to come every night, to prowl, to sniff. Once it crept close to her bed and sniffed her bedclothes as though it were looking for a warm place to nest for the night, but it turned away when the girl stared it directly in the eyes. That had given Elspeth courage, and the seed of a hope that somehow she could defeat the nightmare by the force of her will.

She had to do something quickly, though. The creature was getting bigger; it was now bigger than her father, and its wings were more proportionate, and growing more mature. She might have some chance against such a creature when it was young, but she would have great difficulty with one when it was fully grown.

In late July the creature shed its scales. It was a painful thing to see, and for the first time Elspeth felt something akin to pity for the creature. She watched in fascination right from the start. The shedding began almost as a dance, the creature drawing itself back until it stood erect on its hind legs, then whipping forward to produce a superb rippling along the spine. The rippling raised the scales and sent the looser ones skittering across the floor.

It thrust itself up, then back down again, then began turning every which way. As she thought about it later, Elspeth realized that this torturous twisting and turning was a way of loosening the older layer of scales so they could be shaken off or rubbed off against the post of the canopy bed. As she watched, the creature worked itself up into a frenzy or an ecstasy of pain, the rumbling coming up, then receding, then coming back again as the creature rubbed its sides against the canopy post. In that way, in a ritual dance that seemed to take half the night, it shed its skin the way a snake might if it had legs and rigid spines along its back.

As it did so, from underneath, a shiny new layer of scales emerged, each the size of a man's hand. The new scales were beautiful, with none of the chips or marks such a creature is likely to get in its scales as it grows older. And though they were shinier, they were also darker, a deep green along the back, deepening in hue until the plates on its underbelly were almost black. The edges of the new scales were bright yellow or gold, and in the dim light of the room and the rhythmic glowing of the creature's nostril flame they seemed to shimmer as it moved.

For a moment, Elspeth thought she loved it. It was as beautiful as it was terrifying, and she watched in fascination as this wholly new form of her dream emerged from its infancy into a new, powerful adulthood.

The creature seemed also to sense its new powers. It stretched its wings, now for the first time fully formed, and began a tentative flight around the perimeter of the room, but the space was too small. It thrashed its tail against the walls as it struggled to free itself from its confinement. The flame became enormous, enlarged by the creature's frenzy.

Elspeth grew terrified of the flame. What if it engulfed her? Worse, what if it were to catch the thatch of the roof? She and her father would both be engulfed in the flames. The hard stench of tar was now everywhere, and the heat became unbearable. The creature spat, and a sulfurous venom settled into the worn grooves on the floor. Elspeth struggled for breath. In a desperation of her own, she flung herself at the window, clawed at the shutters, then collapsed in a heap on the floor.

Before she lost consciousness she was aware of a roar or a scream from the creature as it crashed through the upper workings of the canopy bed, and of the creature's wings, pulled in sharply in a craning dive through the window, and of her own cry for her father, and of the terrible but very real fact that her father did not answer her.

She was awake. Or at least she thought she was awake. Scattered across the floor, like sawdust in the butcher shop, there was a thick layer of green scales. Elspeth reached out in a kind of dreamy stupor and picked up one, then another. In a moment, she had perhaps a dozen of the finest of the scales. She held one up to the window as her eyes adjusted to the light. They were hard and very thin, and almost translucent. She thrust them all in a pocket as she began to look more carefully around the room.

The hut was a disaster. The walls were badly damaged, the corner of the canopy bed was splintered away, and the surface of the bedpost was sanded beyond repair. In two or three places on the floor Elspeth saw little viscous pools of red-orange light, thick little pools that looked like dying embers and smelled of tar. She had never seen anything like them. They were like coals, but liquid and smooth, formed in perfectly round globs. They were almost mesmerizing. She knew that such things are real only in dreams. Without thinking she reached out her finger to touch one. She wanted to run her finger across the smooth surface, to see if the glob would move, to see if she could change its shape, to see if this was another dream.

It was a mistake. With a cry of pain she jerked back her hand, her finger now blistered and throbbing. Reflexively she stuck the injured finger in her mouth, sucking hard to ease the pain. The liquid was thick and bitter and it burned her tongue.

This was no dream. She was fully awake, and she knew she was awake. There was a blister on her finger and the burning aftertaste of tar on her tongue. The throbbing pain left her dazed and disoriented, and it was only when its effects had worn off that she realized how frightened she had become. It was also only then that Elspeth fully understood what had happened. The creature had become real. It had not only broken free of its prison in her dream. It had become real and had broken free of the hut as well.

Where was her father? Her father would be furious. What would she do when her father came home? The surge of fear that gripped her now was almost as great as the fear in her dream, when suddenly it deepened and became unbearable. She had not been able to control the dream, it had controlled her. It was as though the creature had a life of its own, had chosen her to give it birth, had incubated itself in her dream. If one such creature could do this in her mind, so could another. The nightmare would destroy her now, would destroy her father, would destroy perhaps the whole village. Where was her father?

The only place she could think to go was Levente's shop, where she found Alcera, working on a dress. The old woman mumbled something like, "It's open," without getting up from her stitching.

Elspeth obeyed, but said nothing.

Alcera had a half-dozen sewing pins in her mouth. She removed the pins and worked them one at a time into the fabric of the cloth, then looked at Elspeth directly. "Sit down, Els," she said.

"I'd rather stand."

"You get in another fight?" She reached out and touched Elspeth's chin, turning her face back and forth for a close inspection. "Come over here into the light," she said, leading Elspeth by the chin until she was near one of the candles.

"It's not what you think, Alcera."

"Let me guess. Your father lost his temper."

"That's not it, either," Elspeth said. "There's some kind of monster in our hut."

"I know that," Alcera said. "He's lost his temper with me a time or two, but I pinned his ears back." She sat back down and reached into the box where she kept her sewing needles and thread, selected a color, and wet the end of the thread with her tongue. She twisted the thread into a fine point, then used the candlelight to aim the thread through the eye of a needle. "You eaten?" she asked, not taking her eyes off her work. For an old woman, she had remarkably steady hands. "There's apples in that bin."

"It's a dragon," Elspeth said. She sat down on one of the work-benches. "At least, I think it's a dragon."

Alcera set her hands down on her lap and looked at Elspeth directly. "A dragon now, is it?"

Elspeth reached into her pocket and drew out some of the scales. "These were on the floor when I woke up."

Alcera held one of the scales up to the light. "Once a dragon sheds its scales it gets mean," Alcera said flatly. "Did your father tell you how it got in the hut?"

"My father says I dreamed it. I told you everything. The dragon escaped from my dream."

"That's not what happened," said the Alcera. "Levente's father had a dragon when they were boys. Dragons don't come from dreams, Els. Somebody's keeping a dragon your hut. Maybe it's been there all along, or maybe it came and went. The main thing is it didn't come from any dream."

"Who would hide a dragon in our hut?"

"I wouldn't be surprised if your father has something to do with this," said Alcera. "That man's got a temper, and dragons love that. But wherever it came from, it's a good bet it'll come back, and when it does, you're going to need help. You're going to have to tell somebody. The sheriff maybe."

"If it was in the hut, why didn't I see it during the day? Why only at night?"

Alcera told her about the mime, but then added a personal observation: "Dragons are strange creatures, girl. They frighten people. And the mind is a strange machine. It has trouble seeing things that frighten it. It pretends that everything is alright. That way it thinks it doesn't have to face the danger. Put those two facts together, and you've got a kind of magic. With magic like that it isn't hard for dragons to turn invisible. If you want to see them—really see them—you have to be willing to face truths that could very well frighten you half to death."

Alcera reached out and touched her arm reassuringly. "It takes courage to deal with a dragon. You have to begin by telling the truth."

"What are you talking about?"

"The truth is that there's a dragon in your hut. The truth is that it's real, not a dream. The truth is that you're going to have to ask for help, even if somebody you love and trust tells you to keep it a secret."

Elspeth was silent. What could she say to that?

"If you don't tell the authorities, I will," Alcera said.

"You won't say a word," a man's voice said. Levente came into the room and dropped a pile of cordwood near the fire. He knelt beside the pile and set the wood in a neat stack. He talked as he worked: "You turn him in, you destroy him."

"She's in danger," Alcera said simply.

"I'll talk to him," Levente said.

"Please, Levente," Elspeth said, "he'll find out I told you. You'll put me in danger."

"You're already in danger, Els," Alcera said. She turned to her husband. "He could hurt her real bad, Levente."

Elspeth agreed. "If you tell anybody, I'll be in greater danger. Let my father and me work this out for ourselves."

Alcera completed her line of stitches, snipped off the thread with a pair of shears. "Watch yourself, Els. If you need us, come here. Right here. Levente can handle your father. Understand?"

Elspeth turned to Levente. "How do you know about dragons?"

"My father was banished from the kingdom for keeping a dragon," Levente said, standing up from his stack of wood. "The night he was banished, the dragon disappeared. Your father should know about that. He couldn't keep away from it, even though it burned his hand once."

Alcera stood and reached out to touch Elspeth gently on the shoulder. "People get this dragon thing all wrong," she said, glancing at Levente sideways. "Levente's father didn't keep that dragon—the dragon kept him."

Elspeth eyed Alcera warily, not sure what to make of such a comment.

"Something happens when a dragon sheds its scales," Alcera said. "It's gets hard to get rid of. It's like the dragon's in charge, instead of the man. Levente's father tied his dragon down with a chain, but it turns out he was the one who couldn't get free. The dragon took over. So you can't just chase it away. Something else has to happen. Besides, when a dragon sheds its scales, it turns dangerous."

"What else?"

"Levente told me once his father got to be more and more like his pet, until it reached the point where the two boys could hardly tell the man from the beast. Now eat something and rest. You've been through a lot, and you'll go through a lot more before you're done with this."

Elspeth gathered up the scales from the seamstress' table, thrust them into her pockets, and made her way quietly down the path that led from the bookbindery to what was left of the hut. When she reached the hut her father was patching a cracked place on the wall above the splintered canopy bed. A pile of yellow scales had been swept into the corner, and the bed was turned around so the sanded post faced against the wall.

"You knew about the dragon all along, didn't you, Father?" asked the girl.

Her father said nothing, but kept working. To Elspeth's mind, the silence was an admission of guilt.

"It's your dragon, then?"

Nothing.

Elspeth went to him and shoved him hard onto the bed to stop the incessant moving of the broom. "Talk to me, Father!"

"I don't know what you're talking about."

"You lied to me!" said the girl.

"*I* lied to *you*?"

"You told me the dragon was a dream."

"I said that because I didn't know whose it was. I thought it might be yours. I was protecting you while I figured out what to do about it."

"Protecting me? You were protecting me? You let me think that the dragon was a dream, that it was something only in my mind, and you say you were protecting me?" Elspeth's confusion was giving way to anger. "How could you do something like that? How could you do that to your own daughter?"

"When dragons are small they're harmless. I didn't know whose it was. I thought that if it was yours we could release it before it shed its scales."

"Harmless like the one that burned your hand?" she said, then realized this had been a mistake and turned her eyes away.

Fletcher stopped working and stared at his daughter. "Who told you that?" he demanded. The tone in his voice was becoming surly. It was a tone the girl had never heard before. He slammed his fist down on the table and demanded an answer: "Who told you that?"

She stood silent, refusing to answer.

He hit her across the face with his open hand. 'Answer me!" He towered over her, so close Elspeth could smell his breath, hard like tar, a fury breathing down upon her. The muscles of his jaw tensed. Alcera had been right. He was a looming, malevolent presence. She stared at his fists, which were closed so tightly his knuckles were bled white. Her father was threatening her with his backhand.

The threat galvanized her courage, but it calmed her anger. She backed toward the door. "Father, where were you when the dragon appeared all those nights?" she asked, in a softer tone, though, as though she were more curious than angry. She supposed that a change of topic might weaken her father's growing fury.

He opened his fist, and his face softened. "Outside, guarding the door."

She breathed in then, and was aware only in retrospect that she had been holding her breath and had nearly passed out from the lack of air. She gulped now, almost convulsively trying to take in enough breath to function. Her father sat down. She leaned heavily against a wall, waiting for her breathing to normalize. Finally, she sat down on the edge of her small bed.

She did not know how long she sat there before she had calmed herself enough to speak to her father again. When she looked up, he had oddly stood and returned to his sweeping.

"That's why I never saw you when I saw the dragon?" she asked.

"That's why," said her father. He turned and looked at her. "I was protecting you, like I said."

"But the danger was all inside the hut."

"I thought the dragon was yours, Els."

"You thought it was mine?" She couldn't believe what she was hearing. "How do you think that the hut got wrecked? You think I did this?"

"First things first. If Ranulf figures out we've got a dragon here, we're in serious trouble. The sheriff'll take us away."

"It's your dragon, Father, not mine," said the girl. "He'll take you away, not me."

Her father's face reddened, and he sent his fist crashing down on the table. "I'm going to say this one more time—I, have, no, dragon. You tell anybody I have a dragon, and they'll take me away, and it'll be your fault. I've got no dragon."

Elspeth felt a pang. No wonder he was angry. But she'd told Alcera and Levente about the dragon, and they could tell the sheriff. And her father would be arrested and sent away, and it would be her fault. Without her father, even this father, she would be lost. She would lose herself. The matter had little, nothing at all, to do with who would take care of her. Whatever else, he was right about this: She had disobeyed him. He had told her not to tell anyone about the dragon because he loved her, and what had she done? She'd gone straight to Alcera. He said she had betrayed his trust, and that much had been right.

But if the dragon wasn't her father's, whose was it? Maybe this was all her fault. The trouble had started when she took the wolf pup from the king's demesne. No, *stole* was the proper term. She had stolen the pup. Maybe that was what had allowed the dragon to slip into the hut. If something terrible happened, it would probably be her fault.

She made up her mind then. No matter what, she would not be the cause of her father's arrest, even if it meant that she had to lie to Alcera, who had told her only the truth. It was a terrible decision, and it cost her something very dear, something she could not quite grasp.

IV

As Ranulf approached the armory, he heard a general commotion. Several guardsmen were arming themselves in anticipation of an immediate need.

"What's going on here?" he asked the sheriff's man, Caedmon.

"Somebody's slaughtered and eaten two of the villagers' animals, m'lord," said the sergeant, then adding, "somebody or some*thing*." He was genuinely frightened. "Left 'em out in the barnyard."

"What do you mean 'some*thing*?'" asked the sheriff. As he talked, he donned his leather fighting vest. "And what animals?"

"Dogs, m'lord."

"Dogs?"

"We don't know what done it, m'lord. It's not that they was killed, but that they was killed in such a peculiar way."

"Calm down, sergeant. What are you talking about?" He reached for his sword.

"Mutilated and burned. It's awful."

"But not a wild animal?"

"That wouldn't explain the burns, m'lord."

"Who would eat dogs?"

"Who or *what*," said the sergeant. He seemed genuinely horrified, which was a surprise to Ranulf. The sergeant was a trained fighting man and had seen more than his share of terrible and sordid things in his day, and even though he was aging now his horror was quite difficult to understand.

"Where did you say this happened?"

"In Wharram."

"Has anyone moved anything or touched anything?"

"I set up a guard to keep the curious away. And the children."

"Very well, then," said the sheriff. "We go to Wharram. Have someone run ahead and summon John the Fletcher and have him meet me at the site. Have the squire saddle my horse."

"Have done so already, sire."

Another of Ranulf's sergeants was waiting when he arrived in Wharram. "There are two victims, m'lord. On two different farmsteads."

"Take me to the closer of the two," Ranulf replied. As they made their way, the sergeant described the scenes in detail. Two dogs. Both horribly mauled. The damage could not have been inflicted by a wild animal—say a wolf or a fox—because of the size of the teeth marks, which measured the full span of a man's hand. Whatever had done this had had a cavernous mouth, with wide jaws. More to the point, he said, the dogs had been burned, scorched, so that their hair and hide had in some places been reduced to charred ruins.

The evidence confirmed the report. It was the charring that had created the havoc among the villagers and the guardsmen.

"In neither site is there evidence that someone struck a fire. No small twigs or logs. No human footprints even."

"Any signs of a struggle?"

"Not what you'd expect, m'lord," said the sergeant, kneeling down on the perimeter of the area. "See here," he said. "There's human footprints all over, but this is a farm, remember, and the farmer's in and out of the paddock all the time. But look close here: Within this circle the human prints have all been trampled by those of the dogs and whatever animal killed 'em." He shook his head. "No hunters here."

The site was indeed grisly. The farmer on whose land this had taken place was anxious to clean up the evidence and bury his animal. He wanted the villagers off of his property. Ranulf nodded his permission and the guards withdrew. They herded the remaining farmers and villagers before them as they left. "Go along, now," one of them was saying. "Sheriff is here. All will be sorted out properly. Due time. Due time. Back to your homes."

"Anything more to be learned from the second site?" Ranulf asked the sergeant.

The sergeant shook his head. "It's the same. They're weird tracks, like a bird. Got talons, maybe, but too large for any bird I ever saw."

"Where is it? The second site, I mean."

"A quarter mile to the south, sire. Down the path that leads along the southern edge of the common."

"Very well, then. Release that site also. Then have the men interview everyone in the village who might have seen or heard anything. I'm interested in the time of the attack. Ask about anything unusual. Dogs barking, for example. Horses disturbed. Things like that. Ask if they saw any flashes of light. Also about unusual footprints. Understand?"

"Yes, m'lord."

"Report back to me at the end of the day."

Just then John Fletcher arrived—Ranulf's most skilled hunter. The man was breathless, tucking his tunic into his pantaloons as he hurried across the farmyard.

Ranulf was waiting for him: "Come with me, will you?"

"Yes, m'lord," said Fletcher. The three men walked back in the direction of the town. Ranulf waited until they were well beyond earshot of the villagers, then he spoke to John, keeping his voice low but direct: "I have no idea what kind of animal did this, Fletcher, but I think it may be a dragon."

"Hasn't been a dragon around here for years," said Fletcher.

The sergeant was more direct: "Didn't your father keep a dragon once, John? When you were a boy? Didn't I hear that?"

"That was years ago," Fletcher said. "And it was Levente's father, not mine."

Ranulf turned and spoke directly to Fletcher: "I want you to hunt it down and kill it. The sergeant will give you any help you need."

"As you wish, m'lord," said Fletcher.

"What're you going to do?" asked Elspeth. Her father had come in after dark, tired and hungry from the hunt. As she fixed him something to eat, he had reported to her about the dragon flying loose in the village.

"It wouldn't be loose if you hadn't opened the window," he said, ignoring the supper she had set on the table.

"Eat something," she said. "You'll feel better."

"That was stupid." Her father doubled his fist and brought it crashing down on the table, breaking a dish and scattering the food she had fixed for him. He flung a chair into the corner of the room, then turned on her. "You're a wicked girl," he said. "People are going to get hurt, and it'll be your fault."

"My fault? You think this is my fault?" She said this despite her self-doubt. "You son of a bitch."

"You don't talk to me like that. You should've been born a boy." He grabbed her by the collar and jerked her upward into the air. "Stand up." He was a large man, but now he seemed immense. "Stand up."

He hit her then, open handed. "For what you did to your mother," he said.

She wanted to cry, but checked herself. Crying would give him the upper hand.

"Shut up," he said, "somebody'll hear you," then he hit her again, with a closed fist this time. The beating lasted until Fletcher was exhausted. He headed for the door, leaving Elspeth battered in the corner of the hut.

"The sheriff told me to find it. I'm going to hunt it down and kill it. I'll try and undo your evil. Don't say anything to anybody else about this. Not a word. You understand me?"

Elspeth held her arms high and in front to protect her face. She understood. At least, she understood what her father was going to do. But she didn't understand why. She had done nothing wrong. Why had she been beaten? She was angry at him for beating her, angry at herself for wanting to cry, angry at her mother for abandoning her. Nothing made any sense. All she knew for certain was that her stomach heaved, and as it did so she found the bitter aftertaste of tar at the back of her throat.

Fletcher hardly slept that night. His dreams were a mix of night sweats and flashing images—orders from Ranulf, and his duty to defend the peasants from any harm that might come to them or their farm animals, and pictures in his head, pictures of Alysse and the girl and the dragon.

He found some beer in the dark and drank it straight from the pitcher, wiping his mouth with the open palm of his hand. He had to figure out what to do about the dragon. And even then, could he do it?

A week passed. Elspeth did not leave the hut, did not go to Levente's shop to work.

Alcera, alarmed, came checking on her, but she answered from behind the door that she was sick. A woman's cramps, she said. Terrible. She would be back when she could.

Elspeth's father came back to the hut for provisions, and sometimes for rest, but he said nothing about his hunt for the dragon. Instead, he was strangely silent and he didn't look at her as he came and went. Sometimes he hunted with Aelric, and sometimes alone. If she asked at all about the hunt, he became either evasive or angry, both of which she thought were born of his frustration at not finding the dragon. Maybe he was afraid. No matter how she turned the matter over in her mind, she could not escape the nagging sense that it was wrong for her father to blame her for what was happening. This wasn't her dragon. Perhaps she should make for the bivouac, and then Wales, but she hesitated because it would not do to encounter the dragon alone in the forest. She was growing in her sense that she didn't deserve her father's anger.

Sometimes she could tell that her father had grown close by the smell of tar that would cling to his clothes. It was a frightening smell, and she admired his courage that he should move so deliberately in tracking down and destroying the creature. Elspeth hated the dragon and wanted it dead. The hatred galvanized her own courage, and from it she drew strength to deal with the terrible sense of danger she felt—for herself, for her father.

During these weeks Elspeth herself sighted the dragon several times. More than once the shadow of its wingspan had swept across the countryside like a fast-moving cloud. Elspeth thought from the size of the shadow that the dragon had become enormous. The shadow frightened her more than the dragon itself; it seemed a symbol for the hold the dragon had on her. This was especially so when it flew against the sun. Then it enfolded her in its darkness as it blotted out the light.

Once, she caught sight of the dragon soaring along the edge of the bluff, no doubt looking for a sheep for prey, then another one moving in a different direction. That sighting had lasted for fully a minute, and Elspeth had watched as the animal drew in its wings tight against its body and dropped like a stone, spreading its wings again hard and fast just when its speed had reached breakneck. When it reappeared, it clutched a mule or a horse in its outstretched claws, spread its wings in a long graceful flight, and disappeared beyond the bluff to the north. Later that day, Levente told her it had been a pack horse, and that the loss for the sheriff had been as much in the equipment it had carried as in the animal itself.

Elspeth was afraid—for herself, for the village children surely, and worse, for her father. Maybe she really was the one who had brought the dragon into the shire, had sheltered it in her dream life, had given birth to it, had unleashed it on the village and the town. Maybe there was a whole roil of dragons. There could be others in neighboring towns, or raiding the villages north of the mountains. Even her prayers did nothing to stop it.

When Elspeth could break free, she began making trips to the bivouac. She took a dress, and an extra pair of pantaloons, and two old tunics she rarely wore, tunics her father would not notice were missing. On one trip she took tools to make a fire, and on another she took a blanket and some of the fruit that had been stored in the lean-to. She had no plan or method in this project, and instead took only what she could rightly call her own. She avoided things that she and her father used frequently, and things that would not have a definite usefulness to a girl who was running from something and needed to travel light.

Unknown to Elspeth, Fletcher was fully aware of developments at the bivouac. His concern for his daughter's welfare combined with his sense of duty as an officer of the law and his curiosity itself. All of it together worked like a magnet drawing him back again and again to check.

He tried to discern the plan the girl was cooking up. Was she meeting someone? A boy? A man? There were boys in the village who had tried to befriend her, but he thought had put a stop to that. He watched and waited, and if the growing stock of material in the bivouac told him nothing else, at the very least it told him that the girl was keeping something from him, and at worst it hinted that she was stealing. She was growing so headstrong. It wouldn't be long before she was entirely beyond managing.

V

ONE HOT NIGHT IN late August Elspeth woke in a sweat. The weight of the bedclothes had become confining, hot, pulsating with heat. She kicked and flailed, thrashing about, struggling to get them off. It was only when she was fully awake that she understood why.

The dragon was in the room, sleeping in her father's bed. One enormous wing was spread out awkwardly over the crosspieces of the canopy, and it hung down low so that it rested heavily on Elspeth's own bed. She had been battling with the wing, a huge diaphragm of tissue and scales, thin enough in places beneath the living scales that the throbbing of the creature's heart and blood was fully visible.

The room reeked of tar. A rhythmic glow came from behind the folds of the canopy curtain. It was a wonder that the creature could sleep.

Elspeth retched, but couldn't vomit. Everything within her reacted to produce a deep loathing, a loathing that was as much physical as it was mental.

Her father had somehow managed to capture the dragon and bring it back alive. But why had he left her alone in a room with a fully-grown dragon?

A wave of anger surged up within her, which mingled with fear and confusion, and made her ant to vomit.

Then, quite suddenly, her mind became very clear. What would she do if the dragon woke up? What if it attacked? She couldn't understand why her own father would expose her to danger in this way, but it hardly mattered now. She would have to take care of herself. She sat up, opening her eyes wide so they could adjust to the dim light of the room.

She strained her eyes in the darkness, searching for her father's crossbow. It was a long time before she saw it, in the glow of the dragon's breath, laid out on the table on the far side of the room. The butt jutted out beyond the folds of the curtain of the canopy bed, beneath the other bat wing. The dragon smothered everything with its wings.

If she were to reach the crossbow, she would somehow have to get past the sleeping dragon. But of course, even then she had no idea how useful a crossbow might be against an animal that breathed fire.

She was just slipping out of bed when she heard footsteps, then knocking at the door, then a voice, demanding entry. It was not the voice of her father. Where was her father? Had he been hurt? Had the dragon somehow hurt her father and forced its way into their hut? But why? Had it come here to lair? Maybe her father had gone for help, knowing that the dragon was sleeping. But why had he left his crossbow? Why had ne not used it?

Elspeth was ashamed again. How badly she had misjudged her father. Something was wrong with her father. He must be in danger somehow.

She had to get to the crossbow. As she moved, the knocking began again, louder and more insistent this time. The voice was louder, too, and for the first time Elspeth could hear it plainly. It was Levente, and he was demanding that she open the door.

Elspeth paused for a moment, torn between the door and the crossbow. It was in that moment that the dragon stirred, then woke up. The knocking had disturbed its sleep. The heavy animal raised its head, rolling back its eyes and looking at her. Just looking.

She dashed for the crossbow, and in a flash stood facing the dragon squarely, eye to eye. She remembered the time she had stared the creature down as it had sniffed at her bedclothes, and she took courage from the fact that then she had turned the beast away.

The dragon did not move and the pause lengthened into a full stare. Elspeth could not tell how long the staring lasted, and she found herself mesmerized by the eyes of the creature that was now half curled up, half crouching, on her father's bed. There was something about the animal's eyes, something she had seen before, something from the dream. She knew now what it was.

The dragon had her father's eyes.

The eyes flashed in a kind of anger that Elspeth had only seen in her father since the night the creature had shed its scales. But there was no doubt at all. The dragon had her father's piercing black eagle-like eyes.

All the while, the creature quieted its breathing, the glowing in its nostrils dimmed, and a thin wisp of smoke appeared in its place. The creature somehow seemed to sense the danger from the voice and the knocking at the door.

All of this happened in what seemed like an hour, but she was aware that in reality it had happened almost between knocks. Levente's voice carried through the door again, with an air of finality about it, as though he was reaching the limits of his patience.

"Elspeth!" he said. "Somebody heard a ruckus in your hut. I need to know that you're alright."

Elspeth did not know what to say.

"Answer me, or I'll have Caedmon come and break the door down."

"Go away, Levente. I hear you. Go away now. I'm sorry. I was asleep."

"Not until I know you're alright," said Levente. "Are you safe?"

Elspeth looked around, and hefted the heavy crossbow. "I'm safe."

"Are you alone?"

"No, I'm not alone," Elspeth said. There was a long pause before she finished. "I'm not alone. My father's here with me. But I'm safe. Go back to your hut. I'm safe."

She didn't wait to hear the sound of Levente's retreat. Instead, she cranked the string of the crossbow back to its locking position and mounted a bolt in its seat. Then, very quietly, very deliberately, she turned to face the monster that she knew sat staring at her with her father's eyes.

The dragon was gone. In its place her father sat upon the bed, his head buried in his hands.

Her father said nothing. What was there to say, anyway? The silence became very long. The smell of tar was gradually replaced by the smell of rum. He was drunk. He laid back. In time, exhausted by the tension, he drifted off to sleep.

The girl sat watching all that night, and through half of the next day too. Through it all she kept the crossbow drawn tight, the arrow aimed quite precisely at her father's throat.

When Fletcher came to his senses he was wandering along the path that led down from the plateau where the villagers had been harvesting their meager crops. His descent led him down into a ravine that had been carved out by the river in spring after spring after spring when the winter run-off turned the meandering river into a torrent. He heard the roar of a waterfall a hundred yards below, and in an odd way was comforted by the torrid, splashing, tumultuous sound of the water. It was a steady deep roar that grew deeper as he descended into the ravine. It seemed to echo the rapid, tumultuous roar of thoughts and feelings within his own head and heart, and just as surely as this river had carved its path out of the granite of the mountain, so also the torrent within him threatened to carve in two his broken mind and heart.

He could not remember very well what had happened in the night. The dragon had been in the hut; that much he knew from the stench of tar that clung to his clothing. His head hurt. Twice as he wandered he stopped to empty the contents of his stomach, but all that came up were dry heaves. Gradually he pieced together what had happened, but the memory was unreal, or at least unbelievable, like a bad dream that had been so vivid it was palpable. The fear had been real, he knew that much. He had been asleep, and had been awakened by movement in the hut, awakened by the girl. When he had come fully awake he had realized to his horror that his own daughter had drawn down a loaded crossbow—his crossbow!—deeply into his neck. He remembered that he had managed to remain calm long enough to deflect whatever anger the girl had felt, long enough at least to allow the moment of danger to pass.

He thought he would be sick. What sort of daughter draws a loaded crossbow on her father? Where before the girl had been troubled and defiant, now she was armed and dangerous. Something had snapped within her, something had forced her across that fine line between *thinking* about something violent and actually *doing* it. What sort of father allows such a thing? He felt ashamed, unspeakably ashamed, for raising a girl who had no gratitude and no respect, for allowing her to threaten him that way, for failing Alysse so miserably, for failing God.

What weighed most heavily on him was that in failing to control the girl, he had completely failed Alysse, and he could not bring himself to accept such an end to his promises to his wife.

He came at last to the pool at the base of the waterfall. He stripped off his shoes and tunic and pantaloons and waded naked into the pool. The water was hard cold on his skin, and he felt the bumps rise on his legs and back. It was a cleansing bath, a kind of baptism. He washed himself then, immersing his shoulders and head, swimming out into the deepest part of the pool, diving deep, then swimming freely through the cool torrent. At last he made his way to the shore again, felt the water running in rivulets from his beard and hair, running down his back. He rinsed his mouth in the water, drank it in, then spat furiously in a frantic effort to cleanse his taste buds from the terrible taste of tar that kept returning from his stomach.

By the time his bath was finished, his head was clear. His resolve returned. He would not allow himself to be the victim in his own home. He would not allow the girl to make such a shambles of his life. Alysse expected better of him. God expected better. Was that not what the priest had said?

He dressed beneath a massive aspen tree that spread its protecting limbs out over the pool and the waterfall. A light rain began to fall, washing the earth clean, washing the air. He waited for the rain to pass. A clap of thunder rolled down the valley and disappeared in a series of echoes in the ravine.

There was no doubt about his duty: What the girl needed was a good beating. His stomach churned again. As much as he hated the very idea, if only for the sake of Alysse's memory, he would have to beat the girl again, maybe within an inch of her life.

VI

ELSPETH DID NOT KNOW how long she had wandered in the village. It was already late when she found herself knocking at the door of Levente's shop. Her instinct that the older woman would still be awake was confirmed by the glimmer of candlelight that pierced the corners of the doorsill. She knocked, then knocked again.

"Is that you, Els?" asked Alcera's voice from the other side of the door.

"Yes, Alcera," replied the girl.

Elspeth could hear the creaking of the floor as Alcera made her way to the door. In a moment the door swung heavily on its hinges and a hand bearing a candlestick was thrust through. The candlestick was followed by Alcera's tired face.

"Good," said the face. "Come in, girl. I knew that you'd come when you could. I've been waiting up for you. Sit down over there by the candlelight, so I can look at you. You look a fright. What happened? Are you alright? Have you dealt with the creature?"

Elspeth slipped inside, twisting her shoulder slightly to the right to avoid hitting Alcera with the crossbow which she held very firmly in her right hand. Once inside, she set the heavy weapon on the table, then sat herself down. Even here, in the safety of Alcera's hut, she kept her hand on the stock and her finger on the firing mechanism.

After a while Alcera stopped talking and there was a long pause. She seemed to be taking the measure of the girl who now sat before her. When she finally spoke again she was more reflective. "What's happened?"

Very deliberately and quietly, Elspeth began to unravel the story you have just read.

"What will you do now?" asked the seamstress.

"I may make a run for Wales. I've got people up in the highlands there."

"Alone? Without provisions?"

"I've been stocking a bivouac in the forest," Elspeth said.

"The king's demesne?"

Elspeth nodded.

"Then you're a fool," Alcera said. "You get caught and it's all over for you."

"It's well hidden. Built into a little knoll near the north fork of the river. Nobody knows it's there."

"You can't run, Elspeth. You'll take your problems with you. Might as well stay here and face them."

"What are you talking about? 'I'll take my problems with me.' What's that supposed to mean."

"What'll you do if you attract a dragon of your own, like the one your father has?" asked Alcera.

"I'm not afraid of dragons. Not any more." She fingered the firing mechanism of the crossbow, then picked up the weapon and held it to her shoulder, aiming nowhere in particular.

"Fear and hatred are two sides of the same coin, Els," said the old woman. "A dragon thrives on one just as well as the other."

"What are you saying?"

"Just because he has a dragon doesn't mean you don't."

Elspeth glared at her.

"Did I miss something?" said Alcera. "Didn't you tell me that you drew down a loaded crossbow on your father? Did I misunderstand what happened last night?"

The very thought made Elspeth's jaw tighten, made her wretch, and the taste of something bitter rose at the base of her throat until her tongue was aflame with it. She went to the door and spat on the ground outside, as if by spitting she could rid herself of the bitter taste, but it was to no avail. The spittle formed up into a viscous little pool of orange-red light, very dim, but the glow was there nonetheless. The dim glow sat there, like an accusation on the ground outside Alcera's door.

"I'll kill him. I swear it," she said. "I'll hunt him down like a wolf in the field." As she spoke she could feel the muscles in his jaw spasm, and a deep, penetrating ache in her stomach.

"And just how do you expect to do that?" said Alcera.

"I've got the crossbow."

"That doesn't mean you're safe. We don't know what your father's capable of doing when he's under the spell of his own dragon."

"I've got his crossbow."

"You intend to carry a loaded crossbow for the rest of your life? What good is a crossbow if you're attacked from behind, or if he catches you in that tiny little instant when you're not paying attention?"

"But I'm young and quick," said Elspeth. "He won't take me by surprise. I'm ready for him." She hefted the crossbow, held it to her shoulder, and aimed at the wall.

"Listen to yourself, Elspeth. You think that by your reflexes alone you can protect against a trained hunter? And the sheriff's sergeant, no less. A crossbow is a one chance weapon. What will you do if your hand trembles and the bolt misses its mark? What if you only graze him, or miss him altogether? Or worse, what if it doesn't? What if you kill him? You prepared then to deal with the sheriff and the rest of his men? Believe me, Els, your father is more than your match. Better give me the bow."

"But I know him through and through," the girl protested. "When he comes, I'll be ready for him."

"The way you were ready for him all those times he beat you? And did you know him through and through when you didn't know about the dragon he was attracting to your hut?"

The girl looked down and away. "You can't have my crossbow," she said simply.

Alcera changed the direction of her comments. "You don't know what you're capable of."

"I know I can kill him if I have to," the girl replied.

"What you know is that you're hurt and angry, maybe so angry that you never want to see him again. But you don't want to kill him. Give me the bow." Her voice had turned gentle this time.

Long pause.

"Give me the bow."

Elspeth fingered the firing mechanism. She held the stock to her shoulder, lowered it again, then gripped it tightly with both hands. She could feel her heart beating nearly out of her chest. Alcera couldn't possibly know what she was asking. Then she removed the bolt from its seat in the crossbow, released the firing mechanism, and returned the bowstring to its resting position. She handed both the bow and the bolt to Alcera. As she did so, a chill shuddered down the length of her spinal column and radiated forward through her rib cage. She was weaponless. What would she do when her father came? What would she do if she saw the dragon?

Alcera placed the weapon in a corner cupboard, locking the cupboard door with a large iron key she took from an apron pocket. When she turned back around, the girl was gone.

The girl was not in the hut, but then again, he hadn't really expected to find her there. She wouldn't be at Levente's shop, either, because that would be too obvious. He sat down on the edge of the canopy bed, thinking.

He would need a weapon. He had no intention of hurting the girl, but she had a crossbow and he had to think also of his own safety. The more immediate question was where she would have fled and who else knew of her flight. Moreover, he had the safety of the villagers to consider: She had a crossbow, and she was both angry and desperate. Who knew what she was capable of?

While he was certain she would not be at Levente's shop, he was clear that she would have visited there after leaving the hut, if only to tell Alcera what had happened and what she planned to do next. Alcera might even know where she was, though almost certainly she would not tell. That left then the bivouac. If she made for the bivouac on foot, he could take a horse and be waiting for her when she got there.

Elspeth's immediate problem was to stay out of sight, and then to move without being tracked. She solved both of these problems by slipping out directly behind the shop building, allowing the structure itself to serve as a blind as she made her way to the woods and the better cover that would be provided by the foliage.

A light afternoon rain made it impossible for her to cover her tracks until she had reached the grassy spaces on the far side of the yard, but seeing no way around this difficulty, she simply forged ahead directly. If her father should track her, he would know that she had taken to the woods, but the tracks would be difficult or impossible to follow once she was in the woods themselves. Everything was a matter of timing. If the rain hardened it might well clear the tracks completely, but in turn it could make her movement more difficult and slow her escape.

Once under the shelter of the woods she paused to take stock of her situation and to make any adjustments in the plan she had so hastily and impulsively put together. She quickly reviewed her assets, now considerably depleted by her visit to Levente's shop. She had neither knife nor crossbow. She did have a little money, but no food. She could seek refuge within the monastery, but Prior Robert would no doubt return her to her father on the grounds that the first duty of authority is to acknowledge its limits. So far as the Prior was concerned, the right of a father to punish his own daughter would be beyond question.

The best course was to strike out for Wales under cover of the rain. She headed for the bivouac, where she could lay low until the storm passed.

She slipped out and around the village, for the sake of time making her circumvention by as narrow a margin as she dared leave, heading south to avoid being spotted by the frequent travelers on the cart path that led northward from the village to the town.

Fletcher went to the armory where he requested and was issued a second crossbow, together with a longbow, a quarrel of bolts, and a quiver of arrows. At his instruction, a squire saddled his horse, which Fletcher rode quickly through the village. He dismounted a hundred feet shy of Levente's shop, tethered the horse, and moved forward on foot. There was no need to alarm either of them, nor, for that matter, was there any need to signal to them that he was approaching. He paused long enough to load the crossbow, which he carried raised, near his right shoulder, so that it could be aimed and discharged at a moment's notice. He wondered whether he would act aright in a moment of crisis. What if the girl shot first? Could he kill his own daughter if it came to that? What if Alcera and the girl were lying in ambush? No, he dismissed the thought, Alcera would have no part of something like that, but alone the girl would be less predictable, and so he guarded his approach, crossbow at the ready in case it might be needed.

When he arrived he found the shop empty and the door bolted. The ground around the shop, revealed two sets of tracks. One set, the larger of the two, obviously Alcera's, led back toward the village in the direction of Fletcher's own hut. If she were headed there, Fletcher reasoned, it would be because Alcera had gone for help, a thought that confirmed his suspicion that the girl was still armed and dangerous.

The smaller set, Elspeth's, led out of the village in the direction of Coventry, opposite that of the king's forest, but Fletcher considered that this would be a ruse. Knowing that she could not hide her tracks in the wet earth the girl would lead out in the wrong direction, then when she was well away from the village would enter the woods and double back, circle the village under cover of the dense foliage, and then make for the bivouac by the shortest route. She would try to stay well clear of the road and any of the footpaths where her movements might be noted by the villagers who would be tending to their farm animals or returning from their business in the town. That meant that she would plot a route to the south rather than attempt a risky crossing of the north road that led to the monastery and town.

The drizzle hardened into a steady rain. Fletcher thought about turning back long enough to ask Aelric to join him with the bloodhound, but the rain would have confused the senses of even Aelric's fine dog, and besides, Aelric would want an explanation, and Fletcher knew that any lie he might fabricate would soon enough unravel, so he decided instead simply to strike out for the bivouac directly. He spurred his horse to the north, making for the bivouac by the shorter route.

Elspeth stopped a second time near a narrow rise to catch her breath and gain her bearings. She crawled out carefully along the rise to reconnoiter. There she lay for the longest time, surveying the countryside for signs of her father. More importantly, she looked to the skies for evidence of the dragon.

There! Emerging from behind the bluff, against the backdrop of the lowering rain clouds, were the wings of a fully grown dragon, making long, slow, craning passes back and forth around the wall of the town. As she watched, it turned and glided out along the path from the town to the village. Elspeth knew what it was looking for. She also knew, instinctively, that in her battle with her own dragon a loaded crossbow is no weapon at all, but that did not matter. What she wanted now was not a defense. She wanted an escape to safety. And somewhere, sometime, she wanted revenge.

A flash of sheet lightning spread out its crackling light along the ridge to the south. Thunder, then a long silence. Only the clouds moved. In the end, what mesmerized Elspeth was not the dragon itself, but its shadow. She could see the shadow even when the dragon passed overhead against the cloudburst. It reminded her that the dragon had engulfed her in darkness. She watched it trace out patterns against the base of the bluff, and then snake down along the river. Lightning again. Now the dragon was gliding back and forth, methodically searching the countryside for its prey.

Fletcher also saw the dragon, though he interpreted its presence in a different way. The animal was tracking Elspeth, but he had no idea why. The girl was armed, but who knew what good her crossbow would be against such a creature? He paused only a moment to follow the dragon's movements. When it left the town and began a flight along the path to Wharram. Fletcher turned his attention once again to the trail.

The bivouac was in such terrible condition that Elspeth nearly missed it in her desperation and haste. There it was, though, even in such a shape still a sheltering refuge against the storm. She was not worried that her father might find her there because she knew for certain that he had no idea about this forbidden retreat in this forbidden forest.

The more immediate concern was the dragon.

She checked out the contents of the bivouac quickly, then made for the tree and the perch she knew some hunter had affixed to a high branch as a lookout for authorities or game. From such a perch she would have a better view of any approaches that might be made, and more importantly could spot and track the movements of the dragon. And her father.

It was a long while before Fletcher arrived at the scene, entering the forest by the more commonly used but longer pathway to the north. Because of the horse, he had kept to the roads where he could move more quickly.

He did not approach the bivouac directly, but rode around behind it. There was no telling what she might do with the crossbow. He dismounted, tethered his horse to a tree, and checked his weapons, drawing the crossbow and seating a bolt in its proper place along the shaft. Then he approached the bivouac from behind. He raised his crossbow to his shoulder and trained his eyes through the rain for the leading edge of the girl's own weapon should she make an attempt on his life.

"Elspeth!" he called out. "I know you're here."

Elspeth looked down from her station in the tree, thankful that she had not sought the bivouac's meager shelter from the rain. What she saw was the foreshortened figure of her father, crossbow at the ready. The wind now played havoc with her father's cloak, whipping it up and back. She had been wrong. Her father must have known about the bivouac. He was here, and she was in serious danger.

A flash of lightning lit the countryside around and below her, throwing up a momentary but terrifying shadow of her father across the mound of the bivouac, a shadow that loomed out and up, growing in size as it engulfed the mound, the flapping of the coat spreading out from the man's torso so that the instant that it took for the lightning flash to dissipate was enough to show the unmistakable outline of a dragon poised for a kill.

Fletcher waited until the rolling thunder passed. "Elspeth, get out here. I won't hurt you."

Then he moved cautiously out and around the mound, crossbow at the ready. When he stood at last on the other side, opposite the entrance he could see that the bivouac was empty. The girl had eluded him, had made her escape by some other route, but what?

He entered the bivouac to escape the rain and plan his next movements.

At this point, Elspeth made a desperate decision. She would take her father's horse. But she had to act quickly, while her father was within the bivouac. She slipped off the perch and began her descent, every branch made slippery by the rain. But she moved too quickly and misjudged her footing, placing her right foot on a smaller branch that could not support her weight. The branch gave way beneath her, and with a single horrifying thud she tumbled out of the tree and onto the ground in a heap directly in front of the opening of the bivouac.

Fletcher, startled, discharged his crossbow in the direction of the thud. He had not aimed the bow, but had released the bowstring reflexively, and the bolt narrowly grazed the girl's back before it lodged itself in the tree. Fletcher was horrified. He had nearly killed his own daughter. In a vast but confused relief, Fletcher ran for the girl, thinking to raise her up and check for wounds.

Elspeth had no time to think. All she knew was that her father had attacked her, had fired on her. Now he was lunging at her. His single bolt gone, he would kill her with his bare hands. She struggled, wrenching herself free for a dash for the horse.

All Fletcher could think was that the girl was unharmed, thank God. But she was fighting even now. How dare she! He grabbed the girl by the tunic, pulling her back and down.

Then. Everything. Stopped. Fletcher's head turned round slowly, painfully, achingly, and it seemed to him that he was engulfed in lightning, and the thunder was rolling around and through him. Not lightning, but burning tar, flash-flooding through him, inside him, in his head, his eyes. He saw the girl, he saw the dragon, he saw Alysse's face in the lightning's flash, he saw Father Thomas preaching, his finger raised in oratory, he saw his duty and he saw how badly he had failed in that duty, he saw the shadow of the devil and the wolf and the pup and Aelric, he saw the truth that his daughter was ruined, he saw Alysse packing her bags in a fury and leaving him, her black eyes flashing through him like lightning, he saw the girl and the horse running wildly for God only knew where, he saw the ruin of everything he held dear and precious, he saw the end of the world, his world, all of it destroyed by this uncontrollable and dangerous youth, he saw his own grave, with the shadow of the girl looming above it. He saw himself and he was terribly alone.

He tackled the girl, threw her to the ground, hitting and hitting and hitting. The girl was fighting back now. He stopped thinking altogether and abandoned himself to his hunter's reflexes and the wash of tar inside him. He went for the girl's throat.

Then he heard a voice. Clear, high, commanding. "Fletcher! Stop! John! John Fletcher! Stop!" Hands were grabbing him from behind. Levente's hands. "Stop, John," Levente was saying. "Stop. It's over."

Caput Secundum
BOOK TWO

VII

"Where'd you get that black eye?"

Elspeth wore a hooded cloak in the hope that no one would notice the eye or the bruise on her left cheek. A week had passed and she was still sore from the beating, and she had thought that the bruises had cleared up enough that she could go back into public. Even so, she had taken pains to avoid people on the street. But Brother Constantine had seen it.

She did not know Brother Constantine well, though she had seen him once or twice a week for years because he came to Levente's shop to give instructions about some manuscript Levente was working on. She thought he might be the supervisor of the scriptorium at the monastery, but he had never spoken to her, at least had never said anything at all that indicated he had noticed her.

"I tripped and hit a rock," she said softly.

"How do you have bruises on both sides of your face, then?" Constantine said. "And why are you limping?"

She was silent. She brushed past him and tried to walk away, but he stepped in beside her.

"Did your father do this?"

She looked away. Why did he think that? Had Levente or Alcera talked about what happened? If he put two and two together, she could be in trouble with her father again. Another beating.

He reached out and took her chin in his fingers, drawing her face gently into the light. "It's serious, Elspeth," he said again. "Let me look at the other one." Very tenderly he brushed aside a stray lock of her hair, exposing the other bruise to better view. "You should come to the monastery and let Brother Gregory look after that," he insisted. Brother Gregory was the herbalist who managed the monastery infirmary. "However it happened, it's serious. He can make a salve."

"I'll be alright," she said. "It's nothing."

It was long after Compline, but Brother Constantine was having trouble sleeping. He rose and made his way down the stairs and out of the sleeping quarters, tracing his way along a sliver of moonlight to Brother Johann's garth, the monastery garden in the center of the cloister. He found a bench beneath one of the arches across from Johann's thick hedge of honeysuckle. Nearby, near enough that he could have touched it, was a bed of Johann's prize roses, gleaming a deep blood-red in the slender thread of light, the last blooms before winter. Above him, dangling from the arch, were baskets and baskets of jasmine.

He told himself he was worried about the girl, and that he had to find a way to help her. It was, he told himself, his Christian duty. This was more than idle curiosity. He had known this girl all her life, had watched her grow from a baby wrapped in a blanket at her mother's funeral. He must have been present at her baptism, though he figured this only because the baptism would have been held in the monastery church. All babies born in Warwick were baptized in the church. He had known little about her or been aware that she even existed until one day she had appeared under foot in Levente's workshop, at first cleaning up scraps and doing the kinds of chores a child might do. And there, because he had been a regular visitor, he had seen her grow, not noticing that she was slowly emerging into womanhood.

Now, as he sat on the bench imagining her face, he realized that he had not really seen her before. She had her mother's Welsh features—he had seen her mother at mass many times before she had died giving birth to the girl. He had even spoken to her. She had been unusual, a peasant woman who could read, and he had sensed a connection with her, a part of her life she could not share with her husband. The girl's father was what? A hunter maybe. Maybe he worked for the sheriff. He was certain he remembered the mother's funeral mass because he had gotten in trouble with Prior Robert for slipping out of the line of monks to sit beside the grieving widower to translate Father Athanasius' funeral sermon. Athanasius had been a daft old fool who believed that the un-lettered peasants in the pews who knew no Latin were close to barbarians, were barely Christian anyway, and should raise themselves to a higher level by discipline and piety. He preached to them in Latin to set a good example, a goal to obtain, but that was little comfort to a grieving widower with a baby girl to raise.

The girl had grown up to look like her mother, *Alysse. That was the girl's mother's name. She has her mother's bright eyes.* Why had he not seen that before? He had seen her in Levente's shop every week for years, had spoken with her sometimes when Levente or Alcera were away and he had instructions to leave for them. Always before, she had been a child. A bright eyed, precocious child, but now that had changed. She was grown. She was beautiful like her mother.

He thought again about her hair—long, dark, worn in a braid as thick as the belfry rope, but loose about the temples in a way that high-lighted those dark, luminous eyes. Her stride had a certain confidence about it—unusual for a girl of her station. She was not delicate so much as athletic, and her athletic body carried itself in a way that commanded an unusual degree of respect for a peasant girl. Her dress was simple, but the embroidered stitching on the bodice was worked in fine detail. It was, he guessed, the work of her own hands, but the design was one he had seen on Alcera's clothing. If it were not for the simplicity of her clothes, a stranger would have thought her royal, or perhaps the pampered, self-assured daughter of one of Warwick's more prosperous merchants.

The fact that she was beautiful disturbed him in a way he did not fully understand, but he told himself she was entitled to be admired, if only from a distance by an aging monk. Even her father would concede the point—she was the image of her mother. A younger monk, less sure of his vocation, might find such a girl a challenge to the call of God. He closed his eyes and thanked God that he did not have to contend with the confusions about women that seemed to plague the whole world outside the protecting walls of the monastery and cloister.

Tonight he had other concerns to ponder: Someone had beaten the girl, and he was worried that she might not be safe.

But that was not why he could not sleep. He could not sleep because he had touched her skin with his fingertips as he checked her bruises, and in that moment, in that split second, the earth had opened up and swallowed him whole. He reminded himself he was a man of God; he tried hard to remember the trials of the novitiate, and then the vows he had taken. Chastity. Poverty. Obedience. This was a deliberate choice he had made, to become a monk, in response to the call of God, a choice made so long ago that he could no longer remember the words of his vow.

He knelt beside the garden bench and tried to pray, partly to force his life as a monk back into the forefront of his mind to dispel the lingering physicality of the girl. He prayed for Brother Gregory the infirmerer, and for Brother Paul the herbalist. He prayed for the scriptorium, and for the younger brothers who came to him each day to join in the communal work of copying manuscripts.

An owl somewhere disturbed his prayer. There was a flutter of wings, a disturbance just beyond the thin moonlight. A small animal, a lizard maybe, scurried up one of the pilasters above the bench and disappeared into the hanging jasmine.

Constantine had touched the girl's skin.

He told himself that he had forgotten the words of his vows because he had long since taken them up into his breathing, his very heartbeat, but even so, in that precise moment, as he touched her skin, as he brushed away her hair to care for her wound, something had risen up within him he had not known was there. He sensed that it had the power to destroy him, and yet . . . . when he had touched the girl's skin he had experienced a kind of relief, and was glad, and knew he wanted to touch her skin again if he could.

Elspeth liked Constantine but had been surprised when he had taken an interest in her black eye. She had smiled and tried to turn her face away in case the bruises might still be visible. Thinking about it later, as she lay on her bed, she found herself inexplicably embarrassed. Embarrassed but pleased, too, in a way that surprised her. *Brother Constantine is a gentleman*, she thought, as she drifted off to sleep. *Imagine that. A gentleman monk.*

Two weeks passed, not uneventfully. Fletcher saw his daughter several times, once at church, and three or four times on the road as she ran errands for Alcera or Levente. The dragon, mercifully, disappeared. To all outward appearances his life continued as before. He ate and drank and worked. He found the resources within himself to care for the livestock, clean the house, and prepare his own meals—all tasks that had been done by Elspeth, but that fell to him now that the girl was living at that bookbinder's shop.

But to the careful observer there were clues that all was not right with John the Fletcher. He did not sleep well. He spent long hours alone. Once, for no reason he could understand, he began to cry as he prepared his supper.

The tears were especially difficult for him. *Christ's bones!* he thought. *Here I am a grown man, crying like an infant that's been abandoned by its mother.*

He was thankful that the girl was not there to see it, but in a way that surprised and confused him, he also ached for her the way he had ached for Alysse. What he missed was not the care she had provided him—the meals, the chores in the barnyard—but the girl herself, the way she had moved in the hut fixing supper, the way her body cut the light as she passed before a window, the silent language of gestures and glances that fathers sometimes have with daughters. He missed the girl way he missed Alysse; it was a dull ache somewhere deep in his core, an ache that could not be eased by dwelling on memories. He reminded himself that she was affianced to a man in Wales, that the end would be the same in any case, but the chance encounters on the road only served to make it worse. Even ale did him no good, and when he drank, instead of feeling better, he felt his world slipping away into maudlin sentimentality and sometimes into a desperate, despairing anger. First Alysse. Now the girl. He would die alone, with an unhealed ache in his belly.

Constantine sat with his brother monks and listened as Prior Robert went down his list of items to be discussed at Chapter. The casual observer would think how much they were alike in their woolen habits and their tonsured heads, but Constantine knew now that they were not alike at all. He was not like the others, not any more. He had come to the cloister as a boy, had taken his vows as a youth, and now after all those years he had touched the smooth skin of a woman and had felt it warm and alive beneath his fingertips. He had wanted to touch her again, to feel again the smoothness of her skin.

He could not remember having touched a woman before. Perhaps he had touched his mother, but he could not remember his mother. He had been told that his parents were killed by Mongolian raiders who had swept into eastern Europe, but it was a memory he could not recover no matter how hard he tried. He did not remember even his mother's name, and so did not remember having ever been touched by a woman, or touching a woman. Not until Elspeth, and touching her had stirred something within him that his brother monks would not understand.

What was he *first*? A monk? Or a man? He had been at the monastery since he was a child, orphaned—he had been told—by an attack of Mongols in Moldavia, which he understood was someplace in eastern Europe.

He realized now that when he had become a monk he had not ceased to be a man, but that he had somehow buried that self beneath his monk's habit. His initiation, his vows, had been a funeral mass for a self he thought had died. Now—because he had touched the girl—he felt that part of himself rising up within him once again. A resurrection. He even felt oddly whole again, and he was grateful to God.

His brother monks would say that this was sinful, but what would they know? What would Prior Robert know? Is it a sin to want to touch a woman, if he touched only her face, her cheek? If it would not be a sin for a layman, outside the monastery walls, then why so for a monk? Was it a sin to want to touch this young woman? How could something so normal for other men be a sin for a monk?

During this time, the dragon seemed to go into a quiet phase. It attacked more sporadically, and took smaller prey. Sightings grew less frequent. The general uproar began to abate, though it never once gave way to abandon, and what had been terror thinned to a kind of mindful caution. Perhaps the animal was aging, or even sick. It very well might die. No one knew very much of the lifespan of dragons, and so such possibilities began to be openly discussed in the villages and town. The caution became cautious optimism. How soon, and in what way, they would be done with the monster, no one knew, but the lessening of the threat came to everyone as a relief.

"Is all well with you, Brother?" said a voice. Constantine turned to find Brother Joachim, one of St Cuthbert's two sacristans, quietly cleaning up after mass. Joachim had spoken without turning his head, softly, as he went about his work. He produced a silver brush with the monogram

IHS engraved into the handle, then used it to brush crumbs of the host onto a silver tray to take to the sacristy for the priest to eat.

"What did you say?" said Constantine.

"I asked if all was well with you," said Joachim. He lifted the edges of the cloth that draped the table, folded them carefully together, and placed it and the remnants of the host together on the silver tray. He did the same with the empty silver chalice that had held the blood of Christ.

"I have a troubled friend," Constantine said. In other circumstances, this would have seemed abrupt, but among themselves monks were spare with language, making every word count. He stepped to the front of the church, knelt, crossed himself, then picked up one of the votive candles to light another.

Behind him, Joachim nodded and picked up the silver tray. "I will pray that your friend finds peace."

Constantine waited until Joachim was well out of the sanctuary, set the candle carefully into place, then stepped back to kneel again at the prayer bench. He ran his fingers along the smooth, carved oak of the railing. Beneath the curve of the railing, some village craftsman had carved deep *bas relief* panels to complement those on the high altar. Constantine knew those images well; he had seen them nearly every day of his life. They were biblical scenes, tracing out the history of the Bible in oak iconography. On the far left, Adam and Eve in their garden, on the far right, the Final Judgment. In between, moving from left to right, an image of Moses with his twin tablets of the law, one of the prophets, his finger raised in oratory, the nativity, the baptism of Jesus, other scenes from Jesus' life, the crucifixion, the ascension, then the Twelve Apostles receiving the Holy Ghost, their heads capped with little wooden tongues of fire. To his left a foot or two, one of the panels contained a deep carving of Jesus and the Woman Taken in Adultery. He looked around to see that he was alone, then quietly moved until the panel was directly in front of him, at his knees. He leaned back so he could view the carving more clearly. The grain in the oak made a vertical, layered, mottled pattern down the woman's cheeks, like a track of dried tears, and he thought about Elspeth's bruised and swollen face. He reached out to touch the carved oaken face of the woman—smooth, hard, cold, lifeless—and thought about Elspeth's face, smooth like the oaken face of the woman, but warm and soft and full of life.

I'm a monk, he thought to himself. *I'm old enough to be her father.*

He looked at the panel again, and remembered the story, how the woman's accusers had all left, ashamed by Jesus' demand that the one without sin should cast the first stone.

To distract himself, he moved to the first pew, and sat, and admired the massive workmanship of the high altar that towered above him, filling the apse with gleaming light. He had seen the altar go up during the years when he had first come to the monastery, before he had become a novice and then had taken his vows. As a child, he had watched as the brothers lifted the timbers into place where they could form the superstructure of the panels. They were oak, heavy, and the day they were raised all hands had been pressed into service to see that they were properly placed. The altar was then finished out entirely in oak, polished and finely finished even in those places that would not show to the public but only to God. Prior Robert, a much younger man then, and newly installed in his office, had made a ceremony of placing the timbers, telling the novices and brothers that participating in the raising of an altar to the glory of God was a sacred and holy act. Constantine had loved the altar ever since.

He stood and made his way to the altar, looked over his shoulder to scan the room. He paused, listening for the movements of other worshipers. When he was satisfied again that he was alone, he stepped to its right side and disappeared behind it.

A casual observer might have thought he had disappeared into the wall, and in a sense that would be right. Behind the altar, one could say beneath it, encased in its massive superstructure, there was an enclosure, closed off by a small door. It wasn't a room so much as a large rectangular niche, twice as deep as it was high, twice as high as it was wide. A fully grown man might stand up nearly straight there, and two could stretch out head to heel on the floor against the wall of the apse. Two or three spiders scurried into the shadows of the niche. He cleared away a single cobweb that showed silver in the candlelight, and wondered how a spider could have built it in the total darkness of the niche. The niche was smaller than he remembered, narrower, a corridor of darkness. When he stepped inside he found it damp and a little musty, and his mind wandered back to times he had hidden there as a boy, taking comfort in its closeness and privacy, and then beyond that to a memory from very early childhood that was alternately very vivid and very dim.

He remembered in fragments, carried by the musty smell of another space shaped like it, but with rougher walls, he thought maybe lined with hewn rock. It was more a memory of touch and smell than of sight, the odd physical memory that relates intuitively to the shape and smell of a place. He must have been seven years old, or maybe a little younger.

Constantine did not know the name of his village. He had been told it was in a small Hungarian enclave at the southernmost tip of Moldavia just where eastern Europe humped up over the backs of the Carpathian mountains, but he did not know where that was either. Knotted strands of memory began to disentangle themselves in the back of his mind. He could dimly picture a root cellar in the hill behind a small house. That must have been his family's house.

He picked at the memory like a loose thread, teasing it out of the knot. The root cellar had always been there, a long walk from the house. Looking back, he thought it might be fifteen minutes or more. It was a primal shelter for the summer fruits and vegetables his family grew. He had a dim memory of his father cursing as he walked back from the cellar in the sweating heat of the summer. He had a fragmentary but clear memory of chasing a butterfly through rows of rutabagas and potatoes at that side of the house. For security, the entrance to the cellar had been placed right next to a tall tree where it could not be seen from the road. He could not remember what kind of tree it had been; he thought maybe pine. The door lay in at the same slope as the hill, and over time the wood had aged to a dull grey that matched nearly perfectly the color of the grey ground around it. It was a good camouflage, at least good enough that somebody would have to be looking for it to see it, and so the earth protected its own, or at least that which Constantine's brother and father had entrusted to it.

The musty smell of the niche brought it back, clearer now than ever. He remembered that the root cellar had been a welcome, cool hiding place where he played sometimes when he was a boy. After that, as an orphan in the care of the monastery, he had sometimes hidden in the niche beneath the high altar when his teacher Brother Basil had been angry with him.

Now, thirty years later, he wondered if Elspeth might need the shelter of the niche the way he had. When he left the church he was surprised by his own sense of hurry. His heart was pounding in a way that surprised him, too, and he could not quite figure out the origin of that. He went to the scriptorium and wrote a simple note, folded it and put it in the pocket of his robe, and headed for the monastery library to find a book. He would hide the note within the pages and slip it to the girl on his next visit to the bookbinder's shop.

VIII

FLETCHER CONTINUED TO GRIEVE the loss of his daughter. Alcera's unending challenge to his patience came to a head in the wake of a thunderstorm late in the fall. There was flooding in the town. Any of the streets that had not yet been cobbled became rivers and then pools of muddied, turbulent water. All available men were called into the service of the common good, filling sandbags, hauling them to various strategic points around the town, stacking them in such a way that the water was diverted from its raging path and sent back to the river, itself swollen nearly beyond capacity.

Thus Fletcher found himself working alongside Levente, sweating in the rain, unable to talk because of the howling wind that enveloped them in a kind of savage fury. Elspeth, he supposed, must be working with the women elsewhere in the town or perhaps one of the villages. The sheriff's man Caedmon was barking orders, and Fletcher thought angrily that Caedmon was too old to carry his weight with the sandbags, but still thought himself able to manage the burden of considerable authority.

Levente worked for an hour before he said a word to Fletcher. "Here, John," he said, pulling one of the heavy sandbags to the back of the oxcart on which he was working. "Can you help with this?" He leapt down from the cart and pulled at the bag from the other side.

Fletcher grabbed hold, adjusted his grip, and the two men muscled the heavy bag to the top of a dam that was growing higher at a rate barely greater than the rising flow of the water. They went back for another, then another after that. For most of the day they worked without stopping, as oxcart after oxcart arrived with fresh supplies of sand and bags and timber.

Then the storm broke and the rain stopped. The river continued to swell as runoff from the hills brought more and more water into the town, but the dykes held, and in time the water crested and then abated and the men paused in their labors to rest. Like the others, Fletcher and Levente were soaked to the bone, dripping water from their hair and clothing and beards. They huddled together under one of the eaves of the monastery, listening to the dripping of the runoff from the roofs of the monastery buildings.

"So how are you doing, John?" asked Levente, even before his heavy breathing had slowed. For want of a bench he flopped down on the stones of the cobbled walkway.

"I've been better," Fletcher replied, breathing heavily between words. Of the two men, he was the younger and had borne the greater part of the workload. "Be sore tomorrow, though. I may find out about muscles I didn't know I had."

Somebody held out a dry towel, and Levente dried his hands. "Can't remember a storm so bad." He laid the towel over the top of his head.

"Over now, thank God." Fletcher leaned back against the monastery wall.

"There are other kinds of storms in life, John," said Levente. "How are you faring with those?"

"I want Elspeth home."

"I think it's better if she stays with us a while longer," said Levente. "We have plenty for her to do, and she needs to earn her keep, you know. Apprenticeship and all that."

"She served her apprenticeship right well before," Fletcher said, "when she was coming home at night. You've got another reason for keeping her." He ran his fingers through his soaking hair.

"What do you suppose that is?" asked Levente.

"I don't give a rat's tail what that is, Levente. I want my daughter back."

Levente looked distant, and John could not figure out what scheme he was cooking up. "I'll tell you what, John," he said. "She has just a few months remaining on her apprenticeship. I'll allow her to return home if I have your word that you will not hit her."

"Nobody tells me what I can and can't do in my own house."

"Then she stays with us," said Levente calmly. He stood and left the shelter of the monastery eaves and made his way across the muddy street to the path, treacherous now with deep mud, that led to the village of Wharram and his shop.

Elspeth, too, was working the storm, carrying food and drink to the men, sometimes helping lift a heavy timber or a sandbag. In no time at all she was soaked to the bone, but still she kept at it. When it was over, she was exhausted. The work had taken a heavy toll on her sixteen-year-old frame. Still a slender girl, she had forgotten her youth and inexperience in the struggle with the river, and had insisted on carrying a woman's full burden of the work. There had been no stopping for rest, and only when the rain ceased and the river crested did she and the others pause from the back-breaking work of feeding the men who were moving sandbags and support timbers against the flow.

Levente was coming along the road. "Elspeth," he said. "Are you alright? Where were you working?"

"Worn thin," said Elspeth, falling in beside him. They walked in silence for a while, focusing what little energy they had remaining on the demanding task of walking without slipping. It was slow going.

"Where were you working?" asked Levente, repeating himself.

"Near the cemetery," said Elspeth. Normally at such a moment she would have picked her way from boulder to patch of grass to boulder. Now she just trudged along through the mud. "I could drop in my tracks."

"Good then," said Levente. "It's over now. We've done enough. Come along home."

"In a little while," she said. "I want to check on my father."

"Be careful," Levente said.

Willem's pub was closed because Willem had joined the sandbag effort in the town, but Sarabeth was standing in the doorway as Fletcher passed by.

"John," she called out. "John Fletcher. Any word of Willem? Have you seen him?"

"I saw him with one of the oxcart drivers, heading back to the paddock on the north side. He should be along soon enough, though."

"Terrible storm," she said.

"We saved the buildings near the foregate," said Fletcher. "The worst is over."

"Ale?" she asked.

Fletcher hesitated. He was weary to the bone, it was late in the day, and the path home was treacherous enough in the waning light. What good would come from delaying? He was still stinging from his confrontation with Levente, and one part of him wanted to be alone.

But another part did not. One part of what troubled him was the blow to his dignity that Levente's words had dealt, but another part was the way Levente had effectively told him he would continue alone. This latter wound only confronted him the more powerfully with the fact that there was no one waiting for him at his hut. When he did get home he would be too tired to make supper. He expected he would just fall into bed. And then finally he thought—or rather was afraid to think—there was no telling how much damage his own hut had sustained in the rains. It would be good not to know for a few more minutes yet.

"Just one flagon, Sarabeth. Then I'll be on my way."

One flagon stretched into two, then two into three.

Elspeth found her father's hut itself in good condition, but the lean-to and the woodshed had sustained heavy damage. Nearly a third of the grape arbor was down. Within the lean-to, several bags of grain were inches deep in standing water, and the cordwood had been dislodged and swept from the shed and nearly lost to the river. She made what repairs she could to the two structures, working quickly to take good advantage of the fading light. Then she salvaged the grain and secured the cordwood against further loss. She would restack it in the morning. It was hard work, but important since the wood was essential if her father was to survive the winter, and the grain was needed for the spring planting in the garden behind the hut.

Before she left, she checked inside the hut itself. Surprisingly there was leakage only near the door, but it made the floor slippery so she cleared the puddled water, sweeping as much of it as she could out the door with the broom, then spreading out the rest so it would dry.

She was now exhausted and she considered staying, but Levente and Alcera would worry. The sun was setting. The high canopy of the forest would deepen the shadows, so she took with her one of the torches her father kept stacked in a corner near the door. She used her father's flint kit to light the torch, returned the kit to its place on the shelf, and headed out into the night.

Fletcher did not make it home. The exhaustion from the work, the lack of food, and the ale combined like air, fuel and heat into a condition that was at best simmering and at worst explosive. Add to that the deep mud and the continuing drip of raindrops from the forest canopy, and he found himself forced out into the middle of the cart-path where the wheel ruts were treacherous pools. Somewhere along the way, he slipped and fell, and could not get up.

Returning to Levente's hut, Elspeth found her father lying in a pool of mud. She called for help, and Willem came, and together they took him to the monastery and placed him in the care of Brother Gregory the infirmerer and Brother Paul his assistant. The brothers washed his body and dressed the cut on his head. Prior Robert was told, and word was sent to Sheriff Ranulf that one of his sergeants in arms had been hurt in an accident coming home that night from working the emergency lines during the storm. Nothing was said to Ranulf about the fact that Fletcher had been drinking. The brothers could be counted upon for discretion because they were monks. It was not so much that Fletcher had been drinking—everybody drank—but that in drinking to excess he had impaired his good judgment and placed in jeopardy his own well-being as well as the well-being of others; this much was clear even without Fletcher having said anything at all. Such information could be damaging to his position in the service of the sheriff. Prior Robert was told everything, and in his great concern to discharge his pastoral office he considered carefully and then concurred with their view that it was best to await developments before taking any step that might be irreversible. For the time being, while Fletcher healed, he was safe.

Elspeth was happy in Levente's shop, not least because she felt safe there. She was returning from an errand, when she realized that Constantine the monk was there before her. He was engrossed in some conversation with Levente and Alcera, though she did not catch enough to get the gist of what he was saying. This was the first time she had seen him since he had commented on her black eye, and she suddenly felt shy because she could not remember how much of the bruising was still visible. Constantine stood to provide her with his chair.

"I'm just finishing up here," he said. She followed his glance to a small stack of manuscripts he must have lugged down from the monastery. "I brought something for you to read," he continued, shuffling through the books and unfinished manuscripts until he located a small volume, with the letter E tooled into the leather binding in a fluid, elegant script. "It's a collection of the letters and poems of Elizabeth of Hungary," he said, handing it to her, "my benefactress."

Elspeth looked at him quizzically.

Brother Constantine seemed to feel a need to fill the silence. "When my parents were killed in Hungary, Elizabeth took me in. She took in a lot of us after the Mongol raids, and had her hands full finding places for us. I ended up here in the care of the monks. I must have been seven or eight years old. She's a saint, if you ask me." He told her that he and several of the other monks had come as a group with a cavalcade of crusaders returning from the Holy Land.

Elspeth held the book up and admired the binding, then opened it to view the handwriting within, line after line of fluid, rounded Carolingian script.

"I copied it out myself," said Constantine, gazing at her. "I also made the leather binding."

"You own books?" said Elspeth. "I mean, other than the Bible? I thought monks took vows of poverty."

"The book belongs to the monastery," said Constantine. "It's my work; it's the monastery's book. God's book, really. My favorite letter is on page eighty-three. When you have a moment to yourself, you might enjoy that one." He turned to Levente and Alcera. "I have to get back." Then he gathered his things and left.

Elspeth would have watched until his figure disappeared around a turn in the path, but was interrupted by Alcera. "Here," Alcera said. "Help me set out this pattern." She turned to the work-table, but as she did this, she thought about Constantine. Here was an unusual monk indeed. How unlike the other monks. How unlike any man she knew, except perhaps for Levente. Certainly how unlike her father.

Later, Alcera went into the kitchen of their modest living quarters, clucking something about Elspeth staying off her hurt leg. Levente excused himself and went out to the privy. Elspeth was alone for a moment. She reached for the leather-bound book of letters from Elizabeth of Hungary, and turned to page eighty-three. There, tucked in firmly between the pages, was a small slip of paper, written out in the same fluid Carolingian script as the book:

I saw you limping. Are you alright? I have something to show you. Try to meet me tonight at St Cuthbert's. After Compline.   --C.

Elspeth glanced at the kitchen door to see if Alcera was anywhere near, folded the note quickly and put it in her apron pocket. A most unusual monk indeed. *And a headstrong one*, she thought. *Or one with something very urgent to say.* That was because he could not speak to her after Compline without violating the Grand Silence that kept the Benedictines mute until dawn.

Fletcher was aware when Elspeth slipped out of Levente's hut. Unable to see her during the day, he had taken to watching for her at night, and sometimes had taken up a watch beneath a tree on the edge of Levente's property. She had slipped out alone, without a torch, clearly intending not to be seen.

Now he had her. God knew she was up to something, but what? Was she stealing at night? Was she going out to attend to that dragon of hers? Where was she keeping it, anyway? A dragon would almost be a relief; at least then she would not be seeing some boy, doing who knew what. He wracked his brain to think of who she might be seeing, but no one came to mind. She never talked about boys. *Or men!* he thought, suddenly alarmed. She was sixteen. She could be seeing a man. She was pretty, like her mother. Other men had noticed her mother—he had seen them staring sometimes in church—and he had been angered by that. Was Elspeth seeing a married man? She would damn her own soul to hell, and his with it, if he did not intervene.

Constantine sat near the back of the nave where he would be less likely to be noticed if Brother Joachim should return to refresh the candles that burned constantly before the high altar. There was a full moon, and the stars were brilliant studs in an otherwise dark, dark heaven. On such a night, Elspeth could move easily along the roads without a lamp or a torch, but would she? He did not know, but would have to wait to find out. He thought of Elizabeth of Hungary and what she had done for him. He caught an image of his family's root cellar. There was a girl in there; he owed her something, too, though the memory was too dim to recover. There comes a time in a man's life when he has to repay his debts. This was his time. While he thought these things clearly, he did not think them in words; they were something he simply knew, a primal truth, the way what had happened in the root cellar, whatever that was, was a primal truth. He would take care of the girl.

So the root cellar represented some kind of security to him, but there was another memory—or rather, an ache where there should have been a memory, just out of reach, but heart stopping anyway—that had imposed a different meaning upon it, a meaning closer to terror. Something had happened to him in his family's root cellar, something that had frightened him, something he knew he could not recover without being emotionally fragmented. The root cellar must have been important in his leaving Moldavia, though he could not remember how.

There was a stir behind him, the quiet opening and the closing of one of the oak doors that led to the narthex. He glanced back to see a small figure in a hood. The figure came to him, slipping quietly down the aisle. She sat beside him, adjusted her cloak, and calmly lifted her hood from her head and laid it back along her shoulders.

He handed her a small slip of paper, on which he had written out instructions.

She held the note up to her face, turning it slowly to catch any stray gleams from the altar. "It's too dark here," she whispered. She stood, and then he did, and they made their way to the front of the church where they could take better advantage of the candles that were burning at the altar. The note said, "If you should need a place to hide…" and then it stopped abruptly.

"What does this mean?" she asked.

He raised his finger to his lips and then gestured with his hand that she should follow him. He led her past the railing and up into the sacred precinct of the apse and behind the altar.

"What?" she said to him.

The door was invisible in the dark, and the light from the altar was cut off by the confession booths. He went to the front and returned with a votive candle.

"Here," he said softly, breaking his silence, keeping his voice down. "There's a door."

She looked toward the back of the church, startled at something. She put a finger to her lips. "Somebody's coming."

There were noises outside in the area of the narthex, an opening door, and the scraping of boots against the rough granite. A knife-thin sliver of light moved behind the crack of the sanctuary door. He handed the girl the votive candle, then opened the door to the niche and urged her inside, following close after.

Outside, the movements of the boots got closer.

He cracked the door a little, hoping that the shadow would be deep enough to cover any danger of light from the candle being seen from the back of the church. He heard the narthex door open, and then close again with a hard thud. The whole sanctuary area seemed to brighten, and Constantine guessed that whoever had come in carried a torch. That ruled out Brother Joachim the sacristan. Constantine closed the door of the niche.

"Elspeth!" a gruff voice called out in the sanctuary. It was her father, looking for her. He was clearly angry. This could take some time. "I saw you come in here," her father said. He said other things as well, but these were harder to make out. Curses maybe. The voice was moving about the church, and Constantine realized Elspeth's father was methodically searching the large inner chamber of the sanctuary. He began with the doors, which Constantine knew were all unlocked. There was some hope in that. Perhaps he would decide the girl had used the sanctuary as a transition-point on the way to somewhere else.

They could hear her father's angry voice outside, speaking low so he would not attract the attention of the sacristan. "If I have to, I'll take this church apart," her father said.

Constantine groaned a little at that. The sound, the smell, the fear in the moment, all of it carried him back to barely recoverable threads of some horror in his early life. Something had happened to him in the niche. Or maybe in that other space the niche reminded him of—the root cellar. But then he was aware that the memory had not been within the root cellar, but outside of it.

It was a confusing memory. Constantine tried to shake it so he could pay closer attention to the real danger outside, but the memory forced itself upon him. In fragments. Not in a connected sequence. In varying degrees of clarity. He had a vivid memory of pressing his back hard against the stones of the root cellar wall. Granite stones, mortared with mud. Some more vivid images coming first, then other memories, prompted and enabled by the first, piling in later. Some of the memories came to him as muscle aches. There was a kind of violence about the memories, something he tried to avoid. It was like being in a cave with bats around his head. He tried to suppress the urge to swat them away from his head, but had only limited success at that. He began to tremble.

The trembling left him ashamed. Had she noticed?

Elspeth handed him the candle, and then lowered herself down into a sitting position, her back against the wall and her legs stretched out in front of her. He looked down then, struck by the gleam of the candlelight across her black hair. She drew the hood of her cloak back up to cover her head, a gesture Constantine thought strange until he realized she was frightened and this was an instinctive gesture, the only self-protective thing she could think to do. He stooped and set down the candle, then sat beside her.

"He'll kill me," Elspeth whispered, looking at him. The candlelight made a little sparkle against the irises of her black eyes, and that only showed by contrast how fair her skin was. She was truly beautiful, even in the shadows of the niche.

He held his finger to his lips and said nothing. Her father must have been watching her. He was a hunter and had probably had no trouble tracking her here. Now he was methodically turning the church inside out, trying the doors, probably even looking beneath the pews. It would only be a matter of time before her father was searching behind the pillars and the sacred furniture of the apse.

They sat there in the silence, listening as her father's movements brought him closer to the apse and the high altar. He thought about his own father, calling out his name near the entrance of the root cellar in Moldavia. He stroked Elspeth's hair to calm her fears. He held his finger to his lips again, and then blew out the candle, and he and the girl were swallowed up in the safety of the near total darkness.

Constantine lay on his cot fully dressed and tried to understand what had happened during the night. It was a stupid, impulsive thing to do, to show the girl the niche, and he had almost been sent to perdition for doing it, but once there he had protected her, and he was glad of that. He told himself he had gained something for her in the process, another option she might use in an emergency. He had no doubt that her father could hurt her, probably badly even, and the thought of that made him squeamish and angry. If Elspeth's father should hurt her, Constantine would find a way to pin his ears back, and then bear whatever consequences might come from that.

This was a settled decision, and he came to it as calmly as he might select what pen to use in the scriptorium or what book to take from the monastery library. Fletcher ought rather to be proud of her. A man who would knowingly harm a child was evil; there was no excuse for that. Constantine refused to believe there was any proper way to understand such a thing.

When he was certain he would get no sleep at all, he rose and opened the window to let in a little of the thin light of morning. A lizard, lounging on the window sill, startled awake and went scurrying away into the darkness.

Constantine settled back down on his hard cot and thought about the girl. Somewhere in the back of his mind, he realized that it had not been worry for the girl or anger at her father that had kept him awake. It was the physical memory of having been so close to her in the dark after he had blown out the candle. They had waited without speaking in the pitch darkness until long after the noises in the sanctuary had died down and the church had returned to its ordinary, sepulchral stillness. Even with the emerging bat-like, flickering memories of Moldavia, he had not wanted his time with the girl to come to an end, and had completely lost his sense that time was continuing to move outside the niche.

He had forgotten everything but the moment, there in the niche, the moment he was living in. He had imagined he had no past, did not consider the past, and then that he had no future. He had had only the present—himself and the girl together in the niche beneath the high altar of St Cuthbert's Church. Eventually, the memories had cleared the way bats finally clear a cave, and he had become aware again of the girl sitting beside him.

Now, awake on his cot, he realized that they had shared something there in the dark, though he could not quite figure out what it had been. Was it the danger? Was it the fact that in all the world, only they two knew this one thing about each other, that they had huddled together in the dark beneath the altar of St Cuthbert's Church? Their paths had crossed in this odd way, and it seemed precious to him, a connection he had known only once before, with his brother's girlfriend, he thought. This was like that. He realized that monks are not supposed to have secrets, at least not the monks of the Monastery of St Cuthbert and St Chad, not with Father Thomas as their spiritual overseer. Was he no longer a monk, that he now shared this secret with a woman?

Oddly, he realized that the shared secret placed him in her power. If she should report what had happened, even casually to a friend, it could get back to her father, who would beat him beyond recognition, or to Prior Robert, who would probably expel him from the monastery. Either way, he could be ruined.

But at the same time he was aware that by responding to his note, by coming to meet him alone in the night, Elspeth had entrusted herself to him as well—another strange experience for a monk. When Elspeth's father had arrived, she had followed him without hesitation into the protected enclave of the apse, had gone with him into the dark, and thinking about it now he realized that it had been a courageous thing to do, or maybe very foolish. To have a girl, a woman, place her safety in his hands this way, if only for a brief moment, spoke to something within him he chose to think of as noble, calling out from him a part of himself he had only dimly realized was there.

He closed his eyes and tried to remember the night. He had not been able to see her very well in the flickering light of the candle, and not at all in the pitch darkness after the candle had been snuffed, but he had taken a kind of sweet pleasure in knowing that she was there beside him, that her body was there beside his. He had listened to her breathe in the dark, and in his own breathing had taken her fragrance into his body. He had breathed in deeply, trying to memorize the subtle smell of her hair. He had wanted so badly to reach out to her, to stroke her hair, to touch her skin.

He had a dim memory of stroking somebody's hair in the root cellar. A girl, bigger than he was. Older, a teenager. He had held the girl, had touched her. He seemed to remember a Hungarian name, but could not quite make it clear. The memory was a loose thread that broke off in his hand. He had been frightened. He had had to be a man, had to protect the girl, and she had been more frightened than he had been, so he had caressed her skin to calm her in a moment that he now realized might have held grave danger, though the memory was elusive at best, and he finally abandoned any attempt to recover it. Something about the root cellar distressed him.

In the niche, too, beneath the high altar, he had wanted to touch Elspeth's skin the way he had touched the girl in the root cellar. He had wanted to hold Elspeth, or to be held by her, the way he had held the girl in the root cellar, but the danger outside in the sanctuary had been the more urgent concern, and he smothered the urge to touch her the way he might smother a candle beneath a cup.

He rose from his cot and looked through the window at the glistening grass of the monastery cloister. The light was brighter now, but still thin. Further out, a pale fog had settled in across the countryside, giving the monastery the appearance of a mystical place somewhere on a cloud. Then quite close by he heard the bells tolling Vigils, and he scrambled to join his brother monks as they gathered beneath the portico of Brother Johann's garth, black-shrouded ghosts lining up to enter the sanctuary and offer their communical prayers that ended the Grand Silence of the night.

IX

THE NEXT DAY FLETCHER found Elspeth working in Levente's shop. He stood outside the door and called out to her, "Elspeth, get out here!"

The door opened and Levente stepped into the doorway. His left hand was visible against the doorjamb, but his right hand he held back, out of Fletcher's line of sight.

"Get Elspeth out here," Fletcher ordered.

"She's working, John," Levente said obstinately. "She can't come to the door."

"The hell she can't," Fletcher said. His mind bristled with thoughts, fragmentary, splintered images, disorganized by his anger. His mind was like a broken mirror, filled with shattered slivers of images. The girl was going to face him whether Levente liked it or not. Here. Now. In the light. Face to face. What did she do last night? Where did she go? *I'm her father, for Christ's sake, and I expect to be obeyed.*

He thought he caught a glimpse of Elspeth, hiding in the shadows of the hut. Alcera was with the girl. Alcera had her arm around her. *They're only feeding her headstrong streak*, he thought. He paused for a moment, the intensity of what he was saying deflected by the splintered images. "She comes when I say she comes."

"No, John, she doesn't," said Levente calmly. "She's my apprentice, she works for me, she comes and goes as I say, and I say she doesn't talk to you. Not right now. Not when you're like this."

Fletcher raised his fist, but Levente stood his ground in the doorway, clearly unafraid of what Fletcher could do. He drew his right hand out into full view, showing a metal fireplace poker. Then he leaned the poker against the doorjamb, and sat on a small bench that was just outside, beneath the thatch overhang. "Listen, John," Levente said, "Let's sit out here in the sun and talk. I'm glad to see you. I need something from you."

"She's got explaining to do," Fletcher said through his teeth.

"Ah, yes," said Levente. "Don't we all? In due time, John. Not now." He closed the door behind him and leaned back against the wall.

Fletcher, confused by these gestures of vulnerability, and by Levente's apparent nonchalance, hesitated just long enough for Levente to wedge a dissembling question into the talk: "Is there any chance you can bag some grouse for my wife's kitchen? We haven't had grouse in months, and I think you may run across some from time to time in the forest. I'll pay you good money."

Brother Constantine straightened his features and ran a hand through his hair, brushing down on all sides from the shaved tonsure at the back. He straightened his habit, smoothing out any wrinkles and looking for any dust that might remain from the sojourn beneath the altar. The morning sun hurt his eyes. He had come out from his cell to join his brother monks at Vigils, but his head hurt from what had been a long and sleepless night. The near silent movements of their black Benedictine robes whispered the only greetings the brothers were allowed before the chanting of the morning office. He had worried about the girl being hurt by her father, and finally, unable to calm himself, he had simply sat silent in the darkness and thought about being alone with her in the niche.

He felt a hand on his shoulder and turned to find Brother Gregory the herbalist examining him closely. Gregory signaled that he was concerned, and that he would check again later, after Vigils when the Grand Silence was ended.

Later, Gregory was back, examining him again. "You're not well," he said. "Open your mouth, let me look." Gregory said.

Constantine obeyed, and Gregory reached up, and turned his head toward the light.

"Your breath is bad, brother," he said.

"I couldn't sleep," Constantine said softly.

"Come over here into the light," Gregory instructed, "and let me get a better look at you."

"A little food, a little rest, and I'll be good as new."

But Gregory was not to be dissuaded. "Back to your cell with you," he ordered. "Better if you take the day slow."

"I'm needed in the scriptorium," Constantine said.

"Something's going on down there. Wouldn't want you infecting the whole monastery. I'll explain to Prior Robert and we'll let the dead bury their dead." He was referring to a well-known saying of Jesus, meaning, in this case, "Let the scriptorium run on its own today."

Constantine lay still on the cot and stared at the ceiling, one hand behind his head. After a while there was a soft knock, and then, without waiting for an answer, Brother Paul came in, carrying a tray with what looked like bread and cheese. A pitcher, too, probably holding water, beaded from the condensation. Brother Paul was a round little man in every sense, with a face as red and merry as a washer-woman, and a huge belly beneath his habit. He puttered around in the cell for a moment, treating it with such perfect familiarity that it could very well have been his own. He moved aside a book Constantine had been reading and set the tray on the small chest where Constantine kept his few belongings.

"Gregory says you're sick. Says your breath smells like tar. Here let me have a look at you. Have you told the prior? Never mind, I'll speak with him myself. Not to worry a bit about this. Not to worry. You need to get some sleep, I think, but first something to eat. I've brought some bread and cheese for your breakfast. No, don't talk. Save your energy. I'll be back later." As fluidly as he had entered, he turned and moved out the door and was gone.

Constantine was trapped in a way, but grateful for the chance to recover the sleep he had lost the night before. He settled back on the cot and dozed until he heard the bells of Terce, signifying the mid-morning prayers. When he woke, he realized that the air was quite stale, even hard to breathe. Maybe Gregory had been right about his breath. He rose, opened the window to let in some fresh air, and was startled when a rather large lizard came in slowly through the window and settled in on a wooden bench near the head of the cot. "Ah! A new friend!" he said softly, and turned to sit on the cot in such a way that he could eat some of the breakfast and have a better look at the lizard. "What's happened to you?" he said, because the lizard had somehow disappeared. He went to the window and looked out, but the lizard was not there, either. When he came back, it was there again on the bench, waiting for him. Whatever it was, it was intelligent. It had tricks.

He broke off a tiny morsel of bread and set it on the edge of the bench where the lizard could take it at its leisure, then broke a larger piece for himself. He sat on the cot and he chewed and sat stock-still to see if the lizard might come out for the bread. He sat for a long while, listening to the Gregorian chant coming from the church and watching the morsel. Then there was a movement, but so subtle he almost missed it. In a moment, the lizard reappeared and made its way along the surface of the bench. When it stopped, it disappeared, and for a moment he thought it had become invisible. Somehow it was still there, an undulating movement as it breathed. All at once, in a snap, the lizard appeared, went for the morsel, snatched it up and stilled itself, and was gone.

Constantine sat back on the cot and thought about the lizard, aware that its camouflage was nearly perfect. He had seen a creature like that before, but was not sure where. He thought he had heard that some lizards were able to change colors to match their surroundings, he had had no idea it could be done with such precision or completeness. He set out another morsel on the far side of the bench where a slant of sunshine struck the wood, and then watched the as the lizard appeared, moved across the bench, stood still, disappeared. The camouflage was nearly perfect even in the light. What gave it away was its breathing, and he reasoned that it could disappear completely if it stood perfectly still, but that no living thing could do that for very long.

Then he thought about the total darkness of the niche and he realized that within that tiny enclave he was nearly invisible, too, a shape, a shadow—as Elspeth had been. Two bodies, sitting together, invisible in the darkness of the niche. He fed the lizard again, and in his mind's eye worked hard to remember the glint of the candlelight on the girl's dark eyes. The flickering of the candlelight had enchanted him—maybe even now he was enchanted—and he thought about touching her skin, and wished he had the courage or freedom inside himself to touch her hair again, to find some way to show her the tenderness she had not received from her father. He wished he were not a monk, that he could have said more to her in the dark—the Grand Silence prevented that—wished he had been able to reassure her that he would not let anyone harm her.

In the end, he realized that the Grand Silence was only an excuse; he would not have known what to say to her anyway.

Then a thought scratched at the back of his mind like a hair-shirt. He had seen a lizard like that when he was a boy, but where? There was a dim recollection of a cavalcade, maybe a thousand men, maybe more. One of the men had a lizard that could become completely invisible.

The lizard stopped taking the morsels. As it ate, it had made a cooing or clucking sound, like a dove or a hen, and Constantine had the sense that it was at ease, contented probably with the food. He watched as it moved to the window, and then out and away into Brother Johann's garden. He realized as it moved that it had not really been a lizard, but a hatchling dragon. He wondered how it came to be here, in the cloistered enclave of the monastery. The creature had wings, too small to be useful, but large enough to be noticeable, and large enough to make it awkward as it walked. He wished he had a cloak of that same skin—whatever the camouflage was, however it worked—to cover his movements in the church if he had need of seeing the girl. Or rather—he corrected himself—to give to her to cover her movements if she should need to come to him for safety.

Then he lay back on the cot and thought about the smell of Elspeth's hair, and his sense of her body, in the stillness of the niche.

Constantine was leaving the church in the company of his brothers from the scriptorium when he was approached by Levente. "Brother, can we talk?"

There was an uncharacteristic urgency in Levente's voice, and Constantine wondered with a pang if Elspeth had said something about what had happened beneath the altar. A knot the size of a grapefruit appeared in his gut, then squeezed its acidic juices into his stomach. "Is everything alright?" he asked, as calmly as he could manage. "Not a problem with the manuscripts, I hope."

Levente put a reassuring hand on Constantine's shoulder. "No, no, nothing like that," he told him. "All is well on that account. No need to worry. But I would like your help on another matter, something quite unrelated to our 'children.'" It was an old understanding between them. Both men, childless, gave birth to books, Brother Constantine playing midwife, and Levente playing nursemaid. Until lately, it would have been enough. He had been content with that until the girl had come into his life, a woman now, and he had begun to wonder what he had missed, raising children, touched by the love of a woman.

Constantine relaxed a little, drawing in a deep breath of relief. Elspeth had said nothing about meeting him in the niche.

"Are you alright, Brother?"

"Something I ate, I think. You said something about the children."

"Not that, Brother. I need your help with something else."

"Of course, my friend," replied Constantine quietly, breathing much more easily now. "Come within the garden here where we can talk without disturbing the others." *And without being overheard*, he thought.

"I have a friend," Levente began mysteriously, "who is in need of your special gifts."

"What? Copying manuscripts? Deciphering something?"

"After a fashion," said Levente. "He's a wounded soul who has tried to make himself palimpsest." He was referring to the copyist's occasional practice of scraping the ink off of a manuscript to free the page for a different text. Such books were called palimpsests. "I want you to try and help this man read what is in the underwriting."

Constantine listened, puzzled. "I'm not a priest," he said simply. He had followed Levente's metaphor perfectly, neatly making the leap from scrawls written and erased from manuscripts to scrawls written and erased from hearts. In the one as in the other, the underwriting never completely goes away. But there was an odd sense within him that within his own soul there was a hidden underwriting, too, made legible now as the events with the girl called it forth from within him. There were things inside him he needed to understand, things too terrible to remember. He had forgotten his village in Moldavia, and things that had been done to him on his way to England. He had all he could handle to deal with that. More than he could handle. Now he had Elspeth's safety to add to his worries. He did not understand, either, his strange attraction to her. He did not need anybody else's troubles to muddy his own waters. How could he make Levente understand that?

"I'm no priest," he said again. "What your friend needs is a priest."

"I'm not asking you to play priest. That's something different altogether. In fact, the priest's role is one we both know you cannot play and must not play. What I'm asking you to do is to help to expose this man's wound to the air and light so he can be healed."

"I'm no healer, either," said Constantine, protesting this proposed shift of roles into territory he found unfamiliar and unwanted. His own soul was scarred by what he remembered, by what he found emerging from his own underwriting. But he could not say that to Levente. Not here. Not now. "I don't know how to do what you're asking me to do," he said flatly. It was as simple as that. He could not do what Levente was asking.

"There you're wrong, my friend," said Levente. He paused, and Constantine had the impression he was sorting out what to say next. "Have you ever watched the infirmerer grind and blend his herbs to make medicines?"

"Who hasn't seen that?"

"In the same way, God grinds and blends the character of His healers. You're such a person, Constantine."

"I'm not ground, Levente. I'm broken."

"What Christian could not say the same thing?" insisted Levente. "Original sin, remember. What'd Jesus say to the Pharisees??"

Images flashed across his mind then. He saw himself, a monk, hiding with a girl beneath the high altar of St Cuthbert's Church, wanting to touch her, wanting to hold her, he saw Jesus turning over tables, taking a whip to the authorities. Christ was raging, and he flinched beneath Jesus' ranting against the Scribes and the Pharisees—"Woe to you, scribes and Pharisees," Jesus was saying, "hypocrites! for you are like whitewashed tombs, which outwardly appear beautiful, but within they are full of dead men's bones and all uncleanness. So you also outwardly appear righteous to men, but within you are full of hypocrisy and iniquity." But then he forced himself to calm a little. He thought of Jesus, addressing the woman who had been taken in adultery, whose image was carved deep into one of the panels of the kneeling bench before the altar. *Original sin, Levente says, what Christian could deny that? Jesus must have thought that, too.* "Let he who is without sin cast the first stone," the Christ had said. "Neither do I condemn you."

Levente waited and said nothing. Apparently he was allowing Constantine his space, his time to weigh the pros and cons of what he was being asked to do. Constantine liked that about Levente. He had no sense of hurry. But what he wanted was impossible. He could not do this thing Levente was asking. When the silence became strained, he said flatly, "Prior Robert would never approve such an arrangement anyway."

"Robert does not need to know," said Levente. "Your work in the scriptorium needn't suffer. I'm not asking for great amounts of your time, only for an hour here or there, maybe once a week as you see necessary, when your other work is finished."

"No!" Constantine insisted. "I can't do what you're asking." He stood and looked at the garden. "It's not possible."

"Maybe you won't have to do anything at all," said Levente evenly. "This is what I think should happen: The man we're talking about may not know he needs help, may indeed actively resist it. I'll talk to him and ask him if he'll see you. When and if he comes to you, you should ask him how he has come to be the man he is. Then question his answers. Inside this man there are large wounds, wounds he's kept secret for a long time, I think even from himself. I want you to find out where his wounds are, and then help him see them, too. That way they come out into the light where they can be healed."

"And if he does not come?"

"Then he'll continue in his agony and you'll continue in your scriptorium. That's his to choose. But I think he'll come."

Constantine was listening, horrified that he was being asked to be for someone else the person he now needed someone else to be for him. "And of his sins?" he asked.

"Some of his wounds will come from un-confessed sins, though I think not all. For the sins he will need the help of Father Thomas. Be gentle, but listen hard," he went on. "Don't let him escape the healing that he needs."

Constantine felt a stab at that—"his un-confessed sins"—but thankfully Levente knew nothing about that. Had his thoughts about the girl been sinful? "I don't know how to do this thing," he said uncomfortably.

"And does anyone?" asked Levente. "We learn as we go. We make mistakes. We learn from our mistakes. And then we go on."

"But I . . . ."

"He really does need your help."

"Why not yours instead?" asked Constantine.

"I'm too close to him. I've got opinions already, and my opinions may keep me from asking the right questions. Better he should talk to someone who can listen with an open mind and heart."

"But I'm a flawed man," Constantine protested again. He stood to go. He felt sick to his stomach even thinking about what Levente was asking of him. "I mean that I am too flawed. Even for a monk."

"There's a theological debate," Levente said. Constantine was aware that Levente often read the books he had been asked to bind, and over time had become no mean theologian in his own right.

Constantine sat back down. Levente was exasperating, but he often talked sense.

"There is a theological debate about the Eucharist," Levente said again. "If the priest who administers the sacrament is fallen, is the sacrament efficacious?"

"I would think so," said Constantine levelly.

"And why is that?" asked Levente.

"Because," he sighed, "the sacrament does not depend upon the spiritual perfection of the priest, but upon the spiritual perfection of the Christ."

"Exactly so," said Levente. "And exactly so *here*. Christ uses fallen vessels, and so we become saints."

Levente stood and walked to the far side of a row of rose bushes, already dormant in preparation for winter. He talked for a while about the tender care they needed if they were to bring forth new growth—the pruning and the fertilizing—and he said that if the roses in Brother Johann's garden were worthy of a monk's time and energy, then surely he could devote a few moments of his time to the care of another of God's creatures. One for whom Christ died.

"Alright," Constantine said at last. Then he sighed, in that way voicing also his sense of inadequacy. "I'll try. I can't offer you anything more, though. I'm not making any promises."

"Good," said Levente. "When he comes to you, make him tell you the story of his inner life. The wounds will appear at the points where the story cracks open. Look for the places where it breaks down or it begins to contradict itself. Listen for the gaps in the stories. Ask him about the contradictions. Make him deal with the gaps. When you find the stories he's afraid to tell, there you will find his wounds."

"And what then?" asked Constantine. He had given in, and now he had to follow along with what Levente was telling him. "How will we go about healing this man?"

"God is both gracious and good," said Levente levelly. He stood, drawing the conversation to a close. "If you find the wounds, and if this man wants to be healed, God will heal them. This is the work of God in the world, my friend." They paused beside an arched pilaster of a wall that was blanketed with a shawl of jasmine. The air was heavy with the fragrance of the luxuriant old growth, not yet lost to the chill of fall. Then Levente did something absolutely unexpected: He lapsed into the Latin he and Constantine shared from their work with the scriptures:

"Infirmos curate,
mortuos suscitate,
leprosos mundate."

They both knew the passage by heart:

"Heal the sick,
raise the dead,
cleanse the lepers."

Constantine, his eyes closed, heard these words with the most profound sense of inadequacy, but also as a prayer, and within the prayer a seed of hope. Whoever Levente had been talking about, and whatever his wounds, if there was healing for that man, perhaps he could find somewhere along the way that there would be healing for himself as well. He felt Levente's hand upon his shoulder. When he looked up he discovered that Levente's eyes, too, were closed in prayer, and he realized that, intended or not, Levente the bookbinder—pious as the need arose—had pronounced a benediction upon his head, as though between the two of them, in the absence of a priest, and without the blessing of the prior, he had been ordained to a task not of his own choosing.

As God is my witness—he shuddered at the thought—*I will do the best I can, if not for myself, then for Levente and for that man*—whoever it was, Levente had not said—*and for the Kingdom of God. I will do this,* he thought, *if God places it in my path.*

Levente had good reasons for asking Brother Constantine to do this thing. He had known him he since he was a boy, newly arrived from the east. His parents had been killed by rampaging Mongols who had invaded eastern Europe in a series of sweeping raids that decimated the general population in the first half of the century. As a child he had first been taken in by Elizabeth of Hungary, of blessed memory, and then as a youth had been brought to England by troops returning from the sixth crusade, whose route had taken them along the lee of the Carpathian Mountains, then through Hungary proper. His English, while precise and proper, remained forever laced with traces of his native Hungarian.

Constantine believed fervently in all things Christian. He was a contemplative by both inclination and training, though he did not understand the contemplative vocation as a retreat from the world. It was instead a matter of being mindfully present in the world, within it and on its behalf no less than in and on behalf of the Kingdom of God. With these two loyalties, human and spiritual, Constantine was ever mindful—mindful of his surroundings, mindful of the things people said, mindful of the things they did not or could not say, mindful of the secret presence of God in the world. The retreat from the world, the Benedictine practice of the Grand Silence that lasted from evening prayers at Vespers until morning prayers at Lauds, the discipline imposed by the horarium that divided the day into alternating periods of labor and prayer—all were integral parts of the monk's spirituality, and Constantine understood them as necessary for the training of the mind as well as the heart, so that the whole person, head, heart and hands, might be devoted to the world in the service of God. Only by being mindful does one see clearly the fallen-ness of the world, and only then can one respond with a redemptive word or a healing touch.

Constantine was one of the copyists in the monastery's scriptorium and had often been granted leave from the cloister to give instructions about books and copying materials to this outsider with whom the monastery so often did business. His copying work was without equal—line after line of neatly scribed, accurate Latin, written out in flawless Carolingian script—which Levente took to be another sign of a careful mind.

Constantine had found books for Fletcher's wife Alysse to read, sometimes even slipping them secretly from the monastery with his other work.

These were the qualities, plus one other, that suggested Brother Constantine as caregiver and guide for John Fletcher. That one other Levente knew from the odd ways their paths had crossed over the years: In one way or another Brother Constantine had been a presence in Fletcher's life for a long time. Nearly thirty years prior, when Fletcher had still been apprenticed to Levente's father, Constantine had come to his aid, taking his side and thus rescuing him from a sound beating Levente's father was determined he had richly deserved. When Fletcher's wife had died in childbirth, it had been Constantine who braved Prior Robert's anger to sit beside the man in church and translate the daft old priest's sermon into English. Brother Constantine was the only member of the monastery community Fletcher might even remotely consider his friend.

The Feast of St Elizabeth came on the fifth of November. The stores of winter cordwood had long since been laid by. The harvest was now in, and life in Wharram settled into the quiet rhythm that marked the late fall and early winter.

Levente, realizing that John Fletcher would be reluctant to seek help from anyone, much less from him, decided that this was as good a time as any to broach the subject of Fletcher's need for a spiritual guide. He went to see him.

"John, are you home?" he called out.

"Get off my property," Fletcher shouted from above. He was on the roof, making repairs to the thatch in anticipation of winter.

"I want to talk to you about Elspeth," said Levente.

"You've said enough already," said Fletcher, climbing down a ladder. This was a rebuff, but the tone of his voice revealed an aching heart. Angry as he was, he invited the other man inside. If Levente had something to say about Elspeth, it would be for his ears alone, and not for the neighbors.

"I think it's about time the two of you worked out your differences," Levente said. He sat down on one of the two wooden chairs that served as the hut's primary seating. "She needs you."

"About time? Listen to the man! How dare you tell me when it's about time to do anything? Who do you think you are? I'm the girl's father, her only kin in the world, and you think you can tell me when or how I'm to—what did you call it? 'Work out our differences?'" He spat out the door.

"Listen, Fletcher," said Levente levelly, refusing to be intimidated. "There's something terribly wrong here and it needs to be dealt with."

"What's wrong is that she's with you, and not home with me."

"That, and something more. There's a wound that needs healing. Inside you, John, where nobody can see. I think you can heal it, but not by yourself."

"If there was anything wrong with me I'd fix it myself."

"Then why have you not done so?" asked Levente.

"There. Is. Nothing. Wrong. Here." said Fletcher forcefully. "Listen, Levente. You're not my priest, and you're not my father. I don't owe you any explanation for what I do or don't do, not in my own house, and I'm not going to be judged by you."

"You and I are like flint and tinder. But there's someone else can help. I think you should talk to him."

"And if I don't?"

"Then Elspeth remains with me. But remember that she has only a few months remaining on her apprenticeship. She finishes in the spring. When she's released she'll almost certainly leave Wharram. You may not have much time to repair the damaged relationship you have with her."

"In the spring, she marries Meurig ap Gwynedd," said Fletcher.

"She's as pig-headed as you are, John," Levente said. "She says that marriage isn't going to happen."

"She'll do as she's told," John said.

"And if she doesn't, you'll beat her again? You almost killed her."

"Fathers beat their daughters, Levente, but what would you know about that?"

Levente ignored the dripping sarcasm in Fletcher's question. "You need to figure out why."

"Discipline," said Fletcher. "I discipline my daughter. Good fathers do that."

"You nearly killed her," Levente said again.

"It was an accident," Fletcher said. "I was startled. I didn't mean to shoot at her."

"I'm not talking about the bolt, John. I'm talking about what happened afterward. Something dangerous happened out there. You need to find out what it was or it could happen again."

Fletcher thought about the times he had beaten the girl in anger. He thought about the wolf pup and the deeply disturbing images that had flashed through his consciousness in that moment suspended in time when he thought he had slit the pup's throat. He thought about the terrible mistake he had made when he had almost killed the girl near the bivouac, and of his relief that he had not destroyed his only living link with Alysse, and then his horror and shame when he realized that the girl had been unarmed. He thought about his discovery of why the girl had been running, why she had stocked the bivouac in the first place. In his gut he recognized that Elspeth, his living totem of Alysse, had fled terrified into a storm because of her fear of what he would do. The fear of the father had been greater even than her fear of the dragon they both had seen hunting along the ridges to the north. *I'll grant the bookbinder this much,* he thought. *There's something wrong here.* But it was none of Levente's business. He would not give the bookbinder the satisfaction of being right. He clenched his teeth. "Get out of my house."

The next day Fletcher found Levente on the road, making his way to Levente's shop. He stepped in beside him: "Alright Levente," he said. "I'll bite. What's this thing you want me to do?"

"I want you to talk to Brother Constantine," said Levente, as though it were the most natural thing in the world to sit down with monks and talk about one's daughters. He shifted his burden to the other shoulder.

"Do I look like I'm wearing motley here? Monks don't know anything about anything, much less about fathers and daughters. What can a monk possibly have to tell me about that?"

"Probably not very much," admitted Fletcher. "But Constantine is very good at listening. I think you should talk to him."

"Right," said Fletcher. "Confess my sins. Do my penance. Seek absolution. But I haven't committed any sin." He turned and looked at Levente more squarely as they walked. "You see? No sin, no confession."

"Constantine's a monk, not a priest."

Fletcher thought again of the wolf pup, and his unhealed grief for Alysse, and his sacrilegious practice of pausing at the niche of the Blessed Virgin, imagining she were Alysse an act he knew the monks and villagers regarded as a sign of special piety, but only because they were unaware of the deeper meaning that act held for him. "So if I talk to Thomas, I get confidentiality. But Constantine's no priest, so whatever I say to him is fair game. He talks to his brother monks, and I end up the laughing stock of Warwickshire. That'd be a fine turn of events, now, wouldn't it?"

"No, John. It wouldn't be like that."

"Or how about this," John went on, ignoring the interruption. "How about he buries me in pity for the sorry way my mind has gone soft since my wife died? That what you want?"

"John, now listen to me. It wouldn't be like that, either. I give my word. I want you to talk to Brother Constantine. You know him; he's as solid as the granite in the church. Everything will be strictly confidential, I swear it on Christ's bones. As confidential as the confession booth." In Catholic spirituality, even the fact that a confession has been made is confidential. "He won't even tell me. And if he did—which he won't—I wouldn't listen."

Fletcher thought back to the agonies of his struggle with his great secret, the hidden well of agony and grief and shame that attended his inner life. He thought about the times he had wandered the shire trying to decide whether he could ever share this troubling part of his life, this shadow that seemed more to emerge out of him than to descend over him. What Levente was proposing would be a relief, at least from the isolation.

But he would not give Levente the satisfaction of knowing that he had touched a sore spot within him. "No," he said firmly. "I can't, I won't."

He turned back and went home to his house, shaking his head.

X

CONSTANTINE WAS WORKING IN the refectory, which was the oldest part of the monastery and the most in need of frequent repair. Heavy snows from a fierce storm had damaged the roof. Two of the support timbers had cracked under the load, and the west-facing ceiling had fallen in completely, making the situation serious enough to require an emergency suspension of all other work as the brothers, Constantine included, turned their attention to the physical work of controlling the damage and repairing the building. Only Prior Robert and Brother Cyril were excused, but that was because they were both old. For several days the brothers continued in this fashion, stopping only to eat and to rest and to turn to the monk's obligatory horarium of prayers.

Fletcher found Constantine on one of the scaffolds that had been set up within the refectory, trowel in hand, repairing a place in the wall where the leakage had been particularly bad.

"Brother Constantine, have you got a few minutes?"

Constantine waited until Fletcher was near, then replied in as practical a way as he could: "Yes, of course, John," he said quietly. "Is this about some matter for the sheriff?"

"No, Brother," said John. "It's personal. Can we talk? In private, I mean? I've got . . ."—here he paused—". . . something to ask you."

Constantine was aware of the size of Fletcher's hands, and the damage they could do to him if he knew that he had shown Elspeth the hiding place behind the niche of the altar. This couldn't be about that. Fletcher's tone was gentler, and from the tentative way he phrased his query, Constantine knew instinctively that this had something to do with the conversations Levente had asked him to undertake. He considered this for a moment, hesitating. If he had known Levente had been talking about Fletcher, he would have flat-out refused. In his mind flashed an image of Jesus upbraiding the hypocrites in Jerusalem—*whitewashed tombs,* Jesus had called them—but then the counterbalancing image of the woman taken in adultery. He was in this too far to back out, but he reassured himself with the thought that he might learn something that would be useful later on.

He climbed down from the scaffold and lowered his voice to protect what little privacy they might have here in the refectory. "Yes, John. I'd be happy to talk with you. Suppose we meet in the church, tomorrow after Terce? We can continue there uninterrupted for as long as we have need."

The look on Fletcher's face was pained, even agonized. "Not the church, Constantine. Is there somewhere less open?"

"The church is enclosed and at least a little warm."

"Not the church," Fletcher said firmly.

Constantine wondered what it was about the church Fletcher found disturbing. If he knew about the niche he probably also knew what had happened, and in that case he would be after him with a club. "My cell is within the cloister," he thought out loud, "that's out. Ordinarily, we could meet in here in the refectory, but as you can see, this too is open." He was aware of the shift of meaning of that term. "Perhaps we can talk in the library," he went on hopefully. "I'll ask Brother Anselm the precentor for a few moments in the library."

"Alright," said Fletcher. "Tomorrow, after Terce."

"I'll meet you at the gate, John," Constantine said by way of closing. "You won't raise any suspicions if you're accompanied by one of the brothers. We shall have our conversation, perhaps others if you like."

"Tomorrow," said Fletcher again, "after Terce." He turned and left the refectory.

The next day dawned clear and bright. The morning sun caught the sparkle in the snow with such force that Fletcher was nearly blinded on his way to the monastery.

Constantine greeted him at the gate and the two men walked together in the direction of the library. Along the way they entered the monastery's flower garden, the plants now sleeping beneath the white blanket of snow. Here they paused to talk, the unplanned stop in their progress prompted by the crisp cold air and the extraordinary beauty of the monastery grounds.

"I expect you know why I'm here," Fletcher began. He did not look directly at the monk, but stood shoulder to shoulder beside him, looking at the mantel of snow that covered the garden. Constantine shuddered at that, but realized that if John Fletcher knew that he had been with Elspeth in the niche, they would be having a very different conversation.

"Why no, John," said Constantine, as levelly as he could manage. "I sensed it was important and that it needed privacy, but I have no idea what you have to say to me."

"Levente said I should talk to you," said Fletcher simply. A gust of wind kicked up the loose surface of the snow and sent it swirling away across the courtyard. On the far side, Brother Anselm the precentor was carrying a pail in the direction of the kitchen, making himself useful in the work of the Lord even as he had absented himself from the library.

"Why do you think that Levente wanted you to talk to me?" asked Constantine. This seemed as good a place to begin as any. He was feeling his way. Did Levente know about what he had done? Had he sent Fletcher so he, Constantine, could come clean on his own, without having been coerced or exposed? Levente was like that. Then—more alarmingly—he realized that he did not know what Levente might do if he had sent Fletcher to hear a confession, and none had come. Would he expose him then? To protect the girl? To force him to accept responsibility for what he had done?

Fletcher cleared his throat, shifting his weight a little, and running his fingers through his thick hair. The two men stood in silence for a long time. "I nearly killed Elspeth in a hunting accident," he said at last.

Constantine's relief was nearly palpable. Fletcher had other business to conduct. This wasn't about exposure after all. At least not for him, not today. But Fletcher was making some kind of confession of his own.

"Your daughter?"

"Right."

"When was this?" His mind raced. Before, or after that first night in the niche? Fletcher had been furious, a raging animal. His back stiffened, remembering the fear they both had felt, hiding in the niche behind the altar. How many times had he seen bruises on Elspeth's face, her arms? This had been no accident, and Fletcher knew it. It had been an explosion of anger. Fletcher had a temper, and he could no doubt ride that temper to the brink of disaster. *Then again,* Constantine thought, *he's here. He's dealing with it, or trying to. Let this unfold at its own pace.* "We all have accidents, John," he said. "Sure that was the whole of it?"

"Well, no. I think Levente was pretty concerned about what led up to the accident, and about what I did afterward."

"First things first, wouldn't you say?" asked Constantine. "Why not start at the beginning?"

Fletcher told him about that day in the king's forest, beginning with the moment he had set out to track the girl.

"Why was she running?" Constantine said, though he thought he knew the answer already.

Fletcher turned his face away and said nothing.

"How did you know she had a crossbow?" asked Constantine, dislodging the silence.

"She'd turned the crossbow on me," said Fletcher, "aimed it right into my throat."

Fletcher hesitated when he realized he was revealing more than he had intended. Why hadn't he thought about that? Constantine would want to know why a daughter would turn a crossbow on her father, and now he'll want to know about the dragon.

But Constantine only nodded and listened, and Fletcher was struck by the fact that he registered neither surprise, nor horror, nor criticism, but simply listened, nodding occasionally to indicate that he had understood. Occasionally he asked clarifying questions, some of which had not occurred to Fletcher himself. Had the girl ever shown any tendency to violence? Fletcher answered no. Why, then, did Fletcher expect violence this time? Fletcher answered that he did not know. Constantine pointed out that Fletcher had known about the bivouac. How was that? He answered that he had been tracking the girl, watching her. Constantine seemed concerned that he had tracked the girl. Was that so bad? For a father to need to know what his daughter was up to? In the king's forest, no less? He had responsibilities, for Christ's sake. Constantine wanted to know if Fletcher had ever confronted his daughter about the bivouac.

Fletcher answered no.

Why not? What had prevented him?

He did not want her to know he had been watching her. She might change her plans.

So the two continued until they heard the bells chime Vespers and they knew their conversation would have to close. What struck Fletcher was the way Brother Constantine embraced him as they parted company at the monastery gate. It was an odd, awkward gesture, uncomfortable but somehow also comforting. He had not been embraced since Alysse had died. Certainly the girl had never embraced him.

"Not to worry," Constantine said. "All is in the hands of God, the healer of all our souls." Could such a man, this gentle monk, be trusted to keep these details of his inner life a secret? Fletcher desperately wanted to believe this, but he knew he would have to wait and see.

At mass the following Sunday, Fletcher found himself sitting in the third row of the north transept, opposite the point where the monastery's chancel choir was stationed for the singing of the Gregorian chant. Constantine entered with his brother monks, filing past Fletcher on his way to his seat in the south transept. As he did so, he nodded slightly and smiled, but he did this so discreetly that these two small gestures went unnoticed by the others in the processional. Fletcher had the uncanny sense that he, archer and huntsman, man of the world, had been caught up in a kind of intrigue with this quiet monk, director of the monastery scriptorium, the two of them co-conspirators, neither willing to give away the other, neither willing to damage the tiny thread of trust that somehow existed between them.

Brother Constantine sat in the choir with his fellow monks and thought resentfully about the cold. He peered out from the protective enclosure of the hood—straining more than peering, really—trying to see across the transept, where John the Fletcher sat beside his daughter Elspeth. Constantine had noticed them during the processional, had even watched for them. More precisely, he had watched for her, his face held rigidly forward, his head down, covered by his hood, which like his brother monks he wore pulled up over his head. They stepped off the processional in that slow cadence dictated by the Gregorian chant, so that they swayed gently as they moved, rocking from side to side like a column of solemn, black-shrouded ghosts.

Constantine looked out obliquely from beneath his hood, glancing across the chancel at the worshippers there—hoping only to catch a glimpse of the girl. He saw John Fletcher, caught his eye briefly, and nodded. Then he gazed beyond Fletcher to Elspeth as she stood beside her father waiting for the liturgy to allow them to sit. He was distressed that she was sitting beside her father. Elspeth stared straight ahead, which Constantine also found distressing. How could he get her to look at him, to signal him in some way that she, too, felt that connection he had felt between them?

Elspeth noticed Constantine's glances and found she took a momentary pleasure in them. *What woman does not enjoy the admiration of a man*, she thought, *even an older man with a tonsure?* But propriety forbade a direct look, and so she kept her face forward and noticed Constantine out of the corner of her eye. It was a safe enough flirtation—given the differences in their ages and the fact that he was a man of God. She had the passing thought that except for his tonsure, he might actually have been handsome.

She thought about the niche behind the high altar. She had liked being there, encased in the little safe world with Brother Constantine. No dragon. No danger. As they sat together in the dark, his age did not matter. The fact that he was a monk did not matter, either. What mattered was that he had taken a risk to tell her about the hiding place, had probably broken some rule to do that. She had been in St Cuthbert's Church a dozen times a month, every month for as long as she could remember, her whole life, and she had not known about the niche. Now as she thought about that, she realized that she had never been allowed to cross beyond the railing that separated the sacred precinct of the apse from the more secular precinct of the nave. Brother Constantine had not only allowed her that privilege, he had invited it; perhaps as he did this he had even violated some sacred rule she did not know about.

She smiled then, thinking what might have happened if she had been alone in such a place with Jason or one of the other boys from the village. Ever since she had moved into young womanhood, and her figure had rounded out, the village boys had swarmed upon her like flies, wanting from what she had heard all men want. They had nothing to offer in return; they were illiterate like her father; they had no futures. But they fawned upon her anyway, which made their intensions clear enough. She did not hate them; she distrusted them and thought they were silly.

Brother Constantine had not touched her, but had been content only to sit beside her in the stillness of the niche, waiting with her until the danger had passed. He was, she realized, a man of self-control; he was unlike anybody she knew, except perhaps for Levente. She considered also how unlike her father he was. Her father was a troubled, troubling man. Sarabeth had spoken dreamily about her father, but Elspeth did not know why. Perhaps a village woman with a hard life wants a man with greater hardness about him. *Hard*, she thought suddenly. *He is that, whatever else!* Her father seldom spoke; he said what needed saying, but little else. He did what needed doing, took his responsibilities seriously, worked hard, but there was a wall around his heart. What would Sarabeth know about that?

Brother Constantine seemed to be her father's opposite. He was tender, kind, trustworthy. He had broken rules for her, had put himself at risk for her, and then had been content to sit beside her in the quiet of the niche and do nothing and say nothing, so long as she was safe. Which of the village boys would have done that?

She was wondering what journey had produced such a man, when she realized ruefully that it was probably because he was a monk. *There's a cosmic joke!* she thought. *God keeps such men for himself and leaves the others for the women! Perhaps that's how he populates his convents.* For a moment she wondered if she might find safety and contentment within the cloister. It was only a thought, fleeting as a summer breeze, and it passed on as readily as it came. She wanted adventures first. And then children. And a thoughtful man like Brother Constantine who would love her and keep her safe.

Brother Constantine sat in his cell waiting for the bells that would signal the first communical prayers at Vigils and the beginning of the new day. He had washed in a small basin by the light of a lone candle on the table near the bed, and had opened the day with a solitary prayer before the crucifix that hung on the wall near the window.

But now he was sitting quietly, reviewing the conversation he had had with John the Fletcher. There were certain aspects of the story that had not made sense, but that was something Levente had told him he should look for. He had a strong sense of progress, he thought in part because he had been able to listen well enough to identify difficulties in the story.

He pulled out a piece of paper and in the careful Carolingian script that marked his work as a scribe, he wrote out the first question that presented itself to him: Why did Elspeth pull a crossbow on her father in the first place? This then led to other questions. What was she capable of? Had he misjudged her? Was this a sign of defiance, as her father thought, or of desperation? Did it signal a pattern, and if so, where did it originate and what other clues and consequences would manifest themselves? What had caused John to hold that information back? Did he think that detail was unimportant, or was he being self-protective? What else was being held back?

It was clear that Fletcher had misinterpreted the girl's actions on this occasion; could it be that he, Constantine, had misinterpreted her on other occasions? He had built up an image of the girl that did not seem to match the image Fletcher had of her. Did Fletcher not know how lovely she was? How much like her mother? What motives had driven Fletcher's tendency to see the worst in her?

It was apparent too that those moments of punishment, which it seemed to Constantine were usually undeserved, and which John had called "discipline," had escalated into something that was clearly other than that. What factors contributed to that escalation? This was violence, but why did Fletcher not understand it so? What self-protective strategies did Fletcher employ that kept him from seeing the violence for what it was?

As he re-read and reviewed this list, it seemed to him that there were underlying patterns already evident in the story the way Fletcher had told it. Fletcher had described moments in which he had reacted to something in an extreme way, out of keeping with what was really happening. Surely this was so. When he had discovered that he had not killed Elspeth, but had only grazed her, why had he beaten her, rather than embrace her? Violence is an odd way to express relief. Then he had justified this action, calling it discipline, even when he had discovered that Elspeth was not defying him except in self-defense.

The gaps in the story seemed to Constantine to be necessary elements obviously left out. If so, they were left out deliberately or they were memories Fletcher would not or could not recall, or that he thought were unimportant. But perhaps that meant that on some level, perhaps more deeply than he himself was aware, Fletcher knew that there was something wrong here.

Levente had told him to look for the places where there were gaps in Fletcher's telling of the story. Then for a moment the reflection turned personal. Were there gaps in his own story he was unable or unwilling to face? As he had been with Elspeth in the niche, he had had to fight a confusing and frightening set of memories, memories that came upon him like bats in a dark cave.

Not a cave but the root cellar. There had been a girl in there. He had been inside the cellar with a girl. Something terrible was happening outside. He had been thrown one day into the root cellar. His house was burning. His brother was carrying him to the root cellar. His brother was lying on his back with an arrow through his throat.

He forced his attention back to Fletcher. The place to begin would be the obvious holes in the story. Fletcher was avoiding something. It was like holes had been torn out of his memory, and then the cloth of what remained had been rewoven to try and disguise the holes. Maybe that was what had happened to Fletcher. Something had happened to him to carry him beyond the edge of his memory and his conscience into that forbidden place where he did what he himself knew to be wrong, but what? What happened when he beat his daughter?

The bells chimed Vigils, and Brother Constantine, copier of manuscripts, director of the scriptorium, and now spiritual guide to this single solitary soul, rose and made his way silently to the monastery church to join his fellow monks as they began their day in prayer.

In the days that followed, Elspeth found herself making regular trips to the monastery to deliver goods to the scriptorium. One such trip took her near the monastery school. Three monks passed by, herding a group of children before them, and she slipped back to allow them to pass. One of the boys threw an apple, hitting one of the brothers squarely in the back, then straightened his features into mock nonchalance so the brother would not pick him out of the crowd. The monk turned and glared.

"You there. Cyril," said the monk. "Who threw that?'

One of the other boys shrugged his shoulders and looked blankly at the monk.

"All of you, line up there," ordered the monk, a little more sternly than the situation warranted. "I ought to thrash you all. Be good for you. No supper for you. Not tonight." He found a switch beside the road, then used it like a riding crop, snapping it against his robe to emphasize his authority. She watched as he formed the boys into a line and marched them off in the direction of the monastery gate. Elspeth had the thought that they looked like one of the sheriff's chain-gangs, marching off that way, more than a group of boys a little too full of life for their small boys bodies to hold. The monk puffed himself up, full of his own importance. *He must have believed too many of Father Thomas' sermons*, she thought. Then she thought that the monks were all like that, all except for Constantine. *Constantine's a gentleman. A shame there were not more like him. A shame there were none her age. A shame he was a monk.*

It was shortly after the midafternoon office at None. Constantine returned to the scriptorium. With him he carried a bulky manuscript, a handwritten copy of the New Testament. Along the way he spoke briefly with the gatekeeper. "John the Fletcher has permission to visit me," he said simply. "Would you please direct him to the scriptorium?"

Fletcher had never seen the scriptorium, and he paused for a moment to take it in. For an officer of the law, and for a hunter as well, the truth is often in the details, and here he looked for clues that would tell him more about the small and mysterious monk who had lately become such a regular and important companion.

A sweeping gaze took in the whole of the room. The scriptorium was a large and light-filled, with a bank of south-facing windows that took advantage of the winter sun. The east wall was filled with a large ornately carved armoire that held manuscripts in various stages of completion. Some very old scrolls were stored there as well. The wall opposite had a simple built-in cupboard to hold the tools of the copyist's trade—additional sheets of vellum, pumice for burnishing the vellum, a supply of coarser parchment, paper for preliminary sketches, knives, ink, quills, blotters. There were desks and seats for maybe twenty monks, who copied in unison from a single exemplar which was read aloud phrase by phrase by a lector at the room's northern side. On the wall behind the lectern there was a large wooden crucifix. Above the door was an inscription, but John could not tell what it said.

Constantine remained where he was at the lectern, reading silently. He looked up when John entered the room, but said nothing until this survey of the room and its contents was completed.

Fletcher stood uneasily beside one of the heavy writing desks. "I thought monks were supposed to be poverty-stricken. Looks like you're doing pretty well."

"I wrestle with that," said Constantine, smiling. "It's easy enough to set aside our possessions, but it's harder to give up our passions. Mine is for books. I pray daily that my passion will not keep me from the Kingdom of God." He waited for a moment, then changed the subject. "Shall we begin by being silent together, John? That would be alright, wouldn't it?"

The two men stood in silence for a while after that; neither one was comfortable with small talk, and yet both were determined to pick up where they had left off. John was not unaccustomed to shared silence; quite often he and Elspeth had spent hours at a time in such silences, though this time he knew the silence was intended to focus attention on the problem at hand. In this context, though, Fletcher found it new and strange, and a little disconcerting. What troubled him was not the silence itself, but Constantine's notion that the noise of talk or work may be a strategy for avoiding things about ourselves we would rather not acknowledge. If Constantine were right about that, silence of this sort might very well lead to exposure, and he could not know in advance what would be exposed. Even so, he bowed his head and waited patiently, as he saw the monk do before him.

Constantine cleared his throat. "I remember once Father Thomas said something about the Holy Spirit, who guides us into all truth."

Fletcher did not look at him directly, fearing exposure, though oddly, he was unaware of what it was he was afraid of exposing.

Constantine said something like, "even uncomfortable truths about ourselves, so that in the end we may seek forgiveness and healing." He turned his eyes away when he said this, and Fletcher had the impression he was being kind, avoiding a harsh and judgmental gaze.

"John," Constantine said, "I've been thinking about the story you told me."

"I expected you would," John replied. He closed his eyes, as though closing his eyes would make this all go away.

"I think that there's something important in the story," Constantine said, "perhaps a message from God. Did you know there's a passage of scripture that says, "Ever since the creation of the world his invisible nature, namely, his eternal power and deity, has been clearly perceived in the things that have been made."

He paused, then went on tentatively: "The question is, how do you find the truth of God that speaks to you in the flight of the bird, or the footsteps in the sand?" The monk picked up one of the manuscripts from the armoire and turned it over absentmindedly in his hand.

Like a hunter, bow drawn, anticipating the movements of his quarry in the field, Fletcher guessed where Constantine was headed, and he did not want to go there. "That's not the question," he snapped. "The question is this: What was God saying to me when he killed my wife? What was God trying to tell me through that? You're so wise, you tell me." He stood and made his way to the window, turning his back on the monk. "What's God saying through that troubled girl of mine?" Fletcher said. Even as he said this, he thought about the dragon.

Constantine dropped the manuscript with a solid, unexpected thud, so suddenly that Fletcher was startled by the noise. "Your daughter, John?" he said.

"Elspeth," John said. "She's turned wild. I should be able to control her, but I can't. She sneaks out at night, God only knows where. I think she's found a man somewhere; she gives me no end of grief over her engagement."

"The girl is affianced?" asked Constantine. He picked up the manuscript and began thumbing through it, distracted again by something Fletcher could not quite make out.

"Son of a silversmith in Aberystwyth. Name's Meurig something. He's well-spoken of, a good man, I think, and she refuses even to talk about it."

Constantine shook his head: "Why do you suppose she refuses?"

"She says that he's not a man of her own choosing, but Brother do you know the trouble I went through to find him? She thinks she's too good for him."

Constantine smiled and changed the subject. "Let's get back to Alysse, John. I want to talk about her death."

"She died, Constantine. What else is there to say? Alysse died and left me with a baby to raise."

"No, you don't understand me. I don't want to talk about her death, but about the way you experienced her death. The way it impacted you—what it cost you, the work you've had to do to let her go or to keep her alive in your heart and memory, the sense of abandonment you say you felt, you still feel. The spiritual truth is bound up in your experience of her death, rather than in her death itself."

"And how are we going find that out?" said Fletcher.

"Have you ever heard of *Lectio Divina*?" Constantine asked.

"What's that?"

"It's a certain way of reading the scriptures," said Constantine. "Some call it 'holy reading,' and others call it 'praying the scriptures.'"

"You know I can't read."

"Hear me out," said Constantine softly. "I think this may help. In *Lectio Divina* we read the scriptures slowly, sometimes out loud, sometimes not. Sometimes we read the same text over and over until it becomes strange to us, so that it is at last like hearing it for the first time. What makes it holy reading is that we listen actively for the voice of the Holy Spirit, that breathing Presence of God who speaks to us within and through what we read. We could try it if you like."

"I can't read," Fletcher protested a second time.

"No, but I can, and you can pray," said Constantine. He opened the Bible on the lectern. "This is one of the Psalms of David. I'll read. We'll listen together, and then we can talk about what we hear." He read aloud from the 77th psalm, translating from the Latin as he read:

"'In the day of my trouble I seek the Lord; in the night my hand is stretched out without wearying; my soul refuses to be comforted.

I think of God, and I moan; I meditate, and my spirit faints. [Selah]

Thou dost hold my eyelids from closing; I am so troubled that I cannot speak.

I consider the days of old, I remember the years long ago.

I commune with my heart in the night; I meditate and search my spirit:

"Will the Lord spurn for ever, and never again be favorable?

Has his steadfast love forever ceased? Are his promises at an end for all time?

Has God forgotten to be gracious? Has he in anger shut up his compassion?" [Selah]

And I say, "Does the right hand of the Most High hang limp by His side?"

Fletcher was surprised that such words were found in Holy Scripture, but following Constantine's quiet prompts, he found the passage opening up for him, and more importantly, opening up his own experience in a new way. The *Lectio Divina* ranged widely over the psalm. Did it mean that even King David had moments like he had had? He thought about the long nights he had spent alone in his agony, crying out for Alysse. Perhaps the psalm meant that even such crying out—even the psalmist's sorry question, "does the hand of the Most High hang limp by his side?"—was a kind of prayer, and therefore an act of faith. Perhaps having faith was more than believing that certain things were true about God. Perhaps it was struggling to find the places where those beliefs connect with the headaches and heartaches of life, even when the connections are unclear. That was what the psalmist had done. The reverberating echoes of the psalm had him clinging to God even when it felt like God had abandoned him. Where was God when Alysse died?

Constantine interrupted his thoughts: "Suppose we practice *Lectio Divina* on your experience, prayerfully listening to that experience as a kind of text through which God may be speaking to you."

"I'm a hunter, not a monk!" Fletcher said, but he meant it not unkindly.

"Exactly!" Constantine said. "You already have the skills we need." He said he thought that the listening of *Lectio Divina* was something hunters do naturally—listening intently to the sounds that came from the shadows and undergrowth of the forest, a breaking twig here, the panting of an animal there. "You should have no trouble with that," Constantine said. "That should be familiar territory."

Fletcher thought about the grouse that were invisible except in outline, and about dragons in mime, invisible to all but the most patient observer. With only a minor shift of metaphors he could imagine that Constantine was describing the same kind of careful listening, but listening directed to the shadows within one's own spirit, listening for the promptings of the Spirit of God. It was a thoroughly uncomfortable idea, partly because it seemed sacrilegious to think of his experience in the same way as holy writ, and partly because Father Thomas taught that only Holy Mother Church had the authority to decide such things. The way Thomas saw it, for a layman to think he could hold a valid theological opinion was simple heresy, not because the layman was un-lettered and might get the logic wrong, but because the idea that he had a right to an opinion was itself heresy. Nevertheless, he forged ahead. "Tell me how to do this."

"Why don't we listen to the story again?" Constantine said. "Can you begin at the beginning?"

They talked like that until the shadows began to creep across the copyists' desks like tall, thin church spires. Fletcher thought of the gar-goyles and grotesques that topped the church's corners, among them a pair of dragons looming over the whole, and he had the uncanny im-pression that they had taken flight, cool stone turned to fire-breathing flesh that threatened to devour him whole. He thought of the dragon he had seen when he had tracked the girl to the bivouac.

Constantine found Fletcher's story both fascinating and disturb-ing. Together they returned to the first time he had beaten the girl. As Fletcher talked, Constantine listened again, this time attending to the incongruities and disruptions in the story, listening to hear if the same patterns he had noted from the first hearing now repeated themselves. As he listened, he asked clarifying questions. He focused his attention finally on the moments just before Fletcher lost control and crossed that line into violence. How could he assist Fletcher in recognizing that pattern of violence on his own? And at the same time, how could he use what he was learning to protect and care for the girl?

"What you do is sometimes extreme, wouldn't you say?" he asked.

"Extreme?"

"The way you beat your daughter like that, for example. She didn't deserve those beatings, at least not like that. That's extreme, isn't it?"

"All good fathers discipline their daughters," Fletcher said flatly.

"Alright, John," said Constantine, reluctant to give up the point. "Let's think about the event at the bivouac. You told me yourself you nearly killed her, then you beat her. Would it not have been more appropriate to hug the girl? Right then, I mean? Why were you angry, rather than relieved?"

Fletcher gave a look of startled consternation, and Constantine had the impression that the idea that he ought rather to have hugged the girl had never entered Fletcher's mind. He could not be sure, though, because Fletcher said nothing. He simply sat there in the darkening shadows of the room.

Constantine focused again on the moments immediately prior to the beating. "What happened then, John?" he asked. "What happened between the moment you discharged the bolt and the moment you began to pummel Elspeth?"

"I rushed out of the bivouac," said John.

"No," said Constantine. "I mean, what did you think? What did you feel? What went through your mind?"

Fletcher did not tell him about the images, but he did tell him about the emotional trauma he felt when the images came. "I nearly drowned in the river once," he began. Constantine listened intently, but said nothing. Fletcher continued: "I was a boy. Probably eight or nine. Some of my friends and I were swimming near a dam in the river. You know the place, I think. It's that dam just above the fork."

Constantine nodded. "Go on."

"The gate-keeper didn't see us. We were right below the dam and out of his line of sight. Since he didn't see us, he opened the dam and the water came over in torrents. I got hit hard in the back and got the wind knocked out of me. I struggled to catch my breath, but I couldn't. I was gasping, and I couldn't breathe. I can still remember my sense of panic. The water continued to pound me from above. I swallowed some of it. A lot of it. I flailed my arms, but the flood kept coming."

"When you get angry it feels like that?" asked Constantine.

Fletcher looked away. "Like I'm drowning."

"How did you get out of the flow from the dam?"

"I went unconscious and got washed into safer water," Fletcher said. "Levente pulled me out. That's what they told me later. I don't remember."

"Thank God for that," said Constantine. "So who pulls you out now, when you're flooded with anger?"

Fletcher thought about that for a long time. "Sarabeth" he said at last. "It's Sarabeth."

"Willem's sister? That Sarabeth? Works in Willem's pub?"

Fletcher nodded. "What of it?"

"I don't think Sarabeth is as helpful as you think," said Constantine. "It's Sarabeth sells you ale."

They were in the niche again, after sidelong glances in church and a quick exchange of notes. Constantine was not clear about why she had wanted to see him. They sat silently for a long while. He reached over and took her hand, hoping just to hold it, but she was trembling. He touched her face gently, and felt her smile. Knowing that her father had beaten her, he had all he could do to keep from gathering her up in his arms and holding her, of being for her the loving and tender father he knew she did not have.

He leaned down to kiss her gently on her forehead, the kind of kiss he remembered his mother giving him when he had been frightened as a boy. He had a dim recollection of such a kiss in a root cellar nearly forty years before. What better way is there to comfort a frightened child? But Elspeth turned her face up at just that moment, so that quite unintentionally the kiss ended upon her mouth, gently as he had intended, but to an effect that completely astonished and frightened him.

"I'm sorry," he whispered then, so quietly she had to ask him to repeat himself. "I shouldn't have done that."

"Am I that ugly, here in the dark?"

"I meant that for your forehead, Elspeth," he said. "You're just a child."

"I'm sixteen," she replied.

"And I'm an old man," he said, "and a monk."

"Is an old man less a man than a young one? Is a monk?"

"I'm old enough to be your father. I meant to kiss you on the forehead." He pulled away from her and sat upright, opposite her with his back against the altar-side wall of the niche.

"Are you sorry to be capable of loving someone like me?" she asked.

Later, in his cell, Constantine's heart beat like thunder—hard, erratic, rolling through him like the precursor of a blinding rainstorm, a signal to run for cover. What had the girl been thinking? Is that what she thought of his care for her, that he would want that from her? But she had not rejected that. In fact, she seemed to him to have invited it, which left him both confused and pleased. Had she been drawn to him, the way he had been drawn to her?

For the first time he realized that he had never had such a connection with a girl.

No, that wasn't quite right. There had been the girl in his family's root cellar, but he could remember her only in fragments. She had had fair skin. Blue eyes. She was older than he was. Maybe she was the same age. The contact with that girl had been different, though; she had not wanted him, not that way. He had touched that other girl's skin, and had been aware that the touch had been a comfort to her, but that had not awakened something within him the way touching Elspeth had awakened something within him.

He had a flashing recollection of leaving the root cellar and finding his father's body outside. There was a body of one of the invading Mongols right near the entrance, and he realized looking back that his father had probably saved his life. He thought he remembered that his father had died in the effort. There was a memory of his house burning. His family was gone. He had another flashback—this time a searing memory—of his brother Cristian, an arrow through the neck from back to front. Cristian had been running for the house to warn or defend or rescue his mother. Such a death was heroic, sacrificial, a thing that the Christ might do, he thought, and in the same breath thought that he would honor the memory of his father and his brother by protecting as best he could this young woman who had so innocently entrusted herself to his care.

Elspeth did not struggle inside herself as Constantine did. She had not intended what had happened, but she did not regret it, either. In her own bed, beneath the safety of her coarse woolen blanket, she drifted into a deep sleep. A village girl takes love where she finds it—arranged marriages notwithstanding. It was sweet that he had been awkward. How different Brother Constantine's kiss had been, not furtive and thieving, the way the boys in the village sometimes had tried to kiss her, and not forced and hard, the way her father had kissed her. Brother Constantine had been tender. She thought about his age, but dismissed that as irrelevant; she was a woman, had been a grown woman for her father for as long as she could remember.

Nothing would come of the kiss anyway, not in the long run; it was just a kiss, but still, she hoped he wasn't sorry.

Elspeth woke up sweating, grinding her teeth, entangled in her bed-clothes. She was visiting home, a sometime visit that Levente was al-lowing now that her father was getting help, but she couldn't sleep. Something had changed in the hut. There was something alive, unreal. At least, that was how it felt. Whatever it was, its arrival had disturbed her sleep, but she was too groggy to tell just how. Perhaps something had changed in the room. Her heart was pounding and she was drenched in hot oily sweat.

She called out softly, "Father."

"Elspeth." Her father slipped out from behind the canopy, but he grabbed her by the arms, the way he sometimes did when he was drunk, and she tried to wrench free, but he was too strong.

"You're hurting me," she said.

"Shut up," her father said. He raised his backhand and threatened her with it.

"The dragon's back in the hut," she said.

"Stop it, Elspeth!" he said. He said this hard, as though he was trying to snap her back into reality or maybe wake her up, but she was already awake, not dreaming. For a moment she thought he was going to hit her, maybe backhand her, to wake her up. She kicked against him to try and get free, but his arms locked onto her like one of Levente's vises, clamping her body down hard.

Her father just stood there, holding her in the dark until she stopped struggling. Then he carried her to his own bed, laying her down where her mother had slept.

"I sleep in my own bed," she said. She turned away from him and tried to get out of bed, but he held her hard against him. When she stopped struggling, he reached out with his free hand to touch her hair. She had the thought that even stinking drunk, he was trying to be ten-der, but he had no tenderness in him, he had never had tenderness in him, and now as his body leaned in over her, she almost shoved him, but did not know whether to resist him or honor his drunken intention to comfort her.

He touched her nightclothes, reaching for the top button.

She almost screamed then, but no one would hear, and he was stronger than she was and she did not know what would happen if she resisted, but she shoved against him anyway, trying to upset his balance. "Father, no."

He grabbed the hair on the back of her head, pulling so hard he hurt her, and then kissed her fiercely on the mouth. "Alysse," he said.

"No," she choked out again, more forcefully this time, then kicked him hard in the groin with her knee, tore herself free, and broke for the door. Behind her she heard her father groan and try to stand. Then she heard a crash and breaking furniture, as though he had tripped and lost his balance. Then silence.

The brothers went to Compline that night through a pounding storm. Constantine was aware of tiny droplets that beaded up against the tight woolen weave of his habit. During the chants of Compline, he heard the back door of the nave open, and looked to see a small figure sitting in the last pew. Several of his brother monks also looked; it was unusual that a worshiper should come in the middle of a storm. Then they returned to their singing. After Compline, the hospitaller would see to her needs. Only Brother Constantine knew the worshipper's name.

After Compline, he filed out dutifully with his brother monks, and then made his way back to his cell. When he was certain the brothers were fully occupied with their private evening devotionals, he slipped from his cell and made his way along the corridor, then opened the door softly and returned to the church, entering from the west end of the nave through the door that opens in from the narthex. The girl was not there. Brother Joachim was in the front near the altar attending to the candles and the elements of worship required by the Benedictine horarium. Constantine slipped into a side pew in the north transept and waited, hoping the sacristan would not notice he was there.

Brother Joachim completed his ministrations and moved silently away without looking back. Constantine waited until he heard the solid click of the door-latch. He removed his sandals, rose, and moved to the south ambulatory, hoping his bare feet would make no sound on the rough granite as he passed along in the shadows. Once near the front, however, he stopped cold and considered his next steps carefully. The altar was full, every candle lit, and there was no way to remain hidden as he moved from the ambulatory where he stood to the confessionals and the opening of the niche. He would have to cross the transept, and ahead to the prayer bench, take one of the votive candles, and make his way back behind the altar. The flaring of the candles would throw his shadow up against the clerestory walls, but that could not be helped. He straightened to his full height and moved out into the lighted area of the apse, walking slowly but deliberately to the prayer bench, where he genuflected and knelt and paused in prayer. He waited there until his breathing slowed, then stood again, took one of the candles from its place, and moved ahead past the railing and around the corner of the altar. Once there, he tapped lightly on the door of the niche.

The door opened slightly, but no light came through the crack. She was inside, waiting in the pitch dark. "Brother," she said softly. "Constantine."

He slipped in, closed the door tightly, and looked around. She was seated abjectly on the floor of the niche, her back against the wall. She scooted over to make room for him. He handed her the candle, then sat down beside her. She set the light between them on the floor, and he turned a little so he could get a better look at her. She was wearing a thin dress, but no cloak or hood. Her hair was wet from the rain, and he was thankful that no one had noticed the trail of water drops on the granite of the sanctuary floor. She trembled a little.

"You're cold," he said.

"I didn't have time to get my coat," she said quietly, her teeth chattering as she spoke.

"What happened?" he asked.

She buried her face in his shoulder. She continued to cry, but she said nothing.

He had broken Benedictine custom by speaking to her during the Grand Silence, but had had what he took to be good reason—the silence could be broken in an emergency—and now with equally good reason he stripped his hood from his habit. It was woolen, a kind of cloak the monks wore over the top of their cassocks. "Here," he said, "take this." The cassock itself was floor-length, made of black wool, knotted at the waist with a rope. As he stripped the hood, it suddenly seemed an odd, symbolic thing to do, as though he were stripping off some inexplicable part of his identity as a monk, and even though he still wore the heavy woolen cassock he felt naked and vulnerable, and for a moment did not know who he was. His head was unprotected, and he felt his cheeks growing hot and red, flushed at the knowledge that he had exposed his tonsure, the shaved physical mark of the Benedictine.

She did not resist, but allowed him to place the hood over her shoulders. She smiled then, and murmured softly, "Thank you."

He said nothing, but adjusted the hood to cover her more completely. He almost reached out to stroke her wet hair, and his mind went back to the girl in the root cellar. He did not remember the girl's name. He did vaguely remember the first time he had seen her—he had interrupted her and his brother Cristian in the root cellar. He did not know why they were in there alone, or why Cristian had tried to hide the girl from view. He had seen her figure, or a portion of her figure, and he had been ashamed of that. Now he wanted very much to cover Elspeth, too, the way Cristian had covered the girl in the root cellar.

The candle flared, throwing their shadows up against the wall behind them. For a moment, he considered offering her his cassock, but almost at once dismissed that because it would violate all propriety. She shuddered again, almost violently this time, and he reached out tenderly and gathered her in his arms. It took a long a moment before he realized she was fighting back more tears.

He was now more alarmed than ever for the girl's safety. He had seen her bruises, watched her limping in the church. Each time she had been battered, the bruises had been more extensive and more serious. Something was escalating, and he was aware that her father could hurt her very badly before she could get help. At the same time, his own hands were tied. Outside of this tiny chamber he could say nothing to her except what might transpire casually between an older man and an apprentice in Levente's workshop.

"I've been thinking about getting a knife," she said. "To keep beside me in my bed." Her teeth continued to chatter.

He shifted his body so he faced her, looking hard at her because of what she had said. He wanted to shake her. She didn't want a fight with anybody, much less John the Fletcher. The man was a trained killer. And he was trying so hard to come to terms with what he had done to her. It was difficult to believe that this was the same John Fletcher he was talking to in the scriptorium. The man seemed to have an enormous sense of self-control. Then again, it was this same Fletcher who had hunted Elspeth into the church that night, who threatened to tear the church down if she did not show herself, who had nearly killed her in a rage in the forest.

He was aware of a rising anger in his own chest, anger he did not know he was capable of feeling. How could anyone hurt somebody like Elspeth? What had she done to deserve this? Then he thought, *Does she even know how to use a knife?* "You don't want to do that, Elspeth," he said. "You'll get yourself killed."

"So what am I supposed to do?" she said. "I can't go to the sheriff."

"Why not?"

"First, he wouldn't believe me, and second, if he did, my father would lose his job. How would that be?"

"You could come here," he said. "You're safe here." Then he added, so softly he was afraid she wouldn't hear, "with me."

She nodded, not lifting her head, but moving so tightly against his chest that he was afraid she might hear his heart pounding.

"It's alright, Elspeth," he said softly. "You're safe here."

She leaned in closer to him in a way that placed more of her weight against his shoulder. It seemed to him that she was burrowing her head in as close to his chest, as close to his heart, as she could. He laid his right arm across her shoulders to provide her with that little bit more warmth, and with his left he touched her hair in what he hoped she would understand as a gesture of comfort. "No one knows we're here," he said again. "You're safe."

He opened his mouth, but said nothing. Instead, he stroked her hair, and smelled her body, and was thankful that she was there. He adjusted his arm so that they settled into a more comfortable position. With his free hand he touched a tendril of her hair, drawing it out between his fingertips like thread being readied for a needle. She relaxed against him completely then, easing into him, as though his body was a protective blanket. He could sense the release of the muscle tension she had brought with her to the niche. He was nearly overwhelmed by the fragrance of her hair, and he stroked it again to reassure her, then reached down and touched her chin, turning her face upwards so he could look directly into her eyes.

And then he kissed her. The way he had seen Cristian kissing the girl in the root cellar. Not furtively. Not on the forehead. But lingeringly, intentionally, he kissed her.

Fletcher woke on the floor, with a splitting headache. When he tried to stand up, his groin hurt, and he sat back on the floor and leaned his back against the bed-frame. Several large pieces of furniture were set at odd angles, moved from their normal places, as though there had been a struggle. They had fought about something, the dragon maybe. He had tried to comfort the girl, tried to take care of her, but she had struck out at him.

But what disturbed him was that mixed in with the dim memories, was the realization that he had done something awful to his daughter. Something terrible and brutal had happened during the night, but it came to him only in bits of light and dark, like the fragments of a wrecked dream. He had been drinking and the girl had been there and he thought she was her mother and they had fought about an animal.

Later, after the effect of the beer had worn off and the ache in his groin was gone, he sat back and tried to sort out what had happened. He poured cold water in a bowl and splashed some on his face, looked around for a clean cloth, and then abandoned that and wiped his face with his tunic. But his memory stayed soft like candle-light, and he realized that he had done something that would have infuriated Alysse. But what did she know? She had left him alone to raise their daughter. What right would she have now to judge him after she had done that?

He heard noises in the yard, the sound of cranking at the well. He opened the door, to find Elspeth outside, drawing water. "Get in here."

She waited until she had completed her task with the water, lugging the heavy bucket so close against her legs that water splashed out against her dress. She did not look at him as she passed him at the door, and instead brushed hard against him, nearly shoving against him to get into the hut. She was so much like her mother. She had Alysse's form, her shape, her weight. Her voice was Alysse's voice.

"What happened here last night?" he said. He closed his eyes and remembered dimly having had a bad dream about Alysse, that in the dream he had tried to make love to her but she had fought him off, had resisted him. Why had she done that? She thought he was not good enough for her. She thought her own thoughts. A tough woman, Alysse, when she wanted to be. It did not surprise him that at night when he tried to sleep, he would sometimes be haunted by the ghost of his dead wife, an accusing ghost that pointed an accusing finger. Why didn't she leave him alone? She had no right to accuse him. She was dead, she had left him. What right did she have? What did she know about raising headstrong young girls, anyway?

"You kissed me, hard," she said simply.

"Fathers kiss their daughters sometimes."

"Not like that," she said. "Fathers don't kiss their daughters that way. You hurt me."

"Listen, Elspeth, you can't tell anybody that," Fletcher said. He gritted his teeth as he said that. *She's lying*, he thought, *but why? Why would she lie about a thing like that? She could get us both in trouble. With the church. With the sheriff maybe.*

"It's the truth," she said.

"You're making that up," Fletcher said. "I wouldn't do that. Not ever."

Fletcher did not visit Constantine for more than three days. Instead, Ranulf sent him as courier to Coventry. During his absence Elspeth fed the livestock and checked daily on the hut. There were no sightings of dragons in the shire, but the townspeople remained wary.

The ride to Coventry was long and tedious because the roads had been made nearly impassable by the winter weather, so Fletcher had his time of enforced silence in which he practiced this skill of holy listening, this *Lectio Divina*, to the beating of his own heart and the Word of God that might be spoken there. *How odd*, he thought. *I'm armed and ready to kill at a moment's notice, and here I am practicing skills more appropriate to monk and monastery.*

In the long silence of the ride he reviewed the story over and over, looking for connections between the violence and the ale. He finally concluded that the ale played a spotty role at best because the violence sometimes happened when he was completely sober. He thought about the wolf pup and the deeply disturbing images he had seen—the blood, the candles in the church, Alysse dressed as the Blessed Virgin. There had been no ale then. But the images were among the details he had deliberately kept back from Constantine. Why had he done that? Perhaps because he himself did not understand their meaning, and so they were frightening to him. What would they tell Constantine that he did not want him to know? That he himself did not want to know? What would Constantine say about the sacrilege he had committed? Would he say that he took a perverse pleasure in the violence? That he, John the Fletcher, archer and hunter, sometimes lost control of his inner life in a way that disgusted and shamed him?

Perhaps when he heard about the images, Constantine would think of that passage of scripture Father Thomas had preached about during Lent in more than one of his finger-pointing sermons, "From within, out of the heart of man, come evil thoughts, fornication, theft, murder, adultery, envy, slander, pride, foolishness. All these things come from within, and they are what defile a man." Just imagining what Constantine would think of him if he heard about the images left Fletcher feeling horribly, horribly alone.

And yet, he thought, he was alone already, bearing the burden of the images within himself like a wound that would not heal. It was always possible things could go the other way. Perhaps if he shared this piece of his inner life, perhaps if he took the risk of exposure, perhaps if he dared. . . . This is where his puzzling stopped. He did not dare to hope, but he determined that the next time he spoke with Constantine he would open up this part of his inner struggle. He would tell everything, without embellishment and without leaving anything out.

When he returned to Warwick, Fletcher did not even stop at the foregate to return his weapons and supplies to the armory. Instead, he rode directly to the monastery and requested an audience with Brother Constantine. He left his crossbow with the gatekeeper.

Constantine met him in the refectory. "We could talk in the church," Constantine said. "No one will be there except for Brother Cyril the older sacristan, and he's deaf and wouldn't hear what might be said anyway."

Fletcher shook his head. "Not the church." The thought of the Blessed Virgin hearing what he said was more than he could imagine.

"The garden then," Brother Constantine said, but Fletcher was aware that he had not missed his reluctance to talk in the church.

A long glance told Fletcher that Constantine was also aware that he had arrived in a hurry. He had arrived at the monastery dressed for travel, with heavy riding boots and a thick winter riding cloak covering his other clothing. The ragged and dirty condition of his clothes and person would tell Constantine that he had come directly from the trip, without going home even to clean himself.

Constantine went directly to the point: "What is it, John?" he said, showing by the tone in his voice that he understood already that the matter could not wait a more leisurely time. "What's this about? Have you learned something?"

"Not learned, Constantine," said Fletcher. "This is something I've known all along, but I kept it from you."

"Go on," said the monk. As he said this he motioned to a bench near the southern entrance to the garden. The two men sat down together, Constantine gathering his robes about him against the cold.

"I had to ride courier to Coventry," said Fletcher. "Long time in the saddle. The whole time, coming and going I thought about what I told you."

"And?" asked Constantine.

"I started thinking about your comment that the ale was a factor in the violence."

Constantine seemed startled and a little pleased, but Fletcher could not tell why.

"Go on," he said.

"Well, there are moments when the violence occurs when there isn't any ale, so I thought I'd tell you that the ale isn't it, see?"

Constantine looked at him, and started to speak but then apparently thought better of it and kept his silence.

"There was this wolf hunt last spring," Fletcher said. "Remember that? There was a wolf out there, killing farm animals."

"We don't get that kind of news in here, John. Is it important?"

"Only that I got sent out to hunt it. I wounded it and it took to the river. I came back the next day with Aelric to finish the hunt with one of Aelric's dogs." He traced the story back to the den and the single wolf pup. He pointed out that he had been sober. Then he told about what had happened, how he had become flooded with images, terrible, disturbing images of violence. He listed the ones he could remember. The blood flying, Alysse, with her hair shimmering in the light, her funeral,

Elspeth as a baby covered with wolf's blood, then later, at various stages of her life. There was one image he found particularly difficult to describe and he paused a long time before he was finally able to put it into words: "You remember when Levente stopped me from beating Elspeth that day in the forest?"

"What about it?"

"Just before I hit her I had a picture in my head, something about Alysse grabbing her things to leave."

"And when you found your daughter running, that came back to you and you thought you were being abandoned all over again?

"I didn't think about that, but it seems right."

"I can see why you found the images disturbing."

"They seemed to come from somewhere deep down inside me, someplace that scares me spit-less."

"And you're telling me that the images come whenever you're violent?"

"It's not the ale makes me do that, but these pictures in my head."

"You say you didn't actually hurt the pup."

He shook his head. "Aelric stopped me. I don't think I would've harmed it anyway, but while the images were there I thought that that was what I was doing."

"John, I think that proves my point about the ale."

"How so?"

"Who knows why we do what we do, but isn't it interesting that you get violent when you've been drinking and when you're emotionally drowned out, like what happened at the dam. Am I right?"

"I can see that."

"When you hadn't been drinking, as was true in the case of the pup, then the images came, but you were able to resist the urge toward violence, so you didn't actually hurt it. Am I right?"

"Right," said Fletcher. There was tone of deep relief on his face because this piece of his inner life was somehow coming into focus. He remembered what Levente had told him about having a blotch on the skin of his back, but being unable to see it without help. "What do we do with that?" he asked.

Constantine pondered this for a moment. "First," he said, "you need to stop drinking. I think that will be hard, and you will be unable to do it alone. I think you should tell Sarabeth that you've stopped and ask her not to sell you any more. Maybe you should stop going to Willem's altogether."

Fletcher had not wanted the conversation to turn in this way. Of course it wasn't the ale. It was the images. He did not have a problem with ale. Why did Constantine?

"I've got no problem with ale," he said, as forcefully as he could without raising his voice. "The ale's *your* problem, but it's not mine."

"Let's move on to the images for a moment," Brother Constantine said. "Maybe we talk about the ale later. You say that the images occurred at other times?"

"Whenever there was violence."

"Today for the first time you used the word *violence* to describe what happens between you and your daughter. But listen to the way you talk about the violence: You say, 'The violence happens when such-and-such happens.' Wouldn't it be more honest to say, '*I get violent* when such-and-such happens?"

Fletcher stood and turned his back on his companion. "First you say I can't handle my ale, and then you demand that I become my own accuser." He was very angry. "I'm no monk. I'm an archer in the service of the sheriff, and I've got the same passions and needs as other men. I've got problems with Aelric sometimes. I've got a problem with you sometimes, like right now. There're times I could wring Levente's neck like a chicken, but I've got no problem with ale."

He turned, left the garden, and stormed out of the monastery. The movement from the darkened shadows of the monastery corridors into the bright sunlight reflected on snow nearly dazzled him, and he was momentarily unable to focus his vision. When his eyes finally cleared, he was looking at a small statue of the Blessed Virgin that stood in a niche on the monastery wall. "No problem with ale!" he shouted at the statue, then, forgetting where he was, he shook his fist and said, "Leave me alone, Alysse."

The following Wednesday, after mid-afternoon prayers at None, Constantine remained in the church and waited, preparing for this conversation by reviewing where they had come, and then by trying to quiet his soul in prayer. It was harder now because in trying to care for both the daughter and the father, he was leading a double life. Respecting the privacy of both, he also felt dishonest to both. Beyond that, his gut told him he was out of line with the girl, but there was something going on that he did not understand, that he did not want, but that he did not seem to be able to resist, either—each time he touched Elspeth, each time he kissed her, he experienced relief. It cannot be said that he thought these things clearly. Rather, they were a mix of sweet and sour within him, a turmoil of emotions he had to struggle to understand, much less regulate.

He was in the middle of these confusions when Fletcher appeared at the back of the church, moving in slowly. Constantine was aware of his presence, but said nothing to him until he was quite close.

Clearly Fletcher had been uncomfortable talking in the church, and now Constantine was as well, though for different reasons. He could not look up without seeing the altar, and then thinking about the niche, and then about meeting Elspeth in the niche. Fletcher's hesitation was harder to understand. Here was a man who attended mass faithfully every week in this very church, indeed, who had taken comfort there following the death of his beloved Alysse, who often stopped to pay his quiet respects to the Blessed Virgin herself, and yet in the matter of his spiritual journey he found the church itself a place of agony.

"Hello, Fletcher," he said. "Thank you for meeting me here."

Fletcher said nothing in reply, but simply slid into the seat beside him. He looked at his hands.

Constantine opened with prayer, secretly praying for his own soul.

"John," he said at last, his prayer completed, "I want to ask you about something you said during our last conversation. Would that be alright?"

"Yes," said John, so quietly that Constantine gave him an enquiring look. "Yes," he said more loudly. He diverted his eyes, and kept his head bowed the way a shy schoolboy might in the presence of a harsh teacher who was bent on reprimand. "Ask whatever you want."

"In our last conversation you said that you'd had a vision of Alysse packing her bags and leaving. Do you remember that?"

"I said that," said Fletcher. "Is it important?" Despite the question, it was clear that he himself considered it important because he was trembling.

The trembling did not go unnoticed by his companion. "Can you tell me where that image came from, John? Was that your way of inter-preting Alysse's death? That she had abandoned you?"

The silence in the room deepened until Constantine could nearly hear Fletcher's heart beating. And beating it was, wildly, feverishly, the way it might beat if he were trapped by a mountain lion while hunting. The pupils of his eyes dilated until they were huge, an involuntary indication of the seriousness of his sense of panic.

Constantine repeated the question, more gently this time. What is the meaning of Alysse packing her bags and leaving? Where did that come from? Was that how Fletcher had understood Alysse's death? But Fletcher could not respond to this question. He allowed the panic to pass, but still could not speak. In the wake of the panic came a deep numbness. He almost bolted the building, but was overcome by the numbness again and was unable to move. He was simply sitting there now, hoping the question would go away, but it seemed to grow louder in the deepening silence.

Finally, he began to cry. Constantine reached out and placed a reassuring hand on his shoulder. The crying deepened into weeping. Constantine was aware that he had struck a deep cord in Fletcher's inner life, but could not identify what it was. He waited for a long time, then probed once again, adding prompts to help John's memory.

"What had happened in your marriage? Think back to the leaving. Was Alysse pregnant at the time?"

"No, that was earlier. She got pregnant after that."

"How do you know that? What clue in your mind tells you that the one event came before the other?"

"I got her pregnant to keep her from leaving, so the image of her packing her bags must've come earlier."

"So you had had a fight?"

"Yes," said John. "A fight. I can't remember how it started, but I do remember how it ended."

"Can you go on?"

"I hit her," he said simply. "No, that's not right. It's true, but it's not the whole truth. I hit her again after that. I beat her. I doubled my fist and beat her, the way I might've beaten a man down in Willem's pub. I hit her. I beat Alysse." His weeping had abated, but now it surged again.

"So the image in your mind of Alysse packing her bags and leaving is an actual memory of the day of the fight?"

"No. That came two days later."

"You mean she left two days later?"

"Yes." His voice was so quiet Constantine had to strain to make out what he said.

"Why did she delay?"

"I'm not sure," said Fletcher. "She never said why. She never talked to me again about that, but I think it must've taken her that long to build up the courage to leave. I think she was pretty frightened by then."

"What did you do during the two days?"

"I was so sorry. Sorrier for that than for anything I'd ever done."

"Remorse," Constantine said.

"I told her I was sorry. I begged her to stay, I said it wouldn't never happen again, I swore it on my mother's grave." As he said this he looked away, glancing furtively at the Blessed Virgin, then at the floor.

"But it did happen again, didn't it?"

"She didn't respond to me, didn't say she'd forgiven me. I tried to get her to look at me, but she turned her face away. I felt like she was turning to stone in front of me. I wanted her back. I needed her back. I loved her, but in a way she was already gone."

"Emotionally?"

"Emotionally. I couldn't live without her. I couldn't see a future without her. So I hit her again."

"Why did you do that?"

"Don't know. It was a panic reaction I suppose. I got beat up real bad by my father, and I remember panicking and then feeling incredibly strong and clear in the moments after the panic. It was like that."

"You mean that hitting Alysse calmed you somehow?" As he asked this, Constantine had a strong mental image of the girl in the root cellar. He had felt powerful there with her in the root cellar. Touching her skin. Cristian had told him to watch over her, to be a man. Thinking back now he realized that he had been the one who had been terrified, and that touching the girl's face had calmed the terror in him.

"I wouldn't say it calmed me," Fletcher was saying, "but it made me feel powerful, just for a moment, like I could handle anything, even this. It didn't last, it never lasts, but it made me feel strong. Real strong. That was when I hit her again. I remember thinking that even her anger would be easier to bear than her turning her face turned away from me like that."

Constantine understood this odd feeling—that a man might feel good after doing something wrong. He had felt wrong about picturing

Elspeth in his mind's eye, about wanting to touch her, to smell her hair, to run his fingers over her smooth skin. He had been ashamed of that, but then, the times he had done this had made him feel relief, too. He had experienced relief after he had touched her. But this conversation was not about him. It was about Fletcher. He forced himself to concentrate. "After you beat her . . . that was when she packed her bags and left."

"Yes."

"What did you do next?"

"I got her with child to keep her from leaving."

"You what?" Constantine could not believe what he was hearing.

"I said I got her with child to keep her from leaving."

These words exploded for Constantine, he felt like he had been hit in the stomach by a catapult stone. Did Fletcher understand their meaning? After a fight like that, with Alysse fully intending to leave, he had gotten her with child. She would never have gone along with that. He must have forced her, must have raped her, if indeed a husband can rape a wife. There was a theological debate about whether such an act is rape, but if ever there were an occasion that deserved that name, this was it. How could he move Fletcher to realize that that was so?

"How did you get her to cooperate and try for a child when she was determined to leave you?"

"She fought back. I forced her."

Constantine continued to probe, leading now in a direction and to a destination he knew would cause Fletcher great anguish but also bring him to the possibility of healing, if only he could understand it.

"What do you mean that she fought back? How did she resist?"

"She scratched and clawed and struggled against me. Scratched me down my shoulders and back. She drew blood. I took her anyway."

"Do you realize, John, what you have just told me?"

Fletcher looked at him, but said nothing.

"You raped your wife."

"Not rape. Oh, no, Constantine. Not rape. She was my wife. I didn't take anything from her that wasn't mine to take."

Constantine repeated his charge, but quietly, as calmly and deliberately as he knew how. He hoped that John would hear this, not as a moral judgment, but as a statement about facts that may well lie at the core of his spiritual and emotional dilemma.

Fletcher sat silently, unable to speak, hoping for the bells of Vespers that would end this interview, hoping that someone might enter the room, hoping for an interruption, any interruption, but in any case unable to move, unable to bolt, unable to do anything. He knew it was a matter of language whether or not what he had done to his wife could be called rape, but in his deepest core he also knew that he had wronged her terribly. He had not taken what was his to take, but what was hers to give. Was it rape, then? Or was it theft?

As he turned this question over in his mind, he realized that it was something different altogether, that he had known all along that it was different, that he was guilty of a mortal sin against her. He felt a chill, cold to the bone, and was suddenly shaking all over, shaking and doing everything he could to suppress the wracking sobs that were coming from him, "Oh my God, oh my God." He began to cry again, and soon was sobbing uncontrollably, his head in his hands, saying those same words over and over again. *Oh my God. Oh my God. Oh my God.*

He thought he heard Constantine calling his name: "John. Come back to me. What happened?"

In the background, a hundred miles or a hundred years distant, Fletcher could hear the bells of Vespers, tolling the beginning of evening prayers and end of their conversation. Constantine must have heard them too, but he just sat there, waiting.

"What happened, John?" Constantine was insisting.

"I didn't rape her, Constantine," Fletcher said. "I killed her. I murdered Alysse."

"You what?"

"I killed her," Fletcher said again. He stood. Began pacing. "If I hadn't forced her, she'd be alive today. She died in childbirth. It was my doing. I brought this on her." His words were coming slowly now as he turned this monstrous event over and over in his mind.

"But women die in childbirth," Constantine said. "There was no way you could have known."

"I forced her, she didn't want to be a mother, not then, anyway."

"Unwilling, but she would be proud of her daughter."

"That's not the point and you know it. The fact that Elspeth came of it doesn't mean anything here. Alysse died because of something I did to her, something I did against her will."

Then the stupor returned. Fletcher did not move for a long time. Neither did Constantine. The two men sat in the silence, the shadow of evening descending on the room where they sat. They could hear the muffled sing-song voice of the reader in the refectory, working his way through one of the psalms as the other brothers ate their simple meal.

Fletcher did not know how much time lapsed before Constantine rose, and went to the door. He could hear him talking with one of the other monks, who had been moving along the corridor on the way to Vespers.

"Brother Anselm," Constantine said when he returned.

"What did you say to him?" Fletcher asked.

"I asked him to wait until after Vespers, and then bring Brother Gregory. Gregory runs the infirmary. I don't want for you to go home tonight, John. We'll find a place for you here. I promise you on Christ's breath that they'll ask no questions, and if they ask, they'll receive no answers. This matter remains between us, at least for now."

"For now?"

"I believe you need to spend some time with Father Thomas," said Constantine.

"Father Thomas won't understand," Fletcher said.

"Of course he'll understand. He's a priest, for Christ's sake. I believe that you have need of something Thomas can provide and I cannot."

John found this puzzling.

"Absolution," Constantine said finally.

John said nothing after that. His eyes focused on the niche in the transept that held the statue of the Blessed Virgin, mother of God, drawing solace from her face, a face that had such a look of beatific serenity that Fletcher knew that even this would not be beyond the reach of grace.

"Shhh, John. Let's be silent together for a while."

"There's something else," John said, interrupting Constantine's imposed silence. "I think I almost molested Elspeth. During the night. Week ago maybe. Maybe I . . . overstepped some boundary, but I'm not sure."

Constantine sat bolt upright. "You did what?"

"I'm not sure what I did. I'd been drinking. I woke up the next morning sore, like I'd been kicked in the groin. Made my ride to Coventry pure hell. I had a dream, it seemed like a dream, in which Alysse was back, the girl looked like Alysse. I must've been really drunk, because I thought she was Alysse."

"But what did you do, John?"

"I'm not sure what I did," Fletcher said again. "I was drinking."

Despite the cold, Constantine was sweating beneath his woolen cassock. He found this last revelation more troubling than the first. That must have been why Elspeth had left the house in the rain, and why she had sought refuge in the niche, crying. She had refused to tell him what had happened, but that was understandable, too, from either direction—she could be afraid of her father, or she could be protecting him from harm. As long as he had known him, John Fletcher had seemed so stable, so normal, and yet he had within him the makings of a monster. How could that be?

He felt stupid—blind. How could it not be visible? Why had he not seen that before? He had known that Fletcher had beaten Elspeth—why had he been surprised to learn that he had beaten his wife also? And if Fletcher could rape his wife, why had he not seen the possibility that he could also rape his daughter?

It would be wrong to see this as a coherent series of thoughts because they were overlaid with anger and a stabbing, sudden fear. What these revelations meant was that Elspeth was in grave danger, and he could not see any way to protect her—he couldn't even warn her, but then again, she needed no warning. She knew all about the danger. The only thing he could think to do was to watch over her at a distance. He wanted to go to her, warn her, make certain she was never alone with her father again, at least not as long as he was capable of violence of this sort.

Fletcher was talking again: ". . . will I ever get her to trust me again?" he said.

"I thought Elspeth was staying with Levente and Alcera," he said, masking his anger and confusion.

"She was home on a visit. Levente allowed it because I'm talking with you. I hate that."

"Talking with me?"

"That Levente thinks it's his to allow."

Constantine took Levente's side in this one: "Doesn't seem like you've been very trustworthy, does it, John? Maybe Levente's right."

The two men sat together, waiting for Brother Gregory, each one pondering what this event meant, what next steps should be taken, and how it would be resolved. So far as Brother Constantine was concerned, it was a moment of the most profound consternation. What John had said told him only one thing—that Elspeth continued to be in danger. And yet he had given his word that he would keep whatever John said in strictest confidence. What action could he take now? How could he keep the girl safe without violating his word?

He resolved this by forming a plan to watch over her in secret. That might even mean slipping from the monastery without Prior Robert's permission, or trailing her without her knowledge, but in the absence of a clear alternative, these were risks he would have to take.

Finally, after a long while, Brother Gregory arrived to take Fletcher into his care. Constantine went along and suggested a small meal for them both. After the enormous emotional and spiritual effort expended in the last few hours, both men needed rest and nourishment.

Constantine folded the last of his manuscripts into quires and set them neatly into the armoire at the front of the scriptorium, took his scrip from its peg near the door, then made his way out to the monastery's small foregate. He paused only momentarily, a physical acknowledgment of a truth he did not want to acknowledge with his mind—that as his fascination with the girl had increased, his sense of the horarium had waned. What made that conscious—and what was his real source of shame—was that he planned in advance what he would say in the event Prior Robert called upon him to account for his absence from the Holy Office, and what he planned to say included nothing about protecting the girl.

But it was important now that he be there for her. More important than anything in his life. He realized that now because he was willing to risk his life—his life as a monk at least—if he needed to if that was what it took to protect the girl. His plan was half-formed. He would position himself within hearing of her father's house, he would watch for her to make certain she was there, and then stand guard over her. Perhaps nothing would happen. Perhaps not tonight, anyway. He would keep this up as long as was necessary, or until he collapsed, or until he was caught—whichever came first.

A light rain had left the dirt-track road slippery, and he found it easier to move along the grass edges, beneath the canopy of leaves. The road to Wharram included a sharp decline to the left, and a long section through heavy forest. Somewhere near half-way he heard voices and slipped deeper within the forest canopy. It would not do to be noticed. He held his breath as a wagon approached and passed, apparently a merchant returning from Coventry with wares for his shop. Guards on horses were posted before and after. He squatted and watched from a low, protected vantage-point beneath the brush.

He had a dim recollection of traveling this way in Moldavia when he was a boy, after his parents had been killed, hugging the edge of the road, hiding in the forest when he heard other travelers on the road. He was carrying a heavy sack filled with something lumpy and difficult. Perhaps he and the girl from the root cellar had found empty wheat sacks and filled them with vegetables to eat as they made their way out of the hills.

They had been trying to get to some large city the girl knew about, hoping to place themselves into the care of Elizabeth of Hungary. But there was a problem with this memory, he realized only in retrospect: He had lost the girl. They had started out together, and he had arrived alone. What had happened to the girl?

The memories came in fragments, each one a stabbing, lacerating picture in his head, like the memory of hiding in the root cellar and then emerging to find his parents and his brother.

He and the girl had stepped into the brush somewhere along the side of the road. He had a sliver of a memory of voices on the road, and he reasoned now that that must have been why they had hidden. Because of the voices. Staccato voices. Strident, high pitched. Punctuated with harsh laughter. They were voices of youths like themselves. At least three. Maybe more. But he and the girl were afraid because these were the voices of strangers.

"Shhh," the girl said, unexpectedly clamping her hand over his mouth and holding him so tightly he could not breathe, and he had struggled with her there in the brush until he had heard her curse under her breath. "You'll get us killed." He submitted then, and they crouched quietly, trying to make out what language the voices were speaking, and when they realized it was not Hungarian, they had quietly moved back, crouching lower in the deep undergrowth.

From his vantage-point beneath the brush he could make out four pairs of legs. No, five. Two were wearing skirts, but with men's boots. They tramped along together in a little rag-tag cluster, a gang of teenagers probably. Thinking about it later, he realized that they had moved with the teenager's peculiar coupling of urgency and aimlessness. From time to time, one or another of the pairs of feet reversed itself as its wearer walked backward to look at the others as they talked. They were strangers here, adventurers; his mother would say they were up to no good.

What was his mother's name? Tasha, maybe. No. Tatjana.

The girl from the root cellar loosed her grip a little, but kept her hand over his mouth until the gang of aimless teenagers disappeared around a bend. Only then did she release her grip completely, and they both relaxed into the green grass, exhausted by the tension of staying alive.

He tried again to imagine the girl he had been with. The girl from the root cellar. She was older than he was. Larger. It bothered him that he could not remember her face very well. He could not remember her name at all.

Constantine could not tell how long they lay there, protected by the undergrowth, but he remembered waking up alone. There seemed to be a gap in his memory, maybe sleep, and he wasn't even certain that he was remembering the same event, but the girl was gone. He remembered feeling cold against his back where she had been sleeping, her arms around him, holding him close for warmth like a pair of spoons. He woke up and rolled over, reaching for the girl with his hand.

"Ildiko, where are you?" He whispered this, but she did not answer him. He had been abandoned.

Ildiko. The girl's name had been *Ildiko.*

He heard voices again, speaking English, and was drawn back to the present, to the dirt-track road on the way to Wharram. Not knowing what else to do, he had come out to watch over Elspeth, and was trailing her, watching her movements from behind the brush on one side of the dirt-track path to Wharram. He would stay discreet, a silent, guarding presence, there in case she needed help, but otherwise out of sight. He would not abandon her as he had been abandoned, by his parents, by his brother, by Ildiko.

It was a painful memory, and Constantine tried to shut it off, but he could not. It came to him as an ache and a fear. Ildiko had left him, had abandoned him in the night.

No, that wasn't right. Something else had happened. He worked the details back and forth in his mind, trying to weave them into a meaningful pattern. They had fallen asleep beneath some underbrush. They must have crawled in there for safety. They had fallen asleep. They had been awakened by voices in the roadway, speaking something other than Hungarian.

No. *He* had been awakened. Ildiko was gone.

Dimly he realized that one of the voices belonged to Ildiko.

"They're mine," she was saying. What were hers? He had taken a quick inventory, but stopped when he remembered the sacks of vegetables. In their hurry to hide they must have left the sacks nearer the edge of the road, where they must have caught someone's attention. He peered out, trying to reconstruct what had happened. A group of men were questioning Ildiko, but in a language she would not understand.

Ildiko insisted: "I dropped them here when I hid in the forest last night."

The men were fierce-looking, filthy, bearded, dressed in leather, with strange sheep's wool caps. He did not see any women, at least at first. Most of the men carried bows and arrows, and long, curved knives. Most were on horseback, but to his surprise they also had a large caravan of supply wagons. Some of the wagons had cages on back, and in the cages were what he thought were giant lizards with wings. Apparently he had seen them before because he had known they were war lizards.

Now he was watching over Elspeth, following her movements from beyond the brush where he could not be seen. He hoped—he prayed—that Prior Robert would not ask about his movements. If he were asked, he would reply that he had been to Levente's shop, which would be true, in a way.

Elspeth never actually saw the dragon, but she felt its presence in the dripping of the trees and the shimmering of the light on the drenched stalks of corn that lined the cart path through the hamlet and village of Wharram.

Noted or not, the dragon was there, stalking her, mimicking her movements, slipping silently into a mime whenever she looked in its direction. Once it mimed a stand of corn so perfectly that Elspeth nearly turned down the wrong path to Levente's shop. The shimmering she saw on the stalks was the dragon shifting shape, subtly moving as all living things must move or die.

But the sense of the dragon was with her all the way, so that by the time she reached the shop she was overcome with dread.

Constantine did not join his fellow monks for breakfast. Like Fletcher, he was exhausted by the events of the day before, and by the extra task of guarding Elspeth from her father. He could not clear his mind of her. Like him she had seen a dragon. The dragon was no fantasy. What her father had said only confirmed it. She had seen something in her hut, an animal of some kind, and it had somehow found its way into her hut. The fact that it had appeared night after night told him something important: It had somehow fixated on her, or maybe her father. His knowledge that she was in danger nearly tore his heart out of him, but what made it worse was that he had no way to help her without destroying himself in the process.

He thought about holding her, about the smell of her hair, the softness of her skin. He relived the kiss, the kisses, the tender caresses.

It was only later, looking back, that he realized that somehow mixed into his horror and shame at what had happened, kissing the girl had brought him that same, odd sense of relief. What puzzled him was that it was a variously-sided kind of relief. It was a taste in his mouth, like something his mother might have made when he was a boy, a heavy eastern European gruel, at first too hot to eat, with subtle mixed flavors that came out in its aroma, then cooling so that he could taste it on his tongue.

The weather had been hot, so it must have been summer. He remembered that his mother had sent him to draw water from the well.

Cristian came bolting through the vegetable garden, trampling the furrows he had laid out so carefully and planted with his father, destroying his own work. It must have been Cristian, but maybe it was his father. He came from the direction of the village, which was maybe a quarter-mile away, down a little further near the base of the canyon where it opened out into a broader valley. He shouted something to Constantine's mother in the kitchen: "Mongols." Constantine remembered having been snatched up by his brother and carried in a panic to the root cellar.

He remembered that his rib-cage hurt from the way his brother held him, hard under his right arm, legs and arms flailing. He struggled to break free, but his brother was too strong. His grip was like the yoke on his father's oxen. Cristian nearly threw him into the root cellar, but then stopped and squatted on one knee so he could hold him firmly by both shoulders. "Now listen to me, Constantine." His shoulders hurt from Cristian's tight grip. "Get back behind the vegetables. Don't move, no matter what."

There was a shifting behind them, and both of them turned to see the dim outline of a girl, deep within the cavern of the cellar. She had stood and was pressing her back deep into the back wall, and she was sobbing nearly hysterically.

"Ildiko," Cristian said, addressing the girl. "You have to be quiet, Ildiko," Cristian said to the girl. "They'll hear you." He turned back to Constantine: "Take care of her. You have to be a man now, Constantine, and that means taking care of Ildiko. Understand?"

Constantine straightened and nodded. He turned and moved back into the recesses of the cellar and reached up to put his arm around the girl. She must have been fifteen or sixteen, and was taller than he was by a foot or more, but she buried her head in his shoulder.

"Whatever you do, stay put," Cristian said. "Don't come out until I come to get you. Understand?"

Constantine, working hard now to gain control of his emotions, said that he would try, and released the girl and they sat together on the floor behind the boxes of vegetables and bags of seed corn.

Cristian said something like, "I'm going back for mother," then slammed the door of the root cellar down hard.

Now, looking back, he realized that he had not taken care of Ildiko. She had taken care of him. He caught a fleeting memory of her being led behind the supply wagon. A glance back. The whispered instruction, "Get down." She had protected him. He remembered shivering in the brush until the caravan had passed, all the while terrified and relieved that he had not been found.

When he kissed Elspeth now in the niche beneath the high altar, the relief was there again, tinged with the same terror he had felt when the strangers had taken Ildiko. He had the thought that the kiss had aroused something within him he did not know was there, and in doing so, it reassured him he was safe from the wrath of God. How could that be? How could a vowed celibate to kiss a girl and feel safe from the wrath of God? But the thought was so clear and penetrating that it felt like a lance in his head. *I do not deserve to die.* It occurred to him then: *What an odd thought. I did not deserve to die.* Who had said he had to die? But Cristian had died, and he had lived. Maybe that was the root of such an odd thought. It was powerful and clear now. He had had that same thought after he kissed Elspeth. He did not deserve to die. How could such a strange and marvelous reassurance be wrong?

He leaned back against the wall of the niche and thought about the root cellar, and then about something that must have come later. The noise outside the cellar had died down. The girl, exhausted by the fright, had fallen asleep, her head on his lap. He had disentangled himself and stumbled outside into the dark.

An orange-red glow came from the village, and he moved off in that direction, stumbling, not knowing or caring what troubles he might find there. Rounding a bend in the path he realized that the glow was coming from the flames of burning buildings. Undulating black smoke billowed upward into the sky, catching the wind—later, looking back, he realized it must have created the wind—smothering the stars behind their rolling waves. He stopped, not daring to get any closer, aware that Ildiko might come looking for him and get herself in more trouble than she could handle alone.

He remembered seeing a massive bird fly into and out of the smoke, making its passes long and sweeping. No, that wasn't right. Several birds. First one, then another. Then four or five together. There might have been ten or more. One of the passes came near directly overhead, and he realized that they were not birds, but lizards, or something like lizards, but they had wings, and were massive—one was bigger than his house. They seemed to call out to each other from within the billowing smoke, deep throated bellows that sounded like a mix between thunder and the screeching of hawks. They continued their attack on the village deep into the night, circling around and back, flying into and out of the smoke, sometimes carrying people or animals in their talons, each time hauling their prey high up near the top of the billowing smoke, where they dropped it back to be impaled on some tree or through the broken roof of a burning building.

When he could take this no longer, he turned and ran, stumbling in the dark, and made his way back to the safety of the root cellar. When he woke the next morning he was curled into a tight ball, shivering, trembling with the cold. Ildiko was there, silent, holding him, stroking his back, staring at the door.

They did not come out of the cellar for three days. When their thirst finally became too great he took a pail and went out to the well, where he found the body of his mother.

XI

The life of the monk is a highly disciplined one, divided into sections of work and prayer, each moment of time subject to the needs of the community and the demands of one's vocation. Even so, within the structure of the horarium, the monks had a few moments of their own between Vespers and Compline, after the day's work was finished and a person's efforts—intentional or unintentional, for good or ill—are drawn to a close and the finished work of the day is offered to God as a kind of daily sacrifice.

Brother Constantine took these moments seriously, hoping through prayer and contemplation to become ever more mindful in his attention to the details of work and worship that made up his existence as a monk. The evening following his conversation with Fletcher, as had often happened, his need for quiet and perspective led him to the monastery church, where he sat in a back aisle of the north transept and offered up the day in private prayer. He considered the problems he and his fellow copyists faced in the scriptorium, a lack of good quality vellum that resulted from the bad weather and impassable roads, the thickening of the ink in its wells during the colder hours at night when the scriptorium was unheated. He prayed for his fellow monks, three of them by name because they had fallen ill or were facing particularly difficult struggles with this or that internal agony.

His thoughts finally turned to John Fletcher and the revealing, disturbing conversation they had had the night before. Whether or not John was actually guilty of murdering his wife, Constantine could not say. He prayed for wisdom, but found only that the answer to this question eluded him. Perhaps Father Thomas would know, but it would not be his to ask. Constantine realized with a sense of relief that this question, while important, was best answered by someone whose vocation and training had dealt with such things as sin and redemption, while his own vocation dealt more with ink and parchments.

As he shifted mental images, he remembered something Levente had said to him, and he marveled at how apt it had turned out to be: Here was a man who had tried to make himself palimpsest.

Setting aside the question of whether or not Fletcher was actually guilty of murder, Constantine reframed the question in terms that were more appropriate to his role as spiritual guide. John Fletcher was carrying an enormous load of guilt, guilt that—actual or imagined—was very very real in its consequences. The guilt must have been overwhelming, which explained why John had worked so hard at avoiding those memories, had glossed them over with more acceptable images, and perhaps had leveraged their power over him by passing his personal blame along to his daughter.

Here at last, Brother Constantine also had a plausible explanation for the violence against Elspeth. The unacknowledged guilt had festered like a deep sore in the back of Fletcher's mind, infecting everything, including his relationship with his daughter. Fletcher was not punishing his daughter, but himself embodied in the daughter.

But there was much more here. He still had not uncovered Fletcher's reason for avoiding meeting with him in the church. That would have to come later. And he determined that in his next conversation he would try to find out what other steps John had taken to deal with the pain. Clearly this was near the core of his spiritual struggle.

The bells rang for Compline, and Constantine joined his brother monks in communical prayer. In his prayers he remembered John the Fletcher, whose wounds were growing ever more clear in the conversations they were having, both in what was being said and in what was being avoided. He prayed for the souls of Károly his father and Cristian his brother, and of Tatjana his mother, and of Ildiko, whom he had failed so miserably. And he prayed for the soul of Elspeth, daughter of John, whom he would not fail, and whose wounds he could only guess.

The following morning Constantine rose early and sought refuge for a few moments in the garden, where he hoped to gain a bit more clarity before the conversation he knew he had to have with Fletcher before long, perhaps later that very day. Even in the dim light that came before the first communical prayers at Vigils he could see that the snow, once so sparkling and pristine, had dirtied with the rising temperatures during the day and the subsequent melt. There was a large pile of frozen mud near the pilasters that marked the south entrance of the garden.

In time his thoughts grew more prosaic. He considered some of the other questions that remained unresolved. Why had Fletcher hit Alysse in the first place? He was aware that some questions might never be answered, since there were obvious gaps in Fletcher's knowledge, and much of it was known only to Alysse herself, and of course Constantine would never be able to ask her. In the end, Constantine decided that the best tack would be to return to something Fletcher had mentioned in the previous conversation: he reported having been beaten by his father. He would start there.

Brother Constantine stood in front of the other monks of the scriptorium, puttering over his tools, preparing for the day's tasks. These were novices, new to the discipline of copying, and he would lecture them for the first hour, then set them various tasks to improve their mastery of their tools. He went to the cupboard and took out vellum and pumice, ink and quills, for the day's lesson. To do this, he had to set out a small stack of books he had brought back from the bookbinder's shop that morning. Protruding from one of the books was a small slip of paper. He opened the book, the paper fell out, and Constantine's heart stopped.

It was a note from the girl. She wanted to see him again. But she had used his name, and her own name, and that was unwise. If the note had slipped out of the book anywhere along the route they were ruined.

As he considered this, he realized the note had plunged him again into a conflict he did not know how to resolve. But the note was also a relief to him. He would find a way to see her, he told himself, for her own spiritual good, even if he had to break his vows to do so. It honored God to care for one of God's children. The relief came from his decision not to tell even the priest or the prior. If they did not know, he would not need to justify his actions to them, and that would preserve his freedom of movement.

They were in the niche again, long after Compline.

Elspeth came right to the point: "I'm going to Wales."

He objected by putting his finger to her lips. "Don't say that," he said. He could hardly bear the thought of her leaving. It would destroy her father once-for-all. It would destroy him, too.

"I want you to come with me," she whispered. He looked at her, her dark eyes glistening in the candlelight. "The bivouac is on the way. I have people in the hills there, cousins I've never known, who'll take us in because I'm family."

"Or hold you in charge until your father comes to claim you." Constantine said.

"Nobody knows but me, and now you, and we could travel together. I'll find you some regular clothes, a hat to cover your tonsure. We could travel as father and daughter. By the time they figure out we're together, we'll be in Wales and a new life."

He found this startling, surprising, even inviting, but also disturbing. The new life she was talking about was the total destruction of his old life, everything he was or hoped to be. But it would be a new life with her. Was that what he really wanted? A life with the girl? "I don't want you to go," he said. "It would break my heart."

He bent down to reassure her and watched himself kiss her gently on the mouth. Literally, that was how it felt to him, like he was split into two people, two people in one body, the self he knew watching the other self, a stranger. But it was a stranger he had met before, this other self, like a long disowned, bastard brother turning up at an unexpected moment to demand his portion of an inheritance. It was a self he did not like, a self that shamed him to the core, and here it was threatening to destroy his life.

She returned the kiss, or he thought she did.

What the other Constantine did next should not be written about in a record such as this one. Out of respect for the girl, let us then draw a curtain of decency over this episode beneath the golden high altar of St Cuthbert's Church. Enough was later said in one of the confession booths. Suffice it to say that it left the girl frightened and the monk deeply confused. They had not made love; that would be the wrong word for what had happened between them. Love is a mutual giving and receiving, a shared intimacy freely chosen, with full knowledge and acceptance of the consequences. They had not done anything at all like that.

But what they had done had consequences, even though they had not reckoned on them or chosen them. What those consequences might be would fill their waking hours and half of their dreams in the weeks that followed.

XII

BROTHER CONSTANTINE AWOKE IN the Church, prostrate before the high altar. Had he actually done what his memory told him he had done? His conscience refused to accept that. It had been a dream, a strange, ethereal dream in which he had said and done what the waking Constantine would never have done. This cannot have happened, it did not happen, he was not to blame, he had done something nearly demonic. Something had overcome him.

As he thought these things, he envisioned himself a boy again, playing near the entrance of the root cellar. It had been a hot day, and he had slipped inside to cool off from the summer heat. He remembered, dimly, that he had done this often when he had been playing, or when he was wandering unsupervised. He had entered the root cellar to smell the warm earth, or to hide from his friends. One day—how old had he been? Six?—he had found his older brother Cristian in there with a girl from the village. Ildiko. He had seen her at church—his family was Orthodox—but at the time he did not know her name. He was aware of having been shocked to find them not fully clothed. Cristian leapt to his feet, shouting that he should get out and stay out, throwing a box of rutabagas at him.

"I . . . didn't kn . . . know," Constantine tried to calm his brother down. "I'm sorry." He had a very vivid memory of having flushed at what had happened, and then was ashamed when he realized he had done something wrong.

Cristian raised his hand, fist clenched, back toward Constantine, but was stopped by a cry from the girl behind him. "Don't." She said that simply, but loudly enough that it had caught Cristian's attention. He stopped moving, but he was breathing hard, and Constantine could smell the hard smell of liquor on his breath. "Don't, Cristian. Leave him alone. He didn't know."

He heard footsteps behind him at the far end of the nave. There was a cough, but no voices. Someone entered the chancel—Constantine did not look, but knew instinctively that it was Brother Joachim the sacristan, bearing a long taper to light the candles for Vigils. Joachim arrived at the transept, then turned and returned to the rear of the church along the north ambulatory. Constantine did not need to think this through, either, but simply knew that he would have gone for Prior Robert, who would be with the others as they gathered for Vigils.

Dimly, in the distance near the rear of the church, he sensed the movement of woolen robes, the gathering of bodies as the brothers assembled for worship. The brothers, not yet aware that he was prostrate on the floor, began their chant and processed slowly the length of the nave along the north ambulatory. At the front, they filed into the pews, then stopped. No whispering, just the last echoes of the Grand Silence.

Someone placed a hand on his shoulder, gently, apparently not knowing if he was in prayer, if he had had a vision, if he had been engaged in some spiritual battle, if he had been sick. Whoever it was said nothing, continuing to observe the Grand Silence. Another brother, probably Gregory the infirmerer, approached him quietly from the side, knelt beside him. Constantine did not move—he could not move—and instead continued to lay prostrate before the altar.

Whoever had touched him, apparently satisfied that he was not sick and so not in need of medical care, had simply re-joined the others in the recitation of the morning office, leaving him alone in his agony. No doubt they prayed for the peace of his soul, but the prayers and chants were distant, as far removed from him as he now was from God. Even so, the chanting of the Divine office made the landscape of his inner life even more surreal, like eating honey and gall in the same bite, the sweetness and the bitterness mingling and warring in the mouth.

After Vigils, the Divine office completed, he found Brother Gregory and Prior Robert beside him, coaxing him to his feet, expressing concern for his well-being. He could not speak, but allowed himself to be escorted to the infirmary. He allowed himself to be settled onto a cot, felt his legs being lifted, his body covered by a blanket. The brothers, crossing themselves and muttering prayers, retreated to the hallway and then no doubt to their breakfast.

Elspeth lay in her bed and traced out the stress lines in the mud coating of the ceiling. A tiny spider crawled across her neck, sending a shiver down her back. Another spider was making a mis-formed, ugly web within the rafters. She watched a small fly struggling to break free of the web, and finally succumbing to its inevitable fate. The spider that had made the web scurried across its silver filaments.

She had not wanted the lovemaking, had found it frightening, even disgusting, but she had said nothing when it happened, nothing to reassure him, and nothing to dissuade him. She had been too shocked to realize what was happening, and now, looking back, she was angry with herself for not resisting him more forcefully.

Alcera was sleeping, and Levente was gone from the hut, and Elspeth was grateful for that. *Probably gathering wood*, she thought.

She drew the covers to her chin and shuddered, cold to the bone. Tears formed up, but she worked to repress them because Levente might come back, and he would ask her about them, and what could she say? Perhaps she was what her father had said she was. She had kissed the monk. She had repeatedly allowed herself to be alone with him, had sought out those meetings even, had allowed him to touch her, to stroke her hair, to kiss her. She had taken her own pleasure in meeting with him, she had encouraged him, had she not? Had she not asked him to run away with her to Wales? Without realizing it, without intending it, she had allowed herself to be drawn into a place of danger, and then, when the decisive moment had come, had not known what to do to protect herself. She was angry with herself for not shoving him or screaming at him or kicking him hard the way she had kicked her father when he had tried to kiss her on the mouth.

The door opened, and Levente came in, stamping his feet on the floor in a vain effort to ward off the cold. She turned her face to the wall, her back to him, and stifled a sob.

"Are you alright?" Levente asked.

"I want to be left alone." She was not alright. She had not wanted the lovemaking, and now, looking back, she was angry at Constantine, too, for failing to protect her. How ironic is that! The protector turns out to be the danger. Alone, beneath the high altar of St Cuthbert's Church, he had promised her—in words, in actions—that she was safe with him, and then, when she was most vulnerable, when she was frightened, he had taken something from her that was not his to take, something that could not be restored.

By the end of the day Constantine was sitting up, which apparently pleased Brother Gregory. "What happened?" Gregory asked.

"I can't talk about it," Constantine said. What could he say? He really couldn't talk about it, and it was surely none of Gregory's business. Gregory was not a priest, but only a lay brother, and so had no business knowing anything about his inner life, or his sins, or what spiritual battles he might be waging. More importantly, he, Constantine, had an obligation to protect the girl, to protect her reputation, to keep from harming her further.

"As you like," said Brother Gregory. He laid a hand across Constantine's forehead. "No fever, but you're weak. We should keep you here a while longer."

"Wine?" asked Constantine. There was a provision in the Rule of St Benedict that brothers who were ill might ask for wine.

"I'll fetch it, if you like," Gregory said.

"Could you make it brandy, Brother? Please?"

Gregory withdrew and Constantine collapsed backward against the hard pillow and closed his eyes and pondered again what had happened. He had made love to the girl. No one knew but the two of them. He had collapsed before the altar in part out of penitence for his broken monastic vow, his terrible failure to recognize his weakness, his shame at knowing that the moment he had touched her he had set the torch to his life as a man of God. He even had the thought that this was her doing, but vestiges of the monk within him rejected that. The more important thing was that she could destroy him, and he did not really know her well enough to know that she would not. It was, he thought, only a matter of time. She held him in the palm of her hand, and now he needed her silent.

And yet—and this was the odd part—despite it all, the potential costs—to him, to her—despite the danger, the terrible inner warfare he was waging—when it had happened, he had had an overwhelming sense had been relief. Why *relief*? The thought returned to him: *I did not deserve to die.*

He closed his eyes when Gregory returned with the brandy. The infirmerer placed the brandy on a small table beside the bed, and left without a word.

He looked out the window and tried to think. The relief was like something he had experienced before. He had had an odd, strange relief that he had survived the burning of his village in Moldavia, relief mixed with equal parts of horror, and anguish, and shame at being alive. This was like that. Relief and anguish.

But it was different too. From the very first time he had touched the girl, he had been struggling against something, a nagging, shoving, pushing urgency inside him, and whatever it was, it had finally won. But then there was shame: Had he struggled hard enough not to think about the girl? The struggle to hold his attraction to her at bay had been a losing battle, maybe a battle not fought hard enough, he realized, and maybe what he felt had been the relief of a drowning man who finally gives in to the pressure of the water and takes that final, fatal breath. Is there relief that comes with acknowledging failure, if it means that the battle is over?

But then, was the battle over? Or had it simply shifted to a new and more dangerous battleground? And who was the enemy? Himself? Elspeth? Was Elspeth an enemy now? Was there something more sinister, even? The inner struggle was demonic, he realized that now, or maybe a struggle with his own evil core, maybe the Devil himself.

Later, the thin light of evening cast shadows around the room, and what seemed to him especially sinister shadows were thrown up against the wall by a single flickering candle Brother Gregory had left burning beside his bed.

Elspeth sent him no word, and did not come to visit him in hospital, but he was relieved by that, too. What would she have to say to him, here in this more public place? And even if she were not angry, what guesses would the brothers make about why he had had a visit from a girl? The less public the connection between them the better, at least until he worked out what to do next.

On the morning of the second day he felt well enough to return to his cell for a change of clothes.

"I'll send Paul," said Brother Gregory. "You need to rest."

"I'm better now, Brother. I need to move. I can't just lay here."

"One more day."

"Clean clothes."

"Alright, but come back quickly."

When Constantine arrived in his cell he was shocked to find the floor covered with dragon scales. How had a dragon gotten into his room? Did anybody else know? He swept up the scales, wrapping them carefully in some old paper, then carried them to the monastery's compost heap, where he buried them beneath some freshly turned leaves.

Before he left the compost heap he did an odd thing: He picked up two or three of the finest examples of the dragon's scales and slipped them into the slit pocket of his robe.

On the trip back to the infirmary, he paused to sit for a moment in Brother Johann's garth. He looked around, and there, to the north, flying against a field of brilliant white clouds, he saw two dragons.

The brothers filed into Chapter in near total silence. Constantine was still unsteady from his experience with the girl, but against the infirmerer's express wishes had hauled himself from his sickbed and joined his brothers in the refectory to hear the prior's thoughts and decisions about their common life. It was important, he realized, in part because in jeopardizing his own good he had jeopardized theirs as well, but he went also because it was important to sustain the impression that all was as it should be, that he give away no clue about what he had done. He selected one of the benches nearest the kitchen, removed somewhat from the lectern on which Prior Robert would stand, and protected from direct view by a pillar. There he settled, his back propped against the kitchen wall.

Robert began with a short reading from one of the psalms, then a passage from the Rule. This was normal, the standard opening. Then followed a routine recitation of chores and assignments, also normal. Laundry day was postponed because of trouble with the well. The architect who had been hired to assess the state of the monastery's buildings had reported damage to the tiles of the refectory; the brothers were asked to watch for leakage. The harvest had yielded a surplus of barley, which the cellarer was instructed to sell to the peasants for a good price.

As Constantine listened, Prior Robert's words faded into a dull drone, and he had to work to appear attentive.

Prior Robert paused then, and turned to a matter that was less ordinary, and Constantine found his attention suddenly caught, like a fly in a spider-web: "Two of our guests have reported smelling tar in the church, and again while they passed near the entrances of the cloister. I'm not yet certain what that means."

"Could it have something to do with the dragon?" said Brother Cyril the elder sacristan.

Constantine fingered the dragon scales in the slit pocket of his robe, but said nothing.

"Why should it spare us?" someone said.

"What's this got to do with tar?" said Prior Robert.

"I've heard," said Joachim, "that people who harbor dragons sometimes smell like tar." Constantine, startled, almost added that Joachim was right, he had seen a dragon on his way to England as a boy, and that the dragon had smelled hard. He had not known what the smell had been, but now looking back, he thought it might have been tar. He checked himself then and said nothing, because Gregory had found that same smell on his breath. Better to wait and see what the others knew. He reached quietly into the pocket of his robe and fingered the dragon scales he had kept when he cleaned his cell, and privately, in his heart, he crossed himself and prayed that the moment would pass.

"They do indeed," said Brother Gregory, bristling. "But medical conditions such as this are best left to those who have studied them. Several conditions exist in which the smell of tar is a common symptom. I see them from time to time in the infirmary." He glanced at Constantine, who flushed and was grateful for the shelter of the pillar.

"I've found scales in the garden," said Johann. "And footprints."

"What sort of footprints?" asked Prior Robert.

"Talons," said Johann, "but too large for a bird."

Robert considered this. "Perhaps one of our guests has brought a dragon among us," he said levelly. "Dragons are dangerous. It's said that they can disappear and reappear at will. In any case, you are all to keep alert." He closed the book in which he kept his accounts and records. "This Chapter is concluded."

Constantine, feeling pale and exposed, rose with the others, and headed for the infirmary. Brother Gregory, bright-eyed and solicitous of his patient, came alongside and placed a reassuring hand on his shoulder as they walked. Nothing was said between them until they reached the quiet and privacy of the infirmary.

"You've been having nightmares," Gregory said when they were alone.

"How did you know?" asked Constantine, startled, and wondering rather desperately what else Gregory might know.

"Do you not think that a doctor should check on his patients as they sleep?" asked Gregory. "Let me help you into your gown." That gesture alone told Constantine that Gregory considered him still sick. Ordinarily the brothers slept in their regular clothing.

Constantine removed his woolen cassock and stood silent as Gregory slipped a sleeping gown over his head.

"What happens when I sleep?" asked Constantine as he lay down.

"You toss and turn. Sometimes you moan, as though you're being hurt. Some nights I sleep here, in the chair beside you."

Constantine was alarmed by this discovery, aware that in dreaming of the girl he might inadvertently betray his secret.

"Sometimes you talk."

"What have I said?" asked Constantine quietly, hoping to maintain the appearance of composure.

"Last night you said a strange word," said Gregory, "which I assumed must be in your native language."

"I haven't spoken Hungarian since I came here," muttered Constantine. "What word? Do you remember?"

"I wrote it down," said Gregory. He opened a drawer of the dresser and took out a small folded slip of paper. He smoothed it out on the dresser top, and glanced at the writing. "Ildiko," he said.

Elspeth lay on her back, counting the spiders that crawled across the ceiling. Lately the hut seemed infested with spiders. Another misshapen web had formed in the corner during the night, small and out of the way, but trapped within it a fly was struggling to free itself. The spider dropped beside the bed, riding a thin filament that showed silver in the moonlight. A moth fluttered through the open window.

She wanted to talk to somebody about what had happened, wanted to get it off her chest, but could not think of who she could tell. At the same time, she did not want to have to say the words out loud. It was as though saying them out loud would make what had happened real—or worse, *public*—even if she whispered them when she was alone in the hut. It was all too humiliating. But she was afraid, too. What would Constantine do now? Would he tell her father? Had he done this to someone else? Would he do to someone else what he had done to her? Should she talk to the Prior? Would the Prior even believe her? If she was not safe in the presence of a monk, with whom could she be safe now? He was a man of God, for Christ's sake. Could she trust the sheriff? If she told the sheriff, he would tell her father, and who knew what he would do to Constantine? Her father would kill Constantine like he killed that wolf, and wouldn't give it a second thought, and that would be her fault, too. Or he would blame her, maybe beat her again for putting herself in danger. Should she go to confession? Had she committed a sin, to be taken by a man, raped maybe, by a man? Did that make her guilty of a sin?

Had it been rape? She thought so, but then her father would not call it that. He would say that she invited it, that she asked for it, that it was her own fault. Her father would say that men cannot control themselves, that that's why women and girls have chaperones, and then he would accuse her of leading the man on—monk, soldier, farmer, wouldn't matter. What if she became pregnant? Her father would blame her for what had happened.

Who would believe her, anyway? She had not been seen with Constantine except in passing. She had protected their relationship, had not let on that she had ever known him in any way at all except for passing greetings. The nod of the head. Casual remarks made as he visited with Levente and Alcera. The loan of a book of poetry. Besides, he was a monk, a man of God. The journey from what they *believed* to what was true would be too great a journey. They would call her cruel, and accuse her of lying to protect somebody else, and then would connect her up with one of the village boys. Or maybe they would link her up with Levente, and he didn't deserve that either.

"Sick?" Levente asked. She did not turn toward him, but stayed silent, forcing back tears. Behind her, she could hear him lighting a fire with his flint kit.

"I just want to be left alone."

But she was not left alone. Just as she was turning her face to the wall, she heard male voices in the front room that served as Levente's workshop, one of them belonging to Constantine. She could not make out what they were saying, but it had something to do with an order of vellum he had placed with one of the village merchants, and some new inks that were coming from Scotland. Then she heard her own name, and she held her breath to hear.

"Is Elspeth here?" Constantine asked.

"She's not well today, Brother," Levente said. "I told her to sleep."

"Not well?" There was a tone of concern or alarm in Constantine's voice, but she was sure Levente would not understand why. "May I see her?" Constantine said.

"She said she wanted to be left alone."

"Ah, well then. Another time. When she wakes up, would you tell her I need to return Elizabeth's letters to the monastery library?"

Elspeth relaxed. She would not have to deal with him, at least not today.

Constantine left Levente's shop with a deep feeling of confusion. He had thought that perhaps she might see him, that he might find in her some reassurance. But she was ill. He had an odd sense of fear, like the fear he had felt when he had been abandoned by Ildiko. Alone. Relief for himself, but terror for the girl.

As an adult, looking back, it came as a kind of shock—a relieved shock—that Ildiko had not abandoned him, so much as protected him, probably at great cost to herself. He thought again about the strange men who had taken her. They had shouted at her, and had tied her hands in front of her, and then had made her walk behind one of the supply wagons like a cow being led to market. Glancing back, she had caught his eye and mouthed some word—"down" maybe, or "back," and he had retreated to the undergrowth.

This made sense to him in retrospect, but his memory was overlaid with a child's ache at having been left alone. He could not have felt more abandoned if she had sneaked off of her own accord.

He had followed the Mongol caravan as long as he could, hoping to find some way to help Ildiko, but that had proven impossible. He had not been able to keep up, and eventually had sat alone on the side of the road, crying, and had been picked up by a family in a farm wagon.

Eventually, the family dropped him at the door of a large grey building in what must have been Buda or Pest, one of the twin major cities of the Hungarian people, and so he had found his way to Elizabeth.

It was later, after Compline. Constantine lay on his cot in his own cell, and looked at the dark corners of the ceiling. What he had done came back to him with the regularity of an antiphonal liturgy—*Thou art guilty, Have mercy upon me O Christ, Thou art guilty, Have mercy upon me O Lord.* Over and over and over again, each time ending with a brief twinge of relief that he had escaped exposure. The next time he is called to Prior Robert's study, will it be about that? But how long would she keep silent? Had she said anything to anyone else? What if she says something in the confession booth? God was testing him. Then it occurred to him that God was testing him in another way. Could he remake his life?

It was later afternoon. Fletcher had come. Constantine had wanted to avoid this conversation, but could not see how without fabricating some lie that would increase his risk of exposure. They were sitting together in the monastery library. They spent a few moments in centering prayer. Constantine read a psalm. Only then, with the business of the day focused into contemplative stillness, did Constantine begin again to move forward in the manner of *Lectio Divina* into a review of Fletcher's story.

"Have you thought about our conversation?" he asked, as gently as he could.

"I didn't find any comfort in that."

Constantine ignored this, and moved forward. "Think there might be a connection between Elspeth and Alysse?"

"What? Like they looked alike? I'm not an idiot, Constantine, I know enough to sort the girl out from her mother. The better question is why I hit Alysse in the first place."

"I was going to ask you that question, John. I think it may be a crucial piece of the puzzle. Let's begin with the obvious question, then work backward to something that I think will be less obvious."

"Pry away," said Fletcher.

"What did you say to yourself to justify hitting your wife when you did?"

"It's the rare man who doesn't beat his wife," said Fletcher.

"Did your father beat your mother?" asked Constantine.

"I remember once when he almost killed her. Told me that that was a man's right, to beat his wife if he didn't like something she was doing. If she disobeyed him. Like that."

"What did you think when he did that?"

"I thought it was awful at the time. Tried to get in the way. I got beat up pretty bad myself that time."

"He beat you then?"

"Shoved me hard. I still got a scar on my left arm from it. He threw me against a wall where there was a scythe leaning, blade up. My arm almost got cut off in the fight."

"But you rescued your mother."

"I suppose you could say that, though I didn't think of it that way at the time. All I remember is trying to stop him. He was a raging bull."

"Can you see why that might be an admirable thing, though, John, trying to protect your mother? A courageous act?"

"It was stupid, that's all."

"Because you ended up nearly losing an arm?"

Fletcher nodded. "Because I nearly lost my arm. My mother thought it was stupid, too."

"Why do you say that?"

"She got rid of me right after that."

"What does that mean, 'She got rid of you?'"

"She sent me away. Got rid of me. It was why my mother fixed me up with that bookbinder. Levente's father. It's how I came here. She sent me away to get me out of the house. She wanted me gone."

"What makes you think she wanted you gone?"

"Because she sent me too far away. She got me out of Wales, see? Sent me here. I didn't think she wanted me to find my way home."

"How old were you when this happened?"

"Seven, I think. Seven or eight. Don't know for sure what was the year I was born. Had never seen a calendar, my parents, but even if they had, they couldn't have read it."

"And that's why they never wrote to you? You did say that, didn't you?"

"I never saw my mother again after that."

"So you were a seven-year-old boy abandoned by your mother. That must have been terrible. You defended your mother, got beat up in the process, and then she 'got rid of' you, as you say. That seems unfair enough for a lifetime."

"You've got no idea. It was terrible. I could never figure out why she did that. I thought she must've been ashamed of me because I'd challenged my father's authority."

"Could it be that your mother was protecting you from your father?" As Constantine said this, he thought about Ildiko, protecting him, near the same age, and how he had misunderstood and felt abandoned, when what she had done had probably been heroic. He reached down absentmindedly into his pocket and fingered the dragon scales he had hidden there.

When he looked up, he was startled to see that Fletcher was staring at him.

"She saw you in a hopeless battle with your father, and realizing that this event might happen again, sent you away where he couldn't get to you. It must've been a terrible shock to her to see you cut up by the scythe."

"There was blood everywhere."

"Suppose the scythe had cut an artery? Or worse, it could have cut your throat. I can see your mother, picturing this happening again, and your father going off in some rage, and throwing you against a wall, or maybe something worse, and in her mind seeing you bleed to death. The very prospect would have terrified your mother."

"My God."

Constantine was working in the scriptorium, scraping off the lettering of one of the palimpsest manuscripts that had been designated for a different use. He worked alone at this, using one of the hard dragon scales as a scraping tool. He held the scale stiff in his right hand, perpendicular to the vellum, and scraped until his fingers ached. It was slow, repetitive, exacting work, but he did not mind. The repetitiveness allowed him to focus his attention elsewhere as he worked.

This time, he thought about the girl. It had been two weeks, and she had not said anything to anybody. He would have been humiliated by the exposure, would have lost the respect of his brothers, the Prior, every single one of them, but even so, just for a moment, he grieved that loss.

He held the scale at a sharp angle and scraped it across the surface of the ink, following the curved lines of the letters he was removing. The copyist had been a careless workman, and the lettering was uneven and inelegant, and he was happy to be removing it from the page.

He thought about something Levente had said to him months before, something about John Fletcher being a palimpsest, and that his task would be to see what could be recovered from the underwriting.

He brushed off the dislodged ink with a soft-bristled brush, then held the manuscript up to the light.

I am too, he thought. *Palimpsest. There's something there beneath my monk's story, an earlier story still.* He set down the manuscript and went to the window and tried to think what that was.

In his mind were flashes of another distant, dreaded memory. There had been a knight who had rescued him from a brutal man with a red face. The knight was a large man, well muscled from the hardships and disciplines of war. Like the others, he took what he needed from the land. One of the older boys who spoke a little English told Constantine he had heard one of the men joking with the officers that stealing while on a Crusade was a good and Christian thing, a chance to involve the locals in the work of God. One of the officers had reminded the man that this was allowed, but within strict limits: The crusaders were to take only what they needed; anything beyond that should be paid for with plunder they had taken from the infidels.

"What did he say to that?" Constantine asked, curious about a form of logic that did not seem Christian at all. He was aware that the greater burden of this practice fell upon the poor and the small farmers, farmers like his father, who could lose a whole field of vegetables to a single night's feasting. "They steal from us, too."

The older boy shrugged. "We're infidels, too."

"But we're Christians," somebody said.

"Not baptized according to the Roman rite," said the older boy.

The nobility and the merchants in the towns fared much better in the general pillaging. Sometimes the more important of the knights were hosted in Christian castles where, Constantine guessed, they told war stories or regaled their hosts with tales of supernatural portents in the heavens foretelling victory on earth.

It was during one such encampment that he had had a disturbing encounter with someone he thought might be one of the nobleman's field hands. The man said something to him in a language he had not understood, but which he now knew was English. It was dark, night maybe, or maybe overcast by storm clouds. He had not seen the man very clearly, but he saw enough to know that the man had a red face, with the white, grizzled stubble of a partially grown beard. He was wearing a rough tunic, woven out of some coarse fabric, Constantine thought maybe flax. He remembered going to the man innocently, expecting some better effort at communication, but the man had grabbed him hard by the arm and marched him out of the firelight and around behind one of the out-buildings.

He did not tell anyone what had happened. What had happened had been painful and humiliating, and when he had begun to cry out, the man had squeezed his arms so hard he was afraid they would break off there in the man's hands like the branches of a dead tree. Then the man had shoved his finger hard against Constantine's lips and made a threatening gesture with his fist, which Constantine understood to mean that he would beat him if he uttered so much as a word.

The following day, when the cavalcade formed up to resume the westward trek home, he had hidden beneath the tarp on one of the supply wagons because he could not walk.

It was an uncomfortable ride. The wagon driver seemed to find every bump in the dirt track they called a road, and worse, it was stifling hot. The air smelled heavily of tar. He bunched a saddle blanket to cushion the ride, and after maybe an hour tried to occupy himself by taking a mental inventory of the equipment with which he shared the ride. Saddle blankets bound up in neat rolls. Tents. Four large cooking pots in a box. Near the pots, an equal number of metal tripods to stand over the cooking fires. Two spits. A stack of crossbows with a box of tipped firing bolts, like stubby arrows. Beyond the bolts, he saw a large cage, like a cage one might have designed for a bird. Inside the cage, he saw a miniature of the flying lizards that had devastated his village after the Mongol attack. He adjusted his position to get a better view. It was too large to be a lizard, and it had talons. On its back were oversized, awkward-looking wings. He guessed that it might be as large as he was, maybe a little larger, but that was difficult because the animal was curled up, staying quite still. He had the impression that it was sleeping, though its eyes were visible through what must have been clear membranes. A red-orange glow came from the lizard's nostrils in a rhythmic pattern as it breathed. He guessed the unusual heat came from the nostrils.

He heard someone calling what must have meant *halt*, the word repeating itself over and over down the column of horses and wagons from front to rear. The wagon lurched to a stop, and he heard the driver's boots on the gravel of the road. There was a general hubbub of people outside, the talk drifting away as the soldiers and their entourage made for the woods to take their toilet, and then found some spot beside the road to eat their lunch.

He slipped around to the opposite side of the wagon and crawled out from beneath the tarp. Then he walked, painfully, until he found some of the other Hungarian boys.

"They have a war lizard," he whispered to one of the others, a bigger boy whose name he did not know.

"A dragon?" said the boy. "They have a dragon?"

"Keep your voice down," Constantine said. "In one of the supply wagons. I saw it."

"They have a dragon," the boy announced to the others.

"Which wagon?"

He counted. "Sixth one back. It's in a cage."

"Let's look," said another boy, his eyes wide with astonishment and curiosity.

"Don't," Constantine insisted. "We'll get in trouble."

But it was too late. Three of the boys made a sneaking sortie to see for themselves. Constantine did not go because his backside hurt, and he still could not walk very well. Instead, he stayed seated and hoped nobody would notice that he was moving painfully. He did not know whether to be excited or afraid.

Then he heard a shout from the circle of men, and in a moment the boys were back, running and laughing as they slid into place in a little cloud of dust. They straightened their features and tried to look as though nothing had happened. The driver was behind them, but not close enough to tell who the culprits had been. He shook his fist and shouted at them in English.

"What did he say?" asked one of the smaller boys. Constantine had talked to him twice before, but did not know his name.

"He said he would fix our wagon if we don't stay away from his," somebody answered, not translating so much as freely interpreting his red face and angry gesticulations. The boys all laughed, all but Constantine. The driver was the red-faced man who had hurt him the night before.

"Did you see it?" somebody asked.

"There's just an empty cage."

But the cage had not been empty. Whatever had been inside—the older boy had said it was a dragon—it must have had the ability to disappear.

Throughout the following week, Fletcher agonized over the fact that what had had done had brought about Alysse' death; it was an untreated, festering wound within him. He was easily distracted as he hunted, and often noted only after the fact that he had been in the presence of the dragon. At mass on Sunday he did not partake of the Holy Eucharist, feeling that what he had done to Alysse, un-confessed and unforgiven, was an insurmountable barrier to the grace of God. Whatever happened, he would not abuse the sacrament.

Finally, when he could bear the guilt no longer, he sought out Father Thomas to make confession and receive absolution. He requested this audience on a Sunday after mass, and while Father was reluctant, he nevertheless agreed to hear his confession.

Fletcher told the old priest everything, holding back only his habit of envisioning Alysse in the statues of the Blessed Virgin. In some sense his task was made both easier and harder by the screen that separated penitent from confessor, for he could not see the priest's face to tell whether he understood the depth of the anguish he felt, but neither could he see the disgust the priest would no doubt feel, and so Fletcher rambled. He told Father about the times he had beaten his daughter, about the rape of his wife, about her death in childbirth. He confessed these things soberly, deliberately, trusting that even murder is forgivable in the grace of God. He said he was prepared for any penance Thomas might require of him.

But Thomas was disinclined to require penance.

Instead he weighed and sifted Fletcher's confession with the mixed skill of a religious scholar whose grasp of canon law made up in clarity of conviction what it lacked in charity and compassion. In any case, his regard for the details of law and piety superseded any regard he might have had for the depth of the wound Fletcher had inflicted upon his own conscience.

Thomas allowed Fletcher to tell his story in its entirety, asking only a few clarifying questions along the way. Finally, he told Fletcher that his reason for not requiring penance was rooted in the exact details of the case: No penance was required because no sin had been committed.

Fletcher was baffled and stunned, but not relieved. Of course a sin had been committed. He had murdered his wife.

Thomas replied that there had been no premeditation, no intent to kill, and so what had happened could at worse be considered manslaughter, but that was a term from secular law and not from canon law. Holy Mother Church knows nothing about manslaughter, and where the law is silent, no violation of the law can occur. While Fletcher might be guilty of manslaughter, he said, he had committed no sin.

Fletcher insisted: "What I did cost Alysse her life!"

"What you did," Father replied dryly, "was entirely within your rights. She was your wife, and you had a right to father a child by her, regardless of your motive."

"But it was rape."

Father was unpersuaded: "I'll grant you that it was cruel and thoughtless, but by definition, a man cannot rape his wife."

"But she fought back against me," Fletcher said then. "She clawed and scratched and struggled against me." Fletcher was fighting for something here, but he could not quite put his finger on what it was. It was as though his awareness of what he had done, of its reality and its consequences, were a precious possession that he was unwilling to give up lightly. He paused for a moment to reflect on that. Why was it so hard to walk away from this, especially when Christ's very vicar was offering him here a clear conscience, free at any rate from a sense of sinfulness? It was because, regardless of the precisions or imprecisions of language, what he had done had been wrong, and he knew it had been wrong. He seemed to know intuitively that if he capitulated that point he would never come to terms with it and it would haunt him forever.

He repeated his comment to the priest: "I took her against her will. She resisted me. Isn't that what rape is?"

"As she should not have done," said the priest. "The scripture is quite clear, as the Holy Apostle Paul writes"—here he drew upon long memory—"'For the husband is the head of the wife as Christ is the head of the church, his body, and is himself its Savior. As the church is subject to Christ, so let wives also be subject in everything to their husbands.' Notice," the priest said, "wives are to be subject to their husbands *in omnibus*—in *all* things. Even this. Especially in this."

But Fletcher was determined to assert his guilt because there seemed to him no other way to obtain absolution. By this time he was in an agony. If the priest refused to require penance and offer absolution, then he was left without a means of restoring his conscience to a right state. How could he hope for redemption? He voiced this agony to the priest: "I know I've committed a sin because I feel my guilt. It's tearing me up inside like a knife."

"It's quite possible for a man to feel no guilt at all, when in fact he's as guilty as the devil," said Father. "By the same token, it is possible to feel guilt where there is none. Where there is no guilt, there is no need for confession or penance either one, and it is not possible for me to grant absolution."

"So what am I supposed to do with this guilt?" Fletcher wanted to know.

"Such things are no concern of mine, at least not as your priest," replied Thomas. "As your priest I am concerned with your sins and your relationship with God and Holy Mother Church. Your failure of conscience is another matter altogether. Absolution is not a salve for troubled consciences; I will not cheapen the institutions of confession and absolution by making them serve some purpose for which they were not designed." Then he finished abruptly: "This interview is concluded." He cleared his throat.

Fletcher heard the priest rise to leave. He was stunned. No penance. No absolution. No way to heal the wound within himself. No way to restore his conscience to wholeness, no way to restore a right relationship with his memory, or with God. No healing for his aching heart. Even if God did not view his actions as sinful, in his deepest core Fletcher did, so that he knew he would not enter the church again with this heavy burden of unresolved guilt weighing upon him. He was worse off now than he had been when this process began.

He staggered out, stunned, into the blinding sunlight.

Alone in his cell, Constantine took up the threads of the memory and tried again to weave them into a meaningful portrait of what had happened in the root cellar. The girl had been named Ildiko. Ildiko was crying, and Constantine, trying to comfort her and quiet her at the same time, reached up to stroke her hair. They sat, and Ildiko laid her head in his lap, and was quiet, but he could feel her body struggling against the wracking sobs she would have made in other circumstances. He stroked her dark hair with his hand, and whispered, "shhh."

From time to time there was the sharp clatter of swords shocking against swords, and then shouting in a language he did not understand. He heard his father's voice again, answering the shouts defiantly, and then—after a long while—nearer the door—the same voice slowly calling out Cristian's name, and then the name of his mother, Tatjana. He heard his father groaning—he must have been just outside—outside the door of the root cellar, and then call out to him weakly, 'Constantine.'

Through all of this, obedient to the instructions they had been given, he and Ildiko stayed crouched behind the sacks of seed-corn and boxes of vegetables. Slowly the light around the door dwindled to a dim glow. The sounds of shouting, and swords, and stampeding horses dwindled down to silence. The terrified beating of his heart dwindled down to a calm, sweating chill. He reached out and touched Ildiko's cheek, running his fingers down along the line of her jaw and then around the outline of her mouth. Comforted by this gesture, she calmed and went to sleep. She was clearly exhausted by the terror, and by the emotional effort of keeping quiet.

He waited for Cristian like he had been told, but Cristian never came, and so finally he did what a person of courage—what a man protecting a woman—would have to do, and felt his way in the dark to the door, and opened it, and went out alone into the night.

"Of course it was a sin. It was a sin against your wife, it was a sin against your own conscience, and it was a sin against God." Constantine was talking now. Fletcher had found him in the refectory, taking his turn washing dishes. Constantine continued to wash, while Fletcher poured out his agonies.

"But Father said . . . ." Fletcher was not so much inquiring as protesting. He was clear that he disagreed with Father Thomas, and was looking for confirmation of that agreement in the mind and heart of his spiritual guide.

"It's a long way from a country priest, preaching from his pulpit in a monastery church in Warwick, to the pope speaking *ex cathedra* in Rome." He explained that the pope is infallible when he makes official pronouncements from the Holy See, but that country priests do not speak *ex cathedra*. "Thomas sometimes gets things out of context," he said.

"How is that?" asked Fletcher.

"Let me see," said Constantine. "Ever notice how a grouse looks different in a cage than it does in the wild. Ever notice that?"

"So what's your point?"

"Change the context, you change the bird," said Constantine. "It's like that with language, too. Change the context, you change the meaning."

"Father does that with Holy Scripture?" asked Fletcher.

"Look again at that passage in Ephesians 5," said Constantine.

"You know I don't read," said Fletcher.

Constantine went to the lectern that stood in the corner of the refectory, where a large Bible had been placed. It is the custom of the Benedictines to hear scriptures read aloud during meals, and the Bible was there for that purpose. He carefully turned the pages to the book of Ephesians. "The passage in Ephesians reads this way: '*Sed ut ecclesia subiecta est Christo ita et mulieres viris suis in omnibus*,'" he said, following the text with his index finger. Let me translate that for you: 'Wives, submit yourselves to your husbands in all things.' Now, read out of context, the 'all things' has nothing qualifying it, nothing that limits its meaning, so it seems to apply to everything, including violence and brutality. But that can hardly be what the Holy Apostle meant. He did not require wives to be subject to their husbands if their husbands wished to commit adultery, or to break the law, or to inflict violence on their children. Look here. Even in this specific text in Ephesians 5, Paul limits the options for the husband. Notice what the text says in the very next verse: '*Viri diligite uxores sicut et Christus dilexit ecclesiam et se ipsum tradidit pro ea.*' That is, the passage goes on to tell the husbands to love their wives in the same way that Christ loved the Church and gave himself for her. This is impossible to do if you beat your wife. For a man to be violent to his wife is to violate the law of God. What you did was a sin, pure and simple."

Fletcher did not know how to feel. On the one hand, there was the relief of knowing that there were forgiveness and absolution to be found, that the grace of God extends even to this, but then there was the agony of knowing that Father Thomas would not agree under any circumstances and so he had no one to hear his confession, assign penance, or grant absolution. He seemed to be no closer to a resolution than before.

"What do I do next?" he asked Constantine. "Father Thomas isn't going to be convinced, and I'm left without a confessor."

"I believe, John," said Constantine, "that the penance of a broken and contrite heart is all that is required of you."

"And confession?"

"Are you not capable of prayer?"

"I can do that."

"Why, then, can you not offer your confession directly to God in prayer?"

"Constantine," said Fletcher, "you're a heretic."

"A heretic indeed. But did the priest in his orthodoxy offer you any solace for your wounded soul?"

"I don't know how to pray in this way," protested Fletcher.

"Ah, but you do," said Constantine. "Perhaps this would be easier if we practiced *Lectio Divina*."

"With what text?" asked Fletcher.

"With the 51st psalm, perhaps," said Constantine. He turned the pages carefully, then translated directly into English, moving slowly so Fletcher could hear and feel the words as the basis of his own prayer:

Have mercy on me, O God, according to thy steadfast love; according to thy abundant mercy blot out my transgressions.

Wash me thoroughly from my iniquity, and cleanse me from my sin!

For I know my transgressions, and my sin is ever before me.

Against thee, thee only, have I sinned, and done that which is evil in thy sight, so that thou art justified in thy sentence and blameless in thy judgment.

Behold, thou desirest truth in the inward being; therefore teach me wisdom in my secret heart.

Purge me with hyssop, and I shall be clean; wash me, and I shall be whiter than snow.

Hide thy face from my sins, and blot out all my iniquities.

Create in me a clean heart, O God, and put a new and right spirit within me.

Cast me not away from thy presence, and take not thy holy Spirit from me.

Restore to me the joy of thy salvation, and uphold me with a willing spirit.

Deliver me from bloodguiltiness, O God, thou God of my salvation, and my tongue will sing aloud of thy deliverance.

For thou hast no delight in sacrifice; were I to give a burnt offering, thou wouldst not be pleased.

The sacrifice acceptable to God is a broken spirit; a broken and contrite heart, O God, thou wilt not despise."

A broken and contrite heart. Fletcher pondered this text, not only for its offer of grace, but also for its absence of a priest to mediate his prayer to God, or to pronounce absolution in God's name. In the spirit—or perhaps in the Spirit—of *Lectio Divina* he allowed the words of the psalm to voice the prayer of repentance he found so difficult to utter on his own. They soaked into his heart, soaked through his spirit, seemed at last to voice his own heart's cry. *Behold, thou desirest truth in the inward being; therefore teach me wisdom in my secret heart.* Was this not at last what Brother Constantine had taught him?

Fletcher did not know what to make of what had happened. Had he really sinned, as his heart told him and his conscience confirmed? If he had not, what was the meaning of his private confession? If he had, was a personal confession adequate? Had he been forgiven? Was he granted absolution? What did it mean that he had performed no penance? Was he reconciled to God? Brother Constantine would say yes. Did he require further action? The priest would say no. Either way, his heart told him there was something that yet remained to be done. Reconciled to God was not enough. The time had come to make confession and ask forgiveness from Elspeth.

Father Thomas removed his pectoral cross and held it up so he could use the polished reverse side as a mirror. His hair was now considerably greyer than it had been when he had been called to this parish. His eyes were deep-set in a replica of his mother's angular patrician face. Lines near the corners of his eyes told him he was less robust than he once had been before he came here, fourteen years prior. His eyesight, he noted, was still clear and sharp, but a slight tremor in his hands blurred the image in the pectoral cross mirror. He had come to the monastery late in life, hoping for a quiet end, but he had discovered that the community was larger than he had been told, that it encompassed also the town and surrounding villages. It was a large responsibility, and he had heard that his predecessor Father Athanasius had succumbed under the burden. He had not. He had so organized his inner life that he could carry out his duties—celebrating mass, preaching, hearing confession—with a clear conscience, and at the end of the day sleep the sleep of the righteous.

Except sometimes. Sometimes what he heard in the confessional brought him to his knees. Today there had been two such moments. Today one of the villagers had confessed to raping his wife—as preposterous an idea as Thomas had ever heard—and then what he had heard from one of the brothers through the screen had so astonished him that at first he had thought the monk had been lying. He knew, of course, the names and stations of both men—he had heard John Fletcher and Brother Constantine in confession for many years—but in deference to the sanctity of the confessional, he schooled himself never to think of confessions with names attached, but instead to discipline his awareness narrowly to the sin, the circumstances, the validity of the confession, and the proper penance leading to forgiveness and the *ego te absolvo* of the absolution.

The monk claimed he had made love to a girl from the village, and had done so within the sacred precinct of the altar. Father Thomas could not conceive of a more grave sacrilege. He was angered that this had happened, but at the same time gratified that the penitent monk had come to him. At first he thought, *Even for this*, but his pastoral consciousness turned the thought to *Especially for this*. What the monk had done had been despicable, but confessing such a thing was an act of sainthood.

He had sent the villager away with a sound theological lesson—hard but right—and in his evening prayers he asked that God would open the man's blind eyes to his proper role as a husband and father.

The monk had come to him late in the day, before Vespers, as he sat silently waiting in the confession booth to the right of the altar in the church. His opening comments had been routine: "Forgive me, Father, for I have sinned." What usually followed was litany of petty infractions against the common good, or the practice of the church, or the clear teaching of the Rule of St Benedict. The monk, his face hidden behind the screen, had lowered his voice so that Thomas had had to ask him to repeat himself. "I have committed a sexual sin with a girl."

"You have what?" asked Thomas, stuttering the question, not trusting his ears. He was so stunned by what the monk told him that at first he had not known how best to proceed. Ordinarily he would ask clarifying questions designed to establish the validity of the sinner's contrition, but in this case he had been flabbergasted, and found himself stammering out his response.

"I have committed the sin of fornication with a girl." The words came more loudly, and Thomas made out that they were halting, as though the sinner had trouble saying them out loud, and yet the diction told him they were well-practiced.

"One time or several?"

"One time, Father.

"Where did this take place?"

"Here, Father, within the church."

Thomas gasped, and for a moment thought he could hear his heart pounding. The tremor in his hands became more pronounced. He had to suppress an urge to leave the confessional, go around to the other booth, take the penitent sinner out of his booth and strangle him there with his own bare hands. Later, reflecting back, he realized that he had such a strong reaction partly out of astonishment and anger, and partly out of shame that such a sacrilege could take place within his own parish. Where had he failed, that such a thing could happen? And yet, the monk was here, facing the truth, asking forgiveness, ready—at least he so claimed—for whatever penance might be assigned him, prostrate before the altar.

"And how, my child, am I to know that your penance is authentic?"

"*Adsum*, Father," said the penitent quietly. "I am here, Father."

"And the girl?" asked Father Thomas. "She was a willing partner in this?" No girl had confessed this to him, and he wondered if there was another troubled soul in need of penance and absolution.

"That I do not know, Father. She was silent. She allowed me to take her without protest." The monk's voice trailed off at this point, and Thomas had to ask again through the screen. "I haven't spoken to her, Father. Not since this happened."

"Do you realize the gravity of what you have confessed?'

"I am prostrate before the altar, Father."

Now, as he readied himself for bed, Thomas looked at himself in the mirrored surface of the pectoral cross and reminded himself of the reasons he ought to take no further action. He held up his fingers as he counted. First, there was the sanctity of the confession booth. Confession and absolution are sacraments, and who was he to question their efficacy or violate their sacred function? To violate the confessional is to imply that the cure of the soul was not fully efficacious—and that was as abhorrent as what the monk had done. Even if the monk were not fully penitent, even if there were further danger to the girl, he could not violate the sanctity of the confessional. Second, what further danger to anyone would there be if the monk were indeed fully penitent? He was as good a judge of character as anyone, and he believed with all his heart that the monk had been fully contrite.

But even as he thought these things, behind them lurked another quandary, this one ethical: What if he misjudged? What if the monk should fall again, in just this way? Would he, Thomas, be responsible, knowing he had done nothing to prevent it? To reassure himself, he reminded himself that he *had* done something—he had imposed a stiff penance. He had sorted the matter out for the monk, and had imposed a stiff penance, and had acted according to the strict instructions of Holy Mother Church.

Throughout these musings, what remained foremost in his mind was the sacrament of confession itself. If he had learned of this in any other way he would have been ethically bound to report the incident immediately to the Prior, possibly even to the sheriff. But the fact that he had learned this in the confessional changed everything. It mattered not one whit if he had misjudged. He would remain silent, even if he was absolutely certain that the monk in question would commit the same sin again. In the end, what settled his conscience was this: Holy Mother Church declared that he must say nothing at all, and there can be no guilt in obedience.

That business settled, he blew out the candle, and climbed into his narrow bed, and slept the sleep of the righteous.

When Constantine went to bed that night, he slept the sleep of the guilty but forgiven. Even so, he could not help but think of the girl who had brought him to this place. What he had done had joined him to her in some important way, and even the disembodied voice of Father Thomas' pronouncement—*ego te absolvo*—could do nothing to change that. They had lain together beneath the golden altar of St Cuthbert's Church, and denying that was like denying the grace of God. It was a connection he could not sever, no matter how important or how hard he tried, but what sort of a connection it was he was unable to grasp. Was this what the scripture meant when it said that the first man and woman had become one flesh? Father Thomas had assigned a hard penance—he was to wear a hair shirt for more than a year, and was to say nothing to anyone about that. The hair-shirt he could endure, but the penance of severing his connection to the girl he felt was now almost beyond imagining. Even the hair-shirt would remind him of her. Perhaps forgetting her was beyond his ability, a task he would find impossible to perform.

After confession he had taken a few moments for himself, and had wandered out to the monastery garden, where he sat on a bench and considered what he had done, and why, and what he must do next. The penance Father had imposed was difficult, but just. Father had shown concern for his soul, had listened intently, had asked probing and right questions.

It was under Father's questioning that he began to realize that the girl had not consented to what they had done, and that he had taken advantage of her at a moment of intense vulnerability. Father had used the word *rape*, but Constantine refused to think that. The word stuck in his throat. Rape. No, it had not been rape. If he himself did not think of it as rape, why did Thomas thinking of it that way make it so?

Father asked if the girl had been a willing participant.

"That I do not know," Constantine replied, adding that he had not spoken with the girl since what had happened had happened.

"When you were finished, did she say anything?"

"Nothing, Father."

"Did she draw herself toward you, or away?"

"Away," Constantine had said.

Now, looking back, he realized that what had happened had not been the girl's wish. If she had consented to the lovemaking, she would have lingered after it was finished, would have gathered herself to him, would have lain close to his chest—instead, she had turned away, and had silently risen and adjusted her clothing, and had left the niche without a word. Even though he could not bring himself to say that what he had done had been a form of rape, the fact that Father Thomas thought of it that way now filled him with shame.

And yet, at the moment that what had happened had happened, in his very depths, what he had experienced had been relief. He had said nothing about that to the priest, but now, considering it, he wondered what it might mean that a man would experience relief after committing such an act of violence against another person.

He considered how Elspeth must feel. Had she felt violated? Used? Misused? And what must she think of him now that he had done what he had done? These were intractable questions, made harder to answer by a certain numbness within him. He thought about David and the 51st psalm. Like Fletcher, he knew that his soul was in grave danger.

He was certain that Thomas would not accuse him. There are very few things a man can be sure of; this was one. And the girl had not yet accused him, despite the passage of several weeks. Or—if she had accused him—to her father, to Levente, to Alcera—that fact was not yet made public, a hopeful sign. It occurred to him that she still might turn up pregnant, in which case her belly would accuse him, and he wondered if it would be best for him to quit the monastery and leave before that might happen. He had violated his vows already, had he not?

He thought about the prophet Nathan accusing David before the court and the Lord God: "You're the man!" Would that happen to him? He pictured Elspeth coming to him, accusing him in public: "You, Constantine, you're the man. You, Constantine, have abused me. You, Constantine, have taken from me something that is mine, that is precious, that you cannot restore to me. You, Constantine, have gotten me with child. You, Constantine, have raped me beneath the high altar of St Cuthbert's Church!" Perhaps in doing what he had done, he had quit the monastery already.

In the distant west the sunset cast an orange-red glow across the horizon, thinning and tapering, and rapidly disappearing to the south and north. As Constantine sat, he became aware of a certain shimmering in the light, and at first he had the uncanny sense that the orange-red glow of the sun had settled itself among the Brother Johann's rose bushes. He threw a rock at the shimmering, and a dragon appeared among the roses. The image was fleeting, a thin outline, but unmistakable nonetheless.

"Go away!" he said, but the dragon did not move. "Go away," he said again. "I'm done with you." The dragon appeared completely, and moved closer to him. He threw another rock, harder this time, but the dragon came to him with the apparent loyalty of a hunting dog.

He reached out and ran his fingers along the scales of the animal's neck. "You have to leave," he said quietly, rubbing hard behind its pointed ears. The dragon leaned into the rubbing, cooing and clucking as it did so, and he had the sense that it really was tame after all, but of course that could not be true. "I can't keep you, there's no place for you here." As he said this, he was filled with an inconsolable sense of loss, as though he were sending away a beloved puppy. The dragon responded with more cooing, a contented pet responding to its master. He warmed his hands at the animal's breath.

This session lasted until well after dark, and was interrupted only by the bells of Compline that signaled the monks to gather for the divine office.

Now, the hymns of Compline still ringing in his ears, he lay in his bed and tried not to think about Elspeth's smooth skin. He tried not to think about her luminous dark eyes, or the sweet smell of her hair. He tried hard not to think about the pleasure he had taken in the tiny movements of her body as she sat beside him in the niche.

XIII

Alcera was sitting at the table, eating her breakfast of long-bread and cheese, washing it down with goat's milk from a pitcher, when she heard Elspeth groan in her bed. She turned to look, but the girl's face was buried beneath her bedcovering. When she groaned again, Alcera rose and went to her side, pulling back the covering to expose her face.

Elspeth opened her eyes and looked her. The look in her eyes reminded Alcera of a deer she had once seen in the woods. The deer, frozen, had looked back, taking her in with large, dark eyes, luminous, probing eyes, eyes that had seemed to concentrate the whole life of the animal into two points. It was only later, looking back, that she realized that the look in the eyes was fear.

That was the look Alcera saw in Elspeth's eyes. The girl was afraid. Her body, like the body of the deer, was somehow both still and quivering. She was afraid.

She felt the girl's forehead for a fever. "You're sick."

"I think I've got the flu," said Elspeth unsteadily. "My head hurts."

Alcera sat down beside her and looked her in the eyes again. "Your breasts," she said, "how do they feel?"

"Sore," Elspeth said. "What kind of flu leaves your breasts sore?"

"When was your last cycle?" asked Alcera.

"Six weeks ago," said Elspeth. "It came again two weeks ago, but was spotty. Hardly anything." Elspeth's eyes widened again. The fear was deepening. "Why are you asking me this?"

Alcera sat back in the chair. "Well, if this isn't a fine kettle of fish," she said. Then she sat there, twisting and untwisting a strand of her grey hair, waiting. "I may owe your father an apology." She paused a moment, then reconsidered. "Or maybe not. The son of a bitch."

"What do you mean?" asked Elspeth.

"Because you're not sick," Alcera said. "You're pregnant."

Caput tertianum

BOOK THREE

XIV

ELSPETH HAD BEEN STUNNED by what Alcera said to her. How could she be pregnant? But it remained so incredibly painful and confusing that even now, days after she had received this terrible news, she was left completely numb, reduced to a stupor. She had had a spotty flow, she could not be pregnant. But what if Alcera were right. *My life is over. Everything is gone.* More than that: Her mother had died in childbirth. Would she?

A rooster crowed in the yard.

"So who did this?" asked Alcera. The old woman was puttering about the bed, trying to knead some softness into the straw pillows. She had said nothing for two days, but apparently felt that the time for silence was over.

"Nobody," said Elspeth. Her head was filled with flax, un-spun, un-worked. What kind of answer was that? Nobody would believe that she had been with Constantine. She thought about the village boys, and the others in the town. They would not believe a story about a monk any more than their parents would. She groaned when she realized what that would mean, that they would think she was now free for the taking.

"You and the Blessed Virgin!" Alcera said.

"What?" She tried sitting up, but could not find the energy.

"People are going to talk, Elspeth. Sooner or later, you're going to start to show, and then people are going to talk. And you know what they're going to say? About you? About your baby? If you tell who the father is, it'll be easier for you. The boy'll have to step up and take responsibility. If you don't, they're going to guess, and they're going to guess it was your father. If it was, well and good. He should face the music same as any man who does this to his daughter, but if not, they'll blame Levente. Are you ready for that?"

"It wasn't my father, Alcera," Elspeth said softly. "It wasn't my father."

"Listen, Els . . ." Alcera said.

"It wasn't Levente, either," Elspeth said.

"I know that," Alcera said. "You stay put here. We'll deal with what comes when it comes. You're not alone."

Brother Constantine had experienced the priest's blessing with an almost shocked relief. He believed with all his heart that when his penance was completed he would be fully reconciled with God, his great sin forgiven. What could that mean but a new start, like returning to the beginning of a celestial chess game, his missing pieces restored?

He rose from his bed and went to the window, glancing about for a sign of the dragon. Nothing. No shimmering in the half-light. No subtle movement as the animal breathed. No scales dropped as the animal had shed. He was free, completely, from what he had done. The dragon was gone.

He went to the wash basin and poured fresh water, intending to begin his morning ablutions, when heard a man shouting something in the distance, the voice coming from the street. He slipped from his cell and made his way out to the foregate, where a number of the brothers and novices gathered in the arched and corbelled doorway, watching as one of the villagers upbraided a woman. He had seen the couple in church sometimes, but did not know their names. They usually sat apart, bolt upright like a pair of cornstalks.

She must have been about thirty years old, but looked older and more careworn than a woman of thirty should look, her hair unkempt and dirty, her cotton dress torn and patched. As he arrived in the fore gate, she was raising herself from the ground. He could not tell if she had fallen or had been knocked down by a blow. The man—her husband, probably—lowered over her, threatening her with his fist, and shouting obscenities.

"What happened?" he whispered to one of Brother Paul, who was wiping his hands with a towel and watching with a look of almost angelic detachment.

"She was driving the cart," he said. "Something spooked the horse, and they drove off the path."

Constantine looked again. Behind the couple, barely visible over the hump of the roadway, he could see the outline of an overturned vegetable cart. Beyond the cart, a lone swaybacked horse was struggling to regain its footing.

He moved out of the doorway and into the road, not knowing exactly what to do, but believing that someone should intervene, somehow, but was stopped by Brother Paul, who grabbed the sleeve of his robe forcefully enough that the cloth tore.

"Don't," Brother Paul said. "He's sovereign in his own house."

Constantine broke free. "King but not pope," he said. "There are limits to his rights." He stepped into the middle of the fracas, taking on his own face a blow that had been intended for the woman. The husband, startled at this sudden intrusion and shocked that he had struck a man of God, hesitated long enough for Constantine to turn and assist the woman to her feet. "Leave her alone," he said to the man. She brushed herself off, smoothing her dress as best she could. Tears tracked streaming lines in the dust that covered her face.

The man doubled his fist again but hesitated, Constantine later thought, because he must have had reservations about striking one of the brothers. Who knew what evil would come of striking a man of God? The man retreated to the wagon. Brother Paul and two or three of the novices rushed past, intending, Constantine supposed, to assist with the rigging and the spilled load of vegetables.

For a moment he was left alone with the woman. "Come and see me after mass," he said quietly, reaching out to touch her bruised lip, already swelling and trickling blood. "I know a place where you can hide."

Later that night, after the monks had completed their communical prayers and had settled down to sleep, Constantine lay troubled on his bed, his head filled with images of the man and his beaten, beaten-down wife. Nothing she might have done deserved the thrashing he had given her.

He lay silently back against his hard pillow, resting his head on his right hand, and pictured the woman's tears, hot and dirty, and wished he could have borne them on his own face the way he had borne the brunt of her husband's blow. He pictured his own fingers, smoothing the furrows from her troubled forehead, his fingertips gently sweeping along the ridge of bone above her eyes, then along the soft edges to the tender skin near the inner corners of her eye-sockets, then along the rough plane of her cheeks. He tasted her saline tears as though they were his own. For a moment he thought he loved her.

The experience of relief that followed drew him in so gently that he found it overwhelming and was unable to resist. In his mind's eye he saw the woman's battered lip, swollen and bleeding from the force of her husband's blow, and he wanted to touch it again, to place his own lips upon it and bring it healing.

It was days before Elspeth could bring herself to think about her situation, but as the numbness wore off, her first reaction was that this was something she would have to endure alone. In a sense, that was right. Who would be there for her? Alcera? Levente? It might very well be that their care for her was based on a certain belief about who she was, what sort of character she had. The pregnancy would destroy that, and then what would they think of her? What would they do when their idea of her came crashing down around her? What about Constantine? Would he come forward and share in her trials? Would her father?

Alcera was surely right. She was not alone in this. The whole village was involved. But Alcera had meant something else: If she did not name the baby's father, people would blame her own father. Rightly, wrongly, wouldn't matter to the knife-tongued gossips in the village. People would think what they would think, say what they would say, and if it went too far it could no longer matter what had actually happened, the end result would be the same as if it were all true. Or maybe they would say that she had no morals, that she slept around. She could hear the wags in the village saying that she couldn't name the father because she didn't know who the father was.

Her father would side with them! Her father had been angry, cruel even, but he had not molested her. He had called her names, and maybe these had proven to be true. If he knew what had really happened, that this had all started when she had allowed herself to be kissed by a monk, he would say that she had brought this upon herself, and maybe even that she had seduced Constantine. Is this what happens when a woman seduces a man? Her father told her once that a man could not help himself, and now he would say that being alone with him was an invitation to what had happened. Had she done that? Had she invited him?

So in the end—or near the end—she thought that in all the world she was most alone, but that thought was immediately subverted by another: She carried a baby—they were in this together. She thought about the baby—who knew what it was like? Girl? Boy? Twins even? How long did she have left before everything in her life changed out from under her?

What would the child bring to her, and what would it cost? She imagined herself alone then, suckling the baby in the darkness, but what she could not imagine was the room in which this would take place. Her father would disown her. Levente and Alcera? She was not sure of them, either, especially if she refused to identify the father. For them to keep her would imply a confession on Levente's part, and she did not know if he would be willing to live with that undeserved consequence.

Perhaps she should run, but where? And how could she do that, carrying a child? The baby had not been wanted, and for a moment she had the feeling that the presence inside her was a hostile one, an accuser growing there inside her, that she carried within herself the seed of her own destruction.

In the weeks that followed, Constantine deepened in his sense that he was forgiven for his sin. The prayer of David had been his prayer, too, but while he knew in his rational mind he should focus on what he had done to Elspeth, he could not drag his attention away from a deeper sin, an older one, and maybe that was the real reason he had gone to Father Thomas for confession. It had something to do with his shame at what one of the knights had done to him, but he was unclear about what that was. There was a dim recollection of relief when he had been released to the care of the monks at the monastery of St Cuthbert and St Chad.

Now, looking back at that, he realized that what the knight had done to him had been behind the relief he had felt when . . . when what had happened with Elspeth had happened. The knight had not been mean-spirited, but the contact had been unwanted, and he had felt shamed by it. Then he was ashamed of feeling badly because the knight had protected him from the wagon driver, and maybe other men in the cavalcade, and had asked nothing in return except to touch him, and so he let him have his way and said nothing.

How old had he been when this happened? Seven, maybe. What options does a seven-year-old have anyway? In the end, the humiliation of what was happening was less frightening than the threats the driver had made, but the contact with the knight continued for weeks as the cavalcade rumbled west across northern Europe toward England. Why had that experience come back to him now, and why did it seem connected to his sense of relief about what he had done with the girl? This was something he would wrestle with for a long while.

So the thing that had happened with the knight was part of it, but not all. There was something else, too, an experience of some kind, something he could only tease out of the back of his mind the way he might tease a loose hair from one of the inkwells in his scriptorium. He imagined his mind was a thread, and the problem a needle, and he pictured himself wetting the thread with his tongue and trying to shape it into a sharp, fine point. The problem had something to do with the red-faced man who had hurt him, and then after that, the knight. The red-faced man had driven that wagon, the one with the dragon in it. The wagon had belonged to this knight, a large, well-muscled man. But as strong as the knight had been, he had had tender eyes, eyes that seemed to see everything, and he was strong and had kept him safe. The knight had watched out for him.

Constantine had been afraid to get back into the wagon because of the dragon and perhaps more importantly because of who the driver was. Instead, he walked alongside the cavalcade with the other boys, trying hard to keep up and equally hard not to cry because he still hurt from what the wagon driver had done to him.

That was when he had met the knight. George, he had called himself. This must have been forty years ago. George? Was he remembering right? *Never mind,* he thought, *that doesn't matter. His name doesn't matter.* "Have trouble there?" the knight had said in broken but understandable Hungarian. Constantine had been aware that he had ridden out from the cavalcade and had watched the group of boys for more than a mile, but Constantine's attention was focused more on keeping up with the others, and his awareness of the knight had been barely more than a glance. Finally, Constantine was aware of the creaking of saddle leather, and the fact that the knight had ridden up alongside him.

"Have trouble there?" the knight said again.

"Can't walk very well," he said.

"Climb here, saddle," the knight said. He took his foot out of the stirrup, leaving it empty for Constantine to use. "Your foot in thing, see?" He reached down and took Constantine by the hand, but Constantine was too short to reach the stirrup. The knight, realizing this, had simply hauled him up by his arm and settled him into the saddle in front of him. Constantine remembered his amazement at the man's strength. "You hurt," George said. "What happen you?"

Glad for once to be with someone who would look out for him, Constantine began a long monologue about the red-faced man and the wagon and the dragon. Looking back from the vantage point of his adult knowledge, he realized that he had probably rambled, but the road was long and the knight had had no reason to cut the story short. When he was finished, the knight had reached down and taken him by the chin, turning his face gently upward. "It not have to hurt," he said. "Later on, I show you. Not tonight. You heal first. When you better, I show you. It not have to hurt."

He was older. Eleven, maybe. Perhaps twelve. He was a student in the monastery school. After their arrival in England, the Hungarian boys had been parceled out to various homes and monasteries, which was how he had ended up in the Monastery of St Cuthbert and St Chad. It was a Sunday morning, and the priest had mounted the rostrum to deliver his sermon. He remembered the day as a cold one, because the church was hard to heat and the children and other parishioners had had to bring wraps and blankets to supplement their thin coats during mass. He and his friends sat like a line of chessmen in one of the rear pews—all pawns except for Brother Basil the schoolmaster, who sat erect at the end of the aisle, looking like the bishop, ready to make them pay if they missed anything. The boys wriggled beneath their blankets and listened to Father Athanasius preach. In this they were unlike the village boys, who jostled one another and sometimes behaved in the most inappropriate ways. For one thing, they had been told that God expected more of them because they were learning to read, and for another, they were aware that Brother Basil would examine them in the morning on the subject of Father's sermon. The subject of the examination would not be Father Athanasius' theology—Basil said they were not old enough to understand theology—but his Latin. *That* he could test.

When Father announced his text at the beginning of his sermon, Constantine knew he was in trouble. This was from the Letter of the Holy Apostle Paul to the Romans, which everybody said was filled with difficult constructions and unusual vocabulary words. He strained to listen, noticing out of the corner of his eye that some of the other boys were mouthing the words of the text silently beside him. Brother Basil did not allow them copybooks. This would come by memory only.

Athanasius was aging, but his voice was clear and high-pitched in the cold air of the sanctuary: "*Propterea tradidit illos Deus in passiones ignominiae nam feminae eorum inmutaverunt naturalem usum in eum usum qui est contra naturam,*" he read. Constantine, moving his lips like the other boys, tried to put that into proper English. There was something about God giving people up to dishonorable passions. Then something about women exchanging natural relations for unnatural ones—he assumed that was relations with men, but who knew?—and then something that stuck out hard in his mind: "... *Masculi in masculos turpitudinem operantes.*" He ran through the words quickly: "Men. Committing. Shameless. Acts. With. Men...." What followed this was a long list of evil character traits, coming at him faster than he could translate, but with cumulative effect because Athanasius was punctuating them with an upraised forefinger and roaring down from the elevated station of the rostrum.

Athanasius then launched his sermon, also in Latin, which was easier to follow because he was only a town priest, and was not actually very skilled with the language of the Church. The sermon seemed interminable, but it focused down hard on the boys because—Athanasius seemed to believe—boys are naturally incorrigible and prone to trouble.

The sermon ended with a flourish. After elaborating the character flaws in the intervening verses, Athanasius turned in to the end to the end of the passage: "*Qui cum iustitiam Dei cognovissent non intellexerunt quoniam qui talia agunt digni sunt morte ....*" Even in his broken translation, the Apostle's meaning was unmistakable, a bludgeon to Constantine's twelve-year-old mind: "Those who do such things deserve to die!"

Constantine remembered this moment as one of supreme horror. His mind had caught a glimpse of the body of his father, near the entrance of the root cellar. And his brother Cristian, and Ildiko weeping, and the village going up in flames, and his mother's body in the well. He saw the knight, George, tied to a stake, burning for what he had done.

"To die!" Athanasius said again, raising his voice for emphasis. "But the Holy Apostle does not mean physical death, oh, no! It is worse than your most fearful imaginings! He means the death of both body and soul. Those who do such things deserve the fires of hell!" By this time his voice was trembling, and Constantine had trembled, too. He remembered his village in Moldavia going up in flames, and burned bodies. Was that what made Athanasius tremble? Was it anger? Was it fear for those among his parishioners who had yet to repent, and make confession, and do their penance, and receive their absolution?

Constantine thought again about the knight George, and the way he had touched him, what he had done to him, and the image of George at the stake returned with shattering vengeance.

"His confessional'll be busy this week," whispered one of the other boys as they filed out of the sanctuary along the south ambulatory. Everybody laughed. Everybody but Constantine.

Later, in a private conversation at the back of the classroom, he confided to Brother Basil that he thought he might enter the monastery and give his life to God. That moment had been a moment of relief, too, not unlike this one. He had not had to work hard to suppress the unspoken question in the middle of his decision to become a monk; the question had gone into hiding, like the young dragon he had seen in the knight's wagon. Hard to see. Elusive. But a powerful presence nonetheless. Was he one of those who commit shameful acts with men, and if so, would he burn in the fires of hell because of what had happened with the knight? Did he deserve to die?

Constantine and Fletcher were sitting in the nave of the church. Their conversations had covered a variety of topics, all of them related to his gradually healing relationship with his daughter or his memories of Alysse. Many times Constantine had tried to broach some subject, but always had backed down.

Finally, Constantine raised the issue point-blank: "I've been wanting to ask you something for a long time, John, but have never found the moment just right." He said this slowly, almost cautiously, as though he were feeling his way in the dark.

"Ask, then." By this time Fletcher seemed to have developed a deep trust in his spiritual guide. Nothing that he had said to him had damaged the sense that that the two of them were working together toward a common goal. Nothing Constantine had said had made John feel judged or condemned or belittled. The monk had kept his confidences as faithfully as a priest keeps confessions.

A single piece remained un-addressed. Constantine raised the question. Fletcher had assented to the question, so Constantine asked point blank: "Why won't you talk to me in the church?"

John had been expecting the question, but even so had not formulated an answer. This last piece of the puzzle remained unsolved, even for him. He looked in the direction of the niche that held the statue of the Blessed Virgin. "It has to do with her," he said simply.

"With the Virgin Mary?" asked Constantine. "What about her?"

"Look at her real close, Constantine," said Fletcher.

Constantine tried hard to see what it was that Fletcher had seen in the statue, but he could not. "What am I supposed to see there?" he asked.

"She looks just like Alysse," said Fletcher.

"No."

"Identical. The two women could've been sisters."

Constantine looked again, more closely, but the connection apparently eluded him. "I'm sorry, John," he said. "I can't see it. How old did you say Alysse was when she died?"

"Nineteen."

"What about the statue in particular reminds you of Alysse?"

"Nothing in particular, really," said Fletcher. *The girl who had posed for the statue might have been about that age*, he thought. Her coloring would have been the same, too, but that was because most of the young women in that part of the shire had similar coloring. "What reminds me is the whole of it. The serenity. The look of contentment she seems to feel. The deep satisfaction she felt in young motherhood."

"But you never knew Alysse as a young mother."

"I mean, the satisfaction I imagine she would've had."

"But you told me she was pregnant because you forced her. She did not choose that child."

"I did say that, didn't I?"

"You said you had raped her."

Fletcher shook his head. "You said that. What I said was worse."

"So why do you think you associated the two women?"

"I connected the two women, not because of the ways they were similar, but because of their differences."

"Go on," said Constantine.

"Alysse was a woman violated, but the Virgin was, was . . . the virgin. I suppose I must've thought that if I connected the two women, I could think of Alysse as a virgin, too. You know. Somebody pure, somebody who hadn't been raped."

"And in that way you could forget who raped her."

"What?" said Fletcher.

"You buried your own guilt by thinking of Alysse as the Blessed Virgin Mary. It wasn't that you imposed Alysse's image on the Virgin, but that you imposed the Virgin's image on Alysse. You knew it was a sacrilege, but you didn't know that that was covering up a worse sin you were unable to face."

"My God. What I have done?"

"The question is, what do we do about this now?" asked Constantine.

Fletcher looked at the statue, really looked at it. The image of Alysse, the powerful, nearly mystical connection he had often seen there, was gone and the statue was just a statue of a nineteen-year-old girl.

It was Monday. Elspeth was stitching quires in Levente's shop. Two of Levente's commissions were being readied for shipment, and Levente, uncharacteristically, was hurrying the work.

Levente and Alcera stood and made their way to the door. "I have to see Constantine in the scriptorium," said Levente. "Alcera has to take the measurement from one of the wives of Warwick. We should be gone for the better part of the afternoon."

Elspeth nodded that she understood, and continued work on the stack of quires she had arranged before her on the table. Her work was simple to describe, but difficult to do nicely—punching tiny holes in the vellum, then stitching the individual sheets into the finished quires. Over the years she had grown expert with the awl.

As she worked, she thought about her father. Her recent contact with him had been restricted to church, and to those inevitable brief encounters as they passed one another in the street. Most often they exchanged nothing more than the greetings and tidbits of gossip that usually passed for conversation between neighbors who lived after all in the same tiny hamlet in the English countryside. A passing stranger would not have thought they were related. More than once she considered telling him about the pregnancy, but she could not find the words, and she was afraid that their still fragile relationship would erupt again into anger. He would find out soon enough. She shuddered at what he would do then. She did not understand him.

Thus that surface impression of casual indifference belied the deeper, keener anguish that also attended their meetings in the street. In the months following the incident at the bivouac Elspeth had seen a deep sorrow developing within her father. He had lost something of himself, as though the vitality had been drained out of him like honey from a cracked pot. His frame, once large and robust, began to wane; his clothing began to sag, and it became clear that he was losing weight. His skin became sallow, and the spark that had often played through his crystalline black eyes seemed to fade like the setting sun. Elspeth began to wonder if she was watching the sun set on her father's life itself.

Then something remarkable had begun to happen to him; even from the distance Elspeth could see it. Among the villagers, only she and Sarabeth noted the regular visits her father had been making to the monastery. Only they noticed that the waning of her father's life had begun to reverse itself. He seemed more in control. The spark in his eyes returned. He stopped drinking.

As transforming as this whole process was, the sorrow remained throughout, a constant reminder that John the Fletcher was at odds with himself, that something within his inner life was not at peace.

Elspeth did not know how to relate to these shifting impressions of her father. On the one hand she was concerned that the losses he seemed to be experiencing were somehow irreparable losses, and she regretted that so much tragedy had come to this man who had brought her into the world. On the other hand, she remained wary, unable to trust that her father would ever be healed of the deep and festering wound God had inflicted upon him.

Throughout this period, Elspeth remained guarded, reminding herself of the dangerous ways in which her father treated her through the years, but especially since last spring, when the dragon had emerged, connected in some mysterious way with her father's rapid changes of mood. She thought about the earliest appearances of the dragon. She thought about the beatings. She thought about the times her father had blamed her for things he himself had done. She remembered the events at the bivouac.

With all of these memories swirling through her head, with her deeply mixed emotions and her inability to trust that her father's intentions toward her were good, it is understandable that she was hesitant when her father appeared at the door of the shop that Monday afternoon.

"Can I come in?" Fletcher asked.

"Nobody's stopping you," replied the girl sullenly, but even as she did this, she looked around him for the reassuring presence of Alcera and Levente, but then remembered that they were on errands for the afternoon. She was alone with him, a situation she found uncomfortable, and apparently unavoidable, now that he stood there in the only doorway. She stopped and looked at him, and palmed the awl in a gesture that she would hoped would call his attention. She did not want to be alone with him. "Levente and Alcera will be back at any moment."

"Elspeth, I've worried about you."

Did he know she was pregnant? He had worried about her before, but how had that turned out? She continued to work on the quire, steadily drawing the thick, stout thread through the neat row of holes she had punched with the awl. "I eat three meals a day. I've got clothes on my back. I'm learning a trade."

"That's part of why I came to see you," said Fletcher. "I've got something to say to you, and I want to get it said it before you leave."

Elspeth set down her needle and thread and put the quire to one side. "I'm listening," she said. She would listen, though she also kept a respectful distance from her father. What her mind did not remember of the beatings, her muscles did, so that her whole body tensed up at what was coming. There was no telling what her father would say, or what it would cost her. She glanced around for the awl and then furtively through the window for Levente or Alcera.

"I want to make a confession," said Fletcher.

Elspeth heard that with astonishment. Her father had never before confessed any sin to her, much less any shortcoming, or any error of judgment. "Go on," she said simply.

Her father hesitated. "Can I sit down?" he asked.

Elspeth said nothing.

Fletcher pulled around one of the chairs that stood near a wall. Elspeth hesitated: "You want to confess to me that you beat your daughter, you can save your breath. I already know that."

"I was trying to be a good father to you," said Fletcher.

Elspeth considered telling him to get out. "You almost killed me," she said simply. "How was that being a good father?"

"It wasn't. I know that now. I was caught up in something I didn't understand. I understand that better now," he said, "thanks to Brother Constantine."

"Brother Constantine?" She shuddered at the thought of that. What had Constantine told him about her? About what they had done in the niche?

"He's been helping me sort myself out." He shifted uncomfortably in his seat.

"Like your dragon?" asked Elspeth. She was relieved, and then confused, unsure of where her father was intending to take the conversation, but was determined not to allow him to avoid acknowledging his role in the difficulties that plagued the two of them.

"Like my dragon," agreed Fletcher.

Elspeth was startled again. This was the first time her father had acknowledged that the dragon had been his, and she was caught off guard. What had Constantine said to him?

"Tell me about the dragon, father," she said.

"I'm not sure how this connection is made, Elspeth, but I think the dragon appears whenever I get angry or frightened. It seems to be drawn to those emotions. I've seen that in dragons before."

"In the dragon Levente's father kept?"

"How do you know about that?" asked Fletcher.

"Alcera told me about it months ago," said the girl. She was thinking of the time they had talked in Levente's shop about the scales and the destruction of her father's hut.

"Well, yes," said Fletcher, apparently not wanting to be distracted from his primary intention. "Like Levente's father's dragon. When this one appeared, I thought it was yours, and I blamed you for it."

"Which is why you beat me?" said the girl. It wasn't so much a question as it was a conclusion.

"There was more to the beatings than my anger at you, Elspeth," said Fletcher. "That's what I came to confess to you."

"Go on." Elspeth was now curious, but her anxiety was growing very deep. Every time the dragon had come up in a conversation with her father there had been a beating. The beatings were undeserved, and she now knew for certain that her father knew that too.

"I don't know how to say this, Elspeth, so I'm going to be blunt. I hope you will forgive me."

"What? What do you not know how to say?" Elspeth could see her father's palms sweating. Her father was normally so brutally direct—direct that is, when he spoke, if he spoke at all. This time he looked away, avoiding eye contact.

"I was unkind to your mother," he said. "I don't want to talk about the details. There isn't anything served by you knowing what I did or why, but there were times when I was cruel to her."

"You beat her?"

Her father said nothing, but the look on his face was enough.

"The way you beat me?"

"Worse."

"More than once?"

"More than once, though once was once too many."

"But you always spoke of her so lovingly," said Elspeth, cautiously.

"I owed her that. After the way I treated her, the least I could do would be to remember her well. Especially to you."

"Then why did she want to make a child with you? Why did she allow you to touch her?"

"She didn't," Fletcher said quietly. He looked away.

Elspeth stood up and moved away from him. "What are you saying?"

"I forced her," he said.

"And I'm the result? Is that what you're telling me? I'm an accident, an unexpected consequence of a fit of anger? Is that what you're saying? That I'm a freak here, too?"

"It wasn't like that," he said.

Elspeth was shocked and confused by her father's attempt to clear the air. More than anything, she was reeling with the discovery that her father had beaten her mother, that he had taken her against her will, that she herself was an accident, unwanted even by her mother. Then suddenly everything spun out of control, and at the same time everything came suddenly clear, while her mind and heart and belly were filled with a surge of anger. She saw her father's eyes, and the dragon's eyes, and the shadow of the dragon at the bivouac, and her mother, as much as she had been told of her mother, and her father beating her, and the terrible things he had said to her and the bullying, raging way he had hit her and hit her and hit her.

"Go to the devil," she said to her father then. "Get out of my sight. I don't ever want to see you again." She stood up and grabbed one of the heavy bookbinder's vises and threw it at him, threw it as hard and as furiously as she could. This was the final straw. Her father had sinned, had sinned against her and against her mother and now he wanted absolution. Well, he would receive no absolution from her, not without penance, not without groveling—not ever.

"Get out of here," she shouted. "I hate you."

"What's got into you?" he said.

"I'm pregnant," she said. "You happy now? Where were you when I needed you? Now I'm pregnant, and I don't have to explain that to you, and I don't ever want to see you again, now get out," and then before he could react, she stormed past him out of Levente's shop, not stopping to gather her cloak against the cold, slamming the door behind her.

Despite the cold, Fletcher was sweating by the time he reached the monastery. Constantine would not see him when he demanded entrance at the monastery gate. "Tell John that I have responsibilities in the scriptorium this morning," he said when the guard reported that Fletcher had come in a high state of agitation. "Ask him if anyone is in physical danger. If not, tell him I will see him in the refectory after the noon meal. If there is danger, bring him to me."

When the noon meal was completed Constantine found Fletcher waiting at the refectory door for the brothers to move along to their afternoon tasks. His demeanor told the story of a man torn between eagerness to talk and reticence to talk where he would be overheard.

Constantine summoned him into the room. Fletcher said nothing until they were seated and Constantine had led in silent, centering prayer—a terribly difficult act given Fletcher's obvious agitation.

"I've ruined everything with my daughter," he said at last.

"Why do you say that?" asked Constantine. "Tell me what happened."

Fletcher told the whole story—his attempt to apologize, the admission that he had beaten Alysse, his confession that he had beaten the girl out of anger for himself, the resulting flash of anger the girl had shown, and the disastrous way the conversation had ended.

"She's pregnant, Constantine."

Constantine's heart stopped. "Do you know who the father is? Maybe one of the village boys."

"She won't talk to me."

"John, did you do this?"

"Maybe, when I was drunk. I have a memory, but it's sketchy. I remember reaching for the top button of her night-dress." Constantine experienced this with terrific relief. If she had been molested by her father, then he was maybe out of the woods. Then he realized what a demonic thought *that* was—to hope that she had been molested twice. He stood and rushed from the church, not caring that John Fletcher might put two and two together and work out what had really happened.

None of that mattered.

He had to see Elspeth.

He needed to explain to her what had happened, to set things right with her, to figure out what to do about the baby. But he was aware that even though she had not accused him to the authorities, she had resisted being alone with him, a fact that now filled him with shame. In a terrible sense, he had wanted to be her rescuer and had ended up becoming her monster.

His fingers were numb from the cold. The sun was high, but a biting wind cut through the coat he wore, so that the mantle of snow that in other circumstances might have seemed pristine, at that moment seemed sinister. The sunlight glinted hard, and his eyes hurt.

He waited for the bells that tolled Vespers, then slipped into the monastery wine cellar unobserved, hoping to drain off a flagon of ale, something harder if he could find it. Ale he did not find; what he found was brandy. He slipped a bottle from its rack and made his way out into the dark. By the time he had reached the edge of the town the bottle was nearly empty. He stumbled uncertainly to a place beneath the bridge that crossed the river, where he tossed back the last of the brandy in a single swallow. The brandy went down Constantine's throat smooth and searing, filling him with a sense of power and strength and fire in his belly. The bottle went into the river.

He was protected only slightly from the wind by the enclosure of the bridge, and he had only his woolen cassock and the hood of his habit to shield his back against the dampness and chill of the water, so that his very body seemed permeated with frost. He shuddered with the penetrating depth of the cold. He pulled his woolen cassock close around himself, thanked God for the comfort of the brandy, and tried to sleep.

He did not sleep well beneath the bridge. He felt the brandy ebbing through him like steaming molasses, washing away any thoughts of Fletcher, of Elspeth, of the baby. He tried to think in words, and instead saw only pictures, slow-moving pictures, with blurred edges. He drifted into a terrible fitful dream, a dream of tar and bats' wings and dragon's breath and flight. The dream was beautiful and terrifying, and the terror seemed to flow through him like the brandy, a slow, hot, searing river, coursing down through his veins to his fingertips.

But through the river, deeper than the river, there ran a current of sweetness, too. He dreamed he could fly, and in his flight he was powerful and free and unencumbered, just as his moral compasses—the constraining forces of his vows, and his loyalty to his brother monks, and his anguish at what he had done to Elspeth—were left behind in his human body and he knew, or at least felt, that he could do or be whatever he chose without having to answer to the priest or the prior or the pontiff. Without his moral compasses, his actions were neither right nor wrong. For a monk to feel that free, even for a moment, was exhilarating, and for Constantine to be free of the anguish of his guilt over what he had done to Elspeth, all of it wrapped him in a blanket of terrible and terrifying power. But the power came at an incalculable price. It cost him his sense of being human, and bound him up in a body with scales and wings and claws, the terror of being trapped in a reality not his own. His thought processes lost entirely the clarity of words, and then, without words, he was thinking with all the hungers and energies and passions of something not human; he thought with pictures, fears, and rage. The terror was that he could not get free of the dragon's body. He clawed at the scales, but it was like clawing at his own flesh; the horror penetrated even into the marrow of his bones.

Worst of all, when he flew, in his talons he carried the body of the girl, carried it to a lair high in the mountains, and laid it across a dragon's hoard of carcasses and skeletons of forest creatures and farm animals.

Then he forgot everything. He forgot Moldavia and the root cellar. He forgot Ildiko, and Cristian, and his parents, and the red faced man, and the knight. He forgot the baby, he forgot the girl, he forgot the skills of lettering and making books in the scriptorium, he forgot the town of Warwick and the Monastery of St Cuthbert and St Chad, he forgot his own name, he forgot that he had ever even had a name. He no longer knew that his actions were neither right nor wrong; they were just actions, driven by the angers and hungers inside him. It was not simply that he could not remember no matter how hard he tried, but rather that he forgot having forgotten, so that except for the girl, such things were completely swallowed up in the appalling reality of the dragon.

"Fletcher!" The voice belonged to Caedmon. "John Fletcher!" He had left the monastery and was making his way across the foregate when he was accosted by the sheriff's man, Caedmon. He wanted to throw up, but found that he needed all of his energies to focus on what Caedmon was telling him. "Fletcher, the sheriff wants to see you. He said something about the dragon having been spotted again. Said to come directly."

"Tell Ranulf I'm coming. I've got to get my cross-bow."

It took him an hour to arrange for a riding horse and a pack-animal, and arm himself with spear, a crossbow with a quiver of bolts, and a longbow and arrows. He rode out alone, without even stopping to confer with Ranulf.

He stopped by Wharram to tell Elspeth where he was, but she was not at the hut. She was not with Levente and Alcera, either, but he left word—it was the best he could do—and then rode out alone to see if he could not put an end once and for all to the dragon.

It was harder than he expected. He was an experienced hunter, and had often faced danger without flinching, but even so, he was over-come by an indefinable but very palpable sense of dread. The fact that he did not know where Elspeth was pulled hard inside his head. He refused to allow himself to consider what might happen if the dragon should return while he was gone, and yet he had not been able to stay in Wharram to protect her.

He left Wharram without even asking where the dragon had been spotted, and instead followed a hunch that drove against the inside of his skull like a hard wind, shoving him forward. Or maybe it pulled against him the way a magnet draws metal to itself, an inner compass. Whatever it was, he found his body moving with a kind of forceful-ness and directness that would have been normal if he were making his normal rounds, or moving along a path he had traveled before, but seemed strange on a hunt for the dragon he had no way of tracking. It disturbed him that he was following hunches, attending to strong intuitive leadings that took him into territory that should have been completely foreign, but that left him with the strange sense of having traveled there before.

He teased out that thread. His mind's eye remembered this path, but from a different perspective. As he worked the path through the countryside, he realized that it was not the path itself that was strange, so much as the ground–level awareness of the path. He had seen it, or maybe dreamed it, from above.

After four hours, maybe five, the path turned upward, and he could see above him a series of switchbacks stitching a ragged line up the side of a mountain. The grade was manageable for a horse, but he could see two or three places where the path thinned to the point where an animal would have been in trouble, so he dismounted and removed the saddle and saddle blanket. He took the pack off the pack-horse, then dug out two halters and tethered the animals in a little declivity beneath a knoll, near water and some grass they could eat if he should not return by nightfall. He took the longbow and the quiver of arrows. He took the crossbow and three bolts—if he needed more than that, the longbow would be better. He took a water bag, thirty feet of rope, and the flint-kit in case he needed to make a fire. He hid the rest of the supplies behind some brush, and turned his attention upward.

The switchbacks disappeared into what he thought must be a cloud. He had not seen this before, either, and would have sworn before a magistrate that as long as he had lived in Warwickshire he had had been unaware that such a mountain existed. But the uncanny sense of familiarity remained, and even grew stronger as he examined the mountain. It was calling him somehow, pulling him forward, drawing him up its side toward the peak.

After an hour of climbing, he stopped and rested on a large granite boulder. He was breathing hard, and sweating harder, even though a bitter wind cut into his face from the north. He wiped his forehead with the back of his hand, and wished he had brought a heavier coat, but then again, the cold only bit into him when he stopped climbing. He looked back and down, and realized that he could no longer see the horses below him.

He considered stopping at the tree-line to spend the night. He could gather some wood, hunker into one of the clefts that were appearing in the face of the granite, maybe make a fire, but when the moment came he simply pressed on. He was unsure of why he did this, and it went against his training and his better judgment—caution was the muse of the hunter—and he just continued on, driven upward.

It was an odd hunt. Prints were unnecessary. The certainty in his gut was clue enough. He climbed into a thick cloud-cover, and then, after another hour or so, emerged into bright sunshine. He stopped to catch his breath, took a drink from the water bag, and then looked back and down. The switchback path was a thin line below him. Ahead, it narrowed to little more than a foot or so, and there would be moments ahead when he would have to face the mountain and move forward in a side-stepping pattern. He wondered who had carved the path, and what compensation there had been that had given a sensible return on such work, but then again the path seemed ancient and little traveled. There were places where it had weathered badly over the years. Sometimes loose gravel appeared under foot, and when he kicked it aside, he could hear it clattering away beneath him, not rolling but falling free. What had started as a steep incline had become a cliff, and when he looked down, the face was almost sheer, a nearly straight drop. He was above the clouds now. Below him, the cloud glinted back such a hard white light that for a moment it seemed almost solid, a barrier that cut off earth from heaven.

When the path widened out a little, he stopped and adjusted his equipment. He slung the longbow over his shoulder, holding it in place against his back, the taut string across his chest. He moved the bolts from his pocket and dropped them into the bottom of the quiver. He patted his other pocket to reassure himself that the flint-kit was there. His knife was there, too. He took another drink from the water bag and continued the climb.

After another twenty minutes, he came to a large boulder that protruded out into the path, narrowing the ledge to barely a few inches. He flattened his body against the boulder, faced inward, and worked his way around the boulder. He had no idea how he would reverse this and return to the animals, and no idea what was on the other side of the boulder. For a moment he was suspended there in time. A breeze came up, blowing a hard, cold wind against his face.

Beyond the boulder he paused to reconnoiter. Ahead, maybe five feet, there was a ledge, and then beyond the ledge, leading back from it, a niche or a cave.

Within the niche he found a hoard of skeletons and carcasses. To his left, near the entrance, was the skeleton of a horse or maybe a pack-mule, and beyond that, what was left of the animal's pack. There were signs of struggles, and he wondered how many of these animals had survived their harrowing journey to this remote place only to meet their end here, in the terrible darkness of the cave. Here a hoof. There the sinuous remains of a spine. He kicked at what was left of an ox, and watched it crumble into dust. He was thankful that he found nothing human.

A dark circle near the rear of the cave suggested a tunnel or a passage of some kind, leading deeper into the granite of the mountain. He went to the pack-animal skeleton and broke a stick from the pack it had carried, then shaved the end of the stick until it would take a spark, and with that and the flint-kit made a small, glowing torch.

Then he moved into the tunnel. After maybe thirty feet—he could not be sure—the tunnel made a hard left, and then further in, it bent around a boulder. An odd, orange glow lit the tunnel from the inside, bright, then darker, then brighter again, as though something were breathing light. He lodged the torch into the dirt, burning end up, and went ahead without it. He could hear the heavy breathing of a large animal.

After another twenty feet the tunnel opened out into a large cave, or perhaps a cavern. At the far side, there was a dragon, sleeping. *Bad place for battle. Could get trapped. Entrance too small. Without light, no escape.* He dropped to his haunches and leaned back against the wall, sizing up the monster and the situation. The ebbing light was too dim to establish very much about the cavern. Unnatural rock formations lined the floor and ceiling. The rhythmic dripping of water echoed against the far wall, creating a strange, eerie rhythm. Closer in, nearer his feet, were little pools of viscous liquid that gave off a smoldering glow. A huge spider web covered the back of the cave.

The dragon itself was enormous, the size of a small house maybe. Maybe his hut. It had a wingspan of forty-five, maybe fifty feet. Maybe more. He could not see its talons or its tail, but even at a distance its eyes were visible through clear membranes.

He decided he would have a better chance if he were nearer the entrance of the cave outside, where the light would be better and there would be little chance of getting trapped. He retraced his steps through the tunnel, went to the skeleton of the pack horse, and dislodged the pack, then dragged it out to the ledge, where he rifled through its contents. There was a spear, several arrows, a rusty sword. He took the spear and arrows, and found a spot well into the niche, out of direct view from the opening, with room enough that he could maneuver as he needed. Then he cocked the crossbow and seated a bolt in its place, setting it where he could reach for it without having to take his eyes off his quarry. Next to it, leaning against the rock at an angle, he placed the spear, point up. He took up the longbow, placed an arrow at the ready, leaned back against the inner wall of the niche, and waited.

He was awakened by the sound of rocks falling from the loose gravel walls within the tunnel, or maybe the wall of the cavern, and then a large, heavy movement within the tunnel itself. He gripped the crossbow, and raised the stock to his shoulder to aim, but otherwise remained still. There were more falling rocks, and then without warning a massive bellow that shook the granite behind him, and following that an echo receding into the hollow of the cavern. The tunnel shot flame.

The dragon was so massive its wings scraped the walls on either side of the tunnel. Fletcher adjusted the stock, placed his finger on the trigger, held his breath to steady his aim, and stopped cold. The dragon was carrying something, or maybe dragging it, a human body maybe. He could see what looked like white flesh and dark hair, then, more clearly, what might have been a foot. A girl. Fletcher's heart stopped. Elspeth. As he watched, the dragon laid her body down slowly—Fletcher would later recall thinking, *gently*—and then reached down and touched her skin with the tip of a talon, making a barely audible clucking and cooing sound, like he had heard before in the bookbinder's shop. It bent its head close and nudged her, as if it were trying to wake her up, but she lay still. Fletcher could not tell if she was alive or dead.

The dragon paused and looked around the cave, aware maybe that something was alive there, and then it stilled its breathing and mimed the surrounding rock. As it did this, it completely disappeared.

Fletcher faded back into one of the recesses in the cave and considered his options. With the crossbow, he could aim the first shot carefully, except that because of the mime he could not see the dragon clearly. A well-placed arrow would bring it out, force it to appear, but a second arrow or a bolt from the crossbow would have to come very quickly then, and he could not risk hitting Elspeth. He held his own breath and peered out of his protective niche, tracing the dragon's outline as a subtle undulation in the rock. It looked as though the rock itself were breathing. Without taking his eyes off the shimmering in the rock, he set down the loaded crossbow and reached out beside him for the longbow, seated the arrow, drew the string, and waited. Sooner or later, the dragon would have to breathe, and when it did the undulations would deepen and the outline would sharpen ever so subtly, and he would have a better chance of hitting his mark without endangering his daughter.

There was a deepening sense of the undulations in the rock, and Fletcher released the arrow into the dead center of the form, then dropped for the floor, rolled, reached for the crossbow and without taking aim discharged the bolt in the general direction of the monster. The dragon appeared then, unable to hold the mime. A bellow told him it was hurt. A flame lighted up the interior of the cave, showing Elspeth trying to sit up on the far side of the cave. The dragon bellowed again and moved between him and the girl, then turned in his direction.

Fletcher threw aside the crossbow, and took up the longbow because of its speed—shot an arrow, then another, then another. Each time, he could feel the percussive force as the arrows thudded into the dragon's body. He was not thinking now, but was working entirely on instinct. He was able to aim for the wings, and once he heard a hard crack as the supporting bone splintered under the impact of the arrow. The dragon swiped at him with one of its massive forelegs, clipping his left arm with a talon and opening a large bloody gash. Then it roared and staggered backward toward the entrance of the cave and the ledge beyond.

Fletcher glanced at his arm only long enough to tell that the dragon had opened an artery. The bleeding was coming in throbbing spurts.

He had. no. way. to. stop. the. flow. He. collapsed. and. everything,   faded

Elspeth swallowed and swallowed and spat, trying hard to clear her throat of the acrid taste of tar that mixed with the gorge from her stomach and made her want to be sick. She had stumbled outside. The morning sunlight glinted hard on the snow in front of Levente's hut.

Her night clothes clung to her body and her hair hung close to the nape of her neck, dripping from the night sweats. She watched her hands opening and closing mechanically, outside of her control. She ran her fingers through her hair, then across her brow, wiping off the perspiration that was beading up on her forehead and dripping, salty and stinging, into her eyes.

She closed her eyes and imagined, wished, that this had been a dream, but like the times the dragon had appeared before, this was as real as she was, as strong a reality as the sweat that laced upon her brow and ran thick salt down into her eyes. But no, she thought, this must have been a dream because she had been aware of having been taken to some horrible place with the rotting carcasses and skeletons of animals, and yet when she awoke she was back in her own bed again, terrified but alive, unharmed, and yet unable to move because of the terror.

It had started out with a dim awareness of a disturbance in the yard, something to do with the chickens or perhaps one of Levente's goats, and still sleeping, she had stumbled into the yard to check. That was when, without warning she had been snatched up by the dragon, had been carried away in the dragon's talons. The flight itself had been frightening, but she had kept her wits enough to stop struggling to wrench free of the talons for fear of falling, but what if the creature were to drop her? Either way—falling or not—she knew that this was the end, and she thought wildly of the life she had dreamed that would never be, the adventures that would not happen, the husband she would never love, the children she would never hold. She thought of the baby growing inside her. She ached to feel safe again, ached for the solid ground beneath her feet, ached to be back in her own bed.

She had been unable to see the creature whole, but only the talons that held her and the massive head and the bat wings spread wide, maybe forty feet or more, all of it dimly illuminated by the glow of a nostril flame that stank of tar and decayed flesh. In the dream she had been taken to a cave in the high mountains, where she had been added to the dragon's hoard of carcasses and skeletons. It had all happened in a reeling, sickening blur of images and sounds and smells. The dragon's roar had been a thunderous bellow that had shuddered down through her skeleton, leaving her feeling nearly dismembered and helpless.

In her dream there had been a colossal battle. A hunter, maybe her father, had tracked the dragon to its lair. She could not remember how the battle turned out, but she believed her father had been hurt.

The memory focused. The hunter had been her father, she was certain of it, and he had been hurt in a battle with a dragon. She hated him for getting her into that, for exposing her to danger that way.

Her father was bleeding, wounded by a slashing blow from the dragon. She thought she remembered applying a tourniquet to an ebbing cut, then finding her way out and down the mountain. Voices were shouting, calling her name and the name of her father. They were called out for Constantine, too—an odd detail that made no sense to her. She had a dim memory of drawing a crude map in the dirt, directing them upward to the dragon's lair, then being lifted into the saddle of Aelric's horse, and Aelric mounting to support her from behind. Then nothing.

She tried to get up to find Alcera, but fell backward into the bed and moaned. A terrible aching pain seemed to wrap itself around her stomach and wring it like a cleaning towel. She heard herself groan, and then she lay softly backward into the bed.

Alcera's face appeared at the door of her small room. "Elspeth?" She felt Alcera's cool hand on her forehead. "My God, girl, you're burning up."

Levente ran for Sister Bertrice, who arrived in time to witness Elspeth struggling with dry heaves. Sarabeth was close behind her. Elspeth nearly passed out, exhausted by the sheer effort of staying alert, but with this trinity of matrons around her bed, she finally collapsed and allowed them to do what they would to her.

She had no way to know how much time passed, but she was aware that the women had stopped whatever urgent actions they had been taking.

Sister Bertrice stood quietly beside the bed, drying her hands on a towel. "She'll be alright," Sister said. "She's exhausted from the work, and maybe has sickness on top of that. She's out of danger, though. Has lost a lot of blood."

In other circumstances, Sister Bertrice would have cleaned up and gone back to the convent, but this time she simply waited, her eyes downturned. There was so marked an awkwardness about her staying that Alcera finally asked, "Is there something else, Sister?"

"Don't know how to say this, ma'am," Sister stammered. "Not sure if you know . . ."

"Know what?" said Alcera.

"There was a baby, ma'am," said Bertrice. "The girl was pregnant. But now the baby's lost."

Fletcher was awakened by the sound of trickling water, and for a moment imagined he had been dragged back into the cavern in the granite. He opened his eyes tentatively. Somebody was wringing a cloth into a basin near his head. A face came into view, hovering calmly, going about his ministrations methodically, carefully. Brother Gregory was bathing his forehead with a damp cloth. Fletcher's arm throbbed, and he was able to glance sidelong enough to see that it was wrapped in a white bandage. A crucifix on the wall told him he was in the infirmary of the monastery.

"What happened?" he asked weakly.

"You tell me," Gregory said. He refreshed the cloth in a basin, wringing it nearly dry, then placed it again on Fletcher's forehead. "Aelric said something about a cave in the mountains. You were brought down by a search party."

"My horse . . . ?" Fletcher said.

"The horse is found," said Gregory. "And the pack-mule. Both safe in the paddock now."

"What about the dragon?" Fletcher asked. "Any sightings of the dragon?"

"Its body was at the bottom of a ravine north of the king's forest. Near the horse and the mule, somebody said. It had a half-dozen arrows in its chest, and a rusted sword through the back of its neck. They found it while they were searching for you."

"I have to tell Constantine," Fletcher said. It seemed to him that the long nightmare was finally over. In killing the dragon, he had freed himself at last from its grip. His head spun with relief. The dragon was dead.

"Brother Constantine?" Gregory said. "You can't, John."

"Why not?"

"Constantine went missing the same day you did. The search parties were looking for all three of you."

Then he remembered that Constantine had fled from their conversation, but he could not remember what he had said that had made him run.

He closed his eyes and tried to untangle the threads of memory. He had tracked the animal to its lair. There had been a battle. He had a dim recollection of a girl. Then, as the threads of the recollection re-knit themselves, he remembered that the girl had been Elspeth. Elspeth had been there in the dragon's lair.

He panicked and tried to sit up, but was too weak for that. Brother Gregory gently urged him back to the pillow. "Elspeth was there," he said. "Is she alright?"

"She's safe, John," said Brother Gregory.

He collapsed and for a moment had all he could do to breathe. Gregory had said something about a sword, and about arrows in the animal's body. He remembered firing the arrows, and their heavy thuds against the animal's body. He had no memory of the sword. He remembered Elspeth calling out to him, but he had to work to remember what she said—"Father, look out."

That was when the dragon had swiped at him with a claw. There was a terrible flame, the heat was awful, but it was not aimed, and Fletcher guessed that the animal was hurt badly, and possibly fading. There were droplets of burning dragon's blood in the air, more fire, and then viscous glowing droppings from its saliva. The animal's wings spread large, and flame lighted up the interior of the cave. He glimpsed Elspeth behind it, struggling to get to her feet. Then—he did not know how—she was on its back. She had something in her hand—that must have been the sword. She must have taken it from the dead pack animal. The memory focused for a moment and he saw her forcing the sword into the dragon's neck from behind. It was an effort that astonished him. The dragon fell backward and out of the cave, where it must have tumbled off the ledge. He heard a strangled bellow receding below the ledge, accompanied by the crashing sounds of boulders being dislodged, and then a hard thud as the dragon hit what must have been a protrusion on the face of the cliff, and after that an avalanche far below.

Then silence.

That must have been when he had passed out. When he came to, there was a tourniquet on his arm. Elspeth, however, was nowhere to be seen.

"Elspeth?" he asked Brother Gregory. "Where's Elspeth?"

Gregory finished his ministrations with the cloth. "Prior Robert sent for her, but she refuses to come."

"Hatred is a heavy burden to bear," said Levente. He and Elspeth had talked for more than half the night. Elspeth told him everything—everything, that is, about herself and her father. She said nothing about Constantine or what had happened in the niche behind the altar of the church. He was gone now, and accusing him would only have been misunderstood as a gesture to protect someone else. Besides, Levente would think less of her for accusing a man of God.

They talked about the events of the past few days. What she could not describe was the intense horror of the kidnapping, the terror and shock of the dragon's lair, the knot in her stomach that stayed with her almost always now. She told him she must have climbed down the mountain, but that she had no recollection of that. She remembering waking in her own bed with night sweats—it was all a dream anyway, but it was a dream so vivid that it had ruined her waking thoughts. How could Levente understand that? She could not tell about the strange grief that had been handed her—to have had a living child inside her taken from her. He did not ask about who had fathered her baby; that also was a story for another time.

Eventually she told about her father's admission that he had beaten her mother, she told about how he now admitted that the beatings had not been deserved, she told about his apology. She told about the fact that his father had forced her mother, and that that was how she learned she had not been wanted.

"And what did you say to that?" asked Levente, referring back to Elspeth's description of her father's apology.

"I told him to go to the devil," said Elspeth. "I never want to see him again. I hate him." She could feel the gorge rise within her own throat, filling her mouth with the hard acrid taste of tar. "I hate him," she said again.

Levente just sat there, waiting.

"You don't know what it's like, Levente," said the girl.

"Don't be so sure about that, Elspeth," said Levente. He reached down, plucked a long blade of grass, placed it in his mouth, and chewed for a long while. "You and I have more in common than you know."

"Because you and my father grew up like brothers?"

"Not like brothers. Never like that. I think I may have resented John because of the attention my father gave him. I can't remember that very clearly now. What matters is that my father was cruel to us both. His mother sent him away into the world—I don't remember how old he was, maybe seven or so—and my father took him in, but my father worked him hard. Never found anything right about his work. Beat him. Shamed him. I saw that happen."

"Did you do anything to stop it?"

"It was happening to both of us. My father didn't approve of me or my work any more than he approved of John's. He beat us both."

"So how come you turned out so different, if you were both treated the same way?"

"What I'm telling you is that I'm not so different from your father. We both carry our wounds from what happened to us. I've come to the place of forgiving my father a little earlier than John did, that's all. It was easier for me, but then, I never suffered the other losses your father did. I never lost a wife in childbirth, and my mother—God rest her—never sent me off to be apprenticed to a stranger in a foreign place. I suppose you might say that of the two of us, I was the luckier. I was older and a little stronger, I had less to forgive, and fewer hurdles to get over. I'm alright most of the time now, I think, but I still have moments when I panic or I feel out of control, just like your father."

"He's got a dragon, Levente," said the girl. "Remember the night his dragon appeared in our hut? It was his."

"Lots of people have dragons, Elspeth. Even some of the monks." She choked when he said that. "Remember the mime?" Levente said. "I suppose I have a dragon of my own. There may be dragons hiding in lots of places in the shire. They're just not always visible."

"Everybody?"

"Who am I to judge everybody? What I mean is that dragons are more common than you think. You seem to have forgotten something about our conversation that night when your father's dragon came out in your hut. Do you remember what my wife said to you?"

"She said that I may have a dragon of my own." Even remembering this filled the girl with such deep anguish that she tasted tar. "So how do I live with that?" she asked Levente.

"You starve a dragon by living forgivingly," said Levente. "It's the only way."

"But that implies that what he has done is alright with me, and it's not."

"Not so," said Levente, speaking more tenderly. "You can't forgive someone until you recognize that what he's done is wrong. Forgiveness isn't the same as saying that something was alright. It *is* the same as saying that whatever happened was wrong—perhaps starkly, violently wrong—but that you're not going to allow it to damage the future. You're going to assign it to its proper place in the past."

"Next you'll to say that Christ commanded us to forgive. What does the scripture say? Seventy times seven. I can't figure that. It's too large."

"Four hundred, ninety."

"How do you do that, when forgiving even one time is too hard?"

"I'm not going to tell you that you have to do that. Forgiveness isn't something that can be conjured up as an act of the will. It comes as a gift of grace. It's not something you do, it's something you wait for, something you search for."

"Well," said the girl, "It isn't coming to me, and if it came, I'd send it back. I don't want anything to do with him."

"You choose to feed your own dragon, then?" said Levente. "Like I said, hatred is a terrible burden to carry around. It's easier if you let your dragon do the heavy lifting."

"You can go to the devil, too."

"Of course," said Levente. "But before I go, let me remind you that you and your father have very much in common. The dragon you hate in him is the father of the dragon you hate in yourself."

"I don't have a dragon, Levente," Elspeth said, but even as she said this she tasted tar and knew it was a lie.

"If you hope to live with yourself, you'd better learn to live with him."

"I hate you, Levente. I hate you."

"Elspeth," said Levente more gently. "If you ever want to be at peace with yourself, you have to find the grace to forgive him."

"What if what he said turns out to be another lie?"

"Forgiving him isn't the same as giving him permission to hurt you again. You can forgive with your eyes open. It's not the same as trusting him. Forgiveness isn't the same as reconciliation. But there comes a time when the danger is over, and then forgiveness is fully proper and appropriate. It's giving him permission to earn your trust again, but you may need to keep your wits about you for a very long time. It may be that you will never feel safe with him again, and maybe you will choose never be alone with him again, not once, but still there is room for forgiveness."

Elspeth began to shake all over. She found this line of reasoning deeply troubling. She hated her father, and would not tolerate being thought in any sense like him. But she also remembered the times she had tasted tar on her own tongue, the times she had lashed out unprovoked, the over-reaction she had had when her father had apologized to her. Why had it been so hard? Could it really be that what she loathed in her father was something she loathed in herself?

Suddenly she was on her feet and through the door. Levente let her go, not even calling out after her. When she reached the street she spat and spat and spat, and where she spat, little viscous pools formed up, round and glowing and hot.

It was Sunday morning. Elspeth was in the church when her father came in. She felt the pulse quicken in her veins, tried to avoid eye contact, tried to leave. Her father, obviously pained, retreated to the door to avoid an encounter that he must have known would be difficult for them both, but was turned back into the sanctuary by Levente.

Levente spoke first. "And who said God does not answer prayer?" he said, then added quickly: "I prayed for you both this morning at mass. God be praised!"

"And for what, Levente?" asked Elspeth. "I don't want anything to do with him. He's dangerous. Now let me pass."

Levente did not. Instead he stationed his aging frame in the doorway to block or at least slow the girl's movement. "Let me answer your question," he said.

"What question?"

"You asked for what God should be praised." He continued to stand in the doorway. "Let's talk together, shall we? All three of us?"

He led them along the covered portico that ended dramatically at the south entrance of Brother Johann's magnificent flower garden. The garden was in fine form, now blossoming out in a riot of color that passed retrospective judgment on the mottled muddied brown of the melting snow.

"John, would you allow us a moment?" he said.

John sat on the stone bench beneath the jasmine that covered the pilasters at the garden's entrance. Levente and Elspeth went into the garden and sat among the roses. Elspeth was aware of several small spider webs between the branches of the rose bushes. The webs were perfectly formed, and still laden with the dew so that they glistened like jewels in the thin morning sunlight.

"It hurts terribly, doesn't it?" asked Levente. He reached over and placed his hand on her shoulder.

"I . . . hate . . . him," said Elspeth. Then more quietly, "I hate him." She stood and spat into one of the rose bushes, too angrily to aim, but hoping to break one of the glistening spider webs. The spittle formed up into a little viscous ball.

Levente merely waited until this little drama played itself out. Then he stood and picked up a stick and systematically cleared the spider web from the rose bush. "No one's asking you to like him, or even to trust him," he said as he worked. "No one wants you to say that what happened was anything but wrong. No one wants for you to say it didn't matter, or that it didn't cost you something." He cleared another web.

"No one believes you weren't hurt by it. Maybe you were damaged in a way that will never be healed. No one wants you to deny that."

They sat again on the bench, and Elspeth buried her head in Levente's shoulder and sobbed. "I don't want anything to do with him. I don't trust him."

"It's hard to give up that power, isn't it?"

"Power? What power?"

"The power that comes from not forgiving."

"What are you talking about?" Elspeth slid sideways a bit so she could turn to look at Levente directly. "What do you mean?" She asked this quietly but firmly.

"By not forgiving your father, you keep control of the future. That's pretty powerful, and it can be very destructive."

"It's self-defense," said Elspeth. "He's wrecked my past. No way I'll let him wreck my future."

"But that's exactly what you're doing to yourself, Elspeth," said Levente.

"What are you talking about?"

"You're letting your anger eat away at you like a cancer. Tell me that won't destroy your future."

"I don't have any choice. I have to hate him. I'm afraid of what could happen if I trust him again."

"Look around you," Levente said. "Do you see the gardener anywhere around here? His name is Brother Johann."

Elspeth looked around. Her father had slipped off the bench and was helping two of the monks unload a wagon of lumber near the barn just beyond the covered portico that marked the southern boundary of the garden. "We're alone here," she said.

"No, we're not. Brother Johann is all over this place. I can see him in the way the grass is trimmed along the walk here, I see him in that bed of roses and the pots of nasturtiums that hang along the west portico over there. When we came in, we smelled Johann in the blanket of jasmine that covers the entrance. Like I said, Brother Johann is all over this place."

"And now you're going to tell me that you smell my father all over me, too," said Elspeth. She looked away

"I like what you've done with my metaphor," said Levente mildly, "but no. That's not it. I was going to say that Johann doesn't have to be here physically for his garden to grow. He planted the bulbs, he fertilized them, then he left. The plants are flowering in his absence."

"And what my father did to me is going to continue for me whether he's here or not."

"It's the way God made us, I suppose. Look out over that hill to the west. Can you see the apple orchard over there beyond the paddock?"

"I played among those trees when I was a girl," said Elspeth.

Levente suppressed a smile—she was still a girl. "Did you know that apple trees have to have a cold snap, below freezing, if they are to bear fruit? In warmer climates, where there is no cold snap, there are no apples. It's their nature. People have a nature, too—human beings, you, me, Prior Robert, all of us have a nature."

"And what's our nature, Levente? That we sprout and grow whatever our fathers have planted in us? Is that what you're trying to tell me? That's not all that comforting."

"No," said Levente. He would not be deflected from his point. "Our nature is this: We harvest our fathers' crops unless we choose otherwise. We can't choose what happens to us, but we can choose what we do with what happens to us."

"It's not that easy," said Elspeth with an unsatisfied sigh.

"What I'm saying," said Levente, "is that you've already made your choice. Fletcher planted whatever seeds of anger and bitterness and rage are taking root in you, but by continuing to hold on to them—by nursing the bitterness in your own heart—you're pruning and trimming and fertilizing them. You're feeding your dragon."

"But I don't trust him," said Elspeth. "I hate him."

"So instead you choose to be exactly like him. I can't think of a better way to honor the violence in the man than that."

"But Levente, can't you see? I mean him no harm, but I just want to be rid of him. I want him to leave me alone."

"Fertilizer," said Levente. He could not resist the temptation to turn to scripture, muttering under his breath the Latin he knew the girl would not understand: "*Via stulti recta in oculis eius qui autem sapiens est audit consilia.*"

"What was that?" asked the girl.

"'The way of a fool is right in his own eyes, but a wise man listens to advice,'" said Levente, translating the quote. "It's from the book of Proverbs."

"Even if I wanted to, I wouldn't know how to forgive him," said Elspeth.

"You forgive a little at a time," said Levente. "You forgive with your eyes wide open. You forgive with hurt left over."

"I can't," Elspeth said again, more softly this time.

She thought about the dragon, and the terrible night in the dragon's clutches, she thought about the night she had confronted her father, and the events at the bivouac. She thought about her mother and whatever her father had done to her, she tasted the bile in her own throat and saw again the dragon's lair on the mountain, and smelled the rotting flesh of the dead animals. "I can't," she said again. Her father could rot in hell for all she cared.

". . . gift of grace," Levente was saying.

Elspeth's attentions were brought up short. "What was that you were saying?"

"It's a gift of grace."

"What's a gift of grace?"

"Forgiveness," said Levente. "I said you're right. You can't forgive. None of us can. Forgiveness isn't an act of the will. Whenever forgiveness happens, it happens as a gift of grace."

Grace, thought Elspeth. *What's that?* Somewhere in one of Levente's books she remembered reading that grace was the power of undeserved redemption. She thought about Alysse, the mother she had never known, who was her most profound point of connection with her father. What would her mother ask of her now? Could she forgive her father for the cruel things she now knew he had done to her mother? Had her mother not deserved better? Did Elspeth even have the right to forgive for something done to someone else, especially now that that someone else was forever beyond forgiveness or judgment? She thought about her lost baby, an innocent, another victim. But of course, she thought, the more immediate problem was whether or not she could forgive her father on her own behalf, whether she had the strength to do that when she neither liked nor trusted him.

Bonggg. . . . .

From the tower of the monastery church close by, Elspeth and Levente heard the bells as they summoned the brothers to their midday prayers, deep and resonating peals that seemed to fill the air around them and shake the ground beneath them. The sound echoed down through the porticoes and cells and halls of the monastery. Levente, reluctant to leave the girl at a moment of crisis, simply gestured with his hand and then bowed his head where he sat, speaking out his prayer in Latin.

Bonggg. . . .

Elspeth bowed her head as well, but instead of prayer she felt herself drawn into a deep and mysterious place within herself, a place of demons and dragons and death.

In a moment, Levente was gone.

The garden was gone.

The monastery was gone.

She was in a wood now, dark and dank with the smells of growth and decay and death. There were demons crying out for her soul, crying out to feast on her soul. From somewhere far off, beneath her level of consciousness, she heard a bell ringing, barely audible above the shouting of the demons and the roaring of a dragon nearby, behind her back.

Bonggg. . . .

She was running now, running through the wood, running from the horrors of her life, running from her father, running from the dragon, running from herself, running from God.

Her heart was beating wildly, her eyes darting every which way. She could feel the heat of a dragon's flame on the nape of her neck. From somewhere ahead of her she heard the cackling laughter of a demon. She tasted the bile and the tar that returned to her throat from her own stomach. She ran this way and that, looking in the underbrush for an opening, a way of escape.

Bonggg. . . .

Around a bend. Over a high hill. Into the brush of the forest again. Running to near exhaustion, and then beyond exhaustion. There were lights now, flickering through the forest canopy, torches carried by only God knew whom, voices calling out her name, searching for her in the darkness.

Somewhere in the far distance the echoing peal of bells seemed to summon her. Was there a church nearby?

Bonggg. . . .

She came then to a fork, a parting in the path, one way leading deeper into the wood, the other up to the brow of a small hill where the monastery church stood bathed in sunlight. She heard the voices again.

Her heart ached in her chest. *The way of a fool is right in his own eyes, but a wise man listens to advice.* The words were echoing now with the same rhythm as the bells. *You forgive a little at a time. You forgive with hurt left over. You forgive with your eyes wide open.*

She hesitated, waiting for direction. The dragon inside her roared. *The way of the fool is right in his own eyes.* She wanted to run, but her knees buckled, and in that instant she knew that she had come to a fork in the road in her own inner journey. She heard Levente's voice again: *If you hope to live with yourself, you'd better learn to live with him.*

Bonggg. . . .

The voices were upon her now, swirling through the little glen where the path parted, swirling through her head. Levente. Constantine. Alcera. Her father. Her unborn baby, now lost . . .

Bonggg. . . .

Then, from somewhere behind them—beyond them—she heard a woman's voice, distantly, barely audibly. It was a voice she had never heard before, high-pitched, and lilting with the rounder tones of Welsh laced in and through the accent.

"Elspeth," the voice was saying. "Elspeth . . ."

"Yes, mother," she called out. "I'm here."

"Elspeth!" The voice ached for her, longed for her.

"I'm here, mother," she called back feverishly.

The voice died nearly to a whisper, and Elspeth had to strain to make it out. "Choose life," it said. "Choose life."

Without a word she turned and started up the path toward the light, the church, the garden.

Bonggg. . . .

Bonggg. . . .

Bonggg. . . .

Levente continued in prayer for some minutes, unaware of the struggle that was going on beside him. When he opened his eyes, the girl was gone. He looked all about him to no sign of the girl, but as he stood to leave he looked out through the portico that formed the south facing border of the garden. The two monks had left off their work on the lumber wagon and were making their way to the church for noonday prayers. On the ground beside the wagon sat two figures, John the

Fletcher and Elspeth his daughter, the one enfolded in the arms of the other.

POST SCRIPTUM

"FLETCHER! JOHN FLETCHER!" IT was Sarabeth, calling his name from the door of *The Pint and Ploughman.*

"Hello, Sarabeth," called Fletcher.

Sarabeth called something unintelligible to Willem inside the hut, then slipped out the door and hurried to catch up with him on the road. She had business in Wharram, she said, and would he mind if she came along?

"Glad of the company," he said. He resumed his journey, walking a little more slowly to accommodate her smaller stride.

"Any news about Constantine?" she asked.

"They've called off the search."

"Pity," Sarabeth said. "He was a good man."

"I owe him my life," Fletcher replied. "Father Athanasius is offering a mass for his soul after the Feast of St George has passed."

Sarabeth sighed and changed the subject: "So how are you this fine morning?" she asked. Her voice was full of the lilting sounds of spring. She waved her arm in an expansive gesture that took in the whole of the Warwickshire countryside. Fletcher followed the sweep admiringly. It was indeed a fine morning. The snow that had blanketed the countryside was nearly all gone now. The sun was bright, but not hot. A breeze swept the grasses that blanketed the countryside in bright green. A small flock of sheep stood guard within the fenced enclosure that was the center of Wharram. Far in the distance, a tinker's wagon was making its way along the road to Warwick, signaling that the roads were open, a sure sign that spring had come at last to Warwickshire. A crow took flight across the path and landed on the branch of a tall hemlock tree, shaking down a last final patch of snow.

"I haven't seen you in a good while," she said.

"I've given up ale," Fletcher said to her. It had not been a difficult decision—he owed that to his daughter and to his memory of Brother Constantine. He owed that to Alysse.

"No reason you can't come along and say hello now, is there?"

John smiled, and looked at her so shyly that she could not help pressing him for the reason, punching him in the ribs with her elbow as they walked.

John picked up a small rock and threw it into the undergrowth, sending a small grouse fluttering away into the trees.

"Willem says he spotted a young wolf on the outskirts of the village," Sarabeth said. "You'll be out hunting soon, now that winter's passed."

"Gave that up, too," Fletcher said. He stretched out his arms to feel the wonderful warmth of the sunshine against his body. He told her he had left the employ of the sheriff, and that through Levente's offices and with Prior Robert's approval he now worked in the monastery, not as a huntsman, but as a builder, helping make repairs to the monastery walls and grounds that came inevitably with the onset of the spring thaw and the arrival of the spring rains. Occasionally he would ride as courier, carrying important documents to the ecclesiastical authorities at Coventry. "But no more killing," he said. "Not for me. A fine, fine day."

"Just look at the way the sunlight catches in the trees," she said.

John looked but was distracted by the way it played red-gold in a free lock of her hair. He reached out and took her arm. "Come a little closer, Sarabeth," he said. He wrapped her arm around his waist, laid his own free arm across her shoulders, and the two of them continued down the road.

Elspeth sat on a small hill, beneath a crab-tree, rolling apples down her nose, trying to catch them in her mouth as they fell. Beneath her lay the road that led north and west from Warwick. A tinker's wagon was making its way along the road, and behind that, there was a lone horseman. She stopped trying with the apples and sat up so she could get a better view of the rider. He was tall and broadly constructed, with well muscled shoulders, maybe twenty years old. He had dark hair, nearly black, and a solid, friendly face. He pulled up beside the hill to ask directions.

"Is this the road to Warwick?" he asked. There was a lovely little lilt in his language that she liked at once.

"It is," she said, absentmindedly drawing her long braid around over right shoulder, smiling at him as he looked down at her from his mount. "Around that bend there."

"And would you be able to tell me how to find the sheriff?" he asked.

"Are you looking for work?" she said, not ignoring his question so much as turning it to her own use. Work would keep the rider here a while, perhaps for a long time. She played with a free lock of her hair.

"Christ's bones, girl," said the rider, laughing out loud in a way that made her blush. "Work? Hardly. I have unfinished business with one of his men."

"What sort of business?" she asked.

"Now aren't we being inquisitive?" said the rider, smiling. "I'd rather not say. It's personal. Between the two of us."

"And aren't we being secretive?" said Elspeth, returning his barb with a smile of her own. But then, so there would be no offense taken, she answered his question: "The sheriff's house is the large one. Stone. Just inside the foregate, two doors down. The guardsman will show you. No, better, I'll show you myself." She began to get up, but slipped on the wet grass of the hill. In a moment he was off the horse and offering her his hand to help her up. She brushed off her embarrassment with a gesture, but was pleased that he had not laughed. Apparently he had not thought her awkward.

They walked as far as the bend in the road before he asked her name. "And who shall I say has been my escort this fine morning?"

"Your name first," she said, challenging him one last time.

"Meurig," said the rider. "Meurig ap Gwynedd. I'm from Wales."